Passion's Paradise . . .

On the soft bed of moss that a benevolent nature had provided for them, Shana lay naked beside Gerard with an arm at his waist, her head on his strong chest, knowing that the cool touch of her lovely skin was exciting him beyond endurance. When she took his hand and moved it to her gently swelling breast, he let his fingers, as though of their own volition, mound it softly, cupping it and savoring its resilience.

She could feel the beat of his heart, even faster than her own as she lay close to him, ruffling his thick hair. Slowly she threw a long and slender thigh across him, feeling the heat of him against her, relishing the uncontrolled pulsation. She kissed him lovingly on the lips, and his response excited her strongly as she felt the tip of his tongue between her teeth, probing. She knew that he was hers now, and she whispered: "You cannot refuse me any longer, I know it."

"And I know it too . . ."

She lay her head on his taut stomach and brushed him with her long, silky hair, driving him to distraction as her lips explored him. He gasped as he felt the kisses and the tiny bites, and then she was raising herself up to kneel over him, a knee at each side of his hard hips.

She grasped him and caressed herself, shuddering, moving slowly back and forth for a very long time. She was moaning, and when she could restrain her emotions no longer she placed him just so and dropped down onto him in an agony of desire . . .

Also by Antoinette Beaudry

DESERT OF DESIRE
RIVER OF DESIRE
STRANDS OF DESIRE
TROPIC OF DESIRE

JUNGLE OF DESIRE

Antoinette Beaudry

Pinnacle Books   New York

Jungle of Desire

An original Pinnacle Books edition, published for the first time anywhere.

First printing,
October, 1982

ISBN: 0-523-41401-3
Cover illustration by John Solie
Printed in the United States of America
PINNACLE BOOKS, INC.
1430 Broadway
New York, New York 10018

JUNGLE OF DESIRE

The jungle was a place of great fascination and to repel. We could be wrong. We could be wrong. We could be wrong. We could be wrong. We could be wrong. We could be wrong. We could be wrong. We could be wrong. We could be wrong. We could be wrong.

Chapter One

The jungle was a place of great fascination and of even greater dangers. In this year of 1825, it was as far removed from civilization as a man could venture.

It was hot and humid and often impenetrable. The trees here towered to enormous heights and even the ferns were forty feet tall or more, so that men moved through them like ants, quite overpowered by the sheer exuberance of the lush vegetation.

In some areas, the trees were so tightly packed together as to make passage among them quite impossible. Sometimes, they were even tied together by creeping liana vines that would travel as much as three miles as they sought out the air, the moisture, and the light. A banyan tree could die and rot and still be held erect by the vines till the sheer weight of them brought it crashing to the ground, to decompose slowly in the mud and supply humus for the growth of yet more trees.

It rained here very often. But this was not rain as Europe or America knew it; the water came down in great sheets from dark and over-laden clouds, turning small streams into raging torrents in minutes, plucking huge trees up by the roots and tumbling them over like matchsticks as they swept on their violent way to reach, finally, the Amazon River itself. There, they would either float down to the sea, or plant themselves crookedly on the banks to continue the struggle for survival.

This was the essence of the Amazonian jungle—the constant effort just to stay alive, for man, beast, and vegetation alike.

The mountain was steep, and the three people who were climbing down it were slipping in red mud, clinging to roots as they moved. Once, the girl said: "I am frightened, Bramwell," and he answered her. "Do not be. I am a Strong Man, and I'll protect you, as is my duty."

But there was something strange about the way he used the term *a strong man*. It was as though he had said: "I am an Engineer," or "I am a Doctor," or "I am an Artist."

I am a Strong Man. . . .

The second man said, smiling: "And I am a Wise Man, and I tell you there is nothing to fear." He too used the term *a Wise Man* as though it were an indication of his profession.

The girl looked at him and laughed suddenly, showing her strong white teeth. "It's never easy to subjugate emotion to reason, is it? But if you both agree that there is nothing to fear . . . then I will fear nothing." She turned and studied the slope below them, worrying about it none the less.

Her name was Shana, and she was a young woman of the most extraordinary beauty. She was tall and slender, carrying herself with an easy, almost feline grace, and her skin, very smooth and unblemished, was light saffron-colored, like a kind of beige in which there was a touch of red. Her eyes, which were large and slightly

2

slanted, were of a most startling pale blue and almost luminescent under finely arched brows that now were drawn together in a slight frown; they were very intent and commanding eyes. Her hair was jet-black and shining like silk, falling to below her waist, and there was a narrow band of woven blue silk around her forehead to control it. Her cheekbones were high, her nose straight and delicate, her lips full and promising. But most of all, there was an unusual air of authority about her, in her looks, in her voice, even in the way she moved, as though she were in complete command not only of herself but of everything and everybody around her.

She wore a costume that was called among her people a *draperi*. It was a length of cloth wound once around the waist and then tossed carelessly over one shoulder or wrapped around the whole body as the weather dictated, and it was some twenty feet long. Now, in the humid heat of the day, she had gathered the excess material into folds and was carrying it on her shoulder, exposing the left side of her upper body from the neck to the hipbone. Her small, firm breasts were set high on her torso, and her legs were longer than might have been thought humanly possible. The *draperi* was pale blue, the same color as her lovely eyes, and it was made of finely-woven silk. The two men wore gowns of the same style, but made from llama wool in its natural color.

The younger of the two men with her, Bramwell, was tall and broad-shouldered and muscular. He carried a machete, about which there was something very strange too; it had been ground down with constant sharpening to less than a quarter of its original breadth, and in the process had lost most of its weight and therefore its efficiency too; but it was all he had. On occasion he would

3

look at it somberly and say: "Perhaps, one day, we will find deposits of iron in our haven, and then we will make these knives and use them to great advantage. Iron is more precious than our diamonds. . . ."

He was blonde, fair, and very handsome, with the saffron-colored skin and pale blue eyes of many of his people. Meeting with him for the first time, a stranger would have thought him to be in his late teens; in point of fact, Bramwell had been born in the year 1785, forty years previously.

Emlyn, the other man in the party was older. He was slighter of build, but still robust and in very good health indeed; he was nibbling now on the apricot kernels he always carried in a small leather bag at his waist. Unlike Shana and Bramwell, he was very fair-skinned, though his eyes were of the same remarkable blue. His face was kindly, his expression very gentle, with a constant half-smile on his lips. Some stranger would have said he was fifty years old, perhaps; but Emlyn was much older, and he was a very wise man indeed.

They dropped down the mountainside together, and came at last to a fast-flowing river, to rest there a while from their endeavors. Shana said, pointing, "We will cross by the boulders there."

Emlyn shook his head. "With respect," he murmured, "it is not a good place. The water is too fast, we should find a safer place upstream." He was the advisor of the party, though Shana, because she was a woman, was in command, and she chose to counter his advice. "No," she said. "The trail the Indians have left is not an easy one to follow, but we have followed it. If we lose it now, we may never find it again." She turned to Bramwell. "Can you get us across the river here?"

The younger man nodded. "Yes, I think we can cross

4

safely. I am only a Strong Man of course, but I know how to use my wits too. I will cut a vine to use as a guideline."

He looked at Emlyn as though awaiting his comments, and Emlyn stared upriver and frowned at the great mass of interwoven jungle growth there. He nodded at last. "Yes, it might be very difficult to follow the course of the river along the bank." He scraped idly with a sandalled foot at the clear prints in the forest's muddy floor. "Perhaps that is why they chose to cross here."

He turned to Bramwell. "Can you cross first, unaided, dragging a vine across as a safety-rope?"

"Yes, I can. As you know, I swim well."

"Good."

The younger man took his fragile machete and sawed through a length of tough liana, and pulled it free of its entanglement until there were more than two hundred feet of it, and cut it off. He wound it around a stump and hauled on it, testing its strength, and was satisfied; this was part of the living jungle, and the jungle was never weak. He walked with the other end upstream as far as it would allow him, tied it around his waist, and suddenly plunged in.

The two of them watched in admiration as his powerful body thrashed against the raging water. It swung him around on the end of his improvised rope, in a wide arc, but he reached a rock in midstream and turned to shout back, laughing: "You are a Wise Man indeed, Emlyn! It is more fierce than I thought! But we will succeed!"

He plunged back into the water, fighting the furious current, and in less than ten minutes he had reached the opposite shore. He strode through the mud and found a root to anchor the rope to, and when he had made it fast he entered the river again and hauled himself along it to rejoin them. He put a powerful arm around Shana's waist and said: "Hold onto the vine with both hands at all times, haul yourself along it, my arms will be around you, on both sides of your body. And you, Emlyn, can you manage without my help?"

Emlyn grunted. "I am not as old and decrepit as you think," he said, mocking. "You take care of Shana, I will be close behind you."

The white curls of foam were boiling on the surface of the deep water as Bramwell took strong hold of the rope, his arms around Shana; and slowly, carefully, they began to ease themselves across. This was a simple and time-tested method of traversing a river, and it presented only the minimum of danger. But in the vengeful jungle, even the most paltry danger was often too much; the jungle seemed to be aware, always, and ready to strike. . . .

In all the time they had rested on the bank, the river had seemed to them to be quite devoid of any hazards other than the power of the water itself. It was running far too fast for piranhas, the deadly fish that could strip a careless animal, or a man, of all the flesh on his bones in minutes, ripping him apart with their voracious jaws as hundreds of them feasted on him. And there had seemed to be very little debris hurtling past them.

But now, a great gnarled tree, uprooted perhaps hundreds of miles upstream, was bearing down on them, tossed on the turbulent water. Bramwell saw it first and shouted, "Faster, Shana, faster . . . !"

He began dragging her along the rope as the tree bore down on them, standing upended only a few hundred feet from them, its huge roots pawing at the sky, almost as though, dead or not, it wanted to show that it was still capable of fight.

It crashed down into the water again with a fearful sound and rushed towards them. They had almost reached the far bank when it broke through the length of lifesaving vine and swept on its way. Bramwell felt the liana torn from his hands, and he swung round and grabbed at Shana and fought the water with her. He saw Emlyn floundering and shouted at him, "The rocks behind you . . ." He saw him reaching for them and turned all his attentions back to Shana, dragging her, forcing her onto the muddy bank. He waited only to assure himself of her safety, and arched back into the water.

He reached the clump of washed-granite rocks, and Emlyn was not there. He dived deeply, and came up with the force of the rushing water more than a hundred yards downstream, searching still, and could find no sign of him at all.

The water was dragging him violently, and he fought it with every muscle in his powerful body. He heard the roar of the falls only moments before he was swept over the edge and falling through space.

It was a long, deep fall, and the rising mist was clouding his vision so that he could only vaguely see the shining boulders below him. He knew that the moment of his death had come, and a split second before he struck, he screamed the one word: "Shana . . ." at the top of his voice. It was not a cry of terror, nor of panic; it was rather an expression, in the last moment of his life, of his devotion to a young woman he had always worshipped, ever since her birth.

It was not possible that, so far away, she could have

7

heard him; and yet, lying on her back at the river's edge, a sharp shock came to her at that precise moment, and she sat up quickly with a slim hand to her throat, her eyes wide with apprehension.

She *knew* . . .

Was the jungle itself, gloating, telling her of his death? Or was some sixth sense functioning among those whose lives, for so long, had been so close?

Shana dragged herself to her feet, shaken but unharmed, and walked unsteadily along the riverbank, clutching for support at the branches around her. She had never been alone before, in all of her life, and she drove the fears of the jungle away by an effort of will. She came at length to the waterfall, and was appalled at its unending depth. She stared down towards the pool, but there was too much mist to see anything, and she began the laborious and dangerous climb down the slippery rocks that flanked it, clambering hand over hand, seeking out footholds that were very hard to find. From the halfway point, where the mist was thinner, she saw Bramwell's broken body lying there, grotesquely twisted, and she caught her breath in pain.

Determined, she clambered on down, and when she reached the pool she found that it was wide and turbulent. She searched for any sign of a whirlpool that might be there and found none, and in a little while she made up her mind and swam out to the wet, grey rocks. She clambered onto them and crouched down beside the body, weeping and bewildered, because death was very strange to her. She wondered what had happened to Emlyn; one of the trio had survived, and perhaps another had too.

She steeled herself and straightened out Bramwell's limbs; his arms, his legs, his back had all been broken in many places, and they were like pieces of cold, wet rag as she tried to reform the body. When she was finished, she leaned down and kissed those dead lips and whispered: "Farewell, my dear friend, we will not forget you, ever. . . ."

She slipped into the pool and swam back to the shore, and she put her hands to her mouth and called as loudly as she could: "Emlyn . . . ! Emlyn . . . ! Emlyn . . . !"

There was no answer, nor did she expect one. She saw pieces of wood drifting lazily out of the pool and along a stream, and she wondered: if he had fallen into deep water, and lived, would he too have been carried this way? She followed the stream in a desperate kind of hope, calling his name refusing to give up, even as the hours passed by relentlessly.

And at last, she heard an answering shout that made her heart leap up: "*Shana* . . . !" The sound was distant and very weak, but she answered it and stumbled towards it as they called to each other repeatedly; his voice seemed to be filled with pain.

She found him at last, staggering to her out of the jungle, moving to a little clearing where the ground was covered with rich green moss, and she gasped when she saw him. His face was white and drawn, and there was blood still pumping from a mangled arm, the bones of which, in part, were visible. He collapsed at her feet and said hoarsely: "Thank God you are alive . . ." And then, he fell and lost consciousness completely.

She knelt beside him and looked at the bloodied arm, and knew what she had to do. She spent a long time looking for a tree she needed, and when she found it she collected a bundle of its broad leaves and hurried back to where she had left him.

Emlyn had recovered consciousness and was sitting up with his back to a tree, waiting for her patiently, and he said heavily: "Have you been hurt?"

Shana shook her head. "No. I brought papaya leaves for your wound."

"Good. And Bramwell?"

"Bramwell is dead."

"Oh, God . . ." His face was white. "He was such a good man."

"Yes. He went over the falls, and landed on the rocks there. And you?"

"I was swept over too, but I fell into deep water, but . . ." There were tears in his eyes. He whispered: "I cannot imagine Bramwell dying. He was so kind, so gentle and considerate. And always so full of life."

Emlyn's voice was heavy with pain that did not stem from his own fearful wound. "It may be," he said, "that Bramwell was my own son."

Shana nodded, wrapping his arm in the leaves. "Yes, I have heard it said."

"But in our society, how can a man be sure?"

She tore a piece of silk from her *draperi* and bound the leaves in place. "Are you in great pain?"

"The leaves are a comfort."

"Was it the fish?"

"Yes. I lost consciousness when I hit the pool at the bottom of the falls, or I would never have allowed myself to be carried along on such slow-moving water. And there were piranhas . . ." He grimaced. "There is nothing in the world like mortal danger to bring a man to his senses, and I reached the bank before they could kill me. For a long time, I tried to find my way back to the falls in the hope that you would be there, And then . . . I heard your voice."

10

"You must rest now."

"Yes, for a while. And then?"

"Then, we will do whatever you say." Her wonderful eyes held his. "Up there, you advised me not to cross the river at that point, and I chose to ignore your advice. And so . . . our dear Bramwell is dead."

"It was not your fault," Emlyn said quickly. "It was apparent that the Indians crossed there, and we should have been able to cross too. Save for the chance of that tree, we would have succeeded. One chance in a thousand."

"And this time, I will take your advice. We can return, or go on, as you say."

"Then we should go on," Emlyn said. "We were given a mission. If we return with it unfulfilled, there will be shame. It is not good for either of us, nor for our people."

Shana nodded. "Very well then. There are uncounted thousands of miles of empty jungle around us, and yet we found each other. Perhaps it is an omen for the success of our mission."

"I am sure it is."

"And when you are rested, and strong again, we will continue. Perhaps in two or three days."

"Tomorrow," Emlyn said, smiling. "Tomorrow, I will be strong again."

"Then we will sleep now, it will soon be very dark."

"Yes, sleep will be good. . . ."

They wrapped themselves in their *draperies* and lay close beside each other on the soft moss, their arms entwined. The night came over them, and in the darkness Shana awoke and saw the moonlight reflected in Emlyn's open eyes. She whispered: "Not asleep?"

"No, awake and yet dreaming." The nighttime jungle

11

sounds were all around them, the screeching of monkeys, the squawking of parrots, the bellowing of frogs; there was the distant cough of a prowling jaguar.

Shana's face was very close to Emlyn's. Only half-awake, she whispered: "Why is it that you have never loved me, Emlyn?"

He too was on the verge of sleep. He sighed, and murmured: "Perhaps because the occasion never arose for you to ask for me as is your right. And for my part . . ." He struggled to put his thoughts in order, and he said gently: "Do you know that you might be my daughter?"

"Oh, yes, of course," Shana said. "My mother told me about you many times, how often you had loved her."

"And I am old enough to suffer still from the inhibitions of our ancestors, which have all been swept away now. In my father's world, incest was a terrible offence against morality."

"Yes, I know, it's quite ridiculous."

"Perhaps." He sighed. "I am known as the wisest of the wise, and yet . . . I cannot be sure. In the days of Dashtu it was forced upon us as a matter of survival, we were simply dying out because there were not enough children being born. Strong measures had to be taken, perhaps in desperation, and this was one of them. We must remember that among the Indians who became part of us, who rescued us from oblivion indeed . . . for them, it was perfectly normal, as it has become for our new generation to which you belong. But I am old, Shana. I remember the tales my father told me. That is why I have never loved you. And you must sleep now, we will need all of our strength for the trials ahead of us."

He slid his hand under the silk of her gown and cupped her breast, and whispered: "You are the most beautiful of all our women."

12

Shana held her hand over his. "No." Her voice was very low. "Alma is more lovely than I am, and so is Thelma."

"No, no . . ."

"And Bianca too. Certainly Bianca . . ."

"No, I deny it. Go to sleep."

They slept.

But in a little while Shana awoke, and she shook Emlyn by the shoulder and whispered urgently: "Emlyn, wake up! A jaguar . . .

There was a soft cough in the recesses of the jungle shrubbery that betrayed its presence, and it was an announcement of mortal danger. The jaguar, strong as a lion, fast as a leopard, more unpredictable than the tiger, was the most dangerous animal in the world. And now, it was out there somewhere close by, coughing the deadly warning that made all the other denizens of the jungle cower in their shelters in the hope of safety.

Emlyn was awake at once. He heard it, and said softly: "A tree. There is a dead banyan close behind us."

"But a jaguar can climb trees too, far better than we can . . ."

"It will not go onto branches that cannot support its great weight, an instinct. The tree is dead, and we will climb high. Come."

Shana tightened the *draperi* around her waist and followed him as they moved from their sleeping place to the great tree, and they clambered carefully up together into the high branches. The limbs were dead, but still strong enough to support them. Emlyn whispered, "Good, it will not follow us here. We will be safe."

They found nesting places and curled up to pass the rest of the night in broad, smooth-barked forks; it was not too uncomfortable, but Emlyn said to Shana, only a

13

few feet above him: "Eden was never like this . . ."

"There was nothing, ever, like Eden," Shana said fiercely. "Though I have seen no other place in all my life, I am sure that this is the truth! Do you think we will find the Indian trail again tomorrow?"

"Yes, it will not be difficult. We will climb to the top of the waterfall, follow the riverbank . . . we will find it."

"Are we far behind them, do you think?"

"I cannot know this. But I think not. The jungle quickly obliterates the tracks of those who violate it, so the trail is recent. I fear the jungle almost as much as the rest of our people do, but perhaps I understand it better than most of them. And I think the Indians are not very far ahead of us."

"Will they be friendly?"

Emlyn answered gravely: "This too, I cannot know. It is my hope that they will be. We come to them in peace."

"The Books tell us that on the Outside, peaceful overtures are not always accepted in peace."

He sighed. "Yes, that is so. And perhaps the essence of our mission is to find out if that is true, or not."

"And we will sleep again now, Emlyn," Shana said. "Goodnight."

"Good night, dear Shana. Tomorrow will be a good day for us, I am sure of it."

Once more, they fell into deep sleep. They were safe up here from the predator; but the jungle, as alive as any of the animals it sheltered, had very many weapons at its disposal, and in the early light of the morning they were awoken by a sharp, crackling sound that racked their senses, and by a trembling of the branches they were in. The trembling became a gentle swaying as they held on tightly and waited in alarm, and Emlyn shouted

14

urgently: "A vine, Shana! Find a vine to hold on to!"

His warning was too late. The great tree crashed majestically and very slowly to the ground, borne down by the great weight of the lianas that had massed in its upper branches. It hung at an acute angle for a moment, and then continued on its way down, rolling to one side as it fought its way through the dense vegetation and drove itself deeply into the mud of the forest floor.

Emlyn was thrown clear, and he screamed in pain as he landed on his injured arm. But he was quickly on his feet again and fighting his way through the great branches as he searched for Shana, sure that the fall must have killed her. . . .

He found her at last, the lower part of her body completely immersed in thick black mud, a long and very heavy branch lying across her waist and slowly forcing her down, deeper and deeper. She was unconscious. He groped in the mud and felt her body for broken bones, and placed the back of his hand at her breast to feel her heartbeat; he was in tears.

For an hour or more he struggled to free her, and could not, and at last she revived and stared at him blankly in the knowledge of her predicament. But she was a woman of very strong character, and when he whispered the question, echoing that which she had asked him so recently: "Are you in great pain?" she shook her head. "No, there is no great pain. I am numbed."

"I found no broken bones, though I did not search well."

"I think none are broken. The mud is very soft."

"And can become suffocating."

"Yes, suffocating . . ."

15

Her head and shoulders were well above the level of the wet earth. But how long would it remain so? Even as he worked, she seemed to be slowly sinking. With his one good arm he was scraping mud away from her at a furious pace, like a wild dog digging for burrowing animals to feed on, and the more he worked the more hopeless his task seemed to be. He dug deeply, and found a massive branch lying squarely across her hips, and below them was hard rock. He strained against the branch, and said urgently: "If it moves, can you crawl out?"

Shana nodded, and he bent his back and strained, and could not even begin to move it. He spent an hour thrusting a furious foot against dead branches and snapping them off to lighten the load, but this was a very big tree and not to be broken up so easily. As he worked, the hole he had dug was filling up slowly with mud again. He wept out his desperation, and said helplessly: "There is rock below you, and you are pinned down by a weight I cannot hope to move unaided. And yet, if I hurry back to our people . . . However fast I move, day and night without stopping, it is a week's journey or more, two or three weeks before I can bring Strong Men to help us. You cannot survive for so long."

Shana said weakly: "The Indians, then."

"Yes, the Indians."

He looked up at the towering trees above them and raised his arms, and shouted: "Bramwell! Where are you now that we need you?"

Her arms were free, and she was very calm. She reached out, touched him, and whispered: "For the first time in my life, Emlyn, I face death. And I find that . . . I do not want to die, there is so very much to live for. Will you find the Indians for me? Find them and bring them here?"

"And if I cannot?"

"We *must*. There is no other recourse."

"Then I *will!*

"How far ahead of us are they?"

"I cannot be sure. But I think we are hard on their heels. Maybe it is a little less than a day, two at the most. I will move fast, the time will be shorter."

"Then bring them."

He sat back on his haunches and thought about it, and he knew that there was no other solution. He muttered: "If only I had a chopping-knife . . ."

"You do not."

"If only Bramwell were still with us . . ."

"But he is not."

He reached down into the mud and pulled up her *draperi*, and wound it about the lower part of her face to make a barrier against the encroaching mud, then doubled up the rest of it to make a cushion for her head. . . . He said quietly, "The Indians have left a very clear trail. I will find it again. I will follow it fast and catch up with them, I swear it. And I will bring them here."

"And if they should be hostile?"

Emlyn did not hesitate. He said gravely: "If they are hostile . . . then we will both die." He kissed her on the lips and said: "You must have courage now, Shana."

She held his eyes. "I have courage. I am a woman."

The image in his mind was dreadful, an image of returning with a dozen husky Indians of whom he knew nothing, and finding her dead. . . . Driven by a fierce resolution, he forced his painful way through the dense foliage to the foot of the falls, and began the slow ascent

17

with only one arm to search out handholds, desperately hoping to find once again the tracks they had lost.

He had no way of knowing that the very clear trail had been left by a group of tribal Indians who were fleeing their pursuers in mortal terror; the trail had been deliberately set to confuse the murderous gang of bounty hunters who were searching for them, a band of outlaws led by a cruel and ruthless *mestizo* named Jao Torres.

And Shana, pinned down in great pain now, fought against the coma, knowing that should she lose her senses she would never recover them.

Chapter Two

In the limitless immensity of the Amazon's jungle, it was easy to imagine that no one could possibly move here. And yet, sometimes hundreds of miles apart from each other, there were scattered men here who sought, for one reason or another, to tame the living enemy.

And the jungle hated them all and vented its spite on them.

One of these men was named Gerard Fletcher. He was twenty-seven years old, a professional mapmaker from New Orleans, hired by the Brazilian Government of the expatriate Emperor Dom Pedro to map the upper reaches of the Amazon River.

He was a man of high intelligence and probity, and in four years in the jungle he had learned not to tame it (no man could do that!) but at least to live with it in a kind of mutual and cautious enmity.

He was tall and strong and ruggedly handsome, with very thick, dark-auburn hair; even in the jungle, he kept himself clean-shaven, save for the bushy muttonchop whiskers that were the fashion of the time. He wore dark blue canvas breeches and a shirt of heavy white cotton, and black boots of jacked-leather up to his knees. His heavy woollen cloak of dark blue wool was habitually carried over his shoulder, and there was always a pistol and a machete in the broad leather belt that encircled his taut, narrow waist.

He was a scholar, a man of great erudition, but the jungle had hardened him physically; it had tried and tested him, and had tried to kill him many times. And now, his physical strength was as keenly honed as his intelligence.

The night was falling, and he had called his party to a halt; travel in the jungle after dark was not only dangerous, it was also unrewarding. There were ten others with him; Dora, his young wife, whom he doted on, Harry Welks and Peter Dunning, his two English assistants, and seven Indians (four men and three women), who served as guides and porters for his meagre supplies.

They were only a hundred miles or so south of the equator here, and the darkness came very quickly once the sun had set. And with it came all the raucous sounds of the night. They could hear a violent crashing through the shrubbery as a herd of wild boar, perhaps as many as a hundred of them altogether, thundered past them.

Gerard waited, listening, till the fearful sound of them had died away. He said to his wife, speaking very quietly as was the custom in the jungle, "If they don't go too far, I will track them down in the morning and bring meat."

She reached out to touch him. "And are you worried, darling?"

He smiled. "Worried, no. Though perhaps I should be. Whatever monies may be waiting for me when we eventually get back to civilisation will undoubtedly have been sequestered." He shrugged. "Perhaps I will be able to find work in the docks until we find our feet again."

"In the *docks?*" Her voice was hushed. "As a common laborer?"

He laughed and said, making a joke of it: "I'm in fine physical fettle, and very strong. I'd make an excellent stevedore. No, I am not worried. A little angry, perhaps."

"And justifiably so, I would say."

It had been a bad day for Gerard. An Indian runner, following on his tracks with the wonderful expertise of the jungle people, had come here from Beranha, the nearest Government river post, ninety-five miles away. He had carried a letter, sealed with red wax and bearing the Brazilian Government imprint. Its contents had shocked him, and he thought of the letter now as he slowly stripped off his clothes.

It had said, in part:

'It is my duty to inform you that the Government of His Imperial Majesty Dom Pedro has seen fit to terminate your services. . . . a matter of certain reports bearing your signature which have deeply offended His Imperial Majesty's most respected Ministers of the Crown . . . to advise you that Governmental policy regarding the indigenous population is not the concern of a hired servant of that Government . . . hereby ordered to return your badge of authority by the present runner . . .

When he had finished undressing, he groped for his wife in the absolute darkness and found that she was naked too and waiting for him. He lay beside her on the cool green moss and threw a thigh across hers, and kissed her breasts. He said, darkly, "They are killing off the local Indians because they stand in the way of further colonization. Surely, in so many millions of square miles

21

there's room for those poor unfortunates too! I cannot keep quiet about their callous slaughter, and I never will."

"I am glad of it." Dora shuddered. Only a week ago they had come across the bodies of fourteen Indians where they had recently been shot. The women had been horribly mutilated, and the left ear had been cut from her head, the sign of the bounty hunter; the ears were collected and stored in a salted leather bag for eventual despatch downriver, where the tally was made at the nearest Government river post, sometimes hundreds of miles and many months distant.

Dora held her husband tightly and whispered: "I will never forget the sight of it. . . ."

"The half-castes," Gerard said, "the *mestizos*. There must be men of goodwill among them, but I have never found one in the jungle."

The *mestizos* here were adventurers, wild-rubber tappers, prospectors, outlaws, murderers. . . . men and women who lived by their wits and their weapons, often killing for the sheer exhilaration of it, murdering for even so fragile a thing as a shirt or a pair of sandals, for a few strips of dried meat or a handful of sugar. He felt that Dora was trembling, and he touched her lips with his and said softly: "But you *must* forget it. It is not good to live with spectres."

"Yes, I know that. But memory is a very obtrusive thing, and not easy to control."

His fingertips were brushing her nipples, caressing breasts that were full and very satisfying to the touch, firm and yet resilient. He kissed them gently and moved his hand down to her thighs, and she opened them slightly for the soft stroking that gave her so much pleasure. The heat and the moistness of the night were no more than her own, and her breath was coming fast as he fondled her.

In the jungle, a new sound was intruding, a gentle and friendly sound where the porters were tapping a drum in a strangely persuasive rhythm. The sweetly-scented smoke from the fire they had made was drifting.

Dora was very young, but sensible and down-to-earth, and physically developed far beyond her years. She laughed a great deal, and the simplest things in the world pleased her—the evening light on a mountainside of palm trees, the rippling of a brook over highly-polished pebbles, the chatter of the parrots, the strange scent of roasting bananas. . . .

She moved her body slighty and stretched out on her back with her arms above her head, lying quite still and expectant. He laughed softly, knowing it was all part of a game she liked to play with him. He gently, carefully, .placed her arms and her legs just so, arranging and rearranging them as though exactitude were the most important thing in the world; and then waiting a moment and doing it all again. From time to time he would kiss her body, and then sit back on his heels and wait, knowing that she was wondering where the next feather-touch would come. . . . For a long while he teased her in this manner, restraining his own urgent needs because of his deep love for her, because he knew that there was great excitement for her in the game.

The moon came creeping through the dense foliage above them in errie beams of striated blue light, the shadows moving over her white body as the branches swayed in the wind.

At last, he could resist his needs no longer, and he rolled over and lay between her thighs. She caught her breath as she always did when she felt the strength and the heat of him, thrusting herself up to meet him with an urgency that had not been dimmed, ever, in the four years they had been married. Time and time again, he took her to the limits of passion and beyond them, and he knew that the only Paradise that existed was in the confines of her arms.

For Dora, the act of love itself was always a fulfillment. She worshipped Gerard, sure that he was the most wonderful man in all the world; and this close embrace was invariably, for her, the culmination of a great desire that could not be denied. During these times of love, she was sure that there could be no happier woman than she living anywhere on the face of the earth. Gerard was strong, his muscles, jungle-hardened, as taut as stranded wire; he was as handsome as any of the great heroes the sculptors had carved into everlasting stone or cast in bronze. He was gentle and kind, and deeply in love with her, and what more could a woman want?

She was conscious that she was crying out in her delirium as the explosions came, and she did not care that she might be heard, either by their two English assistants or by the Indians who were a little further removed, around their own camp fire.

The Indians had heard her indeed, and the cry, repeated again and again, brought them great happiness; they were devoted to Gerard, and therefore to his wife as well.

The Government runner, an Indian himself, was still with them, passing a little time in the company of good friends till he would have to return. He had been telling them, in the gutteral *lingua franca* the tribal Indians shared: "Your Master has been discharged, and now he and his women, and the two white men with him, they

24

will starve because there is no pay." He was a river-Indian, more sophisticated than these simple jungle folk, and he said to them, explaining carefully: "Money is very important to the white people, because they need things that we do not need, and without money, they die." He saw that they were already impressed with his knowledge, and he went on, pushing the point of his learning home to them: "A gun, for example. A white man cannot use a bow and arrow, which you and I make from the trees that grow here, and so, to kill a boar for his supper, he needs a gun. But a gun, my good friends, is not made. A gun is bought. With money."

Heads were nodding at this display of wisdom, and he said: "And will you hear *why* he has been discharged?"

There was a murmur of assent, and the lone drummer changed his gentle rhythm to one that meant, to them, pain and anguish. The runner continued: "Your Master spoke out, in letters to the Government, against the *mestizos* who slaughter us for the bounty they are paid, money for every dead ear they salt down and send to the river posts. One Indian ear, one tally to be exchanged for money . . . Your Master Jer-Hard spoke out against this, and now, he is an outcast. It is good that he has his woman to console him."

One of the porters, older and wiser than the others, nodded and said gravely: "The body of a beautiful woman is consolation indeed in times of trouble. Between her thighs, there is forgetfulness. It is important."

The runner held up the badge that Gerard, in response to his orders, had given him. "I take this symbol back, it is no longer his, because . . ."

He drew on the calabash pipe of tobacco that one of them had given him, and said: "The clerk at the post comes from a tribe that is closely allied with my own. He is a man of great education, he went to mission school and he speaks Portuguese, English, and many of our own languages. He told me something of what your Master Jer-Hard wrote in one of his letters. He said, 'the murder of the Indians is a crime against humanity.'" There was no word for humanity in the dialect, and it came out as goodness to other people. He said, puffing out clouds of blue smoke: "Protect him from all evil, my brothers. Such a man is better for us than arrowheads without number."

Very unobtrusively, as the drummer changed his rhythm again, one of the women began chanting: *Jer-Hard, Jer-hard, Jer-hard* . . . The other two women took up the chant, muting their voices. One of them was very young and sweet, and her name was Gri-Sa-Puni, which meant in her language 'a flower that is opening to the sun.' She was perhaps thirteen or so years old, and she was crying at the calamitous news. One of the men said to her harshly: "Dry your tears, child! Jer-Hard is a strong man, he will not die just because he is a free man now, to go where he wishes, do what he wants, to live as he pleases!"

The two English assistants had heard Dora's cries too. They were playing chess together by the light of a length of string in a small pot of pheasant fat. Harry Welks and Peter Dunning were both in their late twenties. Welks was small and wiry, Dunning tall and angular, and they made a very odd couple indeed. Welks' hair was tousled and unkempt and he sported a very bushy mustache, while Dunning was bald and lacked facial hair.

Listening, Welks murmured: "When I hear that kind of sound, the animal in me raises its welcome head, the cry of a lovely woman in the throes of passion, there's no mistaking it. Your move, and if you don't get your queen the hell out of there, you're going to lose her, and the game."

"A lovely woman indeed," Dunning said. He interposed a knight and laughed. "And now, you're in the greatest danger, don't let the image of smooth white thighs distract you from a very good game. And if you are lusting after our employer's wife, then I don't want to hear about it." Not changing his tone of voice he said: "What would happen if we were to sneak into the Indian camp tonight and search out that pretty little thing called Greasy-Funny?"

"They'd probably cut both our throats."

"It might be worth it, she's got tits on her to drive a man mad. And I haven't had a woman since we left that village, when was it? Six weeks ago?"

"Not even a month," Welks said. "Twenty-seven days, to be precise." He moved a bishop. "Check."

"Twenty-seven days? Christ, celibacy is a pretty dull proposition in a hot climate, isn't it?" Dunning moved a castle and said drily: "Harry Welks, you just lost a damn good game. Two moves to mate. And speaking of mating, when you have the decency to admit defeat and resign, I suggest we join our Indian friends and make a few highly immoral suggestions to that lovely child. That fellow with the limp, is he her father?"

Welks frowned. He had been drinking the liquor the Indians made from hearts of palm, and he was the slightest bit tipsy. "Whose father?"

"Greasy-Funny's father."

"Oh. No, I think he's her husband or something, perhaps just her lover, I don't know." He threw back his

27

head and laughed. "I saw them a few days ago, copulating, a spectacle that raised my appreciation of Indian virility to the greatest heights."

"You did?" Dunning's eyes were wide. "You actually *saw* them at it?"

"Yes indeed." Welks moved a knight and said: "And you're in check again. I came upon them unexpectedly in the very early hours of the morning, and had the good sense to keep absolutely quiet and remain hidden in the bushes. And it's not only check, it's mate, you've no way out at all."

"Never mind about that," Dunning said, "I want to hear about this, dammit!"

"Well . . . She was on her hands and knees, and I swear that he positively *shoved* her for fifty feet before he was finished with her. It was really very exciting."

Dunning tipped his king over, admitting defeat. "Then I think we should absolutely go to the Indian camp and tell them what nice people we are. Drink some of that ghastly liquor they make, and see what happens. They might turn out to be very hospitable. A lot of primitive people are, y'know. Like the Eskimos."

"Actually," Welks said, "their liquor really isn't as terrible as all that. If you can stomach the appalling taste of it, the effect is really quite exhilarating." He stood up, stretched his wiry limbs, and said carefully, "All right, let's do that. But let's be circumspect too, I really don't want to see my own throat slit from ear to ear."

"They share their women," Dunning said, "so why shouldn't they share them with us too? After all, they *like* us. They really do, you know."

"Yes, it's true. All right, let's wander over there, sort of stumble on them by accident, and see what happens." Welks was a cautious man by nature, and he said: "We'll

28

play it by ear, drop a few hints and see what happens. But for God's sake don't take your penis out of its habitual hiding-place and start waving it around."

Dunning said stiffly, "It seems to me that you forget that I am, after all is said and done, a gentleman."

They began to move to the Indian camp, and a shot rang out in the moonlight. It was followed at once by a ragged volley of more than a dozen more at very close range, and a musket ball, more by chance than by expert marksmanship, took the top of Dunning's bald head off and toppled him to the ground.

Welks swung round and ran for his gun. The second volley was fired, and three of the heavy lead balls tore into his body and killed him. There was the sound of urgent yelling from the Indian camp, and a little removed in the shadows Gerard rolled away from Dora and shouted: "Welks! Dunning! Your guns . . . !"

There was a sudden silence as he stared into the dark of the trees. The silence went on forever. Out there in the treacherous jungle, unseen enemies were reloading, no doubt. It took a full minute and sometimes more to reload a musket. The powder had to be rammed down the barrel while the musketeer chewed on a lump of lead to make it more or less round, then the cotton wad rammed down on top of the powder and the chewed bullet after it, all of it prodded firmly in place with the ramrod. And then, the touch of powder in the firing pin and perhaps a check of the flint to make sure there was enough of it left to spark after the first, second, or perhaps the third fall of the hammer.

At the sound of the heavy firing, all the jungle sounds had ceased, and the absolute silence out there was terrifying in its intensity.

Gerard, his rifle in his hands, was crouched beside his

29

wife, and he was still naked and vulnerable. Dora, with a uniquely feminine instinct, was struggling into a heavy cotton gown, trying to subdue her fears by the application of prosaic and mundane matters. She whispered, "Gerard, my love . . . who are they?"

He shook his head. "I do not know. But there are very many of them out there, and they are all around us."

As though to confirm his words, a third volley came from behind them, and then a fourth to one side. Suddenly, he was aware that he was about to die, and the only thought in his mind was for Dora, a woman he loved with a never-ending devotion. But how could he save her now? He was in the depths of desperation.

Gerard waited; and in perfect silence the head porter was crawling to him. His name was Fa-Su-Meta, 'the man who knows' and he whispered in broken English, "Mister Dunning, Mister Welks, they both dead, finish."

"Oh, Christ . . . Who are they out there, Fa-Su-Meta?"

The Indian shook his head. "I not know, is *mestizos*, I think, they got *mestizo* guns. They be all sides of us, no way out."

"How many of them?"

"A lot." It meant nothing; the Indians' system of counting was: one, two, three, a lot . . . He said fearfully, "Many a lots."

"And your men?"

"They are frighted. They gather together by fire, all men and women."

"They must disperse, move apart, away from the fire."

"They not want, is fright, they stay together by fire."

And now, a sound came out of the jungle that was

more terrifying even than the silence; there was the sound of a man chuckling, so close that it must have been only yards away in the impenetrable darkness. It was followed by a deep, throaty voice speaking execrable English and raised to a shout: "I am Jao Torres, Americano! Thinking this name when you dying! Jao Torres . . . Jao Torres! People hear my name they dying of frighten!"

Gerard aimed his gun in the general direction of the sound and pulled the trigger, and he heard only the fall of the hammer. He thumbed it back and tried again, and once again, and saw the spark falling on powder that had become damp with the night air. With an oath, he emptied it and replaced it with fresh powder from his horn and tried three more times; but they had passed through a storm two days ago, and all of his powder was unserviceable. He laid the flintlock down, and found his heavy machete and waited. He whispered to Dora: "Do not move, my love, not till I tell you, stay in the shadows where you are."

There were three more disordered volleys from all around them, and he heard the screams of Indians who had been hit. They had been too frightened to douse the fire that illuminated them, and he yelled: "The fire, throw sand on it!" He knew that they would not; for them, the darkness that might have saved them was more terrifying than the firelight that was their destruction. Three more of them died, and two others were wounded.

There was silence again out there; they were reloading. Gerard whispered: "Dora? Now . . . crawl away, very slowly, keep to the shadows, there is too much moonlight. Find a hiding-place, under heavy shrubbery, curl yourself up there, make yourself as small as you

31

can, keep absolutely still, and silent, not even the sound of breathing . . ."

Her voice was a tremor. "No, Gerard my love. I will not leave you now."

He was furious. "Go . . . !"

She whispered: "No, I will not. If you are to die now, then I will die with you. But do not let me fall into their hands, beloved. Save one shot for me, will you promise me that?"

One shot? His powder was damp. Could he bring himself to drive his machete down onto her skull? He whispered hoarsely: "Remember the great love we have for each other, think of it all the time . . ."

There was another volley, a roar of undisciplined sound from all around them, and there were heavy lead bullets thudding into the tree trunks around them. He heard the raucous voice again: "Your woman, I see her! You thinking I am blind? I take her soon!"

And then, one of those bullets found the broad steel blade of Gerard's sharp machete and drove it with monstrous power into his chest; he keeled over and lost his consciousness completely. . . . And when he recovered and found his senses again, he could not move, and the whole jungle was reeling around him.

He opened his eyes and stared at a quite unbelievable image; there was a short, thick-set, bearded and barrel-chested man squatting close beside him, with long black hair down to his shoulders, dressed in European breeches of gray sailcloth and black Portuguese naval boots with no laces in them, with a broad leather belt at his waist in which were stuffed a machete, two pistols, a knife, and a sword; on a string over his shoulder there was a powder horn and a leather bag of lead lumps to be chewed into shape for the flintlock that was across his broad shoulders. And on top of his head, a black top hat was perched.

It was an incongruous and even ridiculous image, but Gerard quite understood the menace of this strange figure. And he was beset with more trials; there was a booted foot at his throat, holding him down while he gasped for breath that would not come to him.

He looked up and saw a young man of very handsome and even distinguished appearance looking down on him as he twisted the foot at his neck, grinding the heel of the boot in. And he heard the voice of the top-hatted man: "You watch now. When my Carmen finish, I take her too."

The pain was intolerable, and he could not breathe. And even when the foot, booted in fine leather, was taken away from his throat, he could not rise. The blood at his chest was pumping, and when he tried to move there were daggers of the most acute pain driving into his heart; he wondered if he were dying. The coma swept over him, and when it left him again there were strong hands at his chin, twisting his head to one side, and a voice that was not that of the top-hatted man was saying fiercely: "You watch, Americano. You watch . . ."

Gerard opened his eyes. There were thirty or forty people gathered in the clearing, lit by the moon and the earth-bound fire, black men, brown men, white men, savage-looking all of them, the *mestizos* of the man who had called himself Jao Torres.

But he was not concerned with them now. To one side of him, Dora was lying, naked as the day she was born, on a patch of moss in the half-light of the moon. There were two cut poles of bamboo to which her wrists and ankles had been tied, and a woman, only half-clothed, was lying on top of her and moving her hips rythmically up and down as she brought herself to climax on that inert and suffering body. He heard the voice of the top-hatted Jao Torres, a whisper: "My Carmen, I give her your woman, a present. But soon. I playing with her too, is pretty. I liking very much. And you watch, Americano, is good watching."

Gerard made a superhuman effort to arouse himself, screaming out his anger; his arms seemed powerless, and the boot was there again, driving him into the earth, twisting murderously onto his windpipe. He saw the handsome, laughing face, and heard the mocking voice: "Remember me too, Americano, as you die. I am Espada. Espada! Remember the name . . ."

The boot ground into his throat, and he lost consciousness again, and when he recovered he tried to move and could not. There was blood from his wound staining the moss around him, and he dimly heard voices:

"Better we kill him now . . ."

"No. My Gods telling me I meet him again one day is good for me."

"My sword through his heart, Jao."

Jao Torres said stolidly: "No. My Gods tell me one day I meet this man again, I don' kill him now."

"Then I tie him . . ."

"Do that, is good. I take his woman now."

Gerard felt himself being dragged, and he struggled and could not find the strength. Only half-conscious, he felt a rope around his neck being tied to a tree trunk, and he choked on it. And the last thing he saw before the coma swept over him again was the naked body of Jao Torres dropping to his knees between the spread-eagled thighs of his beloved wife. He heard her screams

34

and echoed them, but he was powerless to help her.

He saw too, weaving in and out of his consciousness, that extraordinarily voluptuous woman, black-eyed and black-haired, magnificent hair, sweeping down to below her waist, dressed only in a bark-cloth skirt and crouching beside him, groping for him with strong hands. He felt her sharp teeth on him, the teeth of a jungle animal, and he tried to scream and could not. And then, her face was very close to his, and she was laughing. Her skin was white, her lips dark red and full, and that coarse black hair was still sweeping over him. The rope around his neck was cutting deeply into his throat as she found his mouth, biting his lip savagely, and he heard, coming out of the void: "You like me, Americano? I am Carmen. . . ."

And then, everything was black.

He could not know how much time had passed when he came to himself again.

The neck-rope was half-strangling him, and he groped behind him and struggled with the knot. When he was free at last, he pulled himself to his feet and tried to remember what had happened. His chest was caked with blood, and he was so weak that he wondered if he was dying; he gritted his teeth against the pain. He tried to walk, but the whole forest swung around and around till the earth itself came up to hit him. He fought the coma and forced himself to stand.

The sun had risen now, and the steam was rising from the forest floor as he stumbled to the body of his dear wife. She lay silent in death, and a third bamboo shaft had been driven through her breast; her left ear had been sliced off, an added bonus. Unable to control the violent shaking, he dropped to his knees beside her and wept, and prayed, and cursed all the Gods in his philosophy.

With his bare hands, he scraped a hole in the forest floor and buried her, and explored what was left of the camp. He found the dead bodies of Welks and Dunning, and the Indians too. He looked down at the two mutilated women and wondered what had become of the third, a very pretty young girl named Gri-Sa-Puni, whom his two assistants had always insisted on calling Greasy-Funny; there was no sign of her. He found a single machete that had been overlooked, and a pair of breeches and even Indian sandals. He found the trampled vines where the raiders had left, and the careless tracks that told where they had gone, and he estimated that there were perhaps thirty or forty of them.

He remembered the name Jao Torres, remembered the words: 'Thinking this name when you dying . . .' And the name Espada, a handsome youth with a foot grinding into his throat . . . And a woman called—what was her name? *Carmen* . . . 'I am Carmen' she had said. 'You like me . . . ?"

Gerard Fletcher gripped his machete, and set off to follow their tracks. There was only the thought of vengeance in his heart. This gentle, kindly man had become, in the space of a few nightmare hours, an instrument of implacable revenge.

Chapter Three

Gerard had travelled fast. The pain from the deep
wound in his chest was monstrous, and he had lost a
great deal of blood. The blade of his own machete,
driven by the impact of a lead ball nearly half an inch
across, had sliced into him and broken a rib; but he had
the sense to keep his chest expanded so that the ragged
ends of bone might come together and heal themselves
rather than puncturing a lung. Sometimes, he dropped
to his knees and bit his lip half-through in his pain; but
he knew that it was all a question of time, and he would
not give up.

All through the day and half the night he followed the
tracks, and when darkness made further progress impossible he lay down to sleep, too exhausted even to
move away from the sandbanks of the river he was soon
to cross. He could go no further now.

It was not good to sleep where there were sandbanks.
There were always clouds of innumerable insects swarm-
ing over them, tiny flying creatures so small that they
could hardly be seen with the naked eye. Their name in
the *lingua franca* was no-see-ums.

They descended on his body in their hordes, like a

cloud of angry, living smoke, and when he awoke as the sun came up to drive them away his face was swollen to almost twice its natural size, and his arms and legs were bloated beyond tolerance. He knew that it would pass, because his body was healthy, had it not been, they could easily have killed him.

He moved on very fast, searching out signs of the gang's passage with a practiced eye, still not knowing what he would do when he caught up with them but driven on by his cold hatred. Towards midday he soaked himself in a fast-running stream of cold water, bathing his face to reduce the swelling, drinking his fill but refusing to sacrifice time by looking for food, and close beside him, in the red mud of the brook's edge, he saw a footprint so fresh that the water was still seeping into it. He searched and found other prints, that gave the impression of . . . unsteadiness. They were unevenly spaced, as though the man who had made them were staggering . . .

He crawled on his belly, knowing that he was very close and that there must be great danger now. The trail was to one side of that which he had been following before, and he wondered about it, wondered too about the sandals which had left the imprints; they had been made with *soles*, not draped up over the foot in the Indian fashion.

And then, parting the foliage stealthily, he saw a white man of middle-age, quite naked, squatting in a small pool and bathing an arm that had been terribly lacerated. There was a neatly-folded length of cloth on the moss nearby, and yes . . . those sandals too.

For a long time, Gerard watched in silence; where there was one man, there would undoubtedly be others.

38

But there was no sign of a weapon anywhere, and it puzzled him; a man alone, perhaps, in the jungle, without a gun or even a chopping-knife? It made no sense at all.

Alone? No, he could not possibly be alone!

Gerard moved to one side and circled the area, and found no other signs of life, but when he returned to his original position, he still watched from under close cover for a very long time.

The man had left the water now, binding papaya leaves onto his wounded arm, and he was dressed in the strangest kind of gown Gerard had ever seen—a length of beige wool around his waist and a great folded mass of it balanced on his shoulder.

It was time for action, and Gerard rose from his hiding-place and hefted his machete, ready to do battle.

The stranger wheeled at the sound, a middle-aged man of great dignity, blue-eyed and fair-haired, staring at him in acute surprise as he moved forward.

They looked at each other for a long time in wary silence, each of them gauging the other's capability and possible menace, and Gerard said at last, sure that this could not possibly be one of the men he was pursuing: "If you speak English, sir . . . ?"

The stranger answered: "Of course, I *am* English, as I see by your speech you are too."

"American," Gerard said. "And you have no gun?"

"No gun, sir, nor any other weapon save my depleted wits."

"And you are alone?"

"I am, sir. And you?" They were sparring with each other, both of them unsure and wary. Gerard swung his machete down and embedded it in the soil at his feet, an ancient gesture that meant no combat. He said slowly,

"Yes, I am alone too. My party was attacked recently and I am the only survivor. You know of it, perhaps?"

There was a deep frown on the stranger's handsome, gentle face. "Slaughtered, you say? You have my deepest sympathy, sir. And I see that you have been sorely wounded too."

"It is not as bad as it appears to be, and already beginning to heal. May I know your name?"

"My name is Emlyn. And yours?"

"Gerard Fletcher, an American from New Orleans lately employed by the Brazilian Government, but no longer. I am searching now for the men who killed my friends . . . and my wife."

"Oh God! Your wife too? Then my sympathy is multiplied a hundred-fold. I am a man of sensitivity, and I bleed for you. But I am in need of the most urgent help . . ."

"Tell me first, if you will, where you come from. You are English, and yet your dress . . . It is very strange to me."

"I come from Eden, Sir, a community some two weeks' trek to the north of us. I have been following Indian tracks in the hope of finding that help. I am not a skilled tracker, but the trail they have left is a very clear one . . ."

"I too have seen it," Gerard said, interrupting him. "And it is clear because it is a false trail, deliberately left to confuse their pursuers." Emlyn was staring at him in shock, and he went on: "There is a partridge feather carefully placed every few miles along their path. It means flee the area, there is danger. When an Indian travels through the jungle, Sir, *no one* finds his tracks, not even another Indian."

"Oh, God . . . !" Emlyn was in despair. "I need ten or

twelve strong men, desperately, and you tell me that I have been chasing an illusion?"

"That is all it is. But the help you speak of . . . ?"

Emlyn told him at great length of Shana's predicament, and Gerard listened with growing alarm, and he asked at last: "Two days from here, you say? Then if we hurry, perhaps we can save her. Can you lead me straight back to her?"

"Yes, I am sure of it. But the two of us will not be enough . . ."

"The two of us," Gerard said tartly, "are all we have. The Indians in the area are very few indeed, and even if they were within fifty feet of us, as well they might be, listening to us now, they will never disclose themselves and we will not find them. Come, we must hurry. Two cripples, but between us, we will save her. The need seems to be for a good chopping-knife and a strong back. I have both." There were tears in his eyes now, and he said quietly: "I have lost a woman whom I dearly loved, who died in great pain and sorrow at the hands of monsters. Perhaps, if I can help save the life of another woman, Dora my wife, in Heaven now, will look down and bless us both."

They set out together and fought their way through the jungle for all of the day and most of the night until they were in danger of losing the way in the darkness. They moved on again when the bright moon came up, and found themselves in the middle of a huge stand of palms, and Emlyn said, worried; "I did not come this way, I saw almost no palms at all. . . ."

"Then we move in a straight line to the next clearing," Gerard said calmly. And within the hour the forest broadened out, and there were high mountains visible ahead of them, distantly silhouetted in the moonlight.

41

Emlyn stared at them for a moment, and said: "Yes, the saddle between those two peaks there, it was directly behind me when I left her."

"Then we are moving in the right general direction. It will be daylight soon, and easier for us." And when the sun came up they came upon a giant garlic tree, standing almost alone in a small grassland, and Emlyn said excitedly: "Yes! I remember this tree . . ." He was ashamed to tell Gerard that for the last few hours he had been sure that they had lost the way. It was very easy, in this dense jungle; they could have passed within twenty feet of Shana, or even less, and missed her completely.

But a few hours after dawn, they came upon her . . . She was still alive, but her eyes were closed and she was unconscious. The fallen tree was stable in the deep mud, but its weight had twisted her body atrociously; her head only inches above the forest floor.

They both went to work at once, three strong arms digging the usurping mud away again. And then . . . there was the main problem, that of removing the great weight from her slender hips. Gerard slashed at branches furiously with his chopping-knife to lighten the load, and as the hours went by the giant tree was reduced to a skeleton of its former self.

He stood back, panting hard, and studied the way it lay on her, and said: "A lever now . . ." He cut a great bamboo pole nearly twenty feet long and some eight inches thick, and wedged it under the trunk, seeking out the hard rock that lay below the mud. Even the positioning of it was not easy, but when he was sure it was mathematically right, he crouched under the far end of it, placing it on his shoulder and forcing it up till it would move no further.

He said to Emlyn: "Now . . . both our backs together

42

to raise it. As soon as the trunk begins to move, and a few inches will be enough, you will run to her and drag her out. I cannot raise it alone, but once it is in position, I believe I will be able to hold it there."

They bent their backs under the long pole and heaved. Gerard felt his wound open up with the effort, the blood pumping out again, and still he strained with every strong muscle in his tortured back. The pain was insufferable, but he would not weaken, and the two of them forced themselves up against the lever. Emlyn shouted: "It's moving! A little more . . . !"

There were blinding stars in front of Gerard's eyes, the pain in his chest racking him from head to foot, and still he forced himself to thrust upward with every iota of his diminishing strength. As he slowly, inexorably, straightened his powerful back, he saw the blood from his chest coursing down his thighs, and he prayed silently: "Oh, God . . . only a moment more!"

And then, the tree was slowly rolling over, and he screamed: "Now, Emlyn! Now . . . !"

For a brief moment, he saw her being dragged free; and then, he felt the great weight driving his widely-spaced feet into the forest floor, and he collapsed face down in the red mud and lost all consciousness.

He came to his senses very slowly, in fits and starts. In the first moment there was great clarity, and he saw a young woman of surpassing loveliness kneeling beside him, a hand at his forehead and a look of great concern in the most startling pale blue eyes he had ever seen. Jet-black hair of a very fine texture was falling over his bare chest, and he was seized with an insane desire to fondle it, but found that he could not move his arms; or was he unconscious again?

He awoke once more and she was still there, whispering to him in a soft and very sweet voice: "No, do not try and move, you are hurt, you have lost a great deal of blood. Lie still now."

He saw to his astonishment that she was half-naked, a length of blue silk, very muddied now, wound around her waist and falling to the ground beside him. Her breasts were small but full and very firm-looking, and her skin was the strangest color he had ever seen, a sort of light caramel. Unsteadily, only half out of his coma, he reached up and touched her breast, and he whispered through the haze: "Dora . . . ?"

He heard her gentle answer: "Dora?" I do not know Dora. I am Shana, and you saved my life."

The deep green of the jungle was becoming red, and the ferns were swinging in ever-increasing circles around him till it was all ready to explode. He shouted suddenly: "Dora! Where are you . . . ?"

The soft voice came to him again out of the void: "No, you must sleep now, you cannot walk. . . ." There was a man with her now, and they were both trying to ease him back to the ground, though he was not conscious that he had risen to his feet. He fell back and saw her glorious body wheeling away in fast-diminishing sweeps, not holding its position as he tried to focus his eyes on it, but racing up into infinity, surrounded by exploding stars.

The sun had been hot and strong, but only moments later the moon was shining down on them, and there was a small fire burning close by. He heard the man's voice, sad and yet filled with admiration: "It is hard to believe that he can lose so much blood and still live."

There were tiny, sharp pinpricks of pain at his chest, and before his searching hand was brushed gently away by unknown fingers he found the needle-points of long thorns there and knew that his wound had been sutured, jungle-fashion, by pinning the edges of the cut together.

The voices came to him hazily, as in a dream. "It will take time for the cut to heal, but when he is strong enough to travel, he should come back with us to Eden."

"Yes, I think so. If we can persuade him to do that, then our mission will have been accomplished."

Eden? Where, in God's name, was Eden in this forbidding jungle he thought to himself.

The first rays of the early morning sun struck across his face, and he awoke with a start to find, to his astonishment, that the lovely, naked, young woman was asleep beside him. More, his hand was at her breast, cupping it, and he withdrew it guiltily. He rolled over onto his back to stare up at the green treetops and worry about this strange condition.

She was awake instantly, leaning over him to touch his cheek with delicate fingers. "And did you sleep well, as I did?"

He could not believe the intimacy; she was quite careless of her complete nudity, as though it were the most natural thing in the world. Many of the Indian tribes, he knew, went naked, and her skin color might have meant Indian blood; but if that were the case, how could it be that she spoke English with such ease and fluency? And the man with her, Emlyn; in spite of his outlandish dress, he was undoubtedly English, although he too moved like an Indian, on the balls of his feet. Who were these people? In God's name, where had they come from?

But she was waiting for his answer, and he said quickly: "Yes, thank you, I slept very well."

"And do you feel better? You were very sick last night, and we thought we were going to lose you. Though I think you will not remember."

He looked around. "There was a man with us, Emlyn, I believe?"

"Yes, Emlyn. He has gone to find food for us, he will return soon. He says we must stay here for a few days until we are all strong enough to travel."

"He too has been hurt, I remember."

"Ah yes, the piranhas took the meat from his left arm, down to the bone in places. He is recovering fast, but he says we cannot return to Eden until we are all strong again."

"Eden . . . Emlyn told me nothing but the name."

"Our home. It is ten days or a little more from here, and lies in a hidden and very beautiful valley in the mountains. We would like you to come with us, will you do that? Please?"

Gerard nodded. "Yes, I can do that. I am a free agent now, a man alone."

"Good, I am very pleased. I would like so much to have a son by you. As soon as you feel strong again, we will love each other."

Gerard choked. "You would like . . . ? We will do *what?*"

The lovely young girl shrugged. "Even a daughter. In Eden, we have more women than men, which is to be desired, of course. But we need more male children now. As soon as you are better."

He was in shock as she rose to her feet, incredibly long-legged, her skin as smooth as the finest velvet. She took the length of blue silk, washed now and draped over a bush to dry, and shook it out. It was some three feet wide and about twenty feet long, with tassels at both ends. She wrapped it once around her waist and fastened it, letting the rest of the cloth drop almost to her ankles, and tossed the rest of it over her head, down in the front again, and up once more over her shoulder; she looked like a madonna, standing there tall and proud and very regal indeed. Gerard struggled to his feet and gasped at the sudden access of pain that sliced into his chest. Her arm was around him instantly, and there was a look of deep anxiety in her eyes. "The pain is strong?"

Gerard sighed, "It will pass. And you? You were very close to death, I think."

"Until you saved me, yes."

"There are no bones broken?"

"None. Only a fearsome-looking bruise." Making nothing of it at all, she lifted her gown and twisted her lissome body to one side and touched her naked hip; the skin was torn there, the flesh-tones tinged with blue. She said casually, "This too will pass, it is nothing."

She let the *draperi* drop back into place. Gerard nodded and said, "Emlyn is right. We should all rest for a while. In the jungle, a weakened animal is very vulnerable, as we are now."

His mind was filled with questions, but Emlyn was coming into the little clearing now, carrying three huge papayas and a handful of bamboo shoots. Emlyn smiled when he saw Gerard on his feet and said happily, "We will not starve here, there is fruit in great abundance all around us, and a river nearby teeming with fish."

"And soon," Gerard said, "I will make a spear and find meat too." He cut open the ripe fruit, and as they sat down on the moss to eat, he looked at Shana and said: "And now, will you tell me about Eden?"

A smile lit up her lovely face even at the mention of

47

the name. She whispered, "A place of great beauty and of happiness. We have our own terrible jungle in the confines of our valley, but we never venture into it, and why should we? We have fields and meadows and streams, and the township too is a very satisfying place to be in. I have read all the Books, and I know that our township is not like any other on the Outside."

Gerard was frowning. "A *township*? In the middle of the jungle? But I know only of a few small and scattered Indian villages here, hundreds of miles apart. And how can it be that I have never even heard the name Eden?"

Shana shrugged. "Perhaps because no one knows of it."

Gerard gestured helplessly. "Our Indian guides told us that there is only one very small tribe living between the Ayana River and the mountains, they do not even have houses or tents, but live in the trees . . . and you speak of a *township?*" He threw up his arms. "There is so much that I find hard to understand! In spite of his dress, Emlyn is obviously English, but you, Shana . . ." How could he phrase it? He said: "You are far more beautiful than any English woman I ever saw, no English woman ever had eyes like yours nor skin either . . . And yet, you speak English as though you were born to it!"

"As I was," Shana said, laughing at his puzzlement, and Emlyn took up the tale, smiling that gentle smile of his.

"The mystery will be less for you," he said, "if I tell you that in Eden we are all the offspring of Englishmen, and Indian women, and that for many years now we have been quite cut off from the rest of the world, which we call the Outside."

"And that," Shana said, "is the reason for our presence here. Recently, after being closed in so long by an

48

earthquake, we made a way out, cutting steps up the mountainside, and I was sent with Emlyn and a Strong Man named Bramwell, who was killed, to find news of the outside world." She reached out and touched his hand in an intimate little gesture. "After so long, it was decided that we should try and find out what is happening in the countries beyond our borders. We decided that it was foolish to spend the rest of our lives in total ignorance of the rest of the world. While time has stood still for us . . . a great deal must have been happening out there, and we want to know about it. This is why we have asked you to come with us back to Eden, to enlighten us."

"Cut off for some years?" Gerard thought about it for a while, and said at last: "Well, perhaps the most important event in the last few years . . . Napoleon, the scourge of Europe, died four years ago, in exile, and the whole world can breathe again."

"Napoleon?"

"Napoleon Bonaparte, of course."

Shana said: "I do not know this name."

Puzzled, he stared at her, "But . . . for fifty years now, his name has been a household word, and people trembled at the sound of it!"

"Fifty years? It is not very long."

Gerard felt that his mouth was open, and he snapped it shut. He said incredulously: "You have been cut off for so long? Are you telling me, Shana, that you were *born* in your Eden?"

She nodded. "Yes. And so were my parents . . ."

"As I was too," Emlyn said.

"In God's name . . . how long, then?"

"The year of the Great Earthquake," Emlyn said, "the terrible quake that sealed our valley up . . . was the

49

year 1721. One hundred and four years ago and twenty-one years after the community was founded."

Gerard could not believe his ears. "And since then . . . ?"

"Since then, no other world has existed for us. But we are content. Life is good in Eden, our Queen is a wise and benevolent ruler . . ."

"Your *Queen?*"

"Queen Alma is the daughter of Dashtu, our first Queen, who was Adam Grieg's daughter. Adam, as you will learn when you read the Books of our history, was the man who discovered the valley, perhaps by a stroke of extraordinary luck. The only way in was always through a narrow cleft in the rocky mountainside, high up and concealed by vegetation. A heavy rainstorm had washed the greenery away, and for reasons known only to him, he chose to climb and explore it. As you know, the vegetation here grows very fast after the rain, and in a matter of a few days the cleft must have been invisible once more. The Books do not say what prompted him to climb the dangerous cliff face and search, but they do say that he was looking for Raman-li-Undara; and we are all sure that he knew he had found it. That was in the year 1699."

Gerard felt his scalp crawling. He whispered: *Raman-li-Undara?"*

"Yes, an Inca name. The original inhabitants may have been a branch of the Incas, or closely allied with them."

Gerard could not restrain his excitement. "And do you, perchance, know what the name means?"

Emlyn smiled. "Of course, it is known to all of us. It means the Field of Diamonds."

For a long time, Gerard could not answer. He said at

last, not yet daring to ask the crucial question, "In almost every primitive society, there are legends of hidden valleys containing great wealth in gold, rubies, emeralds or diamonds, lost to civilization for thousands of years and waiting to be rediscovered, attracting adventurers —some honest explorers but most of them rogues— from all over the world. One of those legends concerns a place in the Amazon basin called Raman-li-Undara. Every adventurer on the continent knows of it, almost every Indian too. But not one of them has any idea where it might be."

"It lies ten or fifteen days from here," Shana said nonchalantly, "to the north. The valley that Adam Grieg searched for, and found."

His heart was beating very fast. "But . . . there is no field of diamonds."

"No, not any longer."

Shana was smiling her secret smile. "Once in a while, one of our farmers turns up a stone with his plough, but for the most part they were collected long ago by the people, whoever that may have been, who built our township and then, for reasons that we do not know, abandoned it."

Here in the remote vastness of the jungle, the vision was an extraordinary one—an age-old legend come to life, being discussed so off-handedly and apparently having considerable basis in fact. Gerard echoed her words, "Collected long ago . . . ?"

"Yes." Shana rose and made a strange gesture, touching her fingers together and feeling the sweet stickiness of papaya juice on them. "Shall we go to the stream and wash, before the ants find us and eat us alive?"

"Over here," Emlyn said, and as they moved off.

Shana went on, "Yes, there are several thousand of them, and of what use to us can they possibly be?"

They reached the stream and crouched beside it to rinse their hands and faces. Shana said appreciatively, "Ah, the water is good, and very sweet." Without more ado, she unwrapped her *draperi*, and folded it carefully and set it down, and stepped delicately into the shallow brook. She lay down in the cool water on her side, the shimmering surface of it barely covering her flanks, and cupped some of it into her mouth, drinking deeply. The two men watched her, admiring.

Emlyn said, "How many there are, no one knows. Why should we bother to count them? They are stored in a hidden chamber, which we found, though it cost the lives of ten of our founders."

"They are piled into a great heap," Shana said, splashing in the stream, "And quite useless to us, though the Books tell us that they are of immense value on the Outside. Well, perhaps one day we can use them for trade. For iron, perhaps, which we badly need. Now that at last we have established contact with the rest of civilization . . ."

She looked up at Gerard and held out a hand, and said: "Come, why don't you join me?"

Gerard hesitated. But Emlyn was already stripping off his gown and stepping unconcerned into the water. He too lay down in it, and he smiled at Gerard and said, urging: "The water is very refreshing, come, join us."

Gerard could not bring himself to remove his breeches. There was an old Anglo-Saxon inhibition on him, a relic of Puritanism that would not allow the nudity. He kept them on as he stepped into the stream and lay down; the sun would dry them soon enough.

They stayed there for a little while, and at last Shana

left the water and put on her *draperi* again, and Emlyn followed suit, and they all walked slowly along the riverbank with the unaccustomed feeling that there was no need for haste now, that there was need only for rest and relaxation. Soon, Emlyn found an excuse to leave them discreetly alone and went back to the camp, and Gerard wandered with Shana through the silence of the lush forest, hand in hand but saying very little. The question of the diamonds had been forgotten, and as the sun rose higher they sat together on the edge of a cliff and stared out at the vast green panorama that was spread out below them, an immense vista of dark green trees among which a wide river meandered, winding back and forth in its tortuous course. A toucan sat on a branch and spoke with them in its own curious way, and a brown sloth was moving slowly, upside down, along a branch of a giant fig tree. . . . It was an interlude of the greatest serenity.

Shana wanted to know all about him, and he told her of his distant home in New Orleans, of the Louisiana Purchase when he was a five-year-old child, of the great battle fought there, the final battle of the war, when he was a young man of seventeen years and had carried a gun for Andrew Jackson . . . He told her of his work for the Brazilian Emperor Dom Pedro, mapping the upper reaches of a vast river basin that seemed to go on and on into more and yet still more of jungle eternity, of the drive to wipe out the scattered and infinitesimal Indian population, of his objections to it that had cost him his job.

He said again, thinking of the past: "I am a free man now," and she answered: "I am glad. Eden will be good for you. And you will be very good for Eden."

They wandered slowly back to the little camp that

consisted of nothing more than a resting-place, and when the sun was high they ate a large fish that Emlyn had caught by the age-old process of tickling. . . .

And in the afternoon, they explored the forest together again, and Gerard picked wild flowers and gave them to her, and they found a patch of sweetly-scented moss to lie on, side by side and staring up at the great covering of high branches above them. He wanted so desperately to slide his hand under her gown and rest it on that glorious breast, but he would not; his wife was so very recently dead and there was a prohibition on him, even when she leaned over and kissed him on the lips and whispered: "It is so good to lie beside you, Gerard. . . ."

The twilight came, and they went back to the camp again and ate, and when they had finished Shana said abruptly, an order: "We will sleep now, and dream of Eden, our home." She turned to Gerard: "I cannot wait for the sight of Eden. And when at last we arrive there, Queen Alma will be as grateful to you as both Gerard and I are, you will see."

"He will be welcomed as a hero," Emlyn said. "We were both lost, and now we have been found again."

"I will sleep beside him again tonight."

"Yes, I know it. I have made your bed there under the tamarind tree. There are ferns more than two feet deep so that you may lie together in comfort."

Gerard was quite bewildered. "I thank you, Emlyn . . ."

Emlyn went to his own bed, only a few paces distant from them, and Gerard lay down, wearing still the breeches that had been his only clothing since that terrifying night. He stared up at the filtered moonlight, and it was very hard for him to keep his senses.

Shana stood for a moment above him, looking down on him as he lay there in a certain amount of trepidation. She was a silhouette against the night sky as she unwrapped her *draperi* and folded it with meticulous precision, then laid it down on the forest floor.

He stared up at her lithe young body, her outline etched with the eerie blue light of the moon that laid a edge of luminescence over her profile, her long throat, her breast, her hips and her thighs, and those incredibly long legs. He wanted her not to move at all, so beautiful was the picture she made, but in a moment she lay down beside him and put her head on his strongly-muscled chest, and laid delicate fingers against his cheek.

For a long time there was only silence, and she might have been asleep. But then, she pulled at the canvas of his trousers and whispered: "This is what you call . . . *breeches?*"

He could no longer be surprised. "Yes. Breeches."

"In the paintings we have of Adam Grieg and his men, they wear them. Our *draperies* are better."

"Draperies?"

"The gown we wear is called a *draperi*. Do your people always sleep in their breeches?"

He said awkwardly: "Well, not always . . ."

"We sleep naked, it is better, the night air is very good for the skin. It makes it soft to the touch, which is very desirable."

To his horror, her hand was insinuating itself under his belt, straying over his taut stomach and grasping his manhood, and she whispered: "You are strong. Will you take me now?"

His head was turning from side to side, and there were the tears of remembrance in his eyes. He stammered: "Shana . . . My wife, whom I dearly loved, is but recently dead, horribly murdered. How can I love another woman now? Even though . . . even though I admire her greatly, even though she is lovely beyond all understanding, even though . . ." His voice broke. "Even though she is close to me in more senses than one, and very dear to me too. Shana . . . Forgive me, I cannot."

Shana was truly surprised. "But she is dead! And even if she were alive, how could she lay exclusive claim to you? I am alive, and beside you, and waiting for you!"

He was in agony: "Shana . . . I loved her dearly!"

"But she is gone now!" Those long and delicate fingers were wrapped around him, driving him to distraction, and she said, quite incredulous: "What does it matter that you loved her? She is gone, gone, *gone* . . . !" It seemed almost indecent to her, and she said, quite angrily: "How can you say you will not love me? It is not only a question of your duty! It is very apparent that you too want me now . . ."

Gerard said weakly: "My *duty* . . . ?"

"Yes! Your duty! You are a man, both a Strong Man and a Wise Man, and I want a child from you! It is my privilege as a woman to demand it from you!"

But even as she spoke, she became aware of a most unusual emotion; he was refusing her because of his devotion to another woman, a woman, moreover, who was dead! It made little sense to her, but at the back of her mind there was the feeling that this strange attitude might, perhaps, indicate a very different kind of love that was more praiseworthy than she would have at first imagined.

And as though to reinforce her conclusions, a soft voice came to them out of the darkness . . .

Emlyn was lying down only a few paces from them,

and he was not yet asleep. He said, as though a commentary on Shana's demands were the most natural thing in the world: "It is a foreign philosophy, Shana, which you must accept. Under Alma, and Dashtu before her, Eden has changed the relationship between men and women that is accepted on the outside world. Gerard is bound by the laws of the Outside, which, we see, are just as they were when my father left it. It means one man to one woman, a system that we have long ago discarded. And you must accept this until such time as you can change it."

Gerard whispered to Shana: "Has he . . . has he been listening to us all this time?"

"Of course! Why should he not? We have no secrets from Emlyn, you and I."

"No," Gerard muttered. "We have no secrets from him."

"And is it true? One man to one woman?"

"Yes. It is accepted as the correct way to behave."

"Even though that one woman be dead and gone?"

"There is a period of mourning, yes."

"For how long? Three months, perhaps?"

But he could not put it in such prosaic terms. He clasped her very tightly, and he said: "Bear with me, Shana, please? I have the deepest regard for you, and yet, at the back of my mind . . . there is a prohibition. Can you understand that?"

With the knowledge that she was dealing now with a very strange kind of man from the Outside, her attitude changed. She muttered: "I will *never* understand. But I will wait. The time will come."

She released him at last, and lay still beside him, and she said quietly: "I am too aroused to sleep. Will you talk to me of other things?"

"Oh, Shana . . . please try to understand my distress."

"I do, of course. It is strange to me, but I think that perhaps I understand it. Other things, now."

"Very well." In the excitation of the moment, his hand had found that soft swelling of her lovely breast, and he moved it to her waist. But she took his wrist and moved it back again, and he let it rest there, his strong fingers gently moulding. But he forced himself to think of more prosaic matters, and by a strong effort of will he asked her for more news of Eden. She told him of the clusters of stone houses gathered together that were called *conviveries*, with twenty or thirty people living together in their own complexes . . . of the river water that was piped in through ancient conduits from the river, and now drying up and causing the people great concern. . . .

He said, murmuring: "If there is a river, and the elevation of the township is not too high, it can be remedied."

But another puzzling thought came to him. The earthquake that had sealed off the valley had occurred in the year 1721, one hundred and four years ago. And yet, Emlyn had said that he too was born in Eden . . . that the laws of the Outside are just as they were when his father left it . . . His *father?* Who left it to enter Eden, presumably? But there had been no access to Eden for more than a century, and it made no sense at all!

Gerard turned to him and said quietly: "Will you tell me how old you are, Emlyn?"

But Emlyn, it seemed, had dropped off to sleep after the little exposition of his learning, and Shana whispered: "Emlyn was born in the year of the Great Earth-

58

quake that sealed our valley off, in the year 1721. He is one hundred and four years old now."

She saw the look of surprise on his face, and said: "Many of our people are older. But Emlyn remembers well the days of his parents, when sixty was considered to be a ripe old age, and he tells me that it is something to do with the climate of our valley, or the air we breathe, or perhaps the way we live, without stress and anxiety for the future. Or perhaps because of the food we eat."

She laughed. "Emlyn has an idea all his own, that the apricot kernels we all like so much slow down the aging process. Perhaps it is true, I cannot know. I only know that the Books tell us at what age the original founders died, and that not one of them passed the age of sixty-two. But the second generation lived much longer, and they say the third will live forever, who can tell?"

He was almost afraid to ask, but he had to know. "And you, Shana?"

"I am third generation," Shana said. "I became of age only a few days before we set out to climb the steps, the first position of authority given me on reaching my maturity, which in Eden is considered to be the age of sixteen for a woman and eighteen for a man." She said nonchalantly, "I am sixteen years old, and a virgin still. I want my first child to be your child, Gerard."

"Oh, God . . . if I could only bring myself to forget . . . !"

"You *must!*" Shana said fiercely.

She reached for him again and found him hot and pulsating, but still he turned away from her. He gasped, "No, no . . . I think only of my Dora now."

Her voice was low. "You are strong. It means that you

think of me too, I know it. You think of my breasts under your lips, of my lips finding you and kissing you. I am a child, but the women of Eden have taught me well, as they teach every girl who comes of age."

Gerard was groaning. "No, I may not . . . I will not."

He was determined, and she knew it. But she whispered: "Gerard, you have so much love to give. And where shall that great love fall now? So very much of love, I know it."

He could not answer her, knowing that she was right.

In a moment, she released him again, trying hard to understand his emotions even though they were incomprehensible to her, contenting herself with lying beside him, her head at his powerful chest. She said with infinite compassion: "Then sleep, dear Gerard. It is enough that you are close by my side, enough at least for the moment." Her lovely eyes on his, slanted, bright, the palest of blues, were deeply reflecting her emotion. "We will see what the night has to bring us."

In a little while, he fell into a restless and uncomfortable sleep.

And what the night brought him was a realization that he wanted this wonderful woman more than anything in the world. But even though her slim fingers found him again, and enfolded him all night long, he held onto his determination, saying to himself in those half-awake hours: *"Dora, my wife, my only love . . ."*

The sun came up, and she was fast asleep in his close embrace, and still he had not weakened, even though he found that in his sleep he had slipped his hand between her naked thighs and was cupping her. He withdrew it quickly, and he did not know how long he would be able to resist her. Shana was right; Gerard had so much of love to give.

Chapter Four

The sun slanted through the branches of the high trees, dappling their bodies.

Shana opened her eyes and looked at the man she had wanted so much to love her. He was so beautiful! His beard had grown now to a very thick stubble, and somehow it brought his aspect closer to the looks of the men in Eden, who had no iron for razors. Her fingers touched that dreadful wound in his chest, well-closed now with the thorn-pins and already beginning to look less vivid. He had scorned the use of the papaya leaves they had wanted to bind him with, saying: "No, the pins are enough, it will heal itself now."

She lay quite still beside his sleeping body and thought about him, a man who moved her deeply. But there was another need imposed on her. It was the propagation of her tribe in accordance with Queen Dashtu's urgent demands many years ago: the community cannot survive without more children; where a hundred will perish for lack of hands to do the work that must be done, a thousand may prosper . . .

The word went out to the women, almost all of them Indians, who were fast becoming the dominant factor in the society: If our tribe is to florish and grow in the strength we need, then we must have children, as many as you can give us, by all worthy men, whether they be strangers, or your fathers, brothers, and sons. . . .

To the matriarchal Indian women, there was nothing strange about this; it had been the custom in their own tribe for centuries.

Gerard was the first stranger Shana had ever met, and she had recognized him at once as a very exciting man, a worthy man. . . . And at this moment, her needs were pragmatic and reflexive more than anything else; Gerard represented the addition of new blood to the Eden strain, and so, her bound duty took precedence over her emotions, which now were struggling in her subconscious mind for superiority.

But duty or not, Shana was very much a woman, and she could not subjugate her natural feelings to so ordinary a thing as Eden's *needs*. Gerard's refusal to service her had disturbed her deeply. An extraneous and very strange thought was creeping up on her . . .

She had met, for the first time in her life, with an aspect of true love which was quite unknown to her, a kind of love in which the need for children played very little part. Gerard, it seemed, was still pining for a dead woman, and though this seemed very remarkable to her—indeed, even indecent—she admired him for it, not even realizing that her admiration stemmed from the same kind of feeling for *him* that was slowly taking hold on her.

It worried her. She thought that loving a man for emotion alone might be antisocial; and in Eden, the only crime was antisocial behavior.

She thought about the strange twists of fate that had brought them together, and of his stubborn denial of her. She consoled herself with the idea that even if she could not, of herself, bring him to love her, she could ask Queen Alma to command it the very moment they reached the valley. Even as independent-minded as he seemed to be, he surely would not dare to refuse a direct order from the Queen herself!

She left him sleeping there, and arose and slipped on her gown, winding it around the slim body which she was sure had so aroused him, but which was unsatisfied and pining for him.

Emlyn rubbed the sleep from his eyes when she woke him, and yawned.

"Your arm?" she asked, and he grimaced. "I am slowly beginning to recover the partial use of my fingers," he said. "Of course, it will never be quite the same again. I can bear the thought."

"Good. Then we will stay here no longer. We have rested enough." She would not tell him the reason for her sudden decision, feeling a little ashamed, and aware that he was looking at her curiously.

But he merely nodded. "If you say so. You are sure Gerard is well enough to travel?"

"If you wish me to, I will ask him. But he is very strong. All night long, I was very conscious of his strength."

"Ah . . ." Emlyn's eyes lit up. "Does that mean that he loved you?"

Shana sighed. "No, but it will come." There was a puzzled look on her face, and she said: "He thinks only of a woman who is dead. And I find it very strange. And of one woman only to love. How can that be?"

"Once, it was the same with us, long before your time. Dashtu changed it all when she came to power."

"It must have been terrible in those days."

63

"No, not really. A man can be very happy with only one woman."

"But a *woman*," Shana said tartly, "can surely not be happy with only one *man!*"

Emlyn was smiling at her. "Are you convinced of that?"

There was a distant, dreamy look in her eyes, and she thought about the question for a long time. She said at last, hesitantly: "You read my mind well, Emlyn. Yes, it's true. I believe I could love Gerard to the exclusion of anyone else. And I'm sure that's quite disgraceful." She looked at him. "Would you call it immoral?"

Emlyn shook his head slowly. "No, I would not. I suspect that it means . . . that somewhere in your subconscious mind, you have not forgotten the old ways which died out long before you were born. Perhaps subconsciously you would like to return to them. For my own part, I have always wanted to do that."

"And this resolve of his . . . do you think it will last for ever?"

"No, of course not! A man forgets. More importantly, in this case he can be *made* to forget."

"I tried. All night long I caressed him. He was strong as a bar of the hardest mangrove wood, but still he turned away from me."

"You must keep on trying, Shana, never giving up. Remember that each day and night that passes brings with it a strengthening of his body, which you say is already strong, and also . . . a weakening of that resolve. I have seen how he looks at you, not only when you are naked but when your body is completely covered too. He longs for you, Shana. I know it."

She held his look, and whispered: "You are a great comfort to me, Emlyn."

He laughed suddenly, pleased by her confidences, and said: "It is because I love you too in the old way. And there is nothing at all shameful in your exclusive desire for Gerard."

She turned and followed Emlyn's look. Smiling broadly, Gerard approached them and said cheerfully, "A good morning to you both. Did you sleep well?"

Shana embraced him, and when she released him at last he picked up his machete and said: "We need meat, and we have no gun to hunt with, so. . . ." He found a clump of bamboo nearby and carefully selected the pole he wanted. With one fast blow of his machete he sliced it off at the bottom at a very sharp angle, and then cut it down to a length of some six feet. He squinted along it to make sure that it was straight, felt the point with his finger, and nodded his satisfaction. They watched as he twirled it in the embers of the fire to harden it, and when he was finished he examined it carefully and said: "It is good. I will find meat now."

He left them and went into the jungle, and Emlyn looked at Shana and said: "He is recovering very fast. And he is a worthy man indeed. You must have his child."

"Yes, I will do so. If not before we reach Eden, then soon after. If he is still stubborn, I will call on Alma to order him."

Emlyn smiled softly: "And this is the reason for our sudden return?"

She hesitated, but she could not lie to him. "Yes, it is, and it shames me."

"There is no shame. And I do not believe that you will have to wait so long. That light in his eyes grows stronger every day."

Within the space of two hours, Gerard returned. In

the jungle of the Amazon, it was not always easy to find meat quite so readily, but he was a skilled tracker and had come across the broad, broken path left by a herd of wild boar. He had followed it, and now he was staggering into the camp with a carcass across his shoulders. He said, laughingly, "There were twenty or thirty of them, and this one turned on me, and buried his snout in the mud as they always do, and then charged me. Now, we will have meat enough for the two more days we will be here."

Shana said: "Not two days. We will leave as soon as we have eaten."

He stared at her. "Oh? I thought it was decided. . . ."

"I changed my mind. It is a women's prerogative."

"Of course." For no reason at all, he felt embarrassed. "Is Emlyn fit to travel?"

"Yes, and he asked the same question about you."

"I am fit too."

Shana said calmly, "Then there is no argument."

Gerard was aware of a slight testiness in her voice, and he worried about it. He said mildly, "How should there be argument when we are all agreed? After our meal, I will cut up strips of the meat to dry in the smoke and carry with us, there will be enough for the whole journey."

Emlyn fired up the embers as Gerard skinned the boar. When the meal was over they set about the jungle chores that were to last them for most of the day; they sliced up most of the meat into manageable sections that could be cooked for as long as it stayed fresh, and the rest was cut into narrow strips for drying in the smoke of the fire. . . . They cut the hide up into triple thick soles for their sandal repairs and stitched them into place with leather thongs.

It was late afternoon before they set out, but they moved fast and covered a great deal of distance before the darkness fell, and still pushed on by the light of the moon over gently-rolling hills, mile after mile of them covered with scented wild flowers of a hundred different kinds. As the moon began to set they found themselves in a different kind of forest, enclosed by high rocks studded with gaping caves, and Gerard called a halt, wondering if he had perhaps pushed them too hard; they were both exhausted. He said, "We have done very well today, and this is a fine place to sleep, I think." There was the comforting sound of a running stream coming to them from out of the darkness.

Shana nodded, and sank to the ground on a bed of moss, trying not to show her exhaustion, and Emlyn said, a little wearily: "I will make the fire . . ."

"No," Gerard said, "rest now. I will make it."

They watched as he cut a length of thick bamboo and notched it, and found a length of dry vine and cut that too, and Emlyn peered at the arrangement as Gerard tore out some dry grass and set the notched pole on top of it, holding it in place with his foot, the vine under the cut.

Emlyn said curiously, "To make fire? I have never seen this before . . . and I think that a man lives or dies in the jungle by what he learns."

Gerard laughed as he drew the vine-rope rapidly back and forth through the notch, and he said: "I have seen you twirl a twig on a piece of dried-out wood, it takes a very long time indeed. This is much faster, you will see."

He had scarcely finished speaking when, heated by the friction of dry vine against dry bamboo, the grass burst into flames, and Emlyn nodded. "Faster indeed," he said. "I like your method better than ours, which was taught to us by our Indian ancestors."

Gerard frowned. "Yes, you told me of your Indian ancestry. I still find it remarkable." He was tossing twigs onto the burning grass, and Emlyn went on: "It is all written in our bark-cloth books. Have you heard of the Brazilian gold rush of the year 1693?"

"Yes, of course! Miners and adventurers came here from all over Europe in search of gold. From England, Holland, Portugal, France . . ."

"The various nationalities banded together for security," Emlyn said, "and fought each other for supremacy. The Portuguese won and drove out the English, who were led by a man named Adam Grieg. There were a hundred and nineteen of them, and Adam had heard the legend—who had not?—of a lost valley filled with diamonds, a popular Amazonian legend everywhere. But this one was true, and Adam found the valley, long deserted by its original inhabitants who had built a township there and then, for no known reason, had deserted it."

"We think it was because of an earthquake," Shana said. "Many of the fine houses Adam found were badly damaged."

Gerard speared a hunk of pork and began roasting it over the coals. "And those hundred and nineteen founded the place you call Eden?"

"By no means." Emlyn shook his head. "Had they done so, Eden would not, today, be the place it is. No. One year before its discovery, Adam's party stumbled across a tribe of Indians. It was the year 1699, and they had been reduced by attrition, through Indian attack, malnutrition, disease, exposure to the jungle, to thirty-one men, three women, and two female children. The

68

rest of them had perished. They staggered into the Indian encampment more dead than alive, but the Indians were still terrified of them. The tribe was matriarchal, and their chief was a woman."

"It is common among the Amazonian tribes," Gerard said, and Emlyn nodded. "Yes, so I have read. In their society, men counted for nothing, as fathers only to breed more and still more children to strengthen the tribe's power. And by all reports, they were extraordinarily beautiful people. The history of this strange tribe told of a very long migration as they followed a pillar of cloud by day and of fire by night, a chain of volcanoes, perhaps, from their original homeland to the Amazon. Adam was a man of great learning, and he believed that they might have been one of the lost tribes of Israel who migrated here across Russia, over the Bering Straits which were then joined to North America, and down south to the land of the Incas, a journey that would indeed have taken them hundreds, perhaps thousands of years. Because their culture was rooted in antiquity, it could be possible. Adam even pretended to identify the lost Israelite tribe, Issacher, because their chief, a woman, was named I-Suacher, which in their language meant the lost one." It was all part of the legend of Raman-li- Undara. When Gerard had first heard it, he had been told that the people who built the township were not Incas at all, but a strange tribe who migrated here two thousand years ago . . . It was possible; the Amazonian jungle was known to have been inhabited continuously, though very sparsely, for more than fifteen thousand years.

Emlyn said: "I-Suacher was a woman of great authority and understanding, a very wise ruler. She made a careful count of heads and saw that there were twenty-eight men in Adam Grieg's party who had no wives, so she presented them with twenty-eight young virgins and sent them on their way. She too spoke of the legend of the lost valley and its diamonds, and she could not understand why these worthless stones should be of such importance to anybody. . . ."

Gerard was enthralled as he listened to a legend becoming reality, and Emlyn went on: "Adam's party moved on, sixty-four strong now and strengthened by the addition of Indian women who knew the jungle well, knew its dangers, and knew the cure for its dreadful diseases that had decimated the Europeans. Adam wrote in the Books: 'It is probable that had these women joined us but a year earlier, scarcely any of our people would have died. When I fell ill from the fever, they gave me leaves to chew on that saved my life . . . ! These young women could not understand why the society they had joined was not, like their own, matriarchal, and they never lost the instinct, bred into them over countless generations, for authority. And in the year 1700, by an accident of nature, they found the valley."

The meat was sizzling, and they used the machete to slice off pieces of the outside as it slowly cooked. Gerard said slowly, "And so, Eden became matriarchal too. . . ."

Emlyn nodded. "Yes, when Adam Grieg died and his half-Indian daughter Dashtu moved into his place, with no objection from anybody. She was a young woman of very commanding presence . . . No proclamation was ever made, but as the years rolled by, the women took on more and more authority. For the pure-blooded Indian wives, it was merely a move back to the system they had always known. For their half-English daughters

70

. . ." He shrugged. "They learned quickly from their mothers."

They had finished their meal, and they found the small brook and washed the grease away. Shana took Gerard's hand and said, almost shyly: "And shall we sleep now?"

They found deep green moss to lie on, and Emlyn curled up by himself at a little distance as was his custom. Gerard stretched himself out, relishing the comfort of the soft bed that a benevolent nature had provided for them, and stared up at Shana as she took off her *draperi*, folded it carefully, and set it down.

She saw that he was trembling. She lay naked beside him with an arm at his waist, her head on his strong chest, knowing that the cool touch of her lovely skin was exciting him beyond endurance now. His thoughts were still troubled, she was sure, but when she took his hand and moved it to her gently swelling breast he let his fingers, as though of their volition, mound it softly, cupping it and savoring its resilience; she could feel the beat of his heart, even faster than her own.

She breathed: "The breeches, I will not permit them now . . ."

Her fingers were at the drawstring, untying the knot, and he whispered, but with lessening conviction: "No, you must not . . ."

She said fiercely: "I must, and I will . . ."

She undid the knot and pulled the canvas down over his ankles and tossed it aside. He was as naked as she was, and she knelt beside him the better to enjoy the sight of his lean, muscular body. She said quietly: "You are beautiful, I never saw a more beautiful man. . . ."

She bent down and kissed the scar on his chest, and

he felt the sudden, tiny shocks as she quickly pulled out the thorns of the suture: "It is almost healed, you do not need these any more. . . ."

She lay beside him for a while, ruffling his thick hair as she threw a long and slender thigh across him, feeling the heat of him against her, relishing the uncontrolled pulsation. She kissed him lovingly on the lips, and his responses excited her strongly as she felt the tip of his tongue between her teeth, probing. She knew that he was hers now, and she whispered: "You cannot refuse me any longer, I know it. . ."

"And I know it too . . ."

She lay her head on his taut stomach had brushed him with her long, silken hair, driving him to distraction as he reached down for her breasts and fondled them. Her lips were exploring him, and he gasped as felt the kisses and the tiny bites, and then she was raising herself up to kneel over him, a knee at each side of his hard hips.

She grasped him and caressed herself, shuddering, moving slowly back and forth for a very long time. She was moaning, and when she could restrain her emotions no longer she placed him just so and dropped down onto him in an agony of desire for him. She bit her lips when the little spasm of pain came and quickly went, and when he was deeply contained in her she lay on him so that he could give her breasts the urgent attention they demanded; he feasted on them as he drove his loins up to meet her fervent thrusting.

Her smooth body was moving up and down on him rhythmically, and when the explosion came for both of them she would not cease her movement, wanting more and still more of him.

She lay exhausted on him at last, and as he slowly

withdrew from her she fell into a deep reverie, dreaming about the wonder of him. She lay beside him with her back to him, nestled into him, knowing that his strength would soon return and that he would take her again. She reached down and positioned him between her soft, resilient and smooth thighs, and she whispered: "Sleep now. The women tell me that sleep after love is very good . . ."

"Yes . . . I love you, Shana, so dearly . . ."

"Ssshhh, it is a time for rest."

Soon, she knew by his rhythmic breathing that he was asleep; but even so, that great need was on him, and she felt him easing himself into her again. She whispered, not caring whether he was awake enough to hear her or not: "Yes, yes, my love . . ."

This night was a turning-point in the life of Gerard Fletcher, ex-cartographer to His Imperial Majesty Dom Pedro of Brazil; and to Shana too, one of the beautiful young women of a legendary place known as Raman-li-Undara, the Field of Diamonds.

It was the beginning of a great and enduring love.

Chapter Five

They awoke in the morning very early, and lay side by side in utter contentment, looking up at the beautiful green panoply of the trees, spotted with the brilliant reds of a thousand flowers blooming on a gigantic vine that clambered up the tall trunks in search of sunlight, and air, and of freedom to blossom. For a long time neither of them spoke, but simply held their hands tightly clasped together; and Shana knew that what had happened in the night had bound them together for all of eternity.

Gerard propped himself up on his elbow at last, and looked down into Shana's exquisite eyes, and kissed her on the lips, and he said quietly: "Only once before have I been so deeply in love."

"Your Dora?"

"Yes, my Dora."

"And have you forgotten her now?"

He shook his head slowly. "No. I never will . . . Can you accept that?"

"Yes."

"And even understand it?"

"Yes, that too. It is written in the Books that when

Adam Grieg's wife died, soon after his daughter Dashtu was born, he went out of his mind with pain and grief, even though there were very many of the other Indian women who wanted his seed. He disappeared, and search parties went out, and three days later they found him. He had gone to the terrible swamp that lies in the middle of our own jungle, he had gone there to die, to let the jungle overtake him. . . . They brought him back to the township and nursed him back to health. And in time, he took a new wife. Her name was Andulari, a young half-blooded Indian girl. But he changed her name to Fasti-Serifa. It means 'Memory of Serifa,' in the Indian dialect which was very common then." Her voice was very sad: "Serifa was the name of the wife who had died. Yes. I can understand it."

There was a long silence again, and Gerard thrust away from him the thoughts that gave him so much anxiety. Listening to the gentle sound of the stream, Shana said, "There is a river, shall we find it?"

"Good." He reached for his breeches and sandals, but she put a hand on his arm and stopped him. "It is very close, we will not need our clothes."

"Very well." Gerard took her hand and they ran together along the verdant trail of moss, interspersed with smooth mounds of gray granite that led to the river, coursing slowly over polished pebbles. They could hear the sound of a small waterfall now, not very far away. Shana was about to step into the water, but he laid a hand on her hip and said: "No, wait . . ."

He crouched on his heels and studied the shimmering surface intently, and in a moment he said softly: "I cannot be sure, but I have a suspicion, a sixth sense, perhaps. Don't move."

He ran back on unaccustomed bare feet to the embers of the fire, and saw that Emlyn was still peacefully sleeping. He picked up a lump of the fresh boar's meat and took it back to the river and tossed it in. They stared at it as it lay there, only half-submerged among the rocks and pebbles. In a little while Shana said: "It is safe, I think. No?"

"A moment longer."

"All right, if you say so."

She slipped her hands down to the small of his back and arched her body slightly so that their hips were tightly pressed together and her nipples were lightly brushing his manly chest. She was conscious that his breath was coming as fast as hers, conscious too of that hard warmth against the tender skin of her stomach.

She began to speak, but suddenly there was a furious commotion in the water beside them. The meat was torn from its resting-place as a hundred, perhaps a thousand hungry jaws tore into it and ripped it apart in moments, savage jaws equipped with myriad needle-pointed teeth and an insatiable voracity. The water was churned up to white-topped boiling point.

Shana gasped. With his arms tight about her, Gerard felt the thundering of her heartbeat, as furious as the water itself. In a moment, the churning stopped, and she shuddered out her relief. Gerard said quietly, "I have seen piranhas in faster waters than these. It is not true that they gather only in quiet water, as many a poor Indian has learned to his cost. Come, I will find a safe place where we can bathe."

As they moved along the riverbank hand in hand, he said, smiling, "It is not only the piranhas you must watch for. There are eels that can stun with a strange kind of shock, and stingrays that can paralyze your muscles and leave you sick and close to death for weeks. Always beware the waters of the Amazon Basin."

Her voice was hushed. "Our own streams are so clear and pure. . . . Except, of course, in our own jungle."

"Your own jungle?"

"It lies within the confines of the mountains that form our valley, and is much like any other jungle on the Outside, I suppose. But our people seldom go there, they fear it as much as I do."

"The jungle," Gerard said, "is not really a place to be feared. It is a place to be understood—and respected. And with the understanding comes an appreciation of its great beauty."

He laughed suddenly. "Thousands of miles away in New Orleans," he said happily, "my parents know that I am here. And if by some strange device I could communicate with them now, and could tell them that I am walking along a jungle riverbank with a lovely young girl beside me, and both of us are as naked as the animals . . . I shudder to reflect on what they would think!"

They came to the little fall at last, no more than twenty feet high, a narrow ribbon of white water that splashed lazily down over lichen-covered rocks that were spotted with brilliant flowers. He said, "Here is a good place to bathe." He stooped and plucked a water lily from the surface of the pool and gave it to her, a handsome, pale yellow blossom with black-tipped, bright orange stamens. She placed it in her hair and dropped to her knees on the soft, velvety, very dark green moss. The moss gave out a strong, sweet perfume when it was crushed. She tore up a handful of it and held it out to him: "You know this kind of moss?"

He nodded. "The Indians call it *urisani.*" It grew in

78

tightly entangled clumps that seemed to burst out of the soil, building up in the process little air pockets underneath that made it springy to the touch and good to lie on. "In Eden," Shana said, "we use it for bathing."

He took it from her and nodded. "One of nature's other sponges, and very refreshing."

She stretched her long body out half in and half out of the pool, luxuriating in the kiss of the cold water, and she whispered: "Will you bathe me? Please?"

He crouched beside her and soaked the moss and squeezed it to release the scent that was almost like chamomile, and caressed her body with it, washing her from head to foot very slowly and carefully, leaning down sometimes to kiss the places he loved to touch. She lay quite still under his ardent caress, just as Dora had always liked to do. He thought, with a sudden sense of apprehension, *Can I so easily forget my late, dear wife?* But he knew that he was lost now in the deep passions of a love that had completely taken hold of him to the exclusion even of memories. . . .

In a while, he set aside the sponge and parted her thighs with gentle, demanding pressure, and knelt between them as he lightly touched her silken skin, moving his fingertips over her and wondering if there could possibly be a happier man anywhere in the world. Her eyes were closed in a kind of dreaming, but she opened them now and gasped as she saw the strength of him, a young God on his knees to her, lithe and powerful, the muscles of his chest, his stomach, his thighs, corded and well-defined. She reached out to him with her arms and he waited no longer. He placed his strong hands on either side of her shoulders and lay on her, and slowly, smoothly, firmly entered her. She bit her lip to hold back the spasms that were overtaking her, but she could not control them. She let them come one after another, knowing that she was lost now in a kind of oblivion in which all the strange terrors of the jungle were quite obliterated.

He collapsed on her at last and lay contained within her, and all she could do was gently move her hips in the hope of arousing him yet again. But she too was exhausted by their delirium, and when he eased himself from her and lay still beside her, she welcomed the touch of his lips at her breast.

And now, there was a strange sensation coming over her, an unexpected touch at her ankle; she could not imagine what it might be. She opened her eyes and moved her head to look, and suddenly she tried to scream but could not. . . . A snake had entwined itself around her leg.

Gerard aroused himself instantly. Half-propped up on one elbow, his eyes wide with alarm, he whispered: "Do not move now, Shana, lie absolutely still. . . .It is an *iricuri*, it can kill us both. Do not move a muscle. . . ."

They were frozen together. The *iricuri* was only a small one by Amazonian standards, some six feet long and two inches thick, spotted with green and yellow, a series of raised rings at the end of its tail. It was slithering slowly up Shana's leg, its tongue flickering, and she was turned to stone in her terror. But Gerard's hand was tight on her wrist, and there was comfort in it. He whispered again, almost inaudibly now: "Not a movement of any sort . . ."

The snake was at her thighs, and the bullet-head was probing, thudding at her with a strange kind of animal force as though demanding entry; it made her shudder uncontrollably, and Gerard's grip tightened on her, giving her courage. The Indian blood in her was surfacing, and there were memories of childhood tales of the snake-gods of her forebearers who demanded, and took, the services of human women. She suffered the probing in silence, terrified out of her wits.

There was a legend recorded in the Books, and part of it came to her now: ". . .and the snake-god came to Mari-Sifa from the water as she lay asleep, and found her secret places and impregnated her, and a monster was born to her who was called Itu-Shari, the Slayer of Men . . ."

She was moaning slightly, and Gerard's voice was a zephyr in the silence: "Sshhh, my love . . ."

The snake left her thighs, and that intruding head was moving up over her stomach to her breast, and she heard Gerard's almost-silent voice: "Prepare yourself, my dearest. He is aroused, I must kill him now. When I move, roll quickly away, and run . . ."

The evil head was weaving to and fro, and she lay absolutely still, tensing herself. She felt that dreadful tongue weaving over her breast, flickering at the nipple, and she tried to subjugate her terror and could not. She saw the huge mouth open wide, and then . . .

Then, Gerard's arms were shooting out, and his powerful hands were gripping the snake inches below its head, and the long body was thrashing, wrapping itself instantly around him. He shouted, "The chopping-knife! Back to the camp, quickly!"

Shana ran, screaming, and Gerard fought against the monstrous constriction with every muscle in his body. She raced towards the camp, but Emlyn was already running to her with the machete in his hand. She turned back and led him to the river, both of them running faster than they had ever run before. They closed in on Gerard like avenging angels and found him holding the

81

snake's head with one hand and its tail with the other, trying valiantly to unwrap the coils from around his waist. His face was already blue, and he shouted; "The tail first, cut the tail . . ." He pushed it down onto the ground as Emlyn raised the machete and swung it down in one fast slash. The enormous pressure lessened at once, and Gerard took a long deep gulp and said, more calmly now, "And the head . . ."

With both hands, he held it out for Emlyn to slice through, and when the bloodied head dropped to the earth he unwrapped the still-thrashing body from around his bruised waist and cast it aside. . . . He lay on his back for a moment, then looked up at his good friend and said quietly: "I thank you, Emlyn. I could not have held out much longer. I was lost in . . . in the throes of passion, and I relaxed my vigilance. It is something the jungle never allows. The jungle has a mind of its own, and is sensitive to every weakness we allow ourselves. I promise you, it will never happen again."

Shana was on her knees beside him, trying to control her tears. He struggled to a sitting position, then embraced her, and stroked the luxurious black silk of her hair, as he whispered tenderly: "It is all over now, and behind us."

"Yes . . . but how I long for Eden now . . ."

He rose to his feet and pulled her up. He said, smiling, "Then let us be on our way."

He was very conscious of their nakedness as they walked together back to the camp; but Emlyn seemed to pay no attention to it whatsoever, as though, for him, it was the most natural thing in the world. *And why not?* Gerard thought. In many of the Indian villages he had visited, neither men nor women wore any clothing at all; and for them, too, it was all perfectly normal.

But these strange people were almost English! And the more he thought about it, the more certain he was that Eden must be a very strange place indeed. He, too, was beginning to long for the hidden valley that he had never seen. . . .

For day after long day, they continued the trek to the northwest. The jungle was a constant enemy, but Gerard, very much in command now, was competent to fight it.

Another savage rainstorm came, a deluge that dropped tons of pounding water on them before they could find shelter, great sheets of water lashing the forest and everything that moved in it. Mud was sliding down the mountainside in the most terrifying force, a bright red mud that tore gigantic trees out of the ground in its descent, and Gerard, his muscular chest covered with rivulets of streaming water, shouted over the roar of it: "We must climb now, we cannot stay at this level, in an hour we'll be swept away . . ."

They bowed their bodies into the rain and climbed, pulling themselves up on vines, roots, anything that would provide a handhold, slipping back a pace for every two they climbed. They sank at last, exhausted, on the edge of a granite bluff, and saw a deep river pouring down now over the route they had taken. Gerard said, "We rest now, till it has finished . . ."

The vegetation here was the richest on the face of the earth. It was rain forest, and the branches of the trees were divided into three clearly marked stories, green layers of heavy foliage one above the other, all in magnificent order. The first level was covered by acacias, palms, laurels, myrtles, and begnonias. Figs that were at least a hundred feet high, rubber trees, giant ferns, Brazil nuts, and breadfruits formed the second growth level. The ceiling level contained silk-cotton and cow-trees, reaching to more than two hundred feet, the great garlic tree, and rosewood. Every known species except the conifers was represented in the dense vegetation.

They found some huge boulders to shelter under, and stayed there for half a day till the cluster broke up as the soil beneath it was swept away. They scurried to one side as the boulders began to topple and finally careen down the mountainside on the flood, smashing through every clump of vegetation that stood in their way. They climbed again to further safety . . .

Inevitably, the downpour ended, and they struggled on again through the steam that rose from the forest floor, climbing, always climbing. When they reached the top of yet another mountain they looked across a wide valley through which a great river was twisting and turning. Emlyn looked at the distant silhouette and sank, panting, to his knees. He said, with a kind of triumph in his voice, "You see the horizon there? The face of the girl?"

"The face of?" Gerard stared, and the mountain ridge was indeed like the face of a beautiful young girl, with perhaps twenty miles between the top of her forehead, down over a hooked and authoritative nose, down over full lips to the point of her chin, down her neck to the beginnings of a bust, a very distinctive line indeed. "The mountain is called," Emlyn said, " 'The Girl who Fell Asleep', and its story is written in our Books. Thousands of years ago, a young Indian girl went looking for her lost lover in the mountains. When she could travel no longer she lay down on the crest and fell asleep, and over the years she turned to stone. That is her profile you see there. And that . . . is one of *our* mountains.

Beyond it lie the steps. Another day or two, and we will be home."

Gerard, too, was panting. He said, "The steps?"

Emlyn lay down on the wet earth. "The twelve thousand steps. Let us thank whatever gods there be that we go down them, and not up."

He lay on his back and looked up at the evening sky. Searching as always for knowledge, Gerard crouched beside him and said, "The twelve thousand steps? What steps are those, Emlyn?"

"The steps down into Eden."

Emlyn rolled over onto his side and whispered: "Do not question me now, I beg of you. I am older than I have ever been before, and tired . . ." He was asleep.

Shana was sitting on the ground with her back against a giant tamarind tree, her hands limply dropping to her side, her lovely mouth half-open as she gasped for air. She looked up at Gerard and whispered, "Can we rest for a while, Gerard? Please?"

"Of course." Her exhaustion made him feel guilty, and he said, "Forgive me, I have driven you too hard . . ."

"No. I want to see our beloved Eden as soon as possible, I pine for it. But the climb has not been easy."

"Rest, then." He looked up at the still-hot sun. "It is half-past five in the evening, and we will camp here for the night. I will build a fire, and prepare food, and when the sun goes down, we will sleep till it comes up again."

"Good. I will welcome sleep. . . ."

Gerard put his notched piece of bamboo to work with a length of vine and soon had a good fire going. He put the last of the fresh meat on a spit and roasted it; it was a little ripe now, but very palatable. He said, "From now on, we eat dried meat. The altitude here means, I think, that there will be very little game to hunt. But we can catch fish, we will not starve."

He woke Emlyn and said cheerfully, "A good supper is ready, sizzling over the coals . . ."

They lingered over their meal, and when the meat was finished Emlyn took the machete and said, smiling: "I fell asleep and left all of the work to Gerard. It is quite unforgivable, and I will now try to atone for my dreadful behavior . . .

He went off into the forest, leaving them to chat together, and came back at last with a great hand of unripe bananas. He said: "The rest of our dinner, and am I forgiven now?"

Gerard laughed. He cut off a dozen of the fruit and tossed them onto the coals, and when they were cooked to perfection they peeled them and ate them until they could eat no more . . . And once again, Emlyn discreetly retired and left the two lovers alone. They held hands and stared into the dying embers of the fire, and whispered endearments to each other; and then they too made a bed of ferns and lay down to sleep. So close to their objective they were both restless, Gerard lay beside Shana, reaching up under her *draperi* to mould her breast. He wished he had the strength in him to take her; but he did not, and he knew that she was too exhausted by the physical efforts of the day. Meanwhile he contented himself, and her, with the soft touch of probing hands.

He said quietly: "Are you tired as I am? You must be, even more so."

She took his hand and brushed it against her cheek. "Yes, as tired as I have ever been in my life. But I cannot sleep. Eden is so close to us now . . . and you, my dearest?"

"I have dreamed of Eden for many nights now, and I find it very hard to imagine. A legend come to sudden reality . . . the mind does not easily accept it."

"I know . . ."

"The twelve thousand steps, what are they?"

"Ah, the famous steps . . ." They were tightly clasped in each other's arms. "Once we cross the mountain ridge where the sleeping girl lies, you will see them. They lead down into Eden."

"Steps? Into Paradise?"

"Yes. In the year when Emlyn was born, one hundred and four years ago, the Great Earthquake dropped a mountain across the track that led to the hidden valley that Adam Grieg found . . ."

"The legendary Raman-li-Undara . . ."

"Yes, the Field of Diamonds. Dashtu was Queen then, and she put the men to work to find a way out of the valley, in case it should ever become necessary. She was wise enough to know that though the Originals had fled the valley for no known reason, the reason must have been there. It might one day be just as necessary for her people to flee too, and so, she ordered a stairway to be cut up the mountainside that lies to the south of us. They had very few tools, only a handful of miners spikes left from the old days, and a few chopping-knives. But they made digging-tools of ironwood, sharpened with fire, taken from the swamp which lies in the middle of our jungle, and they went to work. When they began this formidable task, there were only sixty or seventy young men for this work, and it was not enough. This was when Dashtu made her famous proclamation, applying the ancient customs of the Indians. She ordered: 'We must have more and still more children. Father will lie with daughter, brother with sister, son with mother, and Worthy Man with any Worthy Woman. There will no longer be any form of marriage, but only procreation of our tribe, that it may increase a hundredfold. . . .' It was a turning-point in our history. And for work on the steps, children, developing in the course of time into Strong Men or Wise Men, were produced."

"But . . ." Gerard was at a loss. "The steps were built by *children?*"

"No, of course not! They grew into men!"

"But . . . Twelve *thousand* of them, you say? It boggles the mind! Twelve hundred, yes, I can contemplate, though it would be a memorable endeavor. But twelve *thousand?* In God's name, how long did it take?"

"They were carved into hard earth and stone," Shana said. "Great boulders were split with fire, blocks of granite embedded into hard clay, terraces built of limestone to carry the stairs a few feet higher . . . It took one hundred years, almost to the day. Many of the workers, starting when they were twelve years old, were still working when the final cuts were made."

She said, dreaming, "Twelve thousand hand-cut steps. We know nothing of the recent accomplishments of the outside world, perhaps they can match ours or even surpass them. But we like to think that it has been a worthy endeavor indeed."

Gerard was dreaming too, trying to imagine the effort. "And how long does it take to climb them? I cannot bear to think of it."

"It takes six days," Shana said. "There are resting-places. Not even a Strong Man, as Bramwell was, can climb more than two thousand steps in a single day."

She laughed suddenly, her small, strong teeth gleaming. "But now, we go down, not up. It takes only two days. And we will reach the top of them very soon now. Emlyn will send the signals, and they will be awaiting us. And are you still tired?"

"No, I am rested now."

"As I am. Then will you love me? I am aroused."

His heart was beating very fast. "As I am too." He moved her *draperi* aside and kissed her. He began to roll over onto her, but Shana was reaching under her slender body to find what it might be that was digging so obtrusively into her skin. She came up with a tortoise-shell comb and stared at it in acute astonishment.

She said, laughing, "In the middle of the jungle, a thousand miles from anywhere, we chance upon a woman's comb? And it is beautiful . . ."

Gerard stared at it, and he felt his blood running cold.

He took it from her, and his eyes were wide with sudden shock. The comb was large and ornate, and he had seen it before. There was a vision coming to him, a memory in which a white-skinned Spanish-looking woman was on her knees beside him, and she was groping for him with uncouth hands, tearing his breeches open, and there was a rope around his neck tying him to a tree trunk . . . Her long and very coarse black hair was piled up on top of her head and fastened there with this very comb. . . .

The image was changing, and the woman with the hair was lying on top of his Dora, spread-eagled there on the jungle floor with bamboo poles at her wrists and ankles, and the comb was there still, an emblem of her distorted femininity. He remembered seeing it removed, the long black hair sweeping, and there was a foot at his throat holding him down even though he was not physically capable of any movement at all. The white-skinned woman was laughing at him as he tried to see what was happening to his beloved Dora, and the hair was sweeping back and forth over him again as he heard her voice: 'You such a beautiful man, I like you . . .' He was struggling to free himself from the strangling rope, and he screamed: "Dora . . . !"

Shana's arms were around him, pulling him into her breast, and she whispered, in shock: "What is it, my love?"

Gerard tried to summon his senses. He said weakly, "The comb, I have seen it before. It belongs to a woman named Carmen."

Shana said curiously, "And is she a woman you loved too?"

"No!" He was shouting. "She is the woman of the man who killed my wife! It's *her* comb, I know it!"

He dropped it back onto the forest floor and tried to compose himself, without very much success. But he said at last, very quietly, "Forgive me, Shana, it is an old wound opened."

She was reaching for him as she spoke. "Then let me heal it for you. Perhaps I can make you forget . . ."

"No. No one can do that, not even you." He lay on his back and stared up at nothing, dry-eyed in his agony as he thought of Dora's last hours. Shana lay beside him, trembling, knowing that there was nothing she could do to drive away his pain nor even lessen it. She held him tightly, in tears because of her sense of helplessness now in a crisis which she knew to be unconquerable.

For a long time he was silent, but at last, very quietly he spoke. "It means that in all the vastness of this jungle . . . they are not very far away from us. In the rain forest, two men, the only human beings in an area of many thousands of square miles. . . . They can pass within twenty feet of each other, separated by impenetrable vegetation, and each not know that the other is there.

90

But a piece of carved tortoiseshell tells me that they are close by."

She was stroking his face, and her eyes were moist. *"They?"*

"A man named Jao Torres, a monster. Another man named Espada. Torres' woman, whose name is Carmen, and forty or fifty others. Before I die, I swear by all the Gods I know that I will find Jao Torres and kill him for what he did."

She held him tightly and tried to find the words. "How will you ever find them, Gerard? And even if you could, then what could you do, one man against so many?"

"I will confess, I do not know . . ."

"Then sleep now, and think only of Eden, where there is only love."

"Yes, Eden . . ."

He was weeping quietly. Shana lay still beside him until the sleep overtook him; and then she too slept, close in his embrace.

It was so simple a thing that had driven him to the edge of despair! A comb, intricately carved out of a sawed-up piece of tortoiseshell, lost and now found again, but bringing memories with the finding that were painful beyond the point of tolerance.

Even in Shana's arms, Gerard was murmuring the name over and over again: *"Dora, Dora, Dora . . ."* as he tried to drive away the horrors of that fateful night. Shana wept as she listened to him, no longer sure that she had captured his heart.

And when she awoke in the morning, she sat up in sudden shock and caught her breath. Gerard had gone; there was no sign of him anywhere.

Chapter Six

It seemed to Shana that Emlyn was waiting to comfort her. He was sitting on a fallen tree trunk close by the pile of moss that had been his bed, and was wrapping fresh papaya leaves around his arm. As though deliberately making light of her problem he held the arm out for her to see, and said, smiling, "Look, it's healing very rapidly . . ."

The tears were flooding her eyes, and he reached out and touched her gently on the cheek, and said: "Come now, it is not a time for tears." He patted the trunk beside him: "Come, sit down."

She could not restrain her misery as she dropped down at his side. "Emlyn," she whispered, "he has *gone!* He has left us before, I know, to find food, but this time . . . All night long he was weeping for his dead wife, and I'm frightened."

"And it is not a time for fear either," Emlyn said calmly. He embraced her, knowing that he was a tower of strength for her in times of difficulty. "Yes, I saw him go, at the very first light. I was only half-awake, but I saw him studying the ground intently, circling our little camp, and in a while he took his chopping-kinfe and spear and hurried off into the jungle. He did not even know that I was awake, his mind seemed filled with problems of his own, but when he had gone, I too studied the ground to find what it was that had interested him so much. I found footprints, of a man and a woman, several of them. I am not a skilled tracker, as Gerard is, but I am sure they were not very fresh. In one of the deeper prints, seeds were sprouting, in another there was an overlay of mud . . . I take it to mean that the prints are old, though I could be wrong. When first we met with Gerard, you remember, he was tracking the gang that killed his wife and his friends. I think he has found their trail again, though how this could have happened I do not know."

"I know . . ." Shana told him the story of the comb, and even went to find it and show it to him. He stared at the comb in silence as she told him of Carmen, the woman who had worn it, and he tossed it carelessly aside when she had finished.

He stared for a long time at a Brazilian pheasant that was slowly climbing one of the aerial roots of a giant Banyan tree, a strange bird that preferred to walk up to its nest rather than fly there. Wrapped in thought, he went over and stood among the upright roots like a priest among the columns of some jungle cathedral. He began pacing among them, his head sunk on his chest. He smiled at last and said, with great conviction, "What you have told me has not changed my belief that he will soon be back."

Across the intervening shrubbery, Shana's eyes were on him. She said urgently: "Emlyn! Can you be sure?"

"I am convinced." He came back and sat beside her again, and took her hand and said: "What do we have? We have a man of great strength and determination whose wife has been murdered. He has found signs that might, perhaps, lead him to her killers, and therefore he has set out to follow them. But by so doing, he has left us alone and defenseless, because without the chopping-knife that he carries we are at the mercy of the jungle, just as we were when first—so innocently—we left our haven to find out what lies beyond it. I believe that this thought, that we cannot now defend ourselves when we must, will plague him terribly when, in the course of time, he reflects on what he is doing." He paused, and raised a finger at her. "He will return to us shortly, I am convinced of it. So . . . we will wait here for him."

"Oh, God . . ." Shana embraced him warmly, knowing that he was right.

Less than three hours later, Gerard came back to them. His face was dark with his own anxieties, his brows drawn into a frown, and he sat on the ground beside them and waited for a reproach, though none was forthcoming.

He said at last, his voice very low: "Will you both forgive me?"

Shana reached for him, silently pleading, and he took her in his arms and held her close. He whispered: "I lost my senses. I know it."

"Sshhh . . ." Her fingers were at his lips. "Do not reproach yourself for what you felt you had to do."

"I must!" He said fiercely: "I left the woman I love, and a man I respect and admire, quite without the defense that so simple a thing as a steel blade affords. I will never forgive myself, never!"

He sighed deeply. "I found tracks and followed them, one man and one woman. And as I half expected they led me to others, many others, forty or fifty people perhaps. Boots, sandals, bare feet, some Indian women among them . . . They led at last into water, a swamp, and I lost them."

"Perhaps it is just as well," Emlyn said. "One man against so many? What could you have done?"

"Nothing, I know it." He placed his hands on his friend's shoulders and said: "What shall I do, Emlyn? You must help me . . ."

"You ask for my advice?"

"Yes."

"Then I give it to you. I say: Forget all ideas of revenge. Think only that in Eden, among those who will love you and to whom violence is unknown, you can find true happiness once again."

"It is hard to forget, dear friend."

"Shana will help you."

"Ah yes, Shana . . ."

He was deeply confused, not finding it easy to shrug off an old love even though he had found a new one that was growing in importance for him with every passing hour. He turned back to Shana and drew her to him. He said softly, "In my anger and sorrow, I left you unprotected. It will not happen again, you have my promise."

"Oh, my dearest . . ."

She held him tightly and looked up into his somber eyes. His sculptured brows were drawn into a frown, and she felt the deep need to comfort him as Emlyn had comforted her. "The kind of love you have for your dead wife," she whispered, "I want so much to replace with my own. It *is* the same kind of love, exclusive of all others." She was smiling through her tears now. "And that kind of love, which you know so well, is unheard of in Eden."

"You are telling me that there is no true love in Eden? I find it hard to believe . . ."

Shana shook her head vigorously, but before she could answer him Emlyn, that smile of his still there, spoke. "As a member of an older generation than Shana's, Gerard, let me put this matter into its proper perspective. There is so very *much* of true love in Eden . . . In all of my years, I have never once seen a blow struck in anger, nor heard a harsh word from one of our people to another. We live in the most complete harmony, sharing together a love that is almost . . . divine . . ."

Gerard interrupted him. "But sharing your lovers too?"

"Yes! It is not strange for us, though from my studies of the Books I know that beyond the world of the Indians who gave us half of our heritage, this is not common on the Outside. As a man in a society that is dominated by women, I will say that I have loved very many of them, physically, when they have requested my services as is their right and privilege. And on each of these many occasions . . . With each individual woman, I myself have felt something of the kind of love you speak of, and I know that they felt it too. That is to say that the only difference is that . . . in your philosophies love is restricted, to one single woman; and that in mine . . . it is shared." He shrugged, and the gentle smile had not left his lips nor even his eyes. "It may be that our system is better than yours, which was the system of my father. It may also be that my father's ideas, and yours, are better. But you must never forget: We are all part Indian, and the Indian culture is very strong in us."

"Marriage, then?" Gerard asked.

"There is none in Eden. Indeed, for one woman to

demand the exclusive love of one man would be considered highly immoral."

Gerard sighed. "I will *never* understand," he said. "Do you have, at least, a religion?"

Shana nodded. "Oh yes! Some of us pray, when we must, to the God of the Christians and of the Jews. For others, there are the Indian Gods. The Concord would *never* interfere in the personal religion of any of us."

"The Concord?"

"What was known in Adam Grieg's time as Government."

"Elected?"

Emlyn frowned. "Yes . . . I think it can perhaps be called *elected*, if that is important. It consists of Alma the Queen, with her natural heirs, two or three of the older women, and one or two of the Wise Men. I myself serve on the Concord from time to time."

"And a 'Wise Man' is . . . what?"

"Precisely that. A Strong Man who has reached the age of eighty-eight. His accumulated knowledge is considered sufficient to permit him that honorable title."

"And a 'Strong Man'?"

"From the age of fourteen onwards. Sometimes, he can pass from one stage to the other even earlier, if it becomes apparent that he is indeed wise. There are some men who make the transition much earlier."

He turned to Shana, and said earnestly, "Lindsay, I think, is a case in point."

Shana nodded, just as eagerly, anxious for Gerard to understand the intricacies of Eden's society. "Yes," she said. "Lindsay is only sixty-four, and at the next meeting of the Concord he is to be declared a Wise Man."

The great banyan tree was close around them. Even as they spoke together, blood-red passionflowers were opening all the way down the aerial roots, spotting the cathedral with splashes of vivid color.

Gerard rose to his feet, content that he was back with the two people he had learned, in different ways, to love. He looked up at the sun and said quietly: "Because of my stupidity, we have lost a great deal of travelling time. So shall we move on?"

They continued the long journey, down the steep mountainside and up again. They came to a turbulent river, crossed it, and found a waterfall pounding into the depths, an image that saddened Shana as she thought of Bramwell, that good man who had sacrificed his life for them so willingly. When the darkness fell, they made fire and cooked what they all believed might be almost their last meal on the Outside; Eden was very close now.

Emlyn pulled ferns for their beds again, and placed his own very discreetly a little way from theirs. Before he retired he said quietly, "How long is it since we left our home? Little more than a month! And yet, I feel as though I am returning to a place I left in my childhood! I long for the sight of our gray stone houses, of the fragrant meadows, of the fishermen coming back from the river with their nets." He continued gravely, "I have thought about it very deeply, and I have come to the conclusion that the Outside . . . The Outside is not a place I would wish to live in."

Shana was in a very good humor, and she laughed, mocking him. "But we have seen nothing of it! A jungle, like ours! What, have you seen Adam Grieg's London and found it lacking? Or the New Orleans that Gerard came from? If the Books are to be believed as they must be, they are great civilizations out there somewhere, civilizations of which Gerard will soon inform us."

He nodded. "Yes, there are, but they are very far

away. The Amazon itself is as far away from those civilizations as a man can travel. And for myself . . . Now, I think only of Eden."

The moon was very brilliant, an Amazonian moon, and it cast a pale and eerie glow over the trees and the giant ferns around them. The daytime silence of the jungle was gone, and the night birds were screeching, the night monkeys howling, the night insects keeping up their interminable buzz . . .

And above all were the frogs, shattering the darkness with the most raucous sounds that the devils of the night could contrive, a cacophony that reverberated back and forth among the trees. Shana whispered, "The giants of the jungle, they terrify me . . ."

Gerard laughed. "Giants?" he echoed. "No! They are the tiny blue bullfrogs, and quite harmless."

"We have them in our own jungle, and even in the township we hear them calling at night, the voices of evil giants."

"They are smaller than the nail on a man's thumb."

She stared at him. "Surely you jest . . ."

"You have never seen them?"

"No."

"Then come."

He was laughing still, very happily, and he took her reluctant hand and led her to a nearby pool, and crouched down on its bank. Sensing her fear, he said, "No! They are harmful to no one! The monstrous sound they make is nothing more than their defense against the predators of the night."

He watched the frogs for a moment, one on every water lily leaf it seemed, a whole army of them. And in a moment he reached out and snatched one of them with a lightning movement, and sat it in the palm of his hand to show her. It was bright blue in the moonlight, almost luminescent, and no more than an inch in size. It was silent now, and its bulbous, alert eyes were staring . . .

Gerard whispered, "Touch it."

Shana recoiled. "No! I cannot!"

"A finger to its head, it is friendly."

Hesitantly, she reached out and did as he told her; and immediately it opened its tiny mouth and bellowed, the sound of a great cannon being fired. Gerard said, laughing, "There, you see? He loves you!"

She could not believe that so monstrous a sound could come from so tiny a creature, and she stared at it in fascination.

He said gravely, "They are guards for us. When we disturb their serenity they cry out, but when we go to sleep and they know that we will not harm them, then they fall silent. And if danger should approach in the night—a jaguar, or a prowling band of Indians with their poisoned arrows, they begin their roaring again and warn us. They are our friends."

"And I was always so terrified of them . . . !"

"Never be terrified of the jungle creatures. They want to be understood. The jungle itself wants to be understood."

"Even the jaguars?"

Gerard sighed. "You defeat me with my own weaknesses! No. Always be wary of the jaguars, we have made them our implacable enemies, and they are stronger than we are, and more knowledgeable. For generations, man has challenged their supremacy, which is absolute. Man has hunted them because their skins are soft and very beautiful, and they *know* now that we are their enemies. They strike first, a measure of their intelligence. As the Government of Dom Pedro is trying to wipe out the Indians . . . so is the jaguar trying to exterminate us, whoever, wherever we may be. It is a continuing battle. Always be wary of the jaguars. And remember that their intelligence far exceeds yours and mine."

"Adam Grieg was killed by a jaguar," Shana said. "In the jungle that lies to the west of our township. Ever since, the people of Eden have been frightened of them." She smiled, and said wryly: "As frightened as we have always been of . . . of tiny blue bullfrogs, the demons of the night whose only wish is to destroy us."

Gerard laid his temporary captive down on its lily leaf again, and it barked at him once and then plopped into the water with a sudden show of elongated and very muscular legs. He laughed and said, "He has gone to inform his family that we are quite harmless too. You will see, in a moment there will be no more barking." With no change in the tone of his voice, he said, "And will you love me again tonight?"

She brushed his lips with hers. "Yes, oh, yes . . ."

"I am very eager tonight."

"I know. It is apparent."

Hand in hand, they walked slowly back to the moonlit camp. A beautiful swamp deer was peering at them inquisitively from a dark tangle of vegetation, seeming quite unafraid. The blue light dappling its smooth bronze flanks in the shadows, its huge ears were pricked up as it stared at them, and then it bounded away, suddenly aware of danger, crashing through the shrubbery. Shana whispered with a touch of sadness, "Why is it frightened of us? We mean it no harm . . ."

Gerard smiled. "Not of us," he said. "But there is a puma nearby somewhere, I too can smell it."

"A puma?" She was alarmed, but Gerard held her arm tightly. He said, "They almost never attack people, but

102

swamp deer and monkeys are their favorite food. And with such a good meal close by, he will not bother with us."

They found Emlyn happily plucking a pheasant. He held it up to show them, and shouted boisterously, "I caught it in a trap made from hibiscus fibre, did you ever see a plumper bird? Six pounds at least, we shall eat well tonight!"

He saw their flushed looks and said slyly, "I know what is in your minds, but we will eat first. A man must fill his belly before he loves the woman who loves him, it is essential. Otherwise, he is only a shadow, and Eden has no use for children produced by shadows. They must grow up to be Strong Men and Wise Men. . . ."

He took the bird over to the stream and eviscerated it, and brought it back with a length of bamboo through it, then fixed it in Y-shaped twigs over the fire, turning it from time to time as the fat dripped over it. The smell of the roasting flesh was ripe and sweet in the air. They ate hungrily, and when it was quite consumed Emlyn produced three mangoes, more than a foot long and as much as nine inches across, yellow-green in color and smelling like honey. They feasted on the succulent fruit.

At last Emlyn said happily, "I will leave you both now, with your permission, and rest my tired old bones. Do well what you have to do. Good night."

"Good night, Emlyn. In the morning, we begin the last day of our long journey, I think."

"Yes, we are nearly home now, and for myself, I can hardly wait for the sight of Eden. And yet I know that I must. Perhaps this is the essence of wisdom, waiting in patience."

He retired to his own discreetly placed couch of ferns, and Gerard took Shana's hand and led her to their bed.

He sank to his knees before her and fumbled urgently with the knot of her gown. He unfastened it and let it fall to the ground, and clutched tightly at her slender hips, his thumbs resting on the points of the bones, his fingertips softly embedding themselves as he held her tightly. She leaned back slightly as he kissed the saffron-colored skin that was warm to his lips, and grasped his head, moaning as she ran her fingers through his bushy hair.

She felt ecstasy building up very quickly, and dropped to her knees between his and whispered: "Now, my dearest, now . . ."

"Yes, now . . ."

She arched her sinuous body back, knowing that this strong and splendid man was hers for all time. Her knees were wide-spread, her legs tucked back under her, and without more restraint he plunged deeply into her. His hands went to her up-turned breasts, moulding at them, and he planted little kisses on them. She clutched at his back, running her hands over the corded muscles there, and straightened her long legs under him. He whispered, "No one else in the world, my love, no one else, ever . . ."

"Yes, the two of us alone, for this night, at least. Once we reach Eden, it will no longer be possible."

In the throes of his passion, he did not completely understand her. He murmured, "Not possible?"

"In Eden, I will have to share this aspect of your love."

He was slowly coming to his senses. "To do *what?*"

"To share you with other women. But this night, we are alone, and you are mine alone. Let us make the most of it while we can."

He still did not understand, and wanted to ask her

more, but she was crouched beside him now and driving him to the verge of distraction with her attentions as she swept that glorious hair back and forth across his body in slow, rhythmic motions, teasing him, exciting him beyond endurance. And when he could hold back his emotions no longer he almost threw himself on her in a frenzy as she reached out to welcome him eagerly.

All night long she lay beneath him as he exploded within her time and time again. And when the first red-gold streaks of dawn came over the mountaintop they still lay fused together, one entity, bound by the strong chains of a love that would never die.

Chapter Seven

By late afternoon of the following day they were reaching the top of the peak, at the silhouette of the "Girl who Fell Asleep," that extraordinary ridge that showed her sad profile so clearly . . . Gerard could sense the excitement taking hold of his two companions as they climbed; they were very close indeed now to their goal.

Soon, there was a formidable barrier ahead of them, a high, smooth cliff face that reared fully three hundred feet into the sky, pitted and broken here and there, with bright green clumps of widely spaced vegetation clinging to it. It was limestone interspersed with granite, and its upper reaches seemed to totter outward as though about to fall. Gerard stared up at it, and looked at Emlyn with a touch of alarm. "We don't have to climb that, I hope?"

Emlyn laughed. "Only a little way, there is a path of sorts."

"I see no path . . ."

"To the left, where the yellow flowers are. Come, I will lead the way."

"A path of sorts," he had said. It was no wider than

the span of a man's hand, and broken everywhere, branching out from time to time in subsidiary paths that led nowhere. With their backs to the cliff face, they eased their way cautiously, for three hundred feet or more. Gerard said incredulously, "This is the way you came?"

Shana nodded. "Once we found our way through the mountain, there was no other way . . ." They came at last to the creeping mass of yellow flowers, and the sight of the drop below them was terrifying. They were like insects crawling on a gigantic cliff face, clinging to it tenaciously, high above the forest they had left. But here, behind all the greenery, the path widened out and became a tiny plateau of bright red sandstone on which the giant ferns were so tightly packed together that they too became a barricade. Gerard saw that some of them had been cut, perhaps as recently as a month ago, the new shoots were sprouting again already. Showing the way, Emlyn forced his wiry body through them, and Shana followed with Gerard close behind, excitedly awaiting whatever surprises this well-concealed trail might offer.

They came to a hidden cleft in the rock, so very narrow that they had to squeeze through it. Shana whispered, as though raising her voice would bring calamity on them: "We must be very careful now. A little further on the floor drops away into the depths, we must jump over the gap. Finding it for the first time, I nearly fell there . . ."

They came to a crack in the ground and leaped over it, clinging to the rocks and searching out every dangerous handhold. Then at last the cleft widened out and disappeared altogether, and they stood on a broad green plateau where there were tall and very beautiful silk-cotton trees waving their pink blossoms in a cool and refreshing breeze, and stands of huge mulberry trees heavy with their fruit.

Emlyn led them to one side through the trees, and they walked quickly on the springy moss till the plateau dropped suddenly down into the Valley; a brook was playing its gentle melody for them. And they were at the head of the twelve thousand steps . . .

Gerard could only gasp at the distant panorama below him. Even at this great height, the gray stone buildings were plainly visible in the clear, sparkling air, the houses spread out over perhaps ten or fifteen acres, and were surrounded by green meadows, with copses here and there, and giant bamboo, and huge, solitary blue jacarindas; two white-capped streams meandered lazily through the valley. The far-reaching meadows lay to the east, and to the west. On the other side of the town there was a dense jungle that looked, from up here, very much like the jungle they had left behind them. The whole valley was tightly closed-in by the confining mountains, and it was a spectacle of breath-taking loveliness.

Down to it all led the incredible stairway . . . The steps snaked down into the deep valley, turning this way and that as they sought out the contours of the mountain, a multi-colored stairway of red sandstone, burntumber brick, gray granite blocks and split boulders of limestone.

Gerard whispered, "Twelve *thousand* of them . . . ?"

Shana's arm was around him as they stood together on the brink. "Yes. A distance of nearly three miles, and a height that the Wise Men have estimated to be more than seven thousand feet. One full century of effort."

She was trembling, her voice a little hoarse. "My home. It seems so long that I left it."

109

Gerard said gently, "And for my part, I left my home behind me nearly five years ago. Perhaps I will never see it again, who knows?"

"You will find a new home with us in Eden."

"Yes, it may well be."

For the first time, the true enormity of his situation came to him. He was a thousand miles from anywhere, deep in a jungle that was so immense it could not be imagined by those who had not, for year after weary year fought their way through its emptiness. Quite by chance he had stumbled on the legendary Raman-li-Undara, now called Eden, and known in the imaginings of so many adventurers as the Field of Diamonds. He was looking down now on an ancient, hidden township that brought the legend to sudden life, a city abandoned ages ago by whatever strange tribe had built it and now inhabited by—of all things—a new tribe that was half-English and half-Indian. A people, moreover, whose knowledge of history had stopped short in the year 1700, a century and a quarter ago! It boggled the imagination!

And was he to spend the rest of his life here? He could not know. And yet . . . He had met with an astonishing young woman of the most extraordinary beauty whose obvious affection for him was strong enough and exciting enough to make him almost forget the cruelly-murdered wife he had loved so steadfastly. He felt very guilty about this. There was, in his philosophy, a deeply rooted idea of a decent period of mourning; but he could not shy away from the fact that Shana excited him beyond endurance.

He was a very virile man, and the physical act of love was very important to him. His regard for Shana had begun, admittedly, at that physical level, but every passing hour had served to assure him that she was far more than just a stunning beauty; she was blessed with a bright intelligence, kindness, and very considerable courage. There were hidden depths in her remarkable character that he delighted in; and he knew that she was a woman greatly to be prized.

He sat with her at the edge of the bluff, holding her hand, and he looked down onto the valley in utter contentment. His arm was around her waist and cupping the underside of the lovely breast he liked to touch, and her head was nestled into his shoulder. There was the purest contentment on her too.

And what was she thinking, he wondered? He placed his fingers under her delicate chin and looked into those wondrous eyes and found that they were sad. He remembered her words: "When we reach Eden, I will have to share you . . ."

For Shana, the sharing of worthy men was normal and she knew of no other way of life. But she had found a different kind of love now, and it confused her very considerably. Gerard held her tightly and said nothing; it was the silence that sometimes falls on lovers, filled with dreams.

Behind them, Emlyn was making a fire, piling the flames with grasses which he soaked in the stream to make smoke. When it was going to his satisfaction he stood back and looked up at the great blue column that drifted up into the evening sky. He said happily, "There! Now they know we are returning."

He stared down at his distant home and said to Gerard: "The descent takes two full days. It is better, I think, if we rest here now and begin the climb down in the morning."

But it was Shana who answered him. Scarcely con-

111

scious that she was reasserting her lost authority as a woman, she nodded. "Yes. We will sleep here tonight. It is so quiet here, and peaceful . . . After those long days in a hostile jungle, we have come through it all unscathed, save for the loss of Bramwell, whom we all loved. But now, no more dangers threaten us, and I am glad of it."

No more dangers? Shana could not have been more wrong. The danger was not yet close, but it was inexorably growing closer and it was very great indeed; it had begun with the tortoiseshell comb that Shana had found lying on the jungle floor.

It was night, and Torres had left his camp to attend to business of his own in the dark of the forest. His gang, forty men and eight women (most of the women were Indian slaves) were sprawled on the turf by the fire that one of them had made. Jao Torres, dressed in his canvas breeches and leather boots and wearing the top hat perched on his bullet-head, was nearly a mile away on the bank of the river, where a single canon-ball tree was growing, its hard fruit dangling in clusters and ready to fall with thunderous force to the ground below.

He lit a fire from the burning twig he carried, and threw on it the green and red feathers of a parrot he had killed by hurling his knife unerringly at it. He was moving very slowly and quietly, because the silence was important, not to awaken before their time the Gods he was to address . . .

When the acrid smoke filled the air, he squatted on his heels by the fire and began tearing out the parrot's entrails. He placed these on the fire and began a long, low incantation in the dialect of his Kaseka Indian grandfather, a language he did not know very well. He

112

liked to think of himself as a civilized man and preferred
to speak one of the European languages when he could.
This recession into his Indian heritage was shameful to
him, though vitally necessary. He felt he had to keep it
secret from his men, particularly from that arrogant
Espada, who was too damned European for his own
good.

Jao Torres knew that most of his life he had been an
abject failure, and he had come here in desperation to
pray for help from the ancient Gods of his forebearers.
He rolled some cannabis into a papaya leaf and smoked
it, and let the memories of the past come back to him as
he waited for a sign from the heavens. . . .

He was some forty years old, though he was not sure
of his precise age; what could it possibly matter? And for
thirty of those years he had lived in the jungle by his wits
and his brutality. At the age of ten, his half-Indian father
had thrown him out of the house for raping a neighbor's
eleven-year-old daughter. It would not have mattered
too much, but the neighbor was a powerful chief in the
squalid riverside village and had to be appeased. As a
young boy growing to maturity he had taken what the
mestizos he grew up with called "the rubber trail," tapping wild rubber trees and sending the sap in wicker
baskets downriver for eventual payment. He had also
become a bounty hunter for the distant landowners, killing Indians and cutting off their ears as proof for more
payments. He had become a bandit, gathering others
under him and raiding isolated villages for food, drink,
money, women, anything they might have.

At the age of about twenty, he had found a very young
girl in a shack he had plundered, killing the two men
there. She was hiding under a pile of fishnetting, a very
pretty child who, though a *mestiza* herself, was as white-

113

skinned as a European girl of quality. She had drawn a hidden knife on him when he ripped the shift from her plump little body, exposing breasts that were scarcely budding yet, and had tried to sink it into his stomach. Bleeding though not badly hurt, he had beaten her brutally before raping her, and then . . .

Then one of those little scenes was played out that make no sense at all in the course of human relationships. He left the house the next morning and the girl followed him. He took her again, and when he had finished with her he said roughly: "Go now. I don' need you no more."

She would not leave, saying angrily, "My father and my brother dead, you kill them both. So where will I go?"

"I don' care where you go. Go."

"No, I stay with you."

Torres stared at her a long time, and he said at last, disgusted: "What I do with you? You no good, you lie there like a watermelon."

"Then tell me what I must do. I will do it."

There was that long, cold stare again, and the top hat perched on his head. He said at last, "You not virgin when I take you. You tell me who take you first."

"My brother. Then, when he find us together, my father."

"You learn, if I teaching you?"

"Teach me."

Torres grunted. "For three days, then. You don' learn in three days, you go, I don' care what happen to you. What your name?"

"Carmen."

And so, the child learned. In spite of her constant abuse—though Torres would never allow any of his

gang to lay hands on her—she grew up into a voluptuous and passingly attractive woman, though as savage as
he was. She had stayed with him ever since, caring nothing that he slept with every nubile female he could find;
indeed, she brought him other women from time to
time, knowing that this was the best way to hold him.

She was heavy and muscular, though her weight was
in her hips and her breasts more than in her waist and
thighs. Her black, black eyes were very wild and her
look was often the look of madness. Her lips were red
and very full, and even though she habitually wore only
the bark-cloth skirts she had taken from her dead
mother, her skin was still white and fairly free from
blemish.

Her crowning glory was her hair. It was very coarse,
but thick and black and very heavy, hanging down almost to the back of her knees. She sometimes piled it all
up on top of her head and held it there with a beautiful
comb carved from tortoiseshell that Jao had stolen for
her long ago.

She was lying now in an eddy of cool water by the
stream and washing herself from head to foot, something she liked very much to do every two or three
weeks; her bark-cloth skirt was lying on the bank, and
she was naked in the filtered moonlight. All of her
senses were tuned to the jungle; she was a jungle creature herself. She heard the sounds behind her and she
paid no attention to them at all, save that her heart beat
a little faster. She knew exactly what the sounds meant;
a man was moving lithely and expertly through the
bushes towards her, and she knew who it was.

The sound as he entered the water was infinitessimal,
but she heard it. And when the hands came around her
body and clutched her breasts, she turned her head to

115

meet Espada's lips, and savored his probing tongue. She tore her mouth away and whispered, "You must be quick, we do not have time."

"A lie." Espada slipped his hand to her throat and pushed her down into the mud. "We have time, I will not be quick. Damn you, open your legs for me."

His lips moved down to a full breast, and he bit her and drew blood. Carmen swung her body around and struck at him savagely, and hissed: "Scum! Pig! European bastard! You make marks on me! Jao see them, he kill you! I don' mind too much, but he kill me too!"

She was on top of him now, pounding her fists with the strength of a man into his handsome face; but she delighted in the touch of their naked bodies together. She spat at him. "When I finish with you, I find your clothes I burn them, you stay naked. I tell Jao you rape me, we see what he do to you then. He feed your balls to the piranhas, if you got balls."

"I have balls, you know it."

"Then lie still, I take you now if you man enough for me."

"No, I will not lie still."

Covered all over in black and slimy mud he squirmed from under her and wrestled her over onto her stomach. He knelt behind her and pulled her hips up into his and entered her brutally. He reached down and scooped up handfuls of the mud and rubbed it into her back, and found more for her breasts, her thighs . . . And all the time he drove into her furiously, like the animal he was. When he was satiated, he collapsed on her, and she lay very still in the slime, holding him tightly within her.

In a little while, he withdrew from her and rose to his feet, a tall, well-articulated, muscular man of very imposing proportions. He seized her wrists and dragged her out of the water like a carcass, up onto the green moss. He dropped her and lay on his back beside her and said: "Now, you make me strong again, woman."

She was lost in the throes of her passion. She murmured, "Jao come back soon . . ."

"No." He said scornfully, "Jao is an Indian, he has gone to pray to his Indian Gods that he thinks we know nothing of. He will breathe the smoke of the weed until he is incapable, and he will not return till morning, I know it. I have seen it a hundred times. Make me strong."

She crouched over him obediently and aroused him in the fashion that Jao himself had taught her so many years ago. In a little while, she lay under him as he pounded into her, completely subservient to him. She whispered: "I love you so much, Espada . . ."

He grunted. "Be quiet, woman! I do not need your love. I need only your body, and I will take it when it pleases me. So keep quiet."

"Yes, of course."

They separated at last, like animals disengaging, and Carmen washed off the mud and put on her skirt, and tried to arrange her disordered hair. She reached for her comb and could not find it . . .

It was a matter of some concern for her and she searched the recesses of her mind and remembered. She said to Espada, very slowly: "Last night, when we make love, you took out my comb and dropped it to the ground."

"I remember, you must have recovered it."

"No, I did not. It is still there where you left it."

He was alarmed, though he did not wish to show it; he was secretly terrified of Jao Torres, sure that if his master ever found out what was going on he would not live

117

for much longer. He said, with feigned nonchalance, "A comb, nothing of importance."

Carmen was furious. "It is of great importance! A present to me from Jao! What, shall I tell him I lost it! He will beat me half to death!"

Espada shrugged. "Then I will find it for you. We travelled very few miles today, I will go back and recover it."

"It is lost, forever."

"No. We lay together under a banyan tree, its roots dropping down from the branches like the pillars of a cathedral . . ." He broke off and laughed harshly. "Cathedral? What should you know of cathedrals, you are a savage! But I myself . . . I am a man of education, I saw a cathedral once, in Manaus where you have never been. Indeed, if they ever saw you in Manaus they would say 'a savage, give her a wide berth in case she bites, like a prairie dog.' But I will find your comb for you, to make you happy. Because I am a gentleman."

It was necessary to urge him more; she was terrified of what Jao might do to her. She said, mocking him: "What, you can run all that way in the jungle, at night, and still be back before dawn? You are a fool, Espada. No man can do this."

"*I* can do it. I am a jaguar, a *tigre.*"

"And still find a comb in the darkness? No, you cannot."

"I will find the camp we made by the banyan tree, there will be a dead fire there, and other signs. I know where I dropped the comb and it will still be there, on the moss. I will find it and run back with it, so that you may respect me more."

"Go then. Show me what a *tigre* you are in the jungle."

Espada *ran. . . .* He moved like a jaguar indeed, a

118

young man of astounding athletic ability, backtracking without rest and very easily over the signs the gang had left. He found the banyan tree in no time at all, though it took him a little longer to find the comb; he knew precisely where he had dropped it, but it had been moved . . .

He wondered how this could be. A herd of wild boar charging across the ground and dislodging it? No, there were no tracks of wild boar. An inquisitive macaw, perhaps, carrying it off for a few yards and then abandoning it? Possible, and the most reasonable explanation. But he was not satisfied, and it was an intriguing problem for him. He searched the soft soil for signs, reading them expertly when he found footprints, and flattened grasses where bodies had lain.

And then, at a little distance, he found the most compelling evidence of all—the remnants of a small fire that was not their own . . .

Ignoring the need to hurry back, Espada squatted on the ground and studied the signs, and came at last to certain conclusions. He was not quite sure how he could impart them to Jao Torres, but he knew, with the arrogance of his youth, that when the time came the means would come to him too.

He hurried back to where the new camp was, moving as he liked to move when it was possible, at a very fast run for two hundred paces, at a walk for two hundred, and then at the run again.

He covered the five miles back to the camp in less than an hour and a half.

He saw that most of the men were in a drunken sleep, some of them with leather bottles of the awful palm-liquor still clutched in their hands. The Indian captive women were all awake and staring at him as he found

Carmen, half-asleep on a bed of green moss. He dropped to his knees beside her and slipped the comb into her coarse hair. He whispered, "I said I would find it, and I found it."

"Good. You are a better man than I thought, Espada."

"Jao?"

"Not yet returned."

He slipped a hand between her thighs and cupped her, and he whispered: "Then maybe I take you again now."

"Are you mad? He come soon! Scum! Portuguese swine!"

He laughed softly. "I would still do so, save that the Indian women are all watching me, wondering which one of them I will favor tonight."

She hissed savagely: "Then go to them, bastard! What do I care? Let them bite your balls off, I do not need them."

He left her and found one of the younger Indian girls, only recently captured. He took her by the wrist and pulled her to her feet and said to her roughly, not caring whether or not she understood the Indian dialect he used. "You come with me now. If you are not good, I kill you. What is your name?"

She stared at him, wide-eyed, a child-woman. "My name . . . Gri-Sa-Puni."

She was slight of build and very pretty. He said, "Ah, yes, I remember. We captured you when we killed those white men, that white woman. You spread your legs for me now." There was a fire in her eyes that he did not fully understand, thinking (but not quite sure) that it might be caused by the great honor he was paying her . . .

120

He pulled her into the forest, a little away from the others, and an idea came to him that amused him greatly; he decided he wanted her unconscious, so that she would ot move either with him or against him, and he balled up his fist and drove it into the side of her head with monstrous force. She dropped to the ground, and he parted her thighs and set her arms beside her body just so . . .

He slipped out of his clothes, even taking the time to fold them carefully and place them aside. And then he fell on her ruthlessly, driving himself back and forth on that unconscious body till the relief came. For Espada, the sweet little Gri-Sa-Puni, the flower opening to the sun, was a woman, a creature to feast on, and nothing more. He laughed as he pulled himself from her, and he took her head in his hands and said: "Lie there, my love. Perhaps someone else will pass by . . ." He was still chuckling to himself when he found a bed of ferns and lay down to sleep for the rest of the night.

In the morning, all the problems of the previous night's camp answered themselves, as Espada was sure they would. He sat with Jao Torres and Carmen as they ate a good meal of a delectable fish called *pirarucu*, followed by Brazil nuts and avocado pears. He said carelessly, "Jao? I have had thoughts about our last campsite."

Jao was pushing slivers of the succulent fish, grilled over coals, into his mouth. "Our last campsite," he said, "is yesterday. Yesterday is dead."

"No. Yesterday is tomorrow's youth, it is important."

"Then tell me what is important about yesterday's camp." Jao turned to Carmen, and pushed fish into her mouth too. Espada said, "There were footprints there."

"We got fifty-two people," Jao said. "Fifty-two people

121

making footprints. Tell me instead about tomorrow."

"There were footprints there that were not ours."

"It is not possible." Jao lifted his top hat and set it more precisely on his head. "This very large jungle, thousands of miles. We are here. Nobody else here, not possible. You fool, Espada.

"Only a short time ago, we found someone else here."

"Ah yes, we kill them! Three white men, one white woman, am remembering."

He started chuckling to himself. "I taking white woman, very good. You taking her too after I am finishing. But she dead then, how you taking dead woman, Espada? You savage man, Espada."

"But it was good," Espada said swiftly. "And I thank you for your courtesy in letting me love her."

"You my number one man," Torres said grandly. "I make you happy, is good for me." But his small, porcine eyes were hard and filled with venom. "You say footprints, no ours."

"Two men, one woman," Espada said. "One of the men is big and heavy, with a long and powerful stride. The other is lighter and much older. He favors the right leg, as though his left side is hurt. The third print, the woman . . . I found it very interesting. She is tall, with a long step, but light, which means she is very slender. And she moves like an animal, on the balls of her feet, a kind of walking that is rare even among the Indians. Both she and the older man wear sandals of a kind I have never seen before."

"Indian, then."

"No. I can look at the prints left by Indian sandals and tell you the name of their tribe. But these were strange to me, with soles in the European fashion. It disturbs me." He took a long deep breath and continued, "There was one place where the grasses were flattened. There were signs of the big man's heels, driven into the ground, the toes of the woman's sandals between them. They were making love together. And she was on top of him, it might point to a woman of authority, though this is not necessarily so. This idea of mine is bolstered by the fact that she walks ahead of him, which is not natural for a woman, her footprints are frequently obliterated by his. What kind of woman is this? And there is something of greater importance. For no good reason at all, except that there cannot be very many people in the vastness of this jungle, I suspect that the big man whose tracks I have seen is the man you left alive back there when, if you had listened to me, you would have killed him. I think that by some remote chance he has found other companions, one man and one woman, who are neither Indians nor Europeans. I think that he is now moving northwest with them, as we are."

"And *why*? You tell me why now."

"Why should *anyone* be moving through this accursed jungle? Why are *we* moving through it?"

Jao Torres and his men had been wandering for years, constantly searching for the means of sustenance. But at the back of their minds, there had always been one overriding thought . . . Torres stared, and said harshly, "You mean . . . they looking for Raman-li-Undara?"

"The Field of Diamonds," Espada said. "Yes! There can be no other reason for their presence here! And it may be that they have information that we do not have, how can we know? We *cannot* know! But they are here, and moving on a parallel trail to our own!"

For a long time, Jao said nothing. Finally, he said, "You find these tracks last night, you don' tell me, you tell me *now*. Why?"

"Last night," Espada said, "the importance of these footprints did not impinge itself on me."

"Impinge? I am not knowing this word. You talk too fancy, Espada. One day, maybe I kill you for your fancy talk."

"It did not seem important at the time," Espada said lightly. "But now . . . I have had time to think about its meaning, and I have come to the conclusion that I should report my thoughts to you, my leader whom I greatly respect and admire."

Jao Torres thought about it for a long, long time, knowing that the conclusion was inescapable. He said at last, "You going back. You picking up tracks. We follow them."

He found it hard to control his excitement as he thought of the legend of Raman-li-Undara, of the long years he had spent, off and on, in a hopeless search for great wealth. And last night, he had prayed to the Indian Gods for help; could it be that they were so swiftly answering his prayers?

But he tried to mask his agitation. Feigning a casual indifference, he said, "You leave me now, go find them tracks. I love my woman now, I am very strong, I don' want you watch."

"I would never do that," Espada said earnestly. Torres roared at him, "I see you sometimes, watching! One day, I kill you for it!"

"Yes, yes, of course. But remember only my great devotion to you, Jao."

Espada slunk away, and went looking for one of the Indian slave women to take with him on his journey back to the old camp and then on to . . . who could know where? He would find the tracks again, follow them till they indicated the general direction of the strangers travel, and then rendezvous once with his leader.

He found a young girl from the Asrubu tribe, whose women were known for the violence of their passion; she was scarcely more than a child, which pleased him. He dragged her to her feet and slapped her face two or three times to make sure she understood that he was her master. He was very expert in the Asrubu language, and to show off his knowledge of it he said, laughing and showing his white teeth to impress her: "If I find you satisfying, I will load you down with the diamonds that are waiting for us in Raman-li-Undara."

Fifteen, twenty, perhaps thirty of the men had raped her since her capture, some of them time and time again. She was sure that life held nothing for her now.

She spat at him, and answered him in the same language, "Your skin is the color of a snake's belly!" It was the ultimate insult in her people's philosophy. Espada only laughed again and said: "Good! I like a woman of spirit!"

He drew his short sword from his scabbard and cut a length of liana and fashioned a halter to fasten around her neck, and used it to drag her, stumbling, behind him, to be used when he might need her. And so he began tracking down Shana, Gerard, and Emlyn, as they slowly began the entry into the Field of Diamonds, blissfully unaware of this new and mortal danger.

Chapter Eight

Eden was there below them, like a beautiful woman waiting to be known, and loved. Soon after sunrise, they sat on the cool grasses and ate the last of their smoke-dried meat.

Gerard ruffled his heavy growth of beard and murmured, "I am not used to it . . . Through all my years in the jungle, I always went clean-shaven, for one foolish reason or another. A matter of distorted self-respect, I suppose. But now, faced with a meeting I am so anxiously awaiting, I feel the need to shave again. But I cannot, I have no razor now, so what can I do?"

It was almost as if Shana did not know the word. She said, remembering, "Ah yes, the razors. In the old days, our people too scraped off their beards, sometimes two or three times a week."

"But not now?"

"We have no iron in Eden for the blades. And it would seem to be a ridiculous habit, accomplishing nothing."

Gerard said laughing, "That is true indeed."

She was staring down into the deep valley at tiny colored specks there. With great excitement in her voice she said, "They are moving up to meet us, I think."

Emlyn nodded. "Yes, they started at first light," he said. "I watched them cross the meadow to the steps. Four men and three women."

Gerard followed their looks; the specks of color were like slowly moving ants. "So far away," he said, "and you can tell the men from the women?"

"Certain colors for the draperies are worn only by the women, the bright colors. The men mostly wear browns and grays, the natural color of the wool. The women's gowns are always silk, which one of Adam Grieg's English women knew how to weave and to dye. And one of them . . . You see the purple there? It is a royal *draperi*, dyed with indigo, and it means she is a close relative of the Queen herself." She turned to Emlyn: "It is Ferida, I think."

"Yes." Emlyn nodded. "Ferida without a doubt. And they should meet us at the first of the campsites." He turned to Gerard and said, "Climbing down, we can move much faster than they can climbing *up*, it is very laborious." He rose to his feet, smiled, and said, "So shall we begin the descent? I think that for all of us, waiting for so simple a thing as food is a torment."

It was to Shana that he addressed the question; so close to home, she was ready to assume once again her lost authority. Throwing a secret glance at Gerard, she said, "Yes. We will leave now."

They went slowly down the uneven steps. Some of them were less than a foot in depth, while others were at least twice as high, and even on the way down the trek was not easy. But at mid-morning they came to what Shana referred to as Camp Five, a broad and pleasantly shaded area where a small hot spring was bubbling in a scooped-out rocky pool.

Shana said, "A bath here for those who might be exhausted by the effort, there is one at each of the campsites. The water is hot and very good." The scent of it was strongly sulphuric. She went on, "We will rest here for an hour, no more." Without more ado, she dropped her *draperi* to the ground and stepped naked into the steaming pool.

Emlyn said happily, "We have both been wounded, Gerard, and it is here that we begin our cure, the water is very beneficial. It is an introduction for us to Eden itself." He, too, unfastened his *draperi* and entered the water.

In a moment Gerard slipped out of his breeches and sandals and joined them, knowing that he was becoming used to a way of life now that only a few weeks before would have astonished him. The water was hot indeed, as Shana had suggested, but he had long ago met with sulphur springs, and he knew that their healing power was very strong. He watched Emlyn unwrapping the papaya leaves and discarding them.

Emlyn said, "Our medicinal baths, what do I need with papaya leaves any more?"

"Let me see," Gerard said, and Emlyn showed him the once-lacerated arm, the tissues already reforming themselves. "A month," Emlyn said contentedly, "and it will be well again." He flexed his fingers to make the point, and only one of them seemed stiff. "And your own wound?"

Gerard ran his fingers along the scar. "The rib has completely healed, I think. And the flesh wound . . . a matter of time now. And there is nothing better, I know, than this hot sulphur water."

129

"There are springs at all our camps, and in Eden itself there are many of them, each more potent than the other."

Gerard was still searching for knowledge. He said, frowning: "And could this be, perhaps, the reason for your longevity? There are many of these springs in America and Europe, some of them known to cure almost every ailment. What do your own doctors say?"

"Doctors? We have no doctors,? Emlyn said gravely, "because we have no sickness." He shrugged. "Oh, there are herbs, of course, which we all know how to use for minor illness. But once in a while . . ." He looked at Shana, admiring her as she lay back with the bubbling water gently lapping at her breasts, her eyes closed. "Once," he said, "a young girl went too far into the forest in search of bamboo shoots and berries, and she was gored by a wild pig. She died, because there was no one with the knowledge to save her life. And some years ago a man fell from the roof of a high building and broke his back, and he too died. There are several other cases in our long history. But you surely must know that when a man sets out into the jungle, as Adam Grieg did and you did also, then he must give up any thought of doctors. Either he treats himself successfully, or he dies. It is much the same for us today."

"You have had no plagues like those that have decimated Europe in this past hundred years?"

"No."

"Pneumonia? In England, it has been devastating, killing off thousands of people."

"In Eden, we have never had a case of it. We die only of mortal accident or of old age. Once we reach a hundred and twenty years or so, we expect to die, but not before. But you will learn of all these things, and more, when we come to the township, which will be very soon now."

There was a matter which Gerard had long wanted to discuss with both of them, and he said slowly: "Will you answer me another question? Will you tell me about your diamonds? You said they were *collected*. Does this mean a great store of precious stones somewhere in Eden?"

Emlyn nodded. "Yes, that is exactly what it means." He had not lost the smile. "I know more of the Outside and of the old days," he said, "than Shana and others of her generation can possibly know, simply because my father told me, when I was a child, of the Outside and its ways, at firsthand. Whereas Shana has only read of them in our Books. So will you answer me a question too? Does the thought of those diamonds excite you?"

For a long time, Gerard worried about it. He said at last, very slowly, "Yes, I think I must say that it does. But I am also happy to find that they do not excite my *greed*, as I would have supposed. I can't think why that should be except that . . . perhaps something of your character and Shana's is brushing off onto me. Certainly, only a month or two ago the idea of such great wealth would have excited me far more than it does now, though I have never considered myself an adventurer, searching the jungle for its lost treasures. My strongest emotion at the moment is a feeling of the greatest alarm."

Shana raised her lovely eyebrows. "Alarm? But why should that be?"

Gerard said earnestly, "So many legends of a great treasure lost in hidden valleys, and this one, it seems, is true. If word of it should ever reach what you call the Outside, I shudder to think of the ruffians who would descend on your haven."

131

Emlyn nodded. "Yes, I understand. But it is obvious that the original inhabitants, who first found and collected the stones thought of this too. They hid them, and they hid them so well that it was many years before our people found them. But having found them—what could we do with them? They are of no use to us at all. They were simply left where they were first hidden."

"And there are many of them?"

"Thousands. We never bothered to count them. There is a mound of them, two or three feet high in the central chamber of a great maze, which is itself hidden underground."

"A *maze?*"

"Built of great stone blocks beneath what was apparently once a temple of some sort. It is a very complicated maze indeed, as my forebearers learned to their cost. Believe me, Gerard, no one entering Eden could ever hope to find them."

Gerard sighed. He was not at all sure that Emlyn was right, and he knew that knowledge of the great hoard of diamonds was in itself an invitation to disaster. He worried about it, but he said no more.

Emlyn turned to Shana, took her hand, and said gently, "This is perhaps the last chance you will have to regard Gerard as your own. By your leave, I will take his knife and cut staves to help us on the rest of the way down . . ."

Discreetly, he left the two of them, and Shana eased herself up to Gerard and put her arms around him, resting her head on his shoulder, half in and half out of the steaming water. He was aware that she was crying quietly. She whispered, "We will be together in Eden too, but there . . . I will have to share you."

"Yes, you told me, and I still do not understand."

132

But Shana was smiling again suddenly, brushing the tears from her cheeks with a delicate fingertip, and she said: "I have studied Adam Grieg's writings, as we all have, and he was a man of very strong and determined character. He wrote once: '. . . and there is much in life that is not acceptable; if we cannot change it, then we must *learn* to accept it, for it is only through acceptance that happiness can be attained, and through happiness, progress. . . .' Perhaps I should try to find that happiness in sharing you, by accepting it and convincing myself that it is, after all desirable. It is certain that it will be very good for Eden if you father twenty or thirty children for us by as many women." She sighed. "Yes, Adam Grieg was right, as always. And do our customs surprise you so much?"

Gerard embraced her closely and kissed her. "No," he whispered. "There is nothing about Eden that surprises me any more."

They loved each other long and passionately in the hot, sulphurous water. When at last they left the pool, covered all over with a fine yellow powder, Emlyn was returning with his cut staves.

Gerard said amiably, "You came at just the right moment, dear friend. We are ready to continue now."

Emlyn nodded wisely. "Yes," he said, "I know. I did not wish to disturb you prematurely, so I waited under cover until you were finished. Not till then did I show myself."

"Oh. Well, that was very thoughtful of you," Gerard said courteously. They put on their clothes and continued down the astonishing steps. As they descended, the changing, forested mountain took on more and more dark green beauty, cut here and there with rushing waterfalls.

They slept at Camp Three, where Emlyn said happily, "Only six thousand more steps to go . . ." And at Camp One, when Gerard was sure that his legs were frozen into immobility, they met at last with the welcoming party . . .

There were seven of them, smiling their broad smiles of the purest delight and clapping their hands. Shana ran from one to another of them laughing and crying at the same time, as though she had been gone for half a lifetime. Gerard thought he had never seen such a display of overt affection as they hugged and embraced each other, and it delighted him. Moreover, he could only stare at them in astonishment; they were the most beautiful people he had ever seen. . . . There were four men and three women, and he marvelled at their sheer physical perfection.

The men were tall and well-muscled, with tightly curled beards and flashing blue eyes, some with dark hair, and some with light hair. The women, carrying garlands of flowers, were blessed with the most spectacular loveliness. They all had that same caramel-colored skin that Shana had, the same pale blue eyes and firm, athletic bodies and easy articulation. Not one of them seemed to be more than twenty years old. They were all slender and willowy, and they carried their *draperies*—one purple, one scarlet, and one green—as Shana usually wore hers, wrapped once around the waist with the excess material neatly folded and balanced on one shoulder.

Tears of happiness welling up into her eyes as Shana said, "This is Gerard, an Outsider who saved my life when I was dying for need of the help he gave me. Emlyn . . . ?"

Accepting the command, Emlyn said gravely, "I present Ferida, Audrey, and Demara. Lindsay, Clive, Edward, and Lionel. I present also Gerard, who has two names in the fashion of Adam Grieg and our other ancestors. His second name is Fletcher, which means a Bowman. But is is not a Bowman, he is a Strong Man, and a Wise Man, and a Hunter too, of which there are only three in Eden sharing these honorable titles. He is also a skilled Hunter, and a Fisherman, and a Tracker too, besides being a Provider of Food. In short, my dear friends, Gerard must be called the Worthiest of the Worthies, and a man to be greatly admired."

A gasp went up at this disclosure of Gerard's talents, and to his great embarrassment they were clapping again. One of the young women stepped forward and placed a garland of red rose petals around his neck. She said a formal little speech made more touching by the smile in her eyes: "As you have learned, I am Ferida, and the indigo of my *draperi* tells you that I am of royal blood, related to Queen Alma who is my half-sister. I have been sent by her to greet you, as I do now, the first Outsider ever to visit us. You are welcome, Gerard."

She had Shana's strange, slightly slanted eyes, but where Shana's hair was jet-black, Ferida's was ash-gray, and fell to below her waist. Her breasts, half-exposed by the *draperi*, were small and very firm.

Gerard stammered, "Y-your servant, ma'am."

She stood aside, and another young girl was there, just as lovely, with finely arched eyebrows and eyes of the same startling blue. "Demara," she said, and placed another garland around his neck. "We will be lovers soon, I think. It is three years since I had a Worthy Man's child."

Gerard choked as she moved away, and Audrey took her place with yet another garland. She leaned in, embraced him, and whispered, "You are welcome, Gerard, and I too will love you soon. Audrey . . . It is my hope you will remember my name?"

He swallowed hard. "I will remember, ma'am, I assure you. And may I say that this welcome . . ." He was conscious of a certain moistness in his eyes, as he said: "I do not think that I am an overly emotional man, and yet . . . I have never in my life seen such an expression of affection, and as perhaps you can see, it touches me deeply."

She moved away, and then men presented themselves, with great deference as befitted their subordinate position, Lindsay (a giant of a man), Edward, Clive, and Lionel.

A conversation began between the women and Shana that Gerard could only regard as extraordinary. Was Ferida truly a young girl, or a grown woman? He could not tell. She spoke to Shana, very casually: "It is seen that he is a good man. Have you loved him?"

Shana nodded. "Yes, of course, many times."

"You were still a virgin when you left, I think?"

"Yes, I was."

"And it was he who made you a woman?"

"Yes."

"Good. We all thought that on this long journey Bramwell would take you, that you would order him to take you." She was blinking her lovely eyes. "And where *is* Bramwell? You left him on the Outside?"

Shana caught her breath. "Bramwell is dead."

Ferida's hand flew to her throat. "Oh, no . . . !"

"Yes, I fear so." The women gathered round her as she told them how Bramwell had died.

Emlyn said gravely, "He was trying to save my life.

136

Safe on the bank of the river, he hurled himself into the water to help me. We went over the falls together, and while I was thrown clear, Bramwell was not, and he died."

"He was always one of Queen Alma's favorites, it will be hard for her."

"Yes, I know it. It is hard for all of us."

"And we must accept it," Ferida said, "in accordance with Adam Grieg's teaching."

"Yes. We cannot change it."

"And Gerard, you say, saved your life?"

Ferida's eyes were on him as she told them the story of the fallen tree, and when it was finished she murmured: "A Worthy Man indeed. May I take him from you when we sleep tonight?"

"Yes, of course."

Ferida turned to Gerard, touched his arm, and said, "It is decided, you will share my bed tonight and impregnate me. It is time I had another child, and Eden badly needs the new blood that you can provide for us."

He looked helplessly at Shana, but she was smiling gently, and she nodded. "Yes, you will sleep with Ferida tonight. When you have satisfied her, you will return to me."

She looked at Ferida. "Is it not so? I may have him again when you have finished with him?"

"Yes, of course! I will not come between lovers. He is an Outsider, his ways without a doubt will still be the old ways of Adam Grieg, when men and women . . ." She broke off and said slowly, "But . . . might the Outside have progressed in these relationships as we have? We must not assume that they have stood still while we have moved on."

Emlyn looked at Gerard briefly, a brightly amused and very secret expression in his eyes. He said: "No, Ferida, they have not changed . . ."

Gerard lay down that night, for the first time in a very long while uncertain of what would happen now. When the moon was low in the sky both Shana and Ferida approached him. Shana whispered, "I bring you Ferida now, Gerard, who is related to Queen Alma. Love her as you would love me, it is her right."

He could only stare up at them, completely bewildered. Shana turned away and left them alone together. Was she trying to hide tears?

Ferida stood above him in the pale moonlight, dropped her *draperi* to the ground, and stood there in all her naked splendor, her smooth, svelte figure etched in a kind of luminescence; he felt his senses quickening even as he looked at her.

She was unbelievably lovely, with that regal air of authority about her that Shana had in such strong measure. He thrust the sense of shock from him and rose belatedly to his feet, not quite knowing what to do or say. But she placed a hand on his chest, pushed gently, and said: "No, lie down, I will take you now."

He did not know whether he should attempt to refuse her or not, and could think only of Shana's words: *Love her as you would love me.* . . . He lay down on his back, bewildered and yet still conscious of his betraying strength. She lay beside him, and found his manhood with urgent fingers. She whispered, "You are very strong, I am glad. It is a duty for you, but it should be pleasurable too."

"Yes," he said brokenly, " a duty . . ."

"It is not like this on the Outside?"

"No, never like this," He tried to think only of Shana,

138

but her hands and her lips were teasing him beyond endurance, and he felt himself arching his hips uncontrollably to meet her. She rose to her knees when she was ready, straddled him, and plunged down onto him, her head thrown back and her eyes closed. She held tightly till he flooded into her, and she was content. She collapsed on him, kissed him on the lips, and whispered, "It was good, you are very strong, Gerard. In the weeks to come, I will call on you many more times, until we are sure that I carry your child."

For a long time she lay with him, covering his body with kisses and tiny little bites, arousing herself once more. She stretched her long limbs out on the grass beside him at last. Ferida said, "Again now, I am ready."

He groaned as he moved onto her and thrust himself into her, suckling on her breasts as he did so, teasing the tiny, hard nipples with his teeth. He held her wrists above her head in a subconscious gesture of superiority; and when the earth and the sky exploded for him he lay still on her and murmured, a half-moan: "Shana, I love her so much . . ."

Ferida was a very wise woman, and even as she clutched at him she said softly, "And this does not diminish your love for her. Your body is mine for the moment, as it will be again. But your mind is not, and I accept it."

"Yes. There is so much we have to accept. Adam Grieg was right."

"Adam was *always* right. His ideas, and Queen Dashtu's, and Queen Alma's after her . . . they have made a Paradise of Eden."

Gerard sighed. "I have not yet learned to *accept,*" he said. "But perhaps I know the meaning of . . . resignation to the inevitable."

"And was it as good for you as it was for me?"

"Yes, it was good. It will be hard for me to face Shana."

"It should not be so. She *accepts*, too."

"Yes, so she has told me. I still find it very strange."

"In a month or two, when you have loved perhaps fifty of our women, you will find it strange no longer."

There was a question troubling him, a question he was sure was of very little consequence; but he *had* to ask it. Was it that same search for knowledge that always consumed him? Or just idle curiosity? He could not be sure. He thought of Emlyn, a man of seeming middle-age who was one hundred and four years old. He said, not very happy with the question, "I could not ask this, Ferida, except that I am obviously older than you are and can therefore call upon the prerogatives of my age. Will you tell me how old you are?"

She laughed, showing small, white, and perfect teeth of a kind Gerard had seldom seen on the Outside; in this enlightened year of 1825, teeth decayed and fell out even in childhood. She said, "Is it of importance to you?"

"It seems to be. For no good reason, I will admit."

" 'No good reason' is always a very *good* reason, and so I will tell, why should I not? I was born in the year of the great fire that nearly destroyed our township. That was the year 1773, I am fifty-two years old. And you?"

He murmured weakly, "Twenty-seven. I feel a great deal older now."

He touched the smooth, firm flesh of her breasts and her thighs, the body of a seventeen-year-old. He whispered, "It is so hard to adjust myself to this new concept of age . . ."

She kissed him on the lips. "And is it still true that on

the Outside a man dies at fifty or sixty years of age?"

"Yes. Sixty is considered to be ripeness."

"It is sad, is it not? As soon as he is old enough, mature enough, to qualify as a Wise Man . . . he dies. Does it mean that your world is ruled by people of insufficient maturity and therefore of accumulated knowledge?"

"Yes. I think that perhaps it does."

She laughed suddenly, the bright and happy laugh of a very young girl. "You must eat apricot kernels," she said, "as we do. They will prolong your life, and you too will live to be a hundred and twenty or more. A few every day, it is all that is needed. And now, I will send your Shana to you."

Ferida left him, donning her royal purple robe, and in a few minutes Shana was easing her lithe young body onto the fern bed beside him, saucering herself into his back. She reached over to hold him, and whispered, "Was the loving good for you? Ferida is a very beautiful woman, I think, no?"

"Yes, she is lovely indeed. Though not as beautiful as you are."

"Ah . . . How pleasing it is to hear you say that!"

She hesitated, and her voice was tinged with guilt. "Is it really so wrong of me to want you for myself alone?"

"No, I think not. It is more wrong of me to lie with a woman I do not love, while my true love waits for me to return to her."

"But it must be done. In Eden it is not considered right for a man to refuse his services to a woman who wants his child. Indeed, I think it has never happened."

"Any woman?"

"Yes, it has long been laid down as our prerogative."

There was a little silence. Gerard said at last, deeply troubled, "I swear to you that as I loved her, it was your

141

name that was on my lips. Her thighs opening to me were your thighs."

Shana said fiercely, "It is as it should be, I am content. Even though, I am sure, my thoughts are very antisocial, and therefore to be disapproved."

He turned to her and embraced her, seeking comfort in the close touch of their bodies, straining against each other, knowing that their minds, too, were as one.

Shana said quietly, "Remember the wisdom of Adam Grieg, and his words on . . . *acceptance*. Perhaps, in the course of time, you will come to realize that our way is not so difficult after all."

"As long as you can remember," Gerard said, "that my heart is yours, and always will be . . ."

"Oh, my love . . ."

They slept together in each other's arms, till the rising sun awoke them to a new and different kind of day.

And fourteen hours later, they stumbled wearily down the last of the twelve thousand steps, and entered Eden itself.

Chapter Nine

Eden, at last . . . The mere sight of it up close raised Gerard's expectations to impossible heights. He was aware that Shana, beside him, and Emlyn following close behind, were both as excited as he was, though he knew that they had left their home only a month or so ago.

The entrance to the township lay about a mile from the last of the steps, across a cool and verdant meadow through which a small stream was prettily meandering. There was a wide stone archway, flanked by low walls of huge granite stones fitted together without mortar. It came to him as a little surprise that the city was made up of thirty or forty blocks of adjoining houses, each one containing a dozen or more apartments. Each block was separated from its neighbor by very beautiful and well-tended gardens in which the most brilliant flowers and shrubs were growing. There were ancient wooden conduits with fast-flowing water coursing among many of the gardens, with little wooden bridges spanning some of them, some of the streams had stepping-stones instead, and some of them were quite dry. There was an air here of the most remarkable serenity, and of an exquisite beauty.

People by the hundred were streaming out to greet them. Gerard was already inured, knowing that this strange tribe was made up of the most beautiful people he had ever met with. But he could only gape. The men were strong and straight and very muscular, wearing *draperies* of white, gray, or light brown wool; and the women, without exception, were pictures of quite unbelievable loveliness in gowns of brilliantly dyed silks of red, orange, yellow, green or blue. Men and women alike seemed, for the most part, blessed with that same caramel-colored skin and those same light blue eyes, though some had black hair, some were very blonde, and there were a few redheads among them too. One or two of the women had Ferida's ash-gray hair, and there was one young man whose strong beard was streaked with black, white, and ginger.

They crowded around the newcomers, slapping Emlyn on the back and laughing excitedly, embracing Shana with great affection, and regarding Gerard with a kind of restrained curiosity. Everyone seemed to be talking at once, and snatches of conversation emerged from the babble:

"So soon, and you have found an Outsider . . . ?"

"And are there great cities there, as the Books tell us . . . ?"

"And Bramwell, where is Bramwell. . . .?"

"*What?* But he was such a powerful swimmer . . ."

"And Emlyn, your arm . . .?"

He heard Shana telling again of their adventures, and after a little shocked silence the chatter started up again.

"A very handsome man, he looks like the pictures of Adam Grieg . . ."

"No, not really. It's because of the strange breeches he wears . . ."

"Alma is waiting, waiting anxiously ever since we first saw your smoke . . ."

"And all this must wait," Shana said. "It is right that we talk with Alma first. For everyone else, there will be so many evenings on the grass, so much we have to tell you."

He could not believe how quickly the chattering stopped. It was as though a hundred people and more had heard the suggestion from Shana and taken it as a command. Ferida said quietly, "Yes, we will go to her now."

Then suddenly, a very young girl was pushed to the front before him, a child of perhaps nine or ten. He wondered if she could be older too? She was clutching a kind of lyre to her immature breast. She whispered shyly, "May I sing you a song, Outsider?"

"Her name is Anitra," Shana said, smiling, "and she plays the lyre very well indeed."

He fondled the young girl's long brown hair and saw those fascinating eyes looking up at him very somberly. He said gently, "I would like that very much, Anitra." The crowd around them was silent, looking at the girl expectantly. He saw that the lyre was very simply made, a board of highly polished rosewood over a gourd for a sound box, with strings of animal gut. As she touched a chord the music was exquisite, sad, and haunting.

Led by Shana, they were all moving slowly down a path that was paved with granite blocks and interspersed with lines of dark green creeper and tiny pink flowers. On both sides of them were the gray stone walls of the houses, squared-off and fitted together very precisely. There were great archways everywhere. Pools of clear water half-covered over with water lilies were fed by a small stream that was channelled in through open wooden conduits. There were deep green lichen clinging to open, glassless windows and and jacaranda trees crowding their blue blossoms above creeping geraniums in scarlet, pink, and white. The air was still and cool and very clear. They moved down a flight of stone steps and up another, and there were more lichen-covered archways where the houses nestled one into another . . .

The child Anitra, moving ahead of them now like a herald, was playing an old English melody that Gerard knew from his own youth. After a few bars, her child's voice broke in, a song that he had not heard for many, many years:

> There is a Ladye, sweet and kind,
> Was never face so pleased my mind,
> I did but see her passing by,
> And yet, I'll love her till I die . . .

The voice was a sweet, immature soprano, and it brought tears to his eyes as he thought of his beloved Shana.

Now, from narrow side streets on both sides of them, more people were joining the procession, and still that lovely voice continued to the accompaniment of the strings:

> Her gestures, motions, and her smile,
> Her lips, her voice, my heart beguile . . .

146

And when they reached the Throne Room, the song was coming to its end:

> But change she earth or change she sky,
> Yet will I love her, till I die . . .

The door to the Throne Room was huge and heavy, of ancient cut timbers that towered up to the high stone lintel. Shana knocked on it and waited. It was slowly swung open by a well-built and handsome young man who smiled broadly and said, "Come in, please, Alma will see you now."

Gerard sought Shana's hand for comfort, wondering why he should feel so nervous. He whispered, "Do I make an obeisance?"

Shana's laugh was a tinkle of happiness. "No, of course not! Come, we'll talk with her now; you'll adore her."

He stared at the vast room in astonishment as the three of them entered. It was perhaps fifty feet long by as much as thirty wide, and very high, made from the same fitted granite blocks. It seemed that every inch of the walls was taken up with paintings that seemed to depict the daily life of the people of Eden—in the fields, at the streams with their fishing nets, digging in the forest for edible roots, picking berries, setting traps for meat, roasting whole carcasses over great fiery pits, weaving silk and dyeing it, herding llamas—There was a huge and stylized picture of a long line of men engaged in cutting the famous steps up the steep mountainside, digging into the slope with ironwood spikes, splitting granite boulders with fire, cementing stones together with adobe. . . . Interspersed with the paintings were hundreds of carvings of various sizes set in individual niches

147

in the walls, busts of the men and women of Eden, and they were exquisite, marvellously well-executed in highly polished tulip wood that caught the light of the sunbeams streaming down through the windows which ran like narrow strips below the ceiling for most of the room's periphery. There were other windows, much larger, giving a splendid view of the meadows and the mountain beyond them. And by one of these apertures, an old-fashioned naval splyglass was mounted on a tripod, aimed at the peak they had left behind them.

But Gerard's attention was taken by the woman who sat on a carved wooden chair at the far end of the room. Her huge eyes were on him as he approached with Shana, an expression of the purest delight in them. She was dressed in a *draperi* dyed to a rich purple, wrapped entirely around her body now in more formal fashion and even draped over her head. Her hair was blonde and very silky, shining beautifully as though it were constantly brushed, and it hung down under the dress almost to her waist. The same caramel-colored skin, the same slightly slanted eyes of that Edenite light blue . . .

Confused by the matter of age in Eden, he could not begin to guess how old she might be. There was hardly a wrinkle of any sort on her face, the calm and lovely face of a young girl but with an added maturity to it that was quite indefinable. And when she rose to greet them, Gerard saw that she was voluptuous in the extreme, with full, firm breasts under her *draperi,* an hourglass waist and slim but well-rounded hips. He could only think of her expression as . . . *regal,* and quite befitting her high position.

"No obeisance," Shana had said, even laughing about it, and he resisted the temptation to drop to one knee in the presence of a majesty that was really quite awesome.

She moved towards him, and he thought of the word *"gliding."* Her right hand was held out to him, the knuckles uppermost, an English *grande dame* from the late seventeenth century. He took her hand and brushed it with his lips, a gesture he had not used in some years.

He said, bowing gravely, "I am Gerard Fletcher, ma'am, and your servant."

Those remarkable eyes seemed to be peering deep into his soul. Her head was held a little back as she murmured, "Yes, I know who you are, Gerard, word has already been brought to me, and I welcome you to Eden with love and affection. It is my understanding that you saved Shana's life and therefore Emlyn's too. I am grateful to you, as the whole of our township is. Shana is very dear to us all, and Emlyn's death would have been a disaster for us."

She turned to Shana, embraced her, and said, "You did well to bring him here, dear Shana, it is more than we could have hoped for." She put her arms around Emlyn and held him briefly too, saying: "And you too, Emlyn, I thank you for what you have done together. Will you make your report now to the Scribe? It should go into the Books while it is all still fresh in your mind."

Emlyn nodded, smiling. "Of course, Alma. For the last several days, I have been rehearsing the phrases I will use, it is a very exciting story. The Scribe is still Burton?"

"Oh yes."

"Good, he's an old and dear friend, and I'll have much to tell him."

"Shortly, we too will talk."

"By your leave then," he said with old-fashioned courtesy, and bowed himself out. The Queen took Gerard's hand and led him to a divan of rosewood, upholstered in silk-covered kapok. She sat with him there as Shana sank to the ground at their feet and rested her head against Gerard's thigh in a little gesture of intimacy, a very casual sort of intimacy in which Gerard took great pleasure. There were none of the trappings of majesty here, and yet . . . he was aware that he was in the presence of a very remarkable woman.

She said slowly, "Ever since Shana left us, I have been trying to decide what questions I should ask on her return. I did not expect that she would be fortunate enough to find someone who could answer these questions more fully, I am sure. And so . . . I find myself at a loss. Tell me first, if you will, where you come from? You are English, I take it?"

"No, ma'am, I come from America, though I have been in the jungle of the Great River for some years now, a servant once, which I am no longer, of Dom Pedro."

Alma raised her fine eyebrows. "Dom Pedro is . . . ?"

"Brazil is a Kingdom now, ruled by the son of Dom Jao . . . Whose name will not be known to you either, since I believe that you have been out of contact with the rest of the world for a very long time now."

"Yes, since the Great Earthquake in the year 1700, one hundred and twenty-five years ago." She caught her breath and said suddenly, "But in my eagerness to talk with you, I forget my manners. After so hard a journey, you will be tired, and hungry, and thirsty too, I think?"

He shook his head and said honestly, "The pleasure of this meeting is very great for me too, ma'am. I am neither tired nor hungry . . ."

But Shana raised her head and said, "Well, it is some time since we last ate, is it not?"

Alma laughed and clapped her hands. From an open

archway a small boy came running. The Queen said gently, "We will have food and wine, Roland. Please tell them in the kitchens."

Wine too? He could not believe his good fortune. Ever since that disastrous night of the attack on his camp, he had drunk only water. Alma said, as though reading his thoughts, "We make several wines here, and some of them are quite good, I think. From elderberries, gorse, nettles, cowslip . . . Our beetroot wine is excellent, a recipe that Adam Grieg himself left to my people. You know of Adam Grieg?"

"Yes, ma'am, though not yet enough. Shana has told me about him."

"He was a fine man."

She rose from the divan and went to one of the niches in the wall, and brought back a statuette to show him. "Adam Grieg, our founder, immortalized by Leonard, who was a sculptor of great talent."

"But carving," Gerard said, "presupposes sharp knives. I am told that you have no iron here. . . ."

"And that is true. There are eighteen knives of various kinds left over from my grandfather's day, and now, they are reserved, for as long as they might last, for the exclusive use of our artists, we do not allow the builders to use them." She sighed. "And when they wear out at last, there will be no more busts of our people, only the paintings. Unless we make contact with the Outside world which you represent for us. And that contact, Gerard, means *commerce*. Have you heard of our diamonds?"

Gerard nodded. "Yes, ma'am, I have."

"We have thousands of them, though this is all we have to trade, and my grandfather's writings tell us that they are valuable in your world, even if they are useless to us. We thought in terms of simple barter, one diamond for one knife, perhaps . . ." She broke off, seeing the look of shock on his face, and said earnestly: "We *must* have access to tools, Gerard, if Eden's growth is to continue. And this is the essence of commerce, is it not?"

He could hardly find the words. He said at last, "With respect, ma'am, it is apparent to me that you do not know the real worth of your treasure. The smallest diamond would buy a huge amount of tools of every kind. My own good chopping-knife . . . Yes, a tiny diamond would purchase a thousand of them!"

Alma stared at him, and there was a little silence. "Well," she said, "that is astounding news indeed! You are sure of it?"

"Yes, ma'am."

"Then when I send the traders out, I will so inform them. I am grateful to you, Gerard."

He was in the depths of despair for these charming and naive people! And yet, surely their naivete in this respect at least was understandable? Alma was reading his thoughts, it seemed. She said, frowning, "In the Books, there are only seven references to the diamonds— mostly the search for them, you understand—and the only indication of their worth is a comment: '. . . *they are very valuable in the rest of the world, but of what use are they to us* . . . ?' And we have underestimated their value, have we not?"

"Very gravely, ma'am." Searching for help, he took Shana's hand and held it tightly. Gerard said urgently, "But it is not this that disturbs me, there is a matter for much more serious consideration. I cannot take it upon myself to advise you, I am an Outsider. . . ."

"And hereby given the honorable title of *Wise Man*,"

Alma said swiftly, "which gives you the right to advise me at all times."

Startled, he looked at Shana and saw that her eyes were alight with her pleasure. He turned back to the Queen and stammered, "I thank you, ma'am, and I will do my best to advise you well, if I may. In this particular case . . ." He took a long deep breath and continued, "On the Outside, Eden has long been known to us in legend, a place of fabulous wealth called Raman-li-Undara. . . ."

"Its original name," Alma said, "until Adam Grieg changed it when English, rather than the dialect of the Indians, became our language."

"The Field of Diamonds," Gerard said. "A name, until now, in legend only. But I *must* tell you that the outside world is a very rapacious world. If the truth of the legend were to become known throughout the Amazon Basin—and once it is known to only one man it will be known to many—then many adventurers will descend on you. Not to trade, but to steal."

Alma went in silence back to the little niche and replaced the statue of her grandfather. She said sadly: "*To steal* . . . It is a word that has disappeared from our vocabulary altogether. In Eden, there has never, *ever*, been anything stolen."

"It is not the same out there," Gerard said firmly. "I wish it were, but it is not."

Alma turned, and her eyes were flashing now with a kind of imperious scorn. "I will accept this as true," she said, "Indeed, how can I not? But you are forgetting one thing."

"And that is . . . ?"

"Let us suppose that some of your . . . your adventurers do indeed descend on us, hoping to steal from us. I say: Let them try! The diamonds are well-hidden, Gerard. They will *never* find them! Let them search as long as . . ."

Gerard was slowly shaking his head, and she looked questioningly at him. "Their hiding-place," he said, "must be known, I imagine, to several of you?"

"Several of us? *All* of us! There is not a woman, man, or child in Eden who does not know where they are."

"Then it is even worse than I thought. Duress can be applied, ma'am, and the secret will be out at once."

"Duress?"

"Persuasion, ma'am. Persuasion of the worst kind."

Alma paled, a hand at her throat. "Surely not . . . !" He felt Shana's hand tighten in his, and he was desperate to make them understand. He said tightly, "Permit me to be harsh, ma'am, as I feel I must be. Imagine one of the desperadoes I speak of swinging a baby around by the ankles and screaming at its mother, 'Tell me where your diamonds are hidden or I will smash his skull . . .' And believe me, ma'am, there are many ruffians out there in the jungle capable of such murderous behavior." There were sudden tears in his eyes as he thought of Dora. He told her, "I myself have had personal experience on at least one occasion with men . . . with *animals* of the kind I have in mind, and there are very many others of their sort."

"A *personal* experience?" Her eyes were very grave, and her voice was low and soothing. "Will you tell me of it? I see that it moves you deeply, and it is sometimes helpful to talk, I think."

Hesitantly, he recounted the events of that terrible night. When he had finished, to his surprise the Queen embraced him tightly, and whispered, almost in Emlyn's own words: "In Eden, there will be only love for you, and respect and admiration. You must forget."

"Yes, I know it. It is not easy to forget. And with respect, ma'am, you must remember what I have told you."

"As I will indeed. Adam Grieg always felt that the time might come when we would have to defend our home against such people. But since our valley was cut off so many years ago, the need has never arisen. We have no weapons here, and fighting is not part of our way of life, though it was for both our Indian and English ancestors. And what you are suggesting, I think, is that where we have cut a way out for ourselves, we have also cut a way in for others. Is that what you are telling me?"

Gerard nodded gravely. "I cannot believe, ma'am," he said, "that anyone will easily find the hidden cleft in the rock that gives access to Eden's steps. But it might be wise to station men there, at the top of the stairway, who would give you warning should anyone by chance approach. I repeat, I do not think it likely, but . . . A permanent guard there might seem like a wise precaution."

"Then I will see to it." She rose to her feet, took his hand, and led him to the huge glassless aperture that was the window. She said, "Let me show you our spyglass, it can be of great help to us now."

It was a splendid old naval telescope, and Gerard read the inscription on its brass plaque: James Doughty & Sons, Birmingham, 1631 Anno Domini, and under it a smaller bronze insert etched with the handwritten name: Adam Grieg. He peered through the lens and focused it a little better, and studied the plateau at the top of the steps where they had taken that last breakfast together before beginning the long and torturing descent.

Alma returned to the divan and patted the seat beside her for him to sit with her. She said, "But tell me about the world beyond the Amazon. Your own home was in America, you said?"

"Yes, ma'am. A small settlement called New Orleans."

"New Orleans? I do not know of it."

"It was founded in 1718, in Louisiana."

"Ah yes. Then it is French, no doubt? At the time my grandfather fled the gold fields in the south, the French were trying to found a colony at the mouth of a river with a very strange name. The Mississ . . . Mississpupi?"

"The Mississippi, ma'am."

"Ah yes. And what of your largest city, New Amsterdam?"

"Now called New York, ma'am, and flourishing."

"And France? Tell me about France."

"There was a great revolution there only thirty-six years ago, in which many hundred thousand people perished . . ."

The food was brought, a great wooden platter of a splendid fish which he thought might be fillets of a very large *pirarucu* which had been grilled to perfection over coals. And with it there was a wine of a strange topaz color and even stranger taste. "Our honey wine," Alma said proudly, "one of our best. The wine was served to Gerard in a heavy pewter mug. He looked in surprise at the name engraved on it—Adam Grieg again. He glanced at the other two vessels; both Alma and Shana were drinking from highly polished gourds.

The Queen saw his surprise, and there was a lovely smile on her face as she said: "It is what Adam called a tankard, the only one we have. Our own vessels are simpler, made from calabash."

He was touched, and he murmured, "I am deeply conscious, ma'am, of the honor you do me."

"It is well deserved, Gerard. Tell me about Germany, if you will."

And so the talk went on as they ate and drank together like old friends.

"And Russia, tell me of Russia . . ."

"And of India . . ."

"And China . . ."

"And what of Africa?"

Alma's thirst for knowledge was insatiable. Throughout the long conversation Shana sat on the floor beside them, picking at the fillets of fish with delicate fingers and sipping from her calabash from time to time. Her eyes stared wide on him, wondering at the extent of his knowledge, taking in every word he said as he spoke of the Ottoman Empire, of the Great Famine in Japan, of the English East India Company . . . of George Washington, Jefferson, Madison, Monroe and Adams, of William and Mary in England, and of Queen Anne. Whereupon Alma said quickly, "*Queen* Anne? Then they had a matriarchal society in England too? As ours is?"

Gerard smiled. "No, ma'am. The social order changed very little."

Alma stared. "But how could that be? A Queen to rule them instead of a King . . . ?"

"Her ministers were all men," Gerard said dryly, and the Queen sighed. "What a wasted opportunity."

For a long time the questioning continued, and at last Alma arose to signify that the meeting had come to an end. To his delight, she embraced him again, and said, "We will talk again, Gerard, very soon. Meanwhile, you are one of us now, one of Eden's Wise Men to be greatly

157

respected. Accommodation has been arranged for you, and it is my hope, the hope of all of us, that you will spend the rest of your long life among us. I will call on you for advice, and for other services too, from time to time. And you will find that the love you have so clearly earned will be yours in the fullest possible measure."

Shana took his arm as they left the Throne Room, and there was a further suprise awaiting him on the street . . . Outside, the waiting crowd had grown to perhaps a thousand people. As Gerard appeared in the doorway they broke into spontaneous applause, clapping and cheering with a display of devotion that brought tears to his eyes.

Gathered with them were a dozen musicians now, carrying strange-looking instruments—drums, guitars, zithers and bamboo flutes. They struck up an old English ballad as the clapping died down to make way for them. The child Anitra's sweet, bell-like voice came to him:

'Come live with me and be my love,
And we will all the pleasures prove
That hills and valleys, dales and field,
And all the craggy mountains yield . . .'

Gerard felt Shana's hand tighten on his arm. She whispered, "My people welcome you . . . as a hero."

Chapter Ten

The days that followed were a delight for Gerard. The gentle people of Eden, men and women alike, were his constant companions, seeking him out at every accessible opportunity to chat with him about his adventures and about their own way of life. Shana almost never left his side, and in these ideal surroundings their love grew beyond the bounds of ecstasy.

The house they had prepared for him was large and spacious, and like all the other houses consisted of a single room of fitted-granite blocks, with wide and tall apertures that served as windows. Narrow passages led from it to other houses where neighbors lived. A veritable warren of houses were built around a central courtyard in which a fountain played among brilliantly colored shrubs and flowers.

The courtyard served as a communal eating-place for the group in his particular block of houses. There was always food there in abundance at mealtimes—whole roasted boar or venison over charcoal coals, great platters of fish, and fruit of many kinds, peaches, plums, citrus and figs . . .

His room was furnished with a very wide bed made of

teak with leather strappings and a mattress of thick kapok covered with a quilt of scarlet silk, and there were
several armchairs and a divan made of the same materi-
als. There were three splendid paintings hanging—one
of them of Shana herself—and there were ten or twelve
ceramic pots of greenery in niches in the wall. Altogether, it was an attractive and refreshing sort of place,
cool and airy, and imposing in its simplicity.

Shana shared his bed at night, hardly using her own
room, which was next to his, at all, and they spent the
idyllic days together as she proudly showed him the
township, and its meadows, gardens, and forests. Sometimes, they joined the hunters or the fishermen and
brought more food home for their group. The clusters
of houses, she told him, were called *conviveries,* where
thirty or forty people lived side by side in close friendship, sharing their food as well as their leisure hours in
the communal courtyard.

She showed him how the work was distributed, the
names written up on a bulletin board every Monday
morning by the unobtrusive Concord that attended to
these mundane matters:

> This week, Sarah, Daphne, Wendy and Delphine to
> care for the children . . . Andrea, Margot, to cook . . .
> Marcella, Hedda, Elaine to the silk-weavers shop . . .
> Michael, Andrew, to repair roof-tiles . . . Arman, Bene-
> dict, Thomas to catch fish . . . Lindsay, Sterling, David
> to cut grain . . .

So, the schedule was posted in each of the *conviveries*
for its own particular inhabitants, the duties changing
constantly, rotating so that all of the people would become familiar with all of the work that was necessary.

Gerard thought that it was a splendid idea, but he said, "Suppose that Benedict does not want to catch fish this week? What then?"

Shana laughed. "And why should he not?" she asked. She shrugged, and went on, "Oh, it sometimes happens that Sterling will change with Andrew, or Hedda with Margot . . . In fact, Hedda is always changing with one of the cooks for the week because she is never happier than when she is preparing a good meal, at which she is very expert."

"And no one objects to this . . . this flouting of authority?"

Shana could not stop laughing. "No, of course not! Why should they? All that matters is that the work should be done!"

"Yes, indeed . . ."

She showed him the charcoal pits where three men from one of the other *conviveries* were piling adobe over long heaps of smouldering thorn roots, and the silk dyers vats where a score of different wild plants were being boiled and pressed, saffron, indigo, madder, lichen and cotinus . . . She took him to the clay pits where beautiful vessels were being turned on potters wheels. He tried his hand at forming a pot of his own, not very successfully; the laughter at his unskilled efforts was shared by all of them. Shana whispered, "Never mind, within the month you will become as expert as any of us . . ." They moved on to where the hunters of the week were making snares from a kind of hibiscus fibre and helped them form it into nets. Then on to the basket-weaving area, and again he spent an hour or two there with Shana learning how these important containers were made. She said proudly, "Some of us, and I am one of them, can weave our baskets so tightly that they will hold water as well as any clay jar. . . ."

In a very few days, Gerard was simply one of the men of Eden, dressed now in a light brown *draperi* and utterly content with his new way of life. He was secretly wondering when he, too, would be put to work.

Emlyn was with him constantly, and a very deep friendship, hardened by trials that no longer existed, had grown up among the three of them. He showed Gerard the Books, a collection of more than a hundred carefully bound volumes, whose bark-cloth pages were covered with precise and beautiful writing in indigo ink. The *Books* detailed Eden's long history, and Gerard found them fascinating:

. . . and the mountain which we have always called The Sleeping Girl erupted . . . an earthquake of monstrous proportions that shook the foundations of the township itself . . . for two weeks, men searched for a way out of the valley and found none . . . we have been sealed in . . . and Dashtu, daughter to Adam Grieg by Serifa, became Queen of Eden, by common consent . . . even the Indian women have agreed that our sole language shall be the English of our men, even though it be the women who rule us now . . . that skilled men or women be appointed Scribes, to keep our history as long as it may last . . . the diamonds were found at last, an exercise in futility during which ten valuable lives were lost to us forever in the great labyrinth; will their bodies ever be found . . . ? It seems that the key lies in the carved faces that adorn the walls, and in the magical number three . . . a decision that they would remain there, worthless as they are to us . . . and on Dashtu's death this day, Alma became Queen, may she rule as long and as wisely as her mother has ruled us . . .

And then, a note of triumph:

> It is almost one hundred years to the day, and the great
> stairway has been completed! For our first contact with
> an outside world of which we know nothing at firsthand,
> Alma has selected Shana, Emlyn, and Bramwell to
> make the long and difficult journey; our hearts go with
> them on a venture that might well be filled with danger

There was great pleasure for him in the reading, a pleasure that was tinged with a strange kind of awe that *someone* had been wise enough to keep these priceless records of a civilization that had stood still for one hundred twenty-five years in a very progressive world.

It was on the sixth day of Gerard's sojourn here that Emlyn came to him and said, that gentle smile on his handsome face: "With your consent, my good friend, Alma the Queen wishes to see you. With Shana too . . ."

They found Alma in her Throne Room, and she took Gerard at once to the spyglass and gave it to him to look through. At the top of the steps he saw three or four young men from Eden moving about. Alma said quietly, "The guards you suggested. Emlyn has arranged that they will stay there for three months before being replaced by others from among our Strong Men. They will give us warning if strangers should appear, so that we may be prepared for them." She hesitated. "Though what form that preparation might take, I do not know."

"I confess, ma'am." Gerard said, "that I, too, do not know the answer to this vexing problem, although I have thought about it deeply and will continue to do so."

"Good, I hope that you will."

"We may be imagining dangers where there are none. But *any* precaution we can take is much to be desired."

"Yes, Emlyn agrees, and he is the wisest of all our Wise Men." She smiled, and her eyes lit up as she took both his hands. "Now, I think the time has come for you to see our hidden diamonds for yourself. I have instructed Emlyn to take you together with Shana who has seen them before, of course." There was a kind of twinkle in her eyes, almost of mischief. "It is apparent that you do not like to leave her side, nor she yours. And when you have seen them, perhaps you will be able to tell me if they are really as valuable as you suspect."

"I will do so, ma'am . . ."

They went together, Shana, Gerard, and Emlyn, to the town's eastern extremity and entered the ancient stone Temple. Strange faces were carved here and there along with a few full-length figures which seemed to be fitted into unearthly machines with wheels surrounding them in which myriad eyes had been carved. The bodies were winged, four-headed, and quite frightening . . . Gerard thought of his early days and of his father's Bible, and of the passages—what were they in, Ezekiel? . . . *As for their rings, they were so high that they were dreadful, and the rings were full of eyes . . . Behold one wheel upon the earth by the living creature, with his four faces . . . They had the hands of a man under their wings on their four sides . . .*

He felt that his blood was curdling; this was a very holy place of the greatest antiquity, and there were overtones here that were not quite human. They found the almost-hidden steps that led down into the damp bowels of the earth where the cellars were. To Gerard's astonishment there was light coming from great sheets of a pale ivory-colored material set in the high walls. He stared up at them in wonderment.

Emlyn said, his voice low as though this were a hallowed place indeed: "A masterpiece of engineering by whoever built this temple. The lights are quartz, set in channels out in the rock to catch the sunlight above us and reflect it in here . . . We, too, marvelled at it the first time we saw it. And there is something else almost as miraculous."

Emlyn went to the solid wall, where one of those strange figures was carved, though here the four faces were of a man, an ox, a lion, and an eagle. *Ezekiel again*, Gerard thought. He leaned into it only slightly, and a whole section of the wall swung ponderously inward. He said, "It is counter-balanced, though we have not yet discovered by what means. But the balance is so perfect that a five-year-old child can swing it open. . . ."

Beyond it was a wide and high passage, faintly lit by a shaft of light that came from a bore-hole in the ceiling high above them. Emlyn whispered, "The entrance to the labyrinth itself."

Gerard felt Shana's hand trembling in his. "A labyrinth?"

Emlyn nodded. "Yes, a maze. But a maze of marvellous intricacy. You know about them?"

"Yes, of course."

Gerard stared down the dark passageway. Emlyn murmured, "A place of death . . ." A shaft of narrow light was streaming down, illuminating the most intricate carving on the walls, row after row of faces, some grotesque, some of animals, some human, starting high up at the top and reaching to ground level, perhaps as many as a thousand of them on one wall alone. Some were full-face, others looking to the left or right, and looking up at the higher rows, Emlyn said, "Only death, unless the secret is known and followed very, very carefully. There are more than two miles of passages here, each one of them is as intricately carved as this one. The carving alone must have taken hundreds of artists hundreds of years. They are sometimes lit by bore-holes, more often they are in utter darkness, and the secret is in the magic number three and its multiples. For three turns, we follow the look of the third face from the left—always from the left on the left-hand wall—it tells us which way to go. And then . . . six. The sixth face in the sixth row for six more turns. Then nine, and finally twelve. And if a single one of those turns is incorrectly made, then the sequence is lost and there remains only the chaos of tortuous passages that lead, eventually, to dead ends. Ten of our people perished here many years ago trying to decipher the labyrinth's secrets. Years later, we found three of their skeletons, the others have been lost forever. I know the maze well now. But even so, I will confess to an onslaught of abject terror every time I enter it."

"There is terror," Gerard said, "in the very word itself."

He knew all about the frightening idea behind the construction of a labyrinth . . . They had first been invented by the ancient Egyptians, who built them as much as fifteen hundred feet underground, their eventual central chambers shielded from intruders by passage after passage that turned right or left or back on itself, all but the right one leading, after a dozen turns or so, to a dead end or back into the main body of the maze again . . . A good labyrinth would permanently lose an unwelcome visitor in the first ten minutes of his wanderings. After his death from thirst and starvation, his skeleton would perhaps be discovered, sometimes hundreds of years later by other intruders who were lost and who would soon die too . . .

Emlyn led the way, muttering: "Please do not talk to me now, I must concentrate on multiples of three, I have no wish to be lost here. And when we reach the eighteenth of the turns, we must remember that the people who designed the maze played a deadly little trick on us; from that point on, all the directions are reversed. That is to say, the faces look to the *wrong* way, it is very frustrating."

They followed him in silence. The passages were narrow for the most part, and some of them were so low that they had to stoop. Once, they were driven to crawling on their hands and knees as the roof became lower and lower as they moved along it, giving an effect of terrifying confinement. At its end, there was a high and very inviting corridor, lit once again by the sun's rays striking through the bore-holes; but it was to the left, and the stern face on the wall meant *turn right* . . .

They moved on slowly, and at the end of an hour it seemed to Gerard that Emlyn had lost a great deal of his assurance; and Shana was visibly trembling.

Emlyn said hoarsely, "I am losing count, was that our seventeenth turn?"

Gerard shook his head. No, the eighteenth."

"Ah yes." He breathed a sight of relief. "And from now on, we reverse the directions."

In some places it was so dark that they could only study the carved faces with their fingertips. Once Emlyn said, with satisfaction, "Ah, the face of the lion here is chipped. I remember it, good. We are almost at the central chamber now."

167

They turned left because the lion's face indicated right, and moved on to the end of the long, narrow corridor. And then . . .

There was only one way to turn, and it gave on to an open chamber ahead of them, large and very high and lit by a circle of seven bore-holes in the roof above them. Gerard could only stare in stupefaction . . .

The four walls were each perforated with seven narrow openings like the one they had come through and carved in bas-relief with life-sized images of the same strange creatures that he had seen in the Temple cellar. And in the center of the room was the most extraordinary statue he had ever seen.

It was a handsome, imposing, and regal woman, dressed in a long skirt and a bodice open at the full breasts in the fashion of the ancient Greeks or Egyptians. There was a long necklace of diamonds at her throat, two bracelets of diamonds at each wrist, and a belt of diamonds around her slender waist. The diamonds were all cut and polished. . . .

Gerard felt his heart pounding furiously. He whispered, "In God's name, *cut* stones? How can it be?"

Shana's voice was hushed. "No one knows anything about her, who her people were, who she might have been, where they came from . . . No, nor how they learned the secret of cutting diamonds, or what tools they used."

"Nor even *when*," Emlyn said.

"And this is your great wealth? They are priceless, beyond any possible calculation . . ."

Emlyn shook his head. "No. She wears only the smallest fraction of our wealth. I will show you . . ."

The statue was mounted on a raised platform, a circular box some four feet across and three feet high, made of stone with a fitted wooden lid at her feet. Emlyn said quietly, "It seems almost sacrilege to open it . . ." But he slowly pulled back the lid to disclose a mound of uncut stones that filled the hollow platform almost to its capacity, piled up in such abundance that Gerard could not even find his voice. And many of them were *huge*. He stooped and picked up one from the top of the heap and stared at it, and he judged that it must surely weigh in at more than three hundred carats; there were others in the mound even larger, and he could only shake his head in bewilderment. He placed the stone carefully back, and said, "And you thought of trading these for chopping-knives on a *one-to-one* basis?"

Emlyn sighed. "We thought only," he said, "that iron tools might be of more use to us. Merely an idea that came to us once." He slid back the polished wooden lid and said slowly, "But there is another great mystery here you should know of. Have you observed where she is pointing?"

The statue's left arm was slightly extended, the hand half-open; and the index finger did indeed seem to be pointing. Gerard said, frowning, "Why yes. She is pointing to the center door in the wall to the left of the one we came through. An indication, perhaps, that we need the center door on the wall to her right, should we become confused in here. It would be very easy, the four walls are very similar . . ."

Even as he spoke, his eyes were flickering from one wall to another, and as though understanding his thoughts Emlyn said quietly: "Not 'very similar', Gerard. They are *precisely identical*, even down to the broken beak on the eagle's head by the second of the doors, repeated *exactly* on each wall . . ."

There was the slightest rumbling sound, and Gerard

169

swung round in sudden alarm. Behind him, the statue was *moving*, and he stared in bewilderment as it made almost a full quarter-turn. He heard Emlyn's quiet voice: "Yes. That is the mystery I spoke of. At irregular intervals, she makes a turn of many or few degrees to her right, and it means that she points, in turn, to one or another of twenty-eight doors, only one of which is the right one. Once, when I was here, she turned three times in the space of an hour or two, though you will have noticed that all our normal conception of time disappears down here. On another occasion, she turned only once in the course of half a day." He hesitated. "The old word magic comes to mind. There can be no other explanation."

Gerard had recovered his senses. "Not magic," he said. "It is a matter of hydraulic pressure." He could not contain his excitement. "Somewhere there is a pipe channelling water underground to the base of the platform. When the weight of the water builds up sufficiently, it turns a great wheel buried there somewhere, which in turn moves the statue. It is a well-known system of the ancient world, used thousands of years ago for turning lighthouses. And I would give my soul to know who these people were."

He stared at the brilliant stones adorning the mysterious statue. There were fifty of them or more in her necklace, a dozen in each of her bracelets; and in her belt, where they were exceptionally large, there must have been twenty or thirty more. Even in their cut form, not one of them was less than the size of a hazelnut. And those uncut stones in the great repository at her feet? There was vaster wealth here than he could even begin to contemplate, untold millions!

He muttered, "This awesome secret *must* be kept,

Emlyn! The appearance on the outside market of a single stone like these would excite all kinds of conjecture! The adventurers need not *know* that the hoard is here. It will be enough for them to *suspect*."

"Then I will talk with Alma this evening," Emlyn said firmly, "and convince her that our continued serenity is more important to us than the progress that iron tools can bring us."

He looked up at the high roof and saw the reddening of the sky through the fissures there. He said, "There is only an hour of daylight left, we must leave here soon. Without those lighted passages along the interminable corridors of the maze, there is always the greatest danger."

He laughed suddenly, "Many years ago, after very heavy rain, the Queen sent me here to determine if too much water was seeping in, and I stayed rather longer than I intended. And on my way out, I turned a corner where I knew there was a shaft of light . . . and to my horror, there was none. For a moment, I thought I had lost my way, and there was a terrible panic on me, it sickens me even now to think of it. And then, I realized that outside, the night had fallen."

"And you still found your way out in the *dark?*" Gerard asked incredulously.

"No," Emlyn said. "Such an attempt would have led to my death, lost in the labyrinth, I was convinced of it . . . not the action of a Wise Man at all. Instead, I stayed where I was, not moving all night long. I slept on the hard rock of the floor, and when the early rays of the sun came streaming down through a high bore-hole, I could see the sign I needed to find my way out, the sixth carving on the sixth row from the top. And we should leave now."

Gerard heartily agreed. "I have no wish," he said, "to leave my bones in any labyrinth, even in the company of a friend who is dear to me and of the woman I love . . ."

The sun was dropping down to the horizon when they reached the old Temple and at last shook off, with great relief, that awesome, claustrophobic terror of the maze. Emlyn went off to talk with Alma about what Gerard had said as Gerard and Shana, hand in hand, walked back through the evening's fragrant cool to the courtyard of their *conviveri.*

There were visitors from other groups of houses, who came to watch a ballgame played between two rival teams. The game was called by its old Indian name *farsika,* and it was played by two teams of four men each. The ball, a heavy leather bag weighted with stones from the river, was tossed back and forth over a rope strung some ten feet above the ground. Anyone who dropped the ball or failed to clear the rope lost a point for his team. The men had discarded their *draperies* and were wearing leather loincloths, red for one side and brown for the other. It was a trial of strength and agility, and the visitors were losing heavily. As Gerard and Shana stopped to watch, the home team captain shouted, laughing, "We are too good for them by far! Lindsay, drop out of the game and give your place to Gerard!"

Lindsay was the *farsika* champion. He was a giant of a man who seemed (but only *seemed,* Gerard was sure) to be in his early twenties, a muscular, blonde-bearded and very attractive-looking man. He too laughed, and he shouted happily: "Then of a certainty they will beat us!"

They found him a red loincloth to wear, and the captain said earnestly: "The game is very simple. Just toss the ball over the rope to where no one seems to be standing, and be ready for its return where *you* are not standing."

The ball weighed at least twenty-five pounds. Gerard swung it up over the rope successfully and even managed its return, to great shouts of delight, when it came back at him like a thunderbolt . . . They played until the sun began to set. Lindsay called out at last, "The score is four all, there are only a few minutes left of play, and we claim a circle. Gerard has the ball, and he will throw!"

A great burst of applause came from the spectators. Gerard said, panting heavily, "What do I do? What does it mean, a circle?"

Lindsay explained as the rest of them tried to catch their breath. He pointed out two rings of inlaid stones set diametrically opposite each other on either side of the rope. "You stand back in one circle," he said, "and toss the bag over the rope and into the other. It must land precisely within the ring, no edge of it touching the ring itself."

Gerard measured the distance with his eye, and muttered: "A hundred and twenty feet, at least . . ."

"One hundred and eleven, a magic number for the Indians."

"It still can't be done, I have lost you the game . . ."

Lindsay threw back his head and roared with laughter, tossing his young mane like a lion. "Nonsense!" he said boisterously, "I have done it myself no less than seven times in the last ten years. Bernard did it three times, Conrad and Bayard have each done it twice."

"Very well, let us see."

Shana was there close on the sidelines as he walked to the little circle and hefted the leather bag; it was beginning to weigh a ton to his tired muscles. He saw the light of pleasure in her eyes and smiled at her, and was aware of the hush that had fallen over the little crowd. He looked up at the high rope, wondering why it seemed so much higher all of a sudden, and stared at the opposing circle and gauged its distance . . . only a hundred and eleven feet? It seemed twice that, at the very least. He looked at Shana and said lightly, "Well, we will never know until we try, will we?"

To his delight, she was holding up her hand, two fingers crossed. He laughed and wondered where she had learned the ancient good luck gesture.

The silence was acute as he took a firm grip on the bag's neck, and swung it back and forth three or four times, and then stooped low and straightened his legs suddenly as he heaved upward with a monstrous effort and let go. A gasp went up from the spectators as the missile sailed high in the air, four feet or more above the high rope, and for a brief moment he was conscious that all the heads were turning expectantly to watch it fall.

It fell exactly dead center within the circle of stones. A great cheer went up from the little crowd, and they were all running to him, the women kissing him, the men clapping him on the back and shouting their congratulations. The giant Lindsay took him in a bear hug and almost crushed the life out of him, and shouted at the top of his voice: "Gerard! You are a champion among champions!"

Shana ran to him as Lindsay stepped aside, resting her head on his chest, lightly touching the scar there. She whispered, "I was afraid that it would open with the effort . . ."

His arms were tight about. "No, it did not. It means that even after so short a stay in Eden, I am cured."

174

"My love, my love forever . . . if you could only know how happy I am!"

"My dearest . . . My heart is bursting with love for you."

"And mine is so full . . ."

But the others would not leave the young lovers alone. It was the first time in Eden's history that a *farsika* player had ever won a circle on his first attempt, and it was a matter of some consequence for them, bringing great honor to their *conviveri*. Wine was drunk in celebration, and a great deal of boasting and happy laughter prevailed. When the evening meal arrived Shana whispered, "Hedda prepared it, and did I not tell you? She is a wonderful cook!" Afterward they found the opportunity to escape from their good friends and be alone together.

The sun was long since down and the moon bright as they strolled arm in arm together like the lovers they were. The gentle sound of the quietly meandering river was music to their ears, and the scent of dew-dampened herbs was very strong on the air; it was a scene of the greatest contentment and tranquility. Gerard lay beside her in the deep grass; his arms were wrapped around her, his eyes closed as he dreamed of her, wondering at the fortune that had brought them together, thinking of her great beauty and of her love for him expressed in her . . . gentleness towards him. He knew that his old life, the harsh life in the jungle in the employ of a Government he was not very fond of, had come to an end, and he knew that a new life was awaiting him, centered on the most wonderful woman in the world . . .

As they lay silently together, the sound of a lyre came to them out of the darkness. It was the melody of an old

English love song, and to Gerard's astonishment that child's voice broke in:

Early one morning, just as the sun was rising,
I heard a Maiden sing in the valley below:
'Oh, don't deceive me: Ah, never leave me!
How can you use a poor Maiden so . . . ?

Startled, Shana had risen to a sitting position and was staring into the shadows. She whispered, "Anitra? Where are you?"

The music stopped, and the child rose up out of the long grass and came to them, clutching her lyre to her breast. She dropped to her knees beside them and whispered in childlike innocence, "Did you like my song?"

Shana nodded. "Yes, it was beautiful. But should you not be in bed now?"

"No. Brenda takes care of me this week, she always lets me stay up late. She says I'm growing up, I shouldn't go to bed too early."

"And will you tell me what you are doing out here in the meadow, when you should be with your friends in the township?"

"Alma sent me, to find you."

"Alma?"

"Alma the Queen. She wants Gerard to go to her now."

"Oh, I see." Shana sighed and very offhandedly said, "Well, it was bound to come sooner or later, I suppose." She turned to Gerard. "You must go to her now, so shall we return to the town? Come . . ."

She rose to her feet and held a hand out for Gerard, pulling him up. He said, mystified, "I wonder what it is she wants with me at this time of the night?"

Shana laughed, a very pretty and happy laugh. "She wants to love you, of course! What else?"

He stared. "To . . . to love me?"

He well remembered what she had already told him, remembered the time that he had spent bemused and scarcely aware of what he was doing with Ferida; and yet he could still not fully understand this peculiar aspect of the Edenites' lives. He held her tightly, and whispered, "After the time I made love with Ferida, I determined that this would never happen again." He said desperately: "I am in love with you, Shana! How can I lie with another woman?"

Shana was still laughing. "Gerard my love," she said. "What, another woman? Bianca wants you, Antonia wants you, Barbara, Thelma, Dolores, perhaps as many as fifty of the other women want you! And now, the Queen herself! It is your duty to give them your children, how can you possibly refuse?"

"And if I were to do that?" Gerard asked. "If I were to say no?"

Her eyes were very grave, and her voice was hushed. "But you cannot! It would be considered the most awful antisocial behavior! And in Heaven's name, why should you *want* to?"

"But . . . but don't you object? In God's name, we're in love with each other!"

Shana threw up her hands. "And why should I object? It's not your *heart* that you give them! Yes, if it were that, perhaps I would be hurt, but I know that it is not. So go now, give our Queen the child she wants from you, the child of a Worthy Man. And when you return to our chamber . . . I will be waiting for you."

Bewildered, he let Anitra lead him away by the hand, and he found Alma waiting for him in her room. She was

dressed in a loosely woven *draperi* in a different shade of
the same purple; it hung around her waist only, the rest
of it piled carelessly beside her on the deep red silk of
the divan's cover. He gasped as he looked at her, the
dancing light of flares flickering over her remarkably
lovely body. In response to her gesture he sat beside
her. She took his hand and said softly, "I learn from
Emlyn that this might be strange to you, that the ways of
the Outside are still the old ways that we discarded many
years ago when my mother Dashtu was Queen. Can you
accept it, Gerard?"

He said awkwardly, "Only . . . only with a certain hes-
itancy, ma'am."

"You must learn to accept it *readily*. You are an
Edenite now, and will be, it is our hope, for the rest of
your life."

"Yes, ma'am . . ."

"Good." She unfastened the knot of her gown and
cast it aside, and then removed his. She held him tightly
for a moment, kissed him on the lips, and stretched herself out beside him. Her body was strong and very
smooth to his touch, her breasts firm, her saffron thighs
long and slender. Her nimble fingers explored him with
the delicacy of a feather, arousing him formidably. He
tried to force all thought to the back of his mind as she
eased herself under him and he met her thrusting with
his own, plunging deeply into her and feeling her nails
raking his back.

The furious passion came over her very quickly, and
he let himself go, moaning quietly in a mixture of anguish and ecstasy. He heard her whisper, "So strong a
man . . . I will be proud to bear your child, the proudest
woman in Eden. And in the course of time, we will people our township with your offspring . . ."

178

Moved by her repeated ministrations, he loved her twice more in the next hour. At last she said very quietly, "I must let you go now, though I would rather have you stay. Your Shana will be waiting for you." She was smiling, covering his face with little kisses. "I am not so far removed from the old days that I am ignorant of a different kind of love which can sometimes exist between one man and one woman. It seems foolish to me, but . . . perhaps it has merit after all."

In a little while he left her to her dreams, and found Shana in the room they shared lying awake and waiting for him. He tried to compose his thoughts as he too lay awake, secure in the arms of the woman he truly loved above all others.

And in the morning, he found his name written up on the *conviveri*'s bulletin board. With Shana to assist him, he had been detailed to make a study of the town's water supply with a view to its improvement; some of the conduits were drying up.

Shana took his hand, pressed it, and said, her eyes shining with delight, "Now, my love, you are truly one of us and no longer an Outsider." She reached up, kissed him, and said, "One of Eden's Wise Men, and I am glad." It gave him the greatest possible pleasure.

Chapter Eleven

For Gerard, the days and weeks that followed were a gift
from a benevolent God who must, he was sure, be
watching over him and his love. He worked very dili-
gently at the job he had been given, first mapping out all
of the township's water supply on sheets of bark-cloth
with charcoal sticks. He cut lengths of split bamboo and
filled them with water to use for levels. Wherever he
went about his measuring, Shana was at his side jotting
down his calculations and collating them at the end of
each days work.

To everyone's astonishment he found an underground series of conduits accurately built of cut stone
hundreds of years ago. Access to them was by removal
of hidden slabs of granite, and in all the time the people
of Eden had been here they had never discovered them.
They were nearly five feet in diameter, and knee-deep in
fast-flowing water, crisscrossing the township like the
underground sewers in some of Europe's oldest cities,
but blocked here and there with age-old rubble.

And as a side effect of this constant toil, he was
pleased and excited to find that he was getting to know
all the people of Eden and to count them as his friends.

Moving from one *conviveri* to another, he chatted with the Edenites after their day's allotted tasks were completed, he sat with them on their green moss lawns, and he played frequent games of *farsika* and *manko* with them. Manko was more a more sedentary trial of mental agility which consisted of moving pebbles from one to another scooped-out depression in a wooden board, mathematically matching up numbers as the game proceeded. It gave him a little shock of pleasure to find this game played here because he had heard of it before. He thought it was a game invented by the ancient Persians. His trained, methodical mind gave him an advantage, and he quickly learned how to play and became very expert at it. Sometimes, there was a game of chess to be played too, the pieces made from small blocks of polished limestone on which the characters were beautifully painted.

Often during these idyllic evenings, there would be concerts played by the musicians who wandered from *conviveri* to *conviveri*, playing a strange mixture of old English tunes and the equally old atonal melodies of the Indians, using lyres, drums, bamboo flutes, and an odd assortment of whistles. One of the women even had a fiddle which had once been the property of Adam Grieg himself.

He would spend long hours studying the Books with Shana, delighting as she read aloud to him the history of Eden's growth, of the men and women who had struggled so hard for survival in the early days . . . They read of the searchers who had lost their lives in exploring the great labyrinth before its secrets were discovered, of the violent storm that came down one night nearly a hundred years ago and washed away many of the culverts and sluices, of the famous edict put out by Queen

Dashtu which began: *We are in sore need of children,* of the long study, under one of the original women founders, of the cultivation of the mulberry trees and their silkworms and of the inevitable change from bark-cloth to silk for the women's clothing . . . Of teaching the children to read, write, and paint in their very earliest years, of the assumption of authority by the women under Dashtu and of the men's acceptance of it . . . of the wearing-out of their few iron tools and their eventual hoarding for the use of the carvers.

Shana showed him what they called *The Book of the Law,* which he discovered to his astonishment and delight consisted of a single sheet of cloth bound in decorated hide and bearing its inscription and text in Dashtu's own handwriting.

The instruction was short and to the point: "There shall be only one law, in the concept of which are incorporated all the laws of Moses; that is, that all of our people shall love, and care for, their neighbors. Henceforth, this shall be our only law."

Night after night he lay with his love and passed with her all the peaks of ecstasy. Alma sent for him twice again and he loved her too. Antonia from the next *conviveri* came to them one night and sat on their bed to chat for a while in the friendliest possible manner. She said at last, smiling, "Have I your consent, Shana, to take him from you for a while?"

Shana laughed. "With my *consent?* You do not need my consent, dear Antonia, though you have it, of course! I have been waiting for you to take him."

Still bemused, but becoming accustomed to this strange way of life, Gerard went with her and impregnated her. After a few nights Barbara was seeking his services too. And then Candida, and Dolores, and

Alexis, and Brenda, and Ferida again, and many others . . .

When he returned to Shana she was always waiting for him, smiling sweetly and asking, "Was the loving good for you too? I hope so much that it was."

They spent long hours walking together through the verdant meadows where basil, garlic, thyme, nasturtiums, rosemary, sage, lemon balm, and other herbs were growing wild. They watched the farmers working long rows of onions and beets with broad blades of mangrove roots shaped with fire into hoes, and weeding the fields where peppers, squash, peas and sweet potatoes were planted. There were oranges, bananas, pears, blackberries and raspberries growing everywhere, and they picked apricots and ate them, breaking open the pits by crushing them with stones for the kernels. Shana said earnestly, "Too many of the kernels eaten are said to be dangerous, but three or four a day lead to a very long life . . ."

They climbed higher into the hills and found the llamas grazing with their young. Gerard murmured, "You don't ride them here?"

Shana shook her head and laughed. "No! They spit at us too much," she said. "They permit us to take their wool for our looms, but if we try to mount them, they spit. The spit has a most objectionable odor."

"Yes, I have heard it said . . ."

They stood one evening arm in arm together at the top of one of the low hills and looked over Eden's wide domain, at the flower gardens little pinpoints of brilliant color far below them. The sun was beginning to set, and its red-gold gleam lit up the gray stone walls of the houses with great beauty. His arm was tight about her waist, and she moved his hand up to her breast and raised her lips to his for a kiss. In a little while they made love together under the blue branches of a giant jacaranda tree, letting the cool breeze caress their naked bodies.

Shana whispered, contentedly, "And are you truly happy here, my love?"

"By your side," he answered, "Purgatory itself would be Paradise! But here in Eden . . . Yes, I have found the kind of life that a man can only dream of in his wildest imagination. I have never seen so many people sharing so much love and respect for each other! And surely, there is no other place in the world where evil simply does not exist. Has there *ever* been a simple crime committed in Eden? Even a small theft?" Before she could answer, he said, "And if you were to tell me that such a thing once happened, I would not believe you."

Shana shook her head. "There has never been a crime of any sort recorded in our history. At first, our people were simply too busy trying to survive to fight among themselves, and then . . . In the course of time, I suppose they lost the habit of stealing, cheating, squabbling among each other, and learned that living in harmony was not only far more desirable but also a very easy thing to do. No, there is no crime, no greed even, because there is enough of what we share for everybody. No one is rich, and no one is poor, and we all love each other, as we should."

"Eden is well-named."

"Yes. And perhaps it was Dashtu who made it into a Paradise for us, though in the forty years of her reign Alma has been a wonderful Queen for us, kind, understanding, considerate . . ."

Gerard felt a quickening of his pulse. He had long since learned not to be surprised by these disclosures,

185

but he could not mask his astonishment. "Alma has been Queen for . . . forty years?"

Shana nodded. "Yes, since 1785, the year of the great flood that nearly destroyed us, she was only twenty-five-years-old then. It is recorded that our people had to leave the township for ten days before the water subsided."

"Then Alma is . . ." He could hardly bring himself to say it: "She is sixty-five years old now?"

Shana nodded casually: "Yes, we celebrated her sixty-fifth birthday just a week or two before Emlyn, Bramwell, and I left Eden to search for news of the Outside."

He thought of Queen Alma's tight, smooth body, of those grave, imperious eyes with hardly a trace of a wrinkle around them, and he sighed.

Shana, tossing back her long hair, was leaping up. She reached out, took his hand in hers and pulled him to his feet. She said happily, "Will you race me to the bottom of the hill?"

Without waiting for a reply, she ran off laughing, and her beautiful hair streamed behind her as she ran; her easy, powerful leg movements were those of a jaguar. Gerard raced after her and found her very hard to catch; but when they reached the meadow at last he was close behind her, and he threw himself at her and brought her to the ground, rolling over and over with her in the fresh-smelling clover, damp with the evening dew. She wrestled with him for only a few moments, and then lay still under his ardent caresses. She reached for him and found him very strong. She whispered: "So soon . . . ?"

His lips were close to the shell of her ear: "It is because I love you so much . . ."

"Then take me, Gerard . . ."

She lay quite still as he explored her smooth, caramel-cream body. Almost as if it were the first time he had ever touched her, his passion rose with every moment. He pulled her *draperi* aside, and his own too, as he luxuriated in the close contact of their bodies and began the probing. Her arms outspread, she did not move as she awaited him, her mouth open, her breath coming in little gasps of expectation as she clutched at him. She whispered, "Now, my dearest, now!"

He entered her slowly and carefully, and heard her soft moaning as he filled her completely, lying fused with her for a long, long time and only moving very slightly. It seemed to her that the earth itself was moving under her. He flared up furiously at last, unable to restrain himself any longer, and she let her own paroxysm take complete control of her. And when, exhausted, he lay still, she found his lips and kissed them. She murmured, "Before we met, my dearest, the world was an empty place. Even Eden was empty."

He returned her kisses. "So long ago! And yet, it was only yesterday."

"When we first loved each other, it was because I wanted your child. Now, it is *you* I want . . ."

"Oh, my love . . ."

"And I well remember how you came to me, a stranger brought quite unexpectedly by Emlyn, whom I have always adored. Though I was half in a coma I remember seeing you digging furiously at the ground beneath me, striving to raise my head above a sea of mud that was slowly trying to kill me. I remember thinking, 'An Outsider, and he is trying desperately to save my live . . .' There was a livid scar on your chest, and I watched it

187

burst open as you strained at a long bamboo pole, trying to move a great tree that was lying on me . . . This is the memory that is strongest for me, the scar bursting open and the blood pounding out. I tried to find my voice and scream, 'No! Do not kill yourself for my sake!' But the words would not come, and so . . . You saved my life."

Gerard whispered, musing as he caressed her, "And for my part, I remember a terrible glazed look in the loveliest eyes I had ever seen, my heart was bleeding for you too. And Emlyn . . . the sight of his mangled arm was horrifying. But he was forcing himself to use it to good purpose, did you know that?"

"Yes, I saw, I remember it well! As you say . . . only yesterday, and yet so long ago! And shall we return to the *conviveri* now? All our friends will be waiting for us."

"Ah, yes, so many good friends . . ."

"Thelma is waiting to challenge you to a game of chess. She is very, very good."

"Thelma? Do I know her?"

"The woman with the long grey hair who lives in the *conviveri* three removed from ours. She watched you playing with Bernard the other evening, you remember?"

"Ah, yes. I did not remember her name." He remembered her only as a tall and statuesque woman of indefinable age, full-breasted and narrow-hipped, with pale gray eyes under sharply arched brows and a high, intelligent forehead, a woman of unsurpassed beauty. He remembered her dark frown as he moved an unexpected rook's pawn, then her lovely eyes lit up as she laughed suddenly. She had said delightedly, "You have three more moves, Bernard, and then . . . mate!" After those three helplessly defensive moves Bernard had tipped his king over to signify defeat. She had embraced him and said, "You are a fine player, Gerard. But I can beat you. Shall we play soon?"

Now, they went back to the *conviveri* together, hand in hand as always; and Thelma was indeed waiting for him, with the limestone pieces ready on the board. And good player that he was, she defeated him roundly in thirty-four moves.

She had a startling feline quality about her, her golden skin was smooth as ice, her sensuous body was marvellously well-formed, and her *draperi* was wrapped around her waist with the rest of it lying in her lap as she sat opposite him throughout the game. There was an added quality to her that he could not readily find a name for; he thought it might be *carnality*. Her veiled eyes were on his as he tipped his cornered king over, but she turned her gaze on Shana and said nothing. Soon Shana and Gerard retired for a night of the most perfect serenity.

Eden was serene indeed. On the Outside, a vicious storm was approaching the hidden valley. And the on-coming danger was a terrible one.

The heavy rain was lashing down onto the sodden earth, and Jao Torres was in a fury. Over the sound of the rain, he shouted, "Damn you, Espada! You lose them tracks now, I kill you, I kill you dead!"

Espada was reckless in his anger; last night Carmen had refused his attentions, because she feared that Jao was too close by, even though he was praying to his In-dian Gods again and lost in the weed's dementia. He shouted back, "There is nobody can track like me, Jao, nobody! But a storm like this? Every footprint they made is washed away into the river below us, as we will be too if we do not move on!"

189

"We don' move on," Jao roared, "we stay here! To-morrow, next day, storm finish, you picking up tracks again! Now, somebody bringing me drink."

One of his men, a wizened old *mestizo* named Manuel, scurried to him and held out a leather flask. He said, grinning, "Is full, you take all, Jao, you know I your frien' . . ."

Jao took it and drank deeply. It was the sour, bitter tasting liquor which the Indian women made from assorted wild berries. Many of the berries must have been poisonous, but it mattered little to the women.

They were sheltering under giant fig trees that kept off none of the rain, but still served as a kind of camp, their territory of the moment. Jao Torres could not contain his anger. Under Espada's expert guidance, the band of more than forty men and women had been following, with consummate skill, a trail that sometimes disappeared altogether as the living humus of the forest floor, sometimes as much as three feet deep, obliterated it completely. Sometimes Espada and two or three of the men who were almost as expert as he was, would lie on their bellies for long minutes at a time, studying a broken twig, a bent blade of grass or a crushed fern leaf, and trying to decipher what kind of man, woman or animal had passed this way. Sometimes the footprints would be clear enough to follow over vast distances, but more often they would be lost among the dense ground foliage in obscurity.

Now the trail had been washed away completely, and Espada knew that they would have to cast around for hours, perhaps even days, before they might be lucky enough to pick it up again. He knew the general direction, and had it fixed in his mind, it was a great help to him.

With a fine disregard for the stares of the envious men, Carmen had removed her skirt and hung it over a shrub for an impromptu washing in the cloudburst; she had found a seat on a slab of granite and was enjoying the pounding of the warm rain on her naked body. And in a little while, Jao drove the men off and snarled at her: "Lie down, woman, I want you now."

His leather bottle was empty, and he was so drunk that he could hardly find the words. He flopped down onto his back under the wet bushes and fell asleep as she removed his breeches and placed a stone under his head to make him more comfortable. She stretched out her voluptuous body beside him and played with him for a while disgustedly, knowing that he was far too drunk to be of any use to her at all this night. He was even snoring, and the stench of the liquor was awful.

She lay quite still and wondered about this obsession of his, the search for unexpected and quite unattainable wealth. In the past, he had often followed what he thought might be leads to Raman-li-Undara, only to find them, time and time again, evaporating into thin air. Ever since Espada had told him of the three strangers moving so deliberately through the jungle, told him of his belief that they too were looking for the Field of Diamonds and perhaps even knew where it lay . . . ever since that morning the search had become a compulsion for him, driving him beyond the bounds of sanity.

A foolish legend! The Amazon basin was filled with idiots who spent their miserable lives in search of dreams like this, excitable vagrants for whom great wealth of this kind was always just around the corner. Carmen always thought of herself as clear-headed and sensible, and she did not believe a word of it.

Yet, what if the legend were really true? She had

never seen a diamond in her life, but she knew they were priceless. How many fine tortoiseshell combs could she buy with a single stone? How many skirts, not of bark-cloth but of cotton, or perhaps even silk! Might finding the valley and its riches also mean an end to this cease-less wandering in a hostile jungle? A small wooden house, perhaps, in one of the river villages? An escape, even, from Jao himself? She shuddered at the thought.

Carmen would never admit it to anyone, least of all to herself; but she had a secret hankering for a more peaceful life, without the interminable search for food from day-to-day, and without the constant subjugation of her body and mind to a man she detested and de-spised . . . And as she mused on this in the darkness, she suddenly froze; there were fingertips brushing her hipbone, and they were not Jao's.

She had heard no sound at all, though her hearing in the bush was the hearing of a *tigre*; she had not even smelled him, because he was downwind of her. The fingertips were creeping slowly up her naked flank to her breast, fastening on a hardening nipple and squeez-ing it with monstrous force as though daring her to cry out now. There was not even the subdued sound of a chuckle, though she was sure that he was silently laugh-ing to himself at her helplessness.

Her movement was almost imperceptible as she reached behind her with one strong hand, found the tes-ticles, and crushed them. Now let him keep silent too! The pressure on her nipple ceased at once.

That strong manhood was probing and she eased her body only a little to accept it, placing her thigh carefully across Jao's drunken body, not daring even to let her breath come faster, lest he should awake and kill them both. She felt the immense force entering her with infin-

192

itesimal slowness until he was fully contained; she dared not move her hips to meet the careful thrusting, back and forth. There was no sound at all, not even a stirring of the sodden leaves they lay on. She restrained herself when he flooded into her, and she trembled when Jao groaned aloud in his stupor . . . She felt the joy of the soft withdrawal, and heard nothing. As silently as he had come to serve himself on her, showing off both his expertise and his daring, Espada was gone.

In the morning the rain had stopped, and steam was rising off the jungle floor when Jao Torres awoke. He lit a cheroot and stared disconsolately at the hideous ticks swollen with his blood that had fastened themselves to his legs during the night. He placed the fiery tip of the cheroot to them one after the other and killed them. He rose to his feet and stared down at Carmen, fast asleep, and was sure that he hated her. He kicked her in the stomach to awaken her, and growled, "Wake up, woman. Put on skirt, the men are awake."

He stalked into the bush, only fifty feet away, and urinated. When he turned back he roared, "Espada! You find trail now, we moving on!"

Espada said, mocking, "Your servant, Sir! I scouted around at sunup, I found traces still remaining. They are moving northwest, and moving very fast. It may mean that they *know* where they are going and are therefore hurrying to get there. It has always been my belief that a man who does not know where he is going does not move so fast, nor does he travel in a straight line."

He saw that Jao did not fully understand what he meant, and he thought it might be time for a lesson, to impress his master with his own competence. He raised a finger and said, "To track a man is not merely a matter of finding the signs he leaves and of following them, Jao!

It is not enough! A good tracker must learn to *think* like his quarry, to wonder why he stops when he stops, sleeps when he sleeps, and hurries when he hurries."

"And you thinking like they thinking," Jao said sourly; he did not like it that Espada was more expert in everything than he was.

Espada nodded. "Let me tell you about them," he said, gloating. "The woman is tall and slender, with a long stride and very little weight. She wears a gown of pale blue silk, I have seen a dozen threads of it caught on thorns. She is a woman of authority, which I find very hard to understand . . ."

"How you knowing *that?*" Jao shouted furiously. "Is impossible you knowing that!"

"No. She leads the way, her footprints are frequently obscured by those of the two men, it means authority. Both the men have been hurt, and are recovering very quickly. I found discarded papaya leaves stained with blood, it means they know about medicine . . ."

"Indians," Jao said. Espada answered him at once. "No. Their sandals were made by no Indian. They have been resoled once with boar hide, and very skillfully."

Jao grunted, hating every minute of his lesson but still needing to know. Espada went on, "One of the men at least is very expert in the jungle, sure enough of himself to leave meat he has killed for the carrion to devour . . ."

"Carrion?" It was a new word for Jao, and Espada said softly: "You, and me, Jao . . ." Before Jao could work it out, he continued, "He left behind him meat that he could easily carry with him, which indicates that he is an expert huntsman and knows that he can always kill more meat when he needs it, even though he is armed only with a machete . . ."

194

"You are a fool!" Jao screamed, "Maybe he got gun too . . ."

"No. When a man sleeps in the jungle, he props up his gun close at hand, the butt resting on the forest floor. I would have seen the signs . . . shall I go on?"

Jao scowled, conscious that his Carmen's wide eyes were on this handsome young man, marvelling at what he had to say. He said, "No. You tell me again why they hurrying now."

Espada took a long, deep breath. He said gently, "They hurry as a man hurries when he knows *exactly* where he is going. If they are searching, as we are, for the lost valley . . . then it means they know where it lies."

"Then we hurry too!" Jao shouted. "And nobody move fast in the jungle like Jao Torres!"

They pushed on at a forced march, and on the afternoon of the third day they found themselves faced with a huge barrier of unclimbable rock, leaning outward and pitted here and there with clusters of draping fern and creeper. Espada said flatly, "They could not have climbed it, it means that there is a way through it."

All evening he searched and found nothing, and they camped there for the night in the deepest frustration. In the morning Jao found Espada crouched on the ground by the cliff face, staring at a small ring of pebbles he had placed there. Espada looked up at him and said, grinning, "A solitary footprint, I think."

Jao looked at the circle of stones and saw nothing within it, so he said nothing too. His lieutenant went on, "I wait now for the slanting rays of the sun, they will tell me all I want to know. Whether they moved left, or right, or straight on."

Jao squatted beside him, his top hat perched ludi-

195

crously on his head, and at last the sun came round and cast the necessary shadows. Studying the almost indecipherable imprint, Espada said, "They have climbed the bluff, it is apparant."

Jao looked up at the towering face of the cliff and shook his head. "No," he said stolidly. "Is not possible."

Espada was not a man who easily lost his temper where Jao was concerned, if only because it meant great danger to him. He was very overwrought now, because he too was sure that Raman-li-Undara was very close to them, tantalizingly close. He swore volubly and shouted, "I am the best tracker you ever saw in your miserable life! And you tell me I am wrong? No! I am right! Come, I show you!"

When Jao, smouldering, did not answer, he turned on his heel and strode off, searching the ground. In a few minutes he shouted, "Come! Look! See for yourself!"

Jao went to him and stared down at footprints in the soil that even he could see. He said, admitting defeat, "Yes, they go this way. But now, you tell me how they climb that rock, not even a monkey climbing it."

"It indicates," Espada said, more quietly now that he was vindicated, "there is an opening in the rock face, not too far up it. You are right, Jao, as always, they could not climb it for more than fifty or a hundred feet. And if we can find it, we will find where they went. It may also mean that we will have found Raman-li-Undara."

Jao remembered that the legend spoke of *a small way through a great rock, where a man may easily fall to his death* . . . He said stolidly, "This is the rock. We staying here now. We searching."

And search they did. For four long days the men tried

scaling the cliff. They found some of the narrow paths and explored them hopelessly till they petered out. Two men fell like rag dolls to smash into the rocks below them as they climbed, and there was almost a mutiny in the camp when the men decided that Espada had been wrong after all.

Jao roared in furious anger, "We staying here till we finding way through! Days, weeks, months, I don' care if is *years!* We finding i!"

Inexorably, the search went on. In five days time Espada stood on a tiny green plateau halfway up the rock face, and examined the cut fern fronds there. His heart was beating fast as he went to the edge of the little shelf and looked down on Jao and his men milling around down there in frustration.

For a little while, he just stood there, enjoying his solitary satisfaction. And then he cupped his hands to his mouth and shouted, "Jao! Hola there!"

He saw the upturned faces, and called down, "You send the men up, Jao! I have found the way . . ."

Chapter Twelve

With Shana, as always, by his side, Gerard was in the underground conduits, holding her hand in the semi-darkness as they strode through knee-deep water from one extremity of the town to the other. It was dank and eerie down there, and very silent save for the gentle noise of the water, and at every few hundred feet of this main tunnel there were intersections that fed it, coming in from the side where the river lay. Some of these subsidiary passages were completely blocked up, and Gerard paused by the largest of them and saw the water merely trickling in some four feet or so above the main level.

He said, murmuring, "The rubble of hundreds of years, stopping the free passage of the water. And once we clear it, all the conduits will be working again. But it may not be possible to do that from this side, the water has built up very high beyond the obstruction, and so . . ." He began climbing up the broken rocks to the top of the blockage. She watched him as he turned back and said, smiling, "And you must come with me too. When I begin to break it down, it will almost certainly collapse very rapidly. I don't want to see you washed away."

199

Shana nodded and followed him up, and they crawled over and dropped down on the other side into nearly four feet of still water. There were ancient roots of mangrove wood here tangled up with the wreckage, still hard as iron after all these years, and he found one and wrestled with it to pull it free. It came loose at last, and he found that it was some eight feet long and as thick as a strong man's forearm. He nodded his satisfaction.

He began at the top, using the pole as a lever, tumbling the stones and broken roots into the faster water below. He sweated for an hour of more, and with the clearing of each layer of debris the strength of the freed water increased, just as he had predicted; the obstruction suddenly gave way, and they were tossed on the strength of the sudden flow and washed downstream very fast indeed. His arms were stretched out to hold her, and as the frantic rush of water subsided, they found their feet and stood there arm in arm, watching the level rise. When it was up to Shana's waist he whispered, "Only a few inches more, I think, it is settling down now, finding its correct level . . ." He was exultant as he said happily, "We will check for other obstructions, of course, and clear those smaller ones we have already found. But I believe that every conduit in the township will be filled now, even those that have been dry for years. And shall we go and see?"

Shana nodded excitedly, and they waded along the tunnel to its entrance, a great flat stone above their head which Gerard had left open. As they pulled themselves up and out into the daylight, two of the women were running to them excitedly, laughing and clapping their hands. One of them was Barbara, a slender woman of very great beauty and bright intelligence. She called,

"Gerard! What did you do down there? For the first time in thirty years there is water in my *conviveri!*"

He laughed. "The conduit is what, half-full?"

"No, almost to the brim and running fast."

"It will soon recede a little, I think, it should be about a foot deep."

The other woman, Antonia, was very voluptuous and outgoing. She seized Gerard around the waist and did a little jig with him, and said happily, "The luxury of running water, after all these years . . ." She held him tightly and kissed him. Lindsay and two of the other men were striding to them, clapping him heartily on the back and grinning broadly at him. Lindsay said, "What happened? All the conduits that were dry are filling up, it's wonderful!"

Gerard could not help feeling a little smug. "Just a question," he said, "of knowing where to look for what had obviously happened. There's still a great deal of work to be done down there, but in a few days, I think, the system will be as good as it ever was. And *that*. . . was very good indeed, the people who built these sluices, who knows how many hundreds of years ago, knew a very great deal about the movement of water . . .

He broke off. From the far end of the narrow alleyway where they were gathered, the gracefully fragile figure of the child Anitra was racing towards them, and even at this distance, they could see the look of terror on her sweet face.

Gerard was the first to react. He ran towards her, conscious of Lindsay's heavy footsteps only a few paces behind as he sought to overtake him. There was suddenly an awful, unexplained fear in the air. He scooped the child up in his arms and saw the tears flooding her eyes, and she was screaming: "I saw, I saw, I saw one of them die . . ."

He held her tightly and set her down, crouching in front of her and gripping her by the shoulders. "Saw *who* die, Anitra?" he asked gently. She took a hold on herself and said, "Alma the Queen, she sent me to find you. There are strangers at the top of the steps, and they are killing our Strong Men, I saw them . . ."

Gerard was on his feet at once and racing for the Throne Room, his arms and legs pumping furiously, the others following him but dropping behind as the men sought to keep up with him.

He threw open the door and saw Alma at the telescope. She looked back briefly and signaled to him to come as she turned her attention back to the lens. She stood aside as he took it from her, and saw, first of all, one of the Strong Men whose name was Thomas lying dead on the topmost step. He saw two other young men wrestling furiously with dark-skinned strangers; one of them had picked a *mestizo* up bodily and was hurling him over the cliff, even though there was a sabre embedded in his side. He caught the flashes of musket fire which he could not hear, and the frequent reflection of sunlight on sword blades. He saw Carmen wielding a long-bladed knife like the expert she was, and Espada, driving his short, pointed sword into the stomach of his unarmed adversary . . . He saw Jao Torres himself, standing there laughing as he let his men do the brief fighting. He moaned aloud, "Oh, God . . . I have seen our people killed, watched them die so far away! And there is nothing we can do to help them!"

The room was filling with people now, Shana, Barbara, Antonia, Lindsay and his two friends; and Emlyn had hurried there too, white-faced. Gerard gave the spyglass to him, and turned to Alma. He said gravely, "What I feared has happened, Alma. The . . . adventurers are descending on us. And these are not strangers to me. I know who their leader is, one Jao Torres, who murdered my wife after he had cruelly raped her.

There was a terrible break in his voice, and he whispered, "It must be that they followed me here, the fault is mine."

Alma's face was white, but her voice was strong and very authoritative. "It does not matter, Gerard, how they arrived here," she said. "It only matters that they are here. And how can we stop them? They are violent men, I see. Can we somehow fight them off?"

"Without weapons against their guns and swords? They are very heavily armed."

"And they have come for our diamonds?"

"Yes."

Alma held his look. "Then we will send emissaries to them up there," she said clearly, "to give them all the diamonds they want, so that they will leave us in peace. *All* of the diamonds."

"No! They will not leave you in peace! It will not be enough for them! They will want to find out what else Raman-li-Undara has to offer them, and they will quickly find out. They are animals, and the women of Eden are very beautiful, they will want the women too. I will not allow it."

Alma caught her breath. "And so?"

"We cannot fight them. They are only thirty or forty strong, and we have more than five hundred Strong Men. But they have guns and swords, and we have nothing! We cannot fight against armed and skilled fighting men in open combat! What, with our bare hands?"

"Then the answer?"

"The answer is to flee. It is not one that appeals to me greatly, but there is no alternative if we are to save our peoples' lives. The women especially. I will not have the women carried off into shame and degradation because we are too weak to defend them."

Her eyes were wide. "Flee? But to where?"

"To our own jungle."

She stared at him. "It is a terrible place, our people fear it."

"It is not more terrible than the jungle out there, in the hands of a man like Jao Torres. They must be told that only there can we perhaps be safe. I will tell them this, and I will lead them to safety there, every man, woman and child of Eden! We will stay there for as long as we must!"

"And then?"

Gerard's voice was tight with bitterness. "Then? I do not know, Alma. They will search for the diamonds which they know are here, and they will not find them. I do not think they will quickly leave, and somehow we must find an answer to that problem. There is an idea at the back of my mind, not yet properly formulated, and I will not speak of it until it is. At this moment, I know only that we must leave the township at once. Emlyn told me there is a great swamp in the jungle . . ."

He turned to his friend, and Emlyn nodded. "Yes, there is."

"Good. It will not be easy for them to track us through water. And we are warned in time, they cannot descend the twelve thousand steps in less than two days, and it is my belief that they will take longer. During those days, we must conceal ourselves in the swamp and plan . . . plan our counterattack. Which will follow, I promise you. There are the deaths of our guards to be avenged, the lives of our people to be saved!"

The Queen nodded brusquely. "Very well then. Your advice is accepted." She turned to Emlyn and said, "Call the full Concord together at once, we have no time to lose."

Gerard was startled by the sudden change in her, startled too by the angry light in Shana's lovely eyes. As though knowing exactly what he was thinking, she said quietly, "We are a very gentle people, my love. But both the Englishmen and the Indian women we spring from . . . were *fighters*."

"At a time like this," Gerard said gravely, "it is something to be grateful for."

The full Concord was called—Alma, Ferida, Shana, Barbara, Antonia, with Emlyn and another of the Wise Men whose name was Charles, and two of the Strong Men, Lindsay and Bernard. The Queen had invited Gerard to attend, but he had begged to be excused. "A half-hour with Emlyn," he said urgently, "to offer certain suggestions. And then I myself should hurry to the swamp to explore it. If I am to lead a thousand people to safety, I must first discover *where* to lead them. So by your leave, Alma?"

The Queen had agreed at once, and it was Emlyn who, after their long talk together, spoke for Gerard. ". . . and a distillation to be made," he said, "by boiling the flowers of oleander and the seeds of the castor plant, to be poured over the most accessible of the grain pits. Let our enemies find out to their cost that some of the food supplies have been poisoned and therefore fear that they all have . . . A hundred Strong Men to work as best they can at the river where it leads into the main conduit making a dam to dry up all of the township's water supply, so recently restored, so that they will have to leave the shelter of the stone houses to find water and so be more vulnerable to whatever actions we may decide on . . . All the books to be carried into the central chamber of the labyrinth so that Torres, in his violent rage, may not burn the records of Eden's growth . . . We are to leave the township tomorrow after dark, so that they may not see us leave should they have a spyglass, which is unlikely, and not rest until we are deep in the cover of the forest . . . These are some of the things Gerard has asked me to talk of."

And before the books were carried away, the Scribe wrote in the current volume: "By order of Queen Alma, on the advice of Gerard Fletcher, the Great Exodus begins on this twenty-first day of October in the year 1825. And may the Gods of our forefathers be with us all . . ."

Gerard himself was still in the jungle, quickly finding his way to the great swamp and defining its limits, fixing in his agile mind the precise locations of the multitudinous little islands of mangrove trees and other plants there, searching out places where shelter could quickly be prepared among the giant probing roots that sometimes arched as much as twenty feet above the surface of the black mud and crisscrossed each other in wild confusion.

All the time, a plan was slowly taking place in his brain, and its details were falling into place as he struggled through the slime. He found that he was talking to himself:

"There are perhaps forty of them, some Indian women with them too, captives who must not be harmed . . . They must not be allowed to track us into this jungle, because they are expert and will find our tracks, however well we hide them. And how can the tracks of a thousand people be hidden? They will spend most of their energies not looking for us, but for the diamonds . . . If we can find a way to fight them, it must be in the town, which we know intimately but is strange to them, rather than in the jungle where their expertise will be formidable . . . Teams of Strong Men, then, just a few at a time, to return to the city with bamboo spears at night, in silence . . . But can these gentle people be taught to fight so easily? Even . . . to kill? Yes! Because all they hold dear is at stake . . . Can a thousand people successfully be hidden, even in a swamp as large as this seems to be? There will be babies who will cry and betray their presence . . . Will our enemies leave the town in search of the water we have denied them in the daytime, when we cannot creep up on them, or at night? Should I myself lead the first party of raiders, to teach them the pattern? Yes, surely I must . . . How long can this game of cat and mouse endure?"

He returned on the morning of the second day, and saw through the spyglass that Jao Torres and his gang of cutthroats had descended only as far as Camp Five. He could not know it, but Jao was taking his time now that his prey was so close. He had decided to spend the night in the hot sulphur spring there, believing in its healing powers and in the effect it might have on his scarred and battered body; he was convinced that prolonged immersion in the yellow water would strengthen the muscles he used on his Carmen and on any of the Indian girls who might for the moment take his fancy.

In Gerard's absence, Emlyn had done his work well. He had gathered the people together and had instructed them, so that now there were teams of men, women, and children carrying the Books down to the labyrinth. And even here, Gerard had been emphatic in his planning: at every fourth or fifth turning in the maze, a guide had been stationed, to avoid the chance of accident to say: "Two turns to the left, two to the right, one to the left . . . there will be someone else there to direct you . . ." There were eighty men at the river building a dam to dry up the township's water supply, others making the oleander and castor brew with which to poison the grain supplies. And when all was done, they began gathering in columns under the shelter of the walls. Their fear of the journey into the jungle was very heavy on them, but Alma had told them firmly, "We are in Gerard's hands . . ." and all was well for them.

Soon Gerard looked up at the moon and said softly, "The time has come. We move in darkness only till we are well-hidden in the forest and out of their sight. And at dawn, we move into the jungle and the swamp to find our hiding-places. There is nothing to fear." He could sense their excitement and their determination too.

Like a gigantic reptile moving on the valley floor, the columns followed each other in the darkness out of the town and towards the forest, across the lush meadows in silence. Even the babies were silent, chewing on cannabis leaves that he had distributed to the mothers, saying: "It is not harmful in very small doses, but you must not give them more than the one leaf that will make them drowsy . . . and therefore quiet."

With Shana and Alma, Gerard was at the column's head, while Emlyn brought up the rear, and Lindsay had organized teams of runners to maintain contact all along the line. Alma herself was carrying the spyglass with Adam Grieg's name on its plaque. Gerard had said,

"We may need it, Alma, and so priceless a memory of Eden's past should not be allowed to fall into the enemy's hands . . ."

As they approached the dense forest that would soon turn into even denser jungle, Gerard spoke to Dalton, one of the runners. "Hurry back now to Emlyn, please, tell him the time for the false trails has come. He knows what to do."

Dalton, a slim and muscular man no older than fifty, ran swiftly back and gave the word. Emlyn called out, "The four columns now as we arranged, all moving north still but in slightly different and winding directions as though they are not sure where they are going. A mile or two to the north, there is a shallow river, let them all follow it to their left as fast as they can, walking only in the water, until they rejoin the rest of us once again . . ."

The deceptive parties hurried off, led by Dalton, crashing carelessly through the shrubbery, trampling down bushes with great abandon. When at last they reached the river they waded along it to the west, struggling on valiantly in the hope that they would indeed find the main party.

When they reached a great green clearing, Gerard called a halt, and posted guards while most of them slept. And at dawn, he took the spyglass from Alma and climbed a huge cow tree, one of the so-called forest giants that rose to an impressive two hundred feet. He broke through the first layer of thick foliage in some ten minutes and stared down at the tops of the other trees, the first canopy. Fifteen minutes later he was through the second canopy and in a world of his own, with all of the jungle and the forest spread out there below him. He steadied himself among forked branches and used the telescope to study the distant steps with infinite patience.

He saw that Torres and his men had descended as far as Camp Two and were cooking themselves a meal. He made a laborious count of heads; there were thirty-four men at least—more may have been concealed—and eight women, not including Carmen. He watched them for a long time before climbing higher still until the township itself came into his view through a break in the dark green tree tops, and he found no sign of life there at all. He worried about it, having made certain judgements about the way Torres would act now, and then, at last . . .

A movement caught his eye, and he refocused the glass and saw two men, their muskets held at the ready, moving from one of the *conviveries* to another. In the space of half an hour he found two more prowling around with their swords drawn; one of them was also carrying an ancient pistol.

He snapped the telescope shut and fastened it securely at his waist. He found a heavy length of green liana that trailed down to the ground a hundred and fifty feet below him; it was all covered over with the wet green moss that carried the life-giving moisture up to the highest levels of the forest. He tested its firm fastening above him, and slid down it to the earth again.

Shana and Alma were waiting for him expectantly. He said, "They have more than forty fighting men, all well-armed, perhaps many more than that, I cannot be sure. And as I expected, they have sent spies into the town, I saw four of them." He laughed suddenly. "It is a wise precaution! They know nothing of us. It may well be that they believe we are ten thousand strong, all armed with spears and bows and arrows! Then let them worry about that! The longer they are kept in ignorance, the better it is for us."

"And they have reached the bottom of the steps?"

"Not yet, they are at Camp Two, waiting, no doubt, for the return of their spies who will tell them that the township is deserted. Then . . . we can only guess. And shall we soon move on?"

Alma smiled gently. "The decision," she said, "is yours Gerard, not mine."

"Then with your permission, I will give the order very soon. But first, there is a matter that must be attended to. In the space of a few hours—not months, weeks, or even days, but hours! I must teach the men of Eden how to fight against murderers who are intent upon our destruction."

He spent some time instructing Lindsay in the making of a bamboo spear. He said, "Find a shoot that grows straight and true, half as wide as the span of a man's hand. Use my chopping-knife to slice it at the base with a single sharp stroke, at a very acute angle so that the point will be sharp too. It is good to temper the point with fire, but fires would betray our presence now. No matter, untempered shafts are serviceable also. And there is a question I must ask, because our very lives hinge on it, and the safety of the women."

He hesitated, gauging the strength of Lindsay's determination. He said slowly, "It is certain that sooner or later we will have to defend ourselves with improvised weapons. I do not doubt the courage of your men, but . . . after so many years, even generations, of gentleness and serenity, the need has arisen for self-defense. And the only way to defend yourself against a man who is bent on your murder is to kill him first, there is no other

211

way. We are not dealing now with *men* as you and all the other Edenites understand them, but with savage animals; it is not easy to kill a man, even in the heat of battle. Will they be able to do this? Because if they hesitate, not only will our Strong Men die, but so will our women whom it is their duty to protect. And the women will not die easily."

He told him of the savage rape and murder of Dora. Lindsay listened gravely and said at last, "My heart bleeds for the loss of the woman you loved, and is filled with hatred for the man who so brutally savaged her. Yes, you are right, such men do not have the privilege of continued existence, they must be destroyed. To protect its home and its family, Gerard, even the gentlest of animals will fight, and if we must, we will. Have confidence in us. Tell us what to do . . . and we will do it."

"The invaders," Gerard said, "have come here for the diamonds. I think that they will not find them unaided. They will therefore try to capture some of our people, and force them by duress, to tell them where they are hidden. And if, in this endeavor, they even set eyes upon our women who are very beautiful . . . Then I shudder even to think of what will happen."

"I will lay down my life to prevent it!" Lindsay said hotly "and so will all the other Strong Men!"

"Then we will hide ourselves," Gerard said, "for only a little while, in shame that we run from them as we must. But they have killed the guards that I had sent to the top of the steps, they are a dire threat to the women we all love . . . And I swear to you, we will recover our dignity. And in the end, we will defeat them."

"Count on us, Gerard."

"I do so. Fifty men, then, in small groups, four or five working together, to be ready when they are needed.

212

Armed with spears and capable of moving in the night like ghouls."

"It will be done."

"I can have confidence?"

"Yes. We will fight!"

"It is all I ask."

When they reached the swamp at last, Gerard showed them how to hide themselves in the hallows that the giant, barricading mangrove roots created. Shana was by his side constantly searching out more of the openings and encouraging the others to burrow their way into them. She repeatedly said, "Here, there is room for five people or more . . . deeper, deeper, you must not be seen . . ."

They were hiding like animals, in surroundings that were frightening to them. But in the space of a few hours, in a dark and murky swamp, more than a thousand people were at last concealed. Gerard had told them, "We will live on the patches of dry land as much as possible, but at the first sign of danger we scurry into our hiding places, being careful to leave no signs that may be discovered by the enemy when he searches for us here, as he surely will. Find branches of eucalyptus to drag in there with you, it will keep the insects at bay. There will be sentries in the trees around us to give warning when they approach . . . But we will not wait for them to make the first move. Tonight, a few of us will take the first steps in the defense of those we love."

When some thirty or forty of the spears had been cut with the only chopping-knife they had at their disposal, Gerard found a clearing and lined up a dozen of the Strong Men to show them how best the use the new weapon, the first weapon they had ever handled. He showed them how to find its point of balance, how to keep it level for correct aim. "These are not for throwing," he said, "except in emergency, because they are not heavy enough for a throwing-spear. Keep the body well-balanced at all times, on the balls of the feet, the eyes on the enemy and not on the point of the spear; by practice, you must know exactly where that point is. And if it should be necessay to throw . . ."

He cut a blaze on the pith-like trunk of a boabab tree, some two inches square, and retreated for twenty paces and said: "The eyes always on the target for instinctive aiming, the spear held perfectly level at its pivotal point. And then . . . every muscle of the arm, the shoulder, the back, into hurling it straight and true with all the force that you can muster."

He threw his upper body forward as he spoke, and drove the spear foward with monstrous force, watching it embed itself nearly four inches deep into the soft tree trunk, precisely in the center of the target. He said a trifle smugly, perhaps "Like that." He turned to Lindsay and spoke, "Each of these men are to teach others as soon as enough spears are cut for every Strong Man to have one. And every waking hour they must practice with them until we have an army of warriors ready to do battle."

"Just as our Indian forebearers fought with spears," Lindsay said grimly, "so will we, their children."

Gerard left him to his work and went on the incessant rounds of the hiding-places one after the other, giving encouragement where he could and making sure that all of his people knew what had to be done. He found that even in so short a time their fears had been considerably diminished, and in their place was an admirable resolution.

He came upon the child Anitra, clutching her lyre to

her immature breast. He crouched down beside her and said gently, "You understand that you must not even touch the strings?" Her eyes were wide and solemn as she held the instrument out for him to see; the strings were cut. She whispered, "They caught once on a twig, and they sounded. No more. But I have *this* now . . ."

Quick as lightening, she reached under her *draperi* and showed him a short bamboo dagger, fashioned just like the spears he had taught them to make but only nine inches long. "Alma gave it to me," she said, "and they are making more of them, one for every woman who wants one. And I will not be afraid to use it, Gerard." Her strength of will astounded him and filled him with admiration; but the tragedy of it nearly broke his heart.

The refugees waited, no longer as terrified as they had been, filled now with confidence in the Outsider who had so recently become one of them, an Edenite. They had learned to know him well, but more than that, their Queen had said to them: "Trust him. We are in good hands . . ."

Chapter Thirteen

The gang of outlaws had descended on Eden, and had found it emptied of its inhabitants. Their guns were loaded and ready, but there was no one to fire at in the empty township. Jao Torres had been hoping for a great deal of killing and was angry. He had the satisfaction of knowing that his prey was frightened of him, and the terror he represented was very important to him.

He had found the Throne Room, and he stared in awe at the paintings there; art had never been part of his life. He took a wonderful carving of Alma from its niche and ran his calloused fingers over it, touching the nipple of the hard breast that was exposed under the tissue thin *draperi*. The carved wood was so fragile that the *draperi* broke under his crude caress.

He sourly said to Carmen, "Why you don' look like this, woman? I find this girl, I give her fifty young Jaos, all in one night." He thought it was a very humorous remark, and he threw back his head and roared with laughter.

Carmen snarled at him and said savagely, "You don't got nobody better than me, you know that . . ."

217

Espada followed his master around like a puppy dog, and Jao looked at the inscription at the base of the statuette and wondered what it meant, because he was illiterate. He held it out to Espada and said, "You tell me what they write here, my eyes not strong today." Espada took it from him and read, "Alma the Queen, fecit John, 1785."

Jao glared. *"Fecit?"* he said. "I don' know this word, and there you with your fancy talk again."

"Fecit is French," Espada said, "or German, maybe Latin. Yes, Latin, I think. It means he made it. John is the name of the man who carved it. The Queen, her name is Alma."

"We find her, I want her."

"And you shall have her, Jao! I have men out already, following the trail they left."

"And the diamonds?"

"Everyone else is searching for them. They will be well hidden, without a doubt. But we will find them."

"If you don't," Jao said, growling, "I cut off your head."

He stalked to one of the embrasures and put his foot up on a low wall, and looked out over a vista of incomparable beauty. He was a crude and brutal man, but he was not incapable of thought, and he worried about a problem that he was sure would be severe. He turned back to Espada at last and said slowly, "Too many things we don' know nothing. We don' know how many people here, we don' know how many diamonds they got, we don' know what they doing with them. You educated man, Espada, is why I hate you so much. So now, you telling me. When them people running away, they taking diamonds with them?"

"Maybe."

218

"Or hiding them here some place?"

"Maybe that too."

"Maybe, maybe, I don' like *maybe!* Only one thing we do now. We find where them people hiding, we take prisoners, women prisoners, we send word: you telling us what you done with them diamonds you getting your women back, not before."

Espada nodded, because this was precisely his own thinking, and the reason he had sent men to track down the refugees. He said, "Good, good, I like the idea. You are a fine leader, Jao."

"I know. Soon as we find out where they are, we take all men, capture prisoners." He wandered slowly around the walls, looking at the paintings and the carvings, shaking his head in wonderment. He said absently, "We got food here? You find food for the men?"

"There are grain pits everywhere," Espada said. "Some of them are damp, the water seeping in through the roof I suppose, but the grain is still good. The women are making bread now."

Jao grunted. "I don' feed my men good, they turn against me."

It was the custom among the *mestizos* for the Indian women to prepare the food and then sit patiently by till the men had finished eating, after which they would voraciously devour what was left. But on this evening, two of the men died instantly after eating the bread and three more were violently sick. The women drew back, knowing at once that the millet had been poisoned; it was an ancient ploy of their Indian enemies.

Word of the disaster came to Jao Torres as he sat on Alma's Throne and chewed on the smoke-dried pork he liked so much, drawn from his own supplies. He roared in anger, "We don' bake no more bread!" The meat had

219

made him thirsty, and he shouted, "Someone bring me water!"

Espada handed him a flask, and Jao smelled it suspiciously and said, "They poison food, maybe they poison water too." His lieutenant shook his head. "The people who live here," he said, "are simple and not very competent, most of their conduits are dry. But I am having water brought directly from the river, the water there is sweet and very good. They will keep all our own containers filled."

By the riverside, three of the outlaws were carrying twenty-seven flasks made of leather, metal, or pottery. They crouched down and chatted together in the darkness as they filled the bottles, and wondered at the silence here after the nighttime cacophony of the jungle to which they were more accustomed.

Ostrama was mostly Portuguese and fancied himself a little better than the others, Gahuri was dark and swarthy, mostly Indian from the Totaneu tribe though he had no idea who his father might have been, and Zanabis, seldom spoke and liked nothing better than killing anything—man, woman, child, or animal. Ostrama was the really dangerous one of the trio. It was his custom to carve a notch on his knife handle for every man he had killed. There were seventeen cuts; every one of his victims had made the mistake of turning their backs to him.

He scooped up water and splashed it over his heavily bearded face, and said: "You see them paintings?"

While soaking his feet in the stream, Gahuri took off his short leather skirt and sank down to enjoy the cold water. "Paintings? I don't know paintings."

"Pictures," Ostrama said, "they got pictures of their people here, they don't look much like Indians. And their women . . ." He whistled his appreciation, and gestured crudely.

Gahuri laughed. "You telling me we got diamonds *and* women?"

"Not yet we don't. But two–three days we find both of them. I skewer them women till I drop dead, then I go home with my pockets full of diamonds, you see."

Zanabis grunted. "Better we kill them all." He was an old man. Many years ago his enemies had captured him, and had tied him naked to a tree, and had cut off his genitals. They had left him to bleed to death, but Zanabis was strong. He had survived long enough for his friends to find him, and to cut him free, and mound wood ashes on the fearful wound to disinfect it. He had recovered, a changed man with only hatred in his heart. Ever since that dreadful day, his greatest delight was killing women, since he could no longer use them, and there was not an Indian woman in the camp who did not give him a very wide berth indeed.

Ostrama rose to his feet and looked down at Gahuri. He said, "Is it cold, the water?"

"The water is good."

"I don't like it too cold, it makes me sneeze all the time."

"No, it is good, not too cold."

Ostrama kicked off his boots, stripped off his canvas breeches, and laid aside his heavy woolen shirt. He squatted down in the river and looked up at the clouds that covered the moon. The night was dark, and he shivered and rose to his feet again. He said, "No, it is too cold now, I come back tomorrow when the sun is hot, I like the sun . . ."

He stooped to pick up his clothes, and when he straightened up he suddenly screamed and grasped with

221

both hands at the shaft of a thrown bamboo spear that was deeply embedded in his chest. He screamed, "The guns!" and fell to the ground.

The spear had shattered his heart, and its sharp point, not even hardened by fire, had protruded through his back. He was dead, but with the savage resistance of a wild animal he still found his loaded musket and pulled the trigger. He did not even see that the half-inch bullet had ploughed into Gahuri's stomach.

Zanabis reached for his own gun, but he was too late. Five avenging angels were bearing down on them out of the darkness, their fearsome spears stabbing; with only one shot fired, the three invaders lay dead.

Gerard said quietly, "It is good. We retreat now, back to the swamp."

He pulled his spear from Ostrama's dead body, and said quietly, teaching the others, "We never leave our weapons behind us, and we collect theirs too, together with whatever else may be of value. Remember it, Lindsay, and tell all the men. And the reason we retreat now . . . a shot was fired, it will bring others running here very soon, perhaps very many others. It is better we do not stand and fight against an enemy whose strength and competence we do not know, but retreat to strike again."

"I will remember," Lindsay said. He enumerated the booty as the men collected it: three guns, four filled powder horns, five bags of lead bullets, three swords, six knives, one ancient flintlock pistol, and a great number of serviceable water bottles. Like ghouls in the night, Gerard, Lindsay, and three other Strong men, their mettle tested now and not found wanting, were quickly swallowed up by the darkness.

The sound of the single shot had reached the Throne Room where Jao lay in a drunken stupor with Carmen at his side. It was enough to bring him back to partial sobriety. He roared for Espada, but Espada was already racing to the river with a dozen of his men. He found the bodies there, and examined their mortal wounds very carefully. When he reported back Jao swore and said furiously, "Three good men, their guns gone, their bullets, their powder, their swords, all gone! We don' sleep tonight, all men stand ready with their muskets!"

"They are already standing to arms," Espada said. "If they want to attack us here . . . then we are ready for them. But I do not think they will. A hit-and-run attack like this means that there will be others of the same kind when we drop our guard."

"Spears!" Jao said wrathfully. "It means they don' got guns. They got guns, they don' kill my men with bamboo stakes, with poison."

Espada was furious at his commander's incompetence. He said angrily, "No! It might mean they want us to *believe* they have no guns, and so follow them to wherever they have gone! You've seen their paintings! These are not simple Indians! Our first day in Raman-li-Undara, and look what we have lost! One man hurled to his death at the top of the stairs, two men poisoned from eating bread and one other dying now, three killed at the river . . . in one single day! At this rate they can destroy us in ten days, by attrition!"

Jao did not know what attrition meant, but he chose not to show his ignorance. Instead, he said, "You find out where they go?"

"Into the forest, and there are very many of them."

"Women?"

223

"Many women among them."

"They hiding, we find them. We take prisoners, five, ten, twenty women, I don' care how many."

"When ever you are ready, Jao."

"First light," Jao said emphatically. "We don' sit still any more they hit us when we want. We hitting them now."

And so, it was decided. Shortly before the sun rose, Espada called all the men and Carmen together, and led the gang towards the forest and the swamp, following the trail that a thousand people had left behind them. He was deceived by the false tracks that Gerard had made, but at last they came to the place where all the prints disappeared into the slime of the great mangrove swamp.

And Jao knew what to do now. He said to Espada, gruffly, "They find water to hide themselves in, they thinking good. But now, you send men round the swamp, find out if they leaving it. I waiting for you here."

Espada himself led the team of expert trackers that circumnavigated the huge marsh, searching for any signs of exit. It took them more than six hours. At last he returned to Jao and said in triumph, "There are all here, hiding, no doubt, under mangrove roots, which afford excellent shelter."

Jao Torres was the General again, and he sat down on the trunk of a fallen and long-dead rubber tree and gave out his orders. "We got two hours left before night coming. Better you send the men out now, same way you went, stay on all sides of the swamp, two–three men together. Night come, all right, they sleeping. Sunup, they moving into swamp, looking everywhere. You don' hide so many people all one place, this meaning ten people here, fifteen people there, twenty some other place . . .

You telling them I want prisoners. *Women* prisoners. We take five, ten their women . . . We don' lose no more men. And we getting what we coming here for. *Diamonds.* "

By nightfall, the gang had been split up into the small parties that Jao had ordered, and were taking up their nighttime positions on the periphery of the marshes. Jao and Espada sat drinking together from a flask of violent liquor, when Espada said, currying favor, "It will work, Jao. With a few of their women in our hands, the diamonds are ours. I wish I could have thought of this idea myself, but I did not. It is the difference between a brilliant leader and a subordinate."

Jao stared at him for a long time, and said at last, "Yes. You good man, Espada. Maybe I like you after all, even you look at Carmen the way you do. Maybe, we find them diamonds, I give her to you."

"You are generous," Espada said swiftly, "but I would not accept. Carmen is yours, and I have too much respect for her."

"I see the way you looking at her, you don' fool me none."

"Never!" Espada said. "The Indian women are enough for me."

"Her skin white, like yours. You like."

"Yes, it is true," Espada said earnestly. "She is indeed a woman of very great quality. But in all the years I have been fortunate enough to work with you, and therefore to know her, no evil thought has ever passed through my mind concerning her. *Never!* But you have worked too long this day, and it is time to drink." He passed over his flask of palm liquor, and Jao drank deeply. He emptied it within the half-hour and took another from Manuel and emptied that too, and found yet

225

a third and drank heavily again. Espada had long since left him to attend to the business of trapping the fugitives in the swamp; and by midnight he was quite incapable, stretched out on the wet ground and snoring abominably.

Carmen was beside him, and when she pushed him away from her in disgust he was not even conscious of it. She heard a subdued whistle, like the cry of a macaw, and knew what it represented. She stood up and stared into the surrounding darkness, and she smelled the telltale scent. She walked towards it unerringly, and when she had gone fifty paces the body scent was very strong. She said, her voice almost inaudible, "Espada . . . ?"

For a moment, there was only silence. And then, with startling suddenness, there was a strong arm around her waist, sweeping her off her feet. A voice as soundless as her own whispered, "Not here, we are too close . . ."

She allowed him to take her arm in a steel grip and lead her through the forest for a hundred paces or more, until they came to a moonlit clearing. He turned then, and took her in his arms and crushed his lips to hers. And suddenly, he released her and struck her a violent blow across her face, so savagely that she fell to the ground. He kicked her, and hissed, "Pig! Why did you not come to me last night? You knew I was waiting for you! All night long I waited! I could have taken one of the Indian women, but no, I waited for you! And you did not come!"

She was on her feet again in a flurry of violent movement, striking out at his face with two fingers extended to drive into his eyes and blind him. But he caught her wrist easily and deflected the blow, and he laughed softly as he bent her body back over a fallen palm trunk. He lay on top of her, forcing her head back viciously, and he found a length of trailing vine and wound it around her throat. She screamed, "Bastard! You are killing me! Pox-ridden bastard of a whore-mother!"

He said, winding the vine about her neck, "I do not have the pox, unless you gave it to me." He drew his sword and cut a length of vine and waved it over her face, while saying, "I could whip you with it, but Jao would see the blood, and I am not ready to fight him yet, not till we find the diamonds." Instead, he snaked it over her body, across her full breasts and between her thighs. She moaned, and begged him, "Take me, Espada, *now!*" He thrust himself into her, not caring for her own release at all but merely satisfying himself on her. And when he was satiated, he unwound the vine from about her throat. As she clutched at him he said harshly, "Enough, woman. Go to your Jao Torres now. Drunk as he is he may awaken if you have the skill to arouse him, which I doubt."

He watched her stumble off back along the trail that led to the camp, and then followed her to find his own sleeping-place. He dreamed in the night that Jao had found out about his affair with Carmen, and he awoke in a cold sweat of terror. He lay awake for a while, trying to persuade himself that it was all a dream and nothing more.

But in a little while, he moved deeper into the forest and found himself a new place to sleep in, where he might not so easily be found. He pulled the ferns about him until he was thoroughly concealed, and he slept soundly.

In the depths of the swamp, Gerard had made his ar-

duous rounds. And now, quite exhausted, he was asleep
in Shana's arms, though Alma, sharing the tiny hideout
with them, was very close beside them.

He half-awoke in the night to feel a light touch finger-
ing him, and though he grew strong he could not quite
awaken himself. In his sleep, he turned on his side—was
it the left or the right? He could not know—and found a
soft and resilient breast to hold. There were smooth and
silken buttocks cupped into his loins, and he did not
know whose they were.

Was it Shana? Or Alma? Both of them, quite naked,
had been close to him when he had fallen asleep. The
sleep was heavy on him, but in a kind of daze his fingers
left that enticing bosom and moved to a face, lightly exploring the arch of the eyebrows, the curve of a chin . . .
but still, he could not be sure whose probing hands were
on him.

He fell into a deep sleep again, a sleep of utter exhaustion, and the peacock feathers still caressed him.
He thought he heard a whispered voice, or was it still
part of the dream? "Even in sleep, he is strong. Will you
take him now, or shall I?"

There was a slender thigh thrown over his, and *someone* was straddling him, lowering herself gently onto
him, with very slow insistence. He reached up and fondled breasts in his sleep, and he still did not know who it
was that had taken possession of his body. He knew only
that there was a great and welcoming warmth there, as
the utter oblivion overtook him.

And so, both sides were waiting now for the advent of
the new day, and for all the good or evil that it might
bring them.

228

Chapter Fourteen

As the first red rays of the sun found their way through the treetops, illuminating their varied green with a brilliant golden glow, a cat and mouse game was beginning in the jungle. Jao was a fool in many ways, but he was a *dangerous* fool, and he had not survived for so long without a sure knowledge of how unseen enemies, hiding out there and waiting for him to make one false move, could be defeated. Even before there was light enough to see properly, he had moved off with Espada along the swamp's irregular border, creeping through the bushes in a silence that was uncanny.

In a little while, they waited under a tall cannonball tree, listening and searching the black roots of the mangroves ahead of them. From above them, high in the branches, there came the raucous call of a parrot . . .

Espada reached out and took Jao's arm in a viselike grip, and they moved under deeper cover. Espada whispered, "Not a bird, but a man," and Jao nodded.

Espada lay on his back and stared into the foliage, and squirmed his body around for a better point of vantage. He whispered at last, "I see him." As he readied his musket, Jao whispered furiously, "No! You want to tell them all we here? No!"

"Very well." He laid the gun aside, and fastened the short sword more securely in his belt. He studied the configuration of the tree very carefully, because he was well-hidden in thick ferns. The parrot call came again. He laughed softly, and said, "He is not good with bird sounds, a man who has never had to use them before, perhaps. But even with his incompetence, he has warned his people that we are here. And by so doing . . . he has signed his own death warrant."

Suddenly, he leaped to his feet and seized a length of trailing vine, and swung quickly up to the lower branches. He leaped from one branch to another with the speed and agility of a monkey, finding places to land where there were none, balancing his athletic body high above the ground as he showed off his expertise to impress his master, knowing that nobody could climb trees as well and as fast as he could. The man above him was heavily built and bearded, blonde-haired and dressed in the strange costume he had seen in the paintings. There was a long bamboo pole in his hand, its end sliced to a formidable point . . .

Espada leaped through the air, and balanced himself on a slender bough. He seized the weapon as it came at him, and he heard the sentry's anguished shout, *"They are here!"* He wrestled the improvised spear away and dropped it, and drew his sword, thrusting it quickly upwards, aiming at the groin. The weight of the muscular body almost tore it from his hands as the blonde man screamed and fell, crashing through the foliage to lie broken on the ground far below. He sheathed his sword and found a vine to slide down. When he reached the wet earth he stood beside his enemy and ground a boot into the dying throat until the semiconscious struggles ceased.

He said, mocking, "These are the people we have to fight, Jao! And they are not fighting men! But did you hear his shout?"

"I hearing him," Jao said stolidly. "He speaking English. "I don' know what kind people we got here, but I don' care none either."

Now all around the swamp, the outlaws were moving in, equally stealthy in their search. Among them was Carmen, who was more expert than most of the others, and Torres had sent a dour and silent Indian named Krasi with her. She had said scornfully, "I know this mad Indian, he moves through the bush like a herd of two hundred wild pigs, maybe because his father and mother were pigs, I don't want him with me."

"He staying with you," Jao had said, and she had laughed. "All right, I do what you want, like always. You tell me: Carmen, you lie down and open your legs for me, I do that. You say: Carmen, you take this mad Indian with you, all right, I do that too. But if he makes any noise, I will kill him."

And so, the two of them were silently wading in waist-high black slime from one tiny mangrove island to another, pausing every once in a while to listen and watch. And by midday, their patience was rewarded. Carmen stopped, frozen in mid-motion, putting out a hand to stop her bodyguard too. She looked a warning at him, and touched a finger to her nose, signifying that she had smelled something. He nodded, and they both lowered themselves into the water till only their heads were showing in a tangled mass of aquatic fern; and they waited . . .

The sound came to them first, a gentle murmur of dis-

231

turbed water. And then there was the sight at last, a
heavily bearded man who was half-wading, half-swim-
ming very slowly and cautiously through the dark water.
He was approaching them, though he could not see
them, and they drew silently back under closer cover
and watched.

Carmen caught her breath. In spite of the beard, she
recognized him at once as the man they had left for
dead back there in the outside world, so long ago now!
She remembered him lying there only barely conscious
with a cord around his neck, the blood pumping out of a
wound in his chest as she played with him. There had
been the woman too, spread-eagled on the ground with
poles at her wrists and ankles, a very pretty young girl.

There was only silence as she watched, and then
Gerard veered to one side and rose up out of the water
like a young God. He strode to a nearby clump of giant
roots and whistled softly.

First a young man appeared, armed with a spear and
dressed in one of those outlandish woolen gowns, and
Carmen strained her ears to hear what they were whispering to each other. But then, as she watched, a tall
and very stately woman emerged from a hideout that
was less than fifty yards away. She wore a gown of brilliant purple, all muddied with the slime of the swamp.
Another young woman followed her, and Carmen could
only stare in wonder at their physical beauty. Slowly, she
began to realize that the first woman was the one por-
trayed in the statuette and paintings identified as Alma
the Queen; and she knew that all their troubles were
over now.

She heard the low, secretive voices, first from the
man: "Roland, one of our sentries, has been killed, and

our people are frightened. The enemy is here somewhere, in the swamp."

The other young woman was known to her too from
the paintings, and what was her name? Shana? Yes . . .
She saw the touch of hands and heard the whispering:
"The time has come for complete concealment. I have
so advised all those of our people I have found time
to visit, and there are runners warning the others. Tonight, we must attack them in the town again, in much
stronger force, to entice them away from our hiding
place."

The Queen said quietly, "We are in your hands,
Gerard." The other young girl was suddenly clutching at
him and whispering, "Gerard my love . . ."

He said fiercely, "Hide yourselves now. There are
twelve dangerous hours till darkness, we must keep under the closest cover. But at nightfall, I will draw them
away from the swamp, I do not want them here. I will go
now to warn other families, other groups . . ."

The two women and the young man with the spear
climbed back down into the dugout, and Carmen
watched Gerard swim away. She waited till he was long
gone, then whispered, a note of triumph in her voice,
"Go, Krasi. Find Jao, you understand" Bring him here
with ten good men, tell him that I have found their
Queen for him. Bring him here, now!"

The Indian nodded and slunk away, and Carmen
waited. It was more than three hours before Jao appeared; it had not been easy to locate him. He was a
comic, though menacing, figure gliding towards her,
chest-deep in slime but with that ridiculous hat still
perched on top of his head. When he was well concealed, he whispered, "Krasi say you got their Queen."

233

Carmen pointed. "There, where the red flowers are. Follow the line of them down to the black sand, there is a hollow there. Inside it, there is one man with a spear, and two women. One of them is the Queen. You came alone?"

"No, my men are here. It is the Queen?"

"You saw the carving and the paintings, as I did. It is the same woman."

"If it is not, I beat you till you nearly die."

"Beat me, I like you to beat me. But first . . . take their Queen, it is what you wanted." She could not resist an opportunity to please him.

Jao ignored her. He cupped his hand to his mouth and croaked three times like a bullfrog. Immediately, Espada and seven other bandits rose up out of the slime where they had been hidden. Jao said to them, scorning silence now: "The roots, where them flowers are, we use our guns now I don' mind none."

In a broad and deadly line, they advanced on the hideout. There was a flurry of movement there, and a young man was bursting out of concealment, his spear leveled as Gerard had taught him. He drove its point into the belly of the first of the invaders, and then Jao's musket-ball, at a range of only a few feet, shattered his chest and killed him.

Not knowing what else might be down there, Jao Torres was wise enough to send three of his cohorts down into the hiding-place. When they came out, grinning broadly, they were dragging Shana and Alma with them. He stared at Alma, and knew that she was the woman whose image he had seen and drooled over. He reached out and tore the *draperi* from the upper part of her body, and stared in awe at the most splendid breasts he had ever seen in his life. He mauled them savagely with coarse and calloused hands, and reached under the skirt portion of her gown and fondled her, and he said: "I take you soon, woman, you be *my* woman . . ."

He laughed shortly and said, "First time I sleeping with Queen, is very good for me, maybe you like too, is better." He stared at Shana, and said, "Yes, I liking you too."

Espada said quietly, "We leave them a message now, I think, no?" and Jao nodded. He found a *piricuri* tree and sliced off a length of the pliable bark and fashioned a sharp stilo for writing. He scratched out, reading as he wrote, "We have your Queen, a prisoner. Your Chief will come to the village now, and talk, or we will kill her."

Jao laughed out loud. "We don' kill her too soon!" he shouted. "You telling about other woman too."

"Shana," Carmen said, "her name is Shana."

Espada nodded, and scratched, "We have Shana too." He stuck the bark onto a log, using the pen to hold it in place. Jao Torres nodded his approbation. "We going back now," he said. "We waiting now, they bring us *diamonds.*"

Espada found vines with which to bind their wrists behind their backs, and less than three hours later, Shana and Alma were prisoners in the Throne Room, still bound, seated on the floor at Jao's feet as he sat on the Throne and gulped the fearful liquor the Indian women had made in his absence. He was wondering which of them he should satisfy himself on first, wondering also how long it might be before their chief came crawling to him . . . Carmen had told him it was the man they had left to die out there in the jungle, the man named Gerard whose wife he had raped. It had been the occasion for one of their interminable squabbles. He was well

235

aware that she was also trying to tell him what a fool he had been for not killing him there and then. He said to her, menacing, "I telling you before, woman, I meet with this man again one day. Now, I do that, and I getting everything I want."

He struck her savagely across the face, and shouted, "You understan' what I telling you? I am not fool! Clever man! Better you know that!"

Carmen contented herself with laughing, knowing that she could not fight him. She looked at the two bound captives and said savagely, "Why don't you find out what they are like, now? Maybe it will put you in a better temper."

He glared at her, and his eyes were hard and very cold. "My temper good now," he said, "very good, because I got two women better-looking like you, I don' need you no more, just these two, maybe I give you to my men to play with. What you say, woman?"

Carmen tossed back her long black hair over her shoulders and answered, mocking him, "I say you take this woman *now*. I want to watch you take her. She is a Queen, it will make you a King, which you never were."

She was not aware of Jao's sudden stiffening. She was staring at Alma, very conscious of her great beauty, especially of that saffron-colored skin, without a thorn scar on it anywhere, a skin that had so obviously been well-cared for, a woman whose life had been pampered; she was lying there now, helpless, and frightened, no doubt, of the ravishment that was to come. She turned her look to Shana, and saw there an even greater beauty; but in those lovely eyes there was no fear at all, only a stubborn kind of resentment. She hated them both, hated them all the more because of the way Jao was licking his coarse lips as he gloated over them.

She said viciously, "Take them, Jao, both of them. Show me what a strong man you are. I want to watch you take them."

Shana had closed off her mind by a very conscious effort of will. And watching her Queen through veiled eyelids, she knew that Alma had done much the same kind of thing. There was a kind of dispassion on both of them now, it was as though they were both thinking alike: *what must be, will be, however terrible it is . . .*

But there was a loathing welling up inside them for this gross man, a loathing of a kind that was foreign to them, and to all of Eden. They knew that there could be nothing but the cruelest indignities ahead for them now.

But Shana's greatest fear was for Gerard . . .

How long might it be before he would discover that crude message that had been left for him? And then, what would he do? She knew the answer to this second thought, with no doubt in her mind at all; he would come rushing to their rescue, a rescue that had no hope at all of succeeding.

And what would this evil monster do with him? Her thoughts were concentrated on Jao Torres now as she lay on her back and looked up at him through half-closed eyes. He was looking not at her, but at Alma, as he gulped greedily from the leather flask in his hand; he was already quite drunk. She heard that horrible woman Carmen say, scornfully, "Take her, Jao, if you are man enough to lie with a Queen."

And then she dropped to the ground and pulled Alma's fine silk *draperi* from around her waist, bunching it up and putting it to her cheek as though savoring its excellence. Her eyes closed in a kind of ecstasy; she rubbed it back and forth across her breasts and

237

crooned, "You give me this cloth, Jao? It is silk, I never had silk in all my life, I like it so much . . ."

Jao Torres did not answer her. And to her horror, even though it was expected, Shana saw him rise to his feet, a misshapen gnome of a man with the muscles of a bull. She saw him kick off the clumsy boots as he unfastened the broad leather belt at his waist. A pistol and a knife fell to the stone floor with a clatter, but he paid no heed to them as he stripped off his heavy canvas breeches and stood here, his naked body hard as iron, his thighs like twin pillars of the hardest oak.

Shana watched as he threw Alma onto her back and sank to his knees between her long and beautiful legs, forcing them apart for his pleasure. She moaned softly, and turned her face away, but there was a strong hand gripping her chin immediately, twisting her face back. She heard that loathsome woman's harsh voice, "No! You watch, this will happen to you soon too, I promise you . . ."

She wanted to close her eyes to mask the dreadful image, but she could not. She watched and could not control her moaning as Jao threw himself on her and violated her. And there were hands at her own breasts now, Carmen's hands, the fingers digging in deeply as strong teeth found the nipples and drew blood. She bit her lip to hold back the scream, and found Alma's eyes on hers. The hatred that was in her heart was reflected in that always gentle look too, and there were easily read, unspoken thoughts: *We must have courage now.* There were also tears there, and Shana held her breath as a woman's hands found their way to her thighs and clutched at her, a finger probing.

She steeled herself as she saw Alma's far worse subjugation; and suddenly, Jao was bellowing at the top of his

voice, the bellowing of a cruel and savage animal mount-
ing another of his kind. A sweet and gentle woman lay
still under his assault and could still turn those express-
ive eyes on her friend and say with them: *We must have
courage now* . . .

The sound of Jao's assault was furious, and it brought
Espada running into the room, his sword drawn. He
pulled up short when he saw what was happening, and
lounged casually against the pillar of the doorway, a
mocking smile on his handsome face.

He waited till he saw Jao collapse on that soft and
lovely body, and a few minutes more till he saw Carmen
stagger to her knees, holding up two of those strange
silken gowns, one purple and the other the pale blue of
Shana's eyes. He heard her say, begging, "You give me
both of them, Jao? They are so beautiful . . .

There was a dreadful pathos in her voice, and Espada
laughed aloud. He said, "And you give me the other
woman, Jao, what do you say? I like the looks of her."

There was a long, long silence. And then Jao withdrew himself from his victim, and rolled over onto his
back. He rose to his feet and said sourly, "No, I don't
give nobody nothing. Only maybe . . . Carmen."

Her insults were still rankling, and he strode to her
and kicked her savagely in the stomach. Jao shouted, "I
don' need you no more, you fat Portuguese pig, I got
better women now, stay with me always!" In a fury, he
turned on Espada and roared, "I don' give her to you
neither!" He was barely conscious of the sudden fear on
Carmen's face as he thrust a finger under Espada's nose
and shouted, "I tell you what you doing now! You telling
men, first man kill five our enemies here, bring me five
ears, I give him Carmen! I don' need her no more!"

Carmen's face was white, but Espada was very calm.

He said quietly, "You are my Chief, Jao. Whatever you tell me to do, I will do, as always."

"Better you do that, or I kill you!" He found his flask and raised it to his lips to drink, but it was empty. In a paroxysm of rage he hurled it at Espada and screamed, "And I don' got to drink! You bring me, white-skin bastard!"

Espada side-stepped the missile with the agility of a *tigre* and caught it by its strap. He said lightly, "I will bring you liquor, Jao, I am your servant." There was a fixed smile on his handsome face, but his eyes were very hard. "I will find more liquor for you Jao, my dear friend and my master to whose welfare I am devoted, always."

Jao said, grumbling, "You talking too much, Espada."

Espada hid his anger. He turned his heel and stalked out, not daring to look at Carmen. The blood was pounding in his temples.

It took him very little time to find more flasks, taking them unceremoniously from two of the men who were incapably drunk. It took a little longer to reach the grain pits where the poisoned millet was and to trickle a large handful into the bottles. He shook them up vigorously for good measure. When he returned he was smiling gently as he said, "There, Jao, two full bottles, enough to last you all night long."

Jao took them from him, paying no attention at all to the two recumbent captives at his feet; he had quite recovered his good humor. He tossed one of the flasks to Carmen, and said gruffly, "Drink, woman, it make you feel better. Who I give you to, woman? Manuel? He take you ten times every night. I don' care who is, first man bring me five ears."

240

Carmen raised the flask to her lips as she turned her look on Espada, to discover how he was taking all this. And something she saw in his eyes made her blood run cold.

She did not drink. She was aware enough merely to hold the bottle to her lips as she studied the look on his face. And she *knew* . . .

She had long known that one day this moment would come, that sooner or later her secret lover would be driven over the edge of tolerance, that *one day* he would accept the constant humiliation no longer.

Had that time come now? The thoughts were racing through her mind, a mind that was shrewd and devious; hostages had been taken, the stage had been set. The diamonds were almost theirs . . . And in a moment, she feigned a great gulp of the liquor and said quietly to Jao, "It is good this time. The last time, it was sour."

"It is true," Espada said swiftly. "The last time, it was carelessly made, and I whipped the women who made it. So . . . this time it is good, the best we have ever had. And by your leave? There are sentries to be posted."

He held Carmen's eyes only briefly as he left, and there was just time to see that Jao was drinking heavily from the first of the poisoned flasks. At the door, he turned and looked down on Shana and Alma, delighting in their naked perfection. He said, not trying now to hide the scorn in his voice, "Perhaps you will give me both of them, Jao. But only after you tire of them, of course."

He was gone, and Carmen was unaccustomedly trembling as she wondered how the changeover from one of her lovers to the other might affect her personal fortunes. The door shut behind him, and she crawled to the drunken Jao on all fours, like an animal, holding out her flask to him. She said, "Drink my love. The liquor is better than it has even been before."

He took it from her and drank deeply, and he muttered: "Yes, taste good, is different this time, I liking too much." He stared down at Shana, and looked into her wide open and very aware eyes, and said thickly, "Soon, I taking you too, you very lucky woman . . ." His head was swaying from side to side as the poison worked on him, and he said, slurring, "I taking you, I taking diamonds . . . I don' feel too good . . ."

"You are sick, my love," Carmen said, urging him. "Drink, the liquor is a sure cure."

His hand was trembling as he raised the flask to his lips again. She whispered, "You have the fever, from the insects, you must fight it, with strong drink." His face was grey, the color of wood-ash as he gulped again. Suddenly he rose to his feet and bellowed like a wounded bull, and fell to the ground on his back, his legs thrashing wildly. He twisted and turned and clutched at his stomach in agony, and through the veil that was over his eyes he saw his woman leaning toward him, and he felt her pouring more of the liquor down his throat. She whispered, "Drink, Jao, a sure cure for the fever . . ."

When he was quite still, and silent, she spat into his face and hissed at him: "Now, Espada tie you down for the ants to feed on, you don't get no burial at all."

She went out to look for her lover, to tell him that Jao was dead. At the doorway she turned back and saw the probing look in Shana's eyes. She said softly, "You think Jao was bad? You wait. You see what Espada do with you now, both of you."

She went out and searched and could not find him. She told three of the sentries, "When you see Espada, tell him to come to the Throne Room, I have news for him."

She went back to wait for him; but she pulled up short at the entrance and stared in horror and bewilderment . . . Jao was not on the floor where she had left him. Instead, he was on the bed, lying on his back with his mouth wide open and snoring abominably. She moved to him, unbelieving, and his cruel eyes opened to stare up at her. He said thickly, "Too strong . . . too .. strong, the liquor, maybe I drinking . . . drinking little bit too much. I sleep now." He was asleep again.

Jao was a man whose stomach, through long abuse, had become resistant to almost everything, like a cast-iron cooking pot that can suffer the most abominable treatment and still function well. There was enough of the deadly poison in him to kill ten men, and yet, he was still alive and recovering fast. Carmen's eyes were on the knife he had dropped when he had first stripped off his clothes to enjoy Alma's body, but she could not bring herself to use it; too many of the gang worshipped Jao, and how could she explain a knife wound to them?

She stared at him for a while, wondering what Espada would have to say when he discovered that his scheme had gone awry.

But all was not lost, not yet. She lay down beside Jao and threw a thigh over his naked loins, and in the yellow light of the flares she saw that the two captives were both watching her closely, perhaps even understanding.

She said furiously: "Sleep! You sleep now, don't look at me like that! Sleep, we see what happens tomorrow!" In a while, she too fell into a restless, troubled sleep.

Chapter Fifteen

It was dark when Gerard returned from his rounds, and he was in despair. He had found one of the hideouts violated on the far side of the swamp; the two Strong Men there had been killed, and the three women who had shared it—Bianca, Hilda, and Yvonne—had simply disappeared.

He moved fast through the swamp to bring the dreadful news to Alma the Queen and to his Shana. When he arrived at the mangrove root shelter he whistled in the prearranged signal before he even saw the Strong Man's body lying there, almost covered over now with the encroaching black mud. In sudden alarm, he wormed his way into the hollow and found it empty. His blood froze when he found the piece of *piricuri* bark and tried to read the message scratched on it; but there was not enough light . . .

And so began the interminable business of finding dry grasses and a dry length of vine in a wet swamp, to make a fire to read by. And it was nearly an hour before he was able to make a flare and to decipher, by its light, the crude scratchings on the bark-cloth. He cupped his hands to his mouth and made the cough of a jaguar, three times, and Lindsay came hurrying to him in answer to the call, wading through waist-deep black mud.

Gerard tried to stifle his anguish and could not. He said, his voice broken: "They have taken Shana and Alma . . ."

"Oh God!"

"And I suspect they have three other women too, Hilda, Yvonne, and Bianca, they have just . . . disappeared. Henry, who was guarding them, has been killed." The good Lindsay stared at him in the darkness, unable to find words. Gerard said quietly, "Emlyn is close by, I think. Will you find him for me and bring him here?"

"Yes, at once . . ." Lindsay hurried off, and Gerard sank to his knees and covered his face with his hands, letting the tears flow now that he was alone. When Lindsay returned with Emlyn, he took hold of himself and told his friend what had happened, and showed him the bark-cloth with its message. His voice tight with his anger, his face pale and drawn, Emlyn said flatly, "If they have hostages, Gerard, we must attack the town at once, and try to effect their release."

"No." Gerard shook his head. "If we do that, they will almost certainly kill the women, perhaps one by one in an effort to hold us off. That is the purpose of hostages, to ensure no action on the part of the enemy."

"And that is our only option? No action?"

"Read the message again, Emlyn," Gerard said. "It gives us another option." Emlyn read aloud: *We have your Queen, a prisoner. Your chief will come to the village now . . ."*

He broke off and stared at Gerard, knowing what was in his mind. He said hoarsely, "You are the Chief now,

Gerard. But you cannot do this! You must not even consider it!"

"I can, and I *must.*"

"No! You will be killed . . . !"

"Perhaps not. They cannot kill me till I tell them where the diamonds are hidden. After all, it is for this that they came here. There is little else of importance in their evil minds."

"Gerard!" Emlyn said desperately, "We can summon up more than five hundred Strong Men, armed with spears now! We are stronger than they are! An attack on the town, I beseech you!"

"No." Gerard was very emphatic. "The risk is not acceptable. "At the first sign of such an assault, we would learn of the hostages' fate . . . How, I do not know, perhaps a severed head displayed on the walls as a warning to us. And we are *not* stronger than they are. In numbers, yes. But untrained men armed only with crude spears . . ."

"And their anger . . ."

"Yes, their anger too, which makes them all the more vulnerable! A mere thirty or forty skilled fighting men, as they are, armed with muskets and swords, can wipe out the kind of force we have in a matter of hours! A sharpened bamboo pole, Emlyn, is of little use against an expert swordsman, and of no use at all against a gun which can kill at fifty paces or more. I will not allow the slaughter of so many good men."

Emlyn was trembling visibly. He could not argue the point, and yet, in his desperation he was driven to do so. He said slowly, "You have told me what an evil man this is. Do you believe that you can make an honest man of him . . . with *talk?*"

247

"I know that I cannot."

"If you offer him the diamonds in exchange for the women . . . Do you believe that he will keep his part of the bargain and release them unharmed?"

"I know that he will not."

"And so . . . ?"

Gerard took a long, deep breath, and said slowly, "I know only one thing, Emlyn. And that is Shana, whom I regard now as my wife, and Alma, who is my Queen, are in the gravest danger. I know only that I *must* go to them. And the message that Jao Torres left has given me that opportunity. I will take it. What may happen then . . . frankly, I cannot imagine. I know only that I cannot help them by remaining here and defying Torres' orders while I weep for them. And so, I will go to this monster, and plan each step after the last has been taken."

"Very well," Emlyn said. "Then I will come with you."

"No." Gerard embraced his friend and said, "You are needed here to hold our people together and keep their courage up. They are unaccustomed to dangers of this kind, and they need you now."

"Then take some of the Strong Men with you . . ."

"They would be killed at once. No, I will go alone. But if you do not hear from me in the space of twenty-four hours, one way or another, then you must take it to mean that I have failed. And if I have failed, it will mean that I am dead and can no longer serve Eden. In that case . . ."

He sighed, and took Emlyn's arm, and said softly, "In that case, the swamp can no longer be a sure refuge for you. But you must not, in your anger, attack the town in force! They will slaughter you! Instead, mount a series of nightly raids, and destroy them by a process of attrition. And if even a single one of them should escape, knowing

248

that they have started a battle they cannot win . . ." He raised a warning finger. "If only one man escapes from Raman-li-Undara, then there is one more thing the people of Eden *must* do."

Emlyn saw the gravity in his eyes, and asked quietly, "And that is . . . ?"

"You must destroy the steps," Gerard said.

"What?" Emlyn's eyes were wide, and Lindsay was staring at him too. "What? Destroy the labor of a Century?"

"If one man escapes," Gerard said stubbornly, "he will return, with others of his kind, perhaps even a thousand strong. They will tear Eden down stone by stone till they find what they want. News will leak out too of the beauty of our women, with results I dare not even think of. Eden will become a known source of wealth . . . and of women. It must not be allowed to happen. It means the destruction of the steps, it means sealing off the cleft in the rock by whatever means you can devise. Even so . . . if the secret ever gets out, it will mean the end of Eden's cherished serenity."

Emlyn sighed heavily. His arms were around his friend's shoulders as he said simply, "We are in your hands, Gerard. First, we must worry about the hostages."

Gerard looked up at the moon and murmured, "It is hard to control my impatience, but I must time my arrival in the township for sunup. They must be sure that I come alone, and unarmed. We have a little more than an hour on our hands before I leave."

He turned to Lindsay. "Will you bring me one of the guns we took last night? Together with the bags of lead and the powder flasks?"

Lindsay hurried off. When he returned, Gerard gave

him a lesson in the complicated business of loading and firing a musket . . .

First, the chewing of the lump of lead till it was roughly rounded to the size of the barrel's bore; then the ramming down of the powder, followed by a wad of cloth torn from his *draperi,* and then the bullet itself. He showed him how to prime the firing pin with more powder, and turn the flint to make sure that it would spark, if not on the first drop of the hammer then on the second or third. He showed him how to squint down the long barrel to bring it into some sort of alignment with the target, and he said wryly, "These are very ancient muskets that can still kill, many years after the men who first used them have been laid to rest. Men die, but their weapons do not, they live on. Remember that your gun will probably not fire at the first pull of the trigger, it happens very rarely unless the flint is good—and good flints are hard to come by—and the powder is bone-dry and well-spread. Always keep your powder dry. But by the time you are ready for the second attempt, it may well be that your target, if he is running fast, will have advanced until he is almost on you, and this is usually the killing shot. If the gun still does not fire, then you must reverse it and use it as a club."

"A sentry," Lindsay said, learning fast. "Standing perhaps on a wall a hundred paces away. Can I use a musket on him?"

"A hundred paces?" Gerard shook his head. "No, the ball may not even reach him, even if it is expertly aimed by a trained marksman. And training in musketry is not a question of a single lesson, years of practice are needed. Never fire your gun at such long range, it will merely disclose your position. In such a case, creep up to sixty paces, no more."

He laughed bitterly in the darkness. "The rule of thumb is, if you can see the pockmarks on your enemy's face, then he is within range. And I fear I am subverting the gentle people of Eden, and teaching them the violent fashions of the Outside. It distresses me deeply."

He was genuinely upset, and he looked at the sinking orb of the moon and said, "I must go now." He took Emlyn's hand. "If you do not hear from me in twenty-four hours . . . And tell our people that by all that I hold most holy, I will bring back the hostages, or die in the attempt."

Overcome by his deep emotion, he turned away, and strode off with no further word.

He left the swamp behind him and walked purposefully through the bordering forest, and as the sun crept over the high mountain behind him he was crossing the meadows. He saw a solitary llama with her cub standing serenely on a small summit; he smelled the sweet scent of the basil in which he had rolled with Shana and had loved her; he saw the red-gold dawn touching 'The Girl Who Fell Asleep' and illuminating her profile; and he steeled his mind to the effort that was ahead of him, ignoring its dangers altogether.

Two men with drawn swords and guns slung over their backs rose up out of the long grass very close to him, grinning broadly, and he paid them no attention at all, knowing that it was the expected message being delivered to him: *You are being watched . . .* He saw from the corner of his eye that they were searching the land behind him, assuring themselves that he was indeed alone, and he was glad that he had made the decision not to come here in the concealing darkness. The daylight would give them confidence, and for them this could perhaps be a mistake that could be turned to advantage; it was the little things that mattered now.

He moved on towards the stone walls of the buildings. More of the outlaws, their muskets ready, were disclosing themselves from under cover, not moving once they had shown themselves, but conveying their menace to him by their very stillness. He strode through the first of the archways into the narrow street that led to the Throne Room, and there were three men with drawn swords blocking his way.

The elegant, dandified man in the middle was the one who had said to him: *"Remember, too, the name Espada . . .* He would *never* forget it!

The man named Espada said, showing his teeth in a broad smile, "Gerard, I believe. Come, we will escort you to where Jao Torres is waiting for you."

Gerard scarcely broke the pace of his brisk walk. He said coldly, "I know where Torres will be, *scum*. I do not need an escort." He saw that handsome face harden, but he brushed past them all and went to the heavy door to the Throne Room and leaned into it until it slowly swung open. He was conscious that Espada and the two others were behind him as he looked. At the far end of the long, stone-walled room, Jao Torres was seated on Alma's Throne; there was an exquisite painting of her on the wall behind him. He was dressed in his boots and canvas breeches, and his black top hat, but there was a purple *draperi* thrown carelessly around his sturdy shoulders now. Alma's *draperi*. The sight of it sickened Gerard.

At Torres' feet, Carmen had discarded her bark-cloth skirt and had wrapped herself in Shana's pale blue silk *draperi*. Gerard's heart missed a beat. And on either side of the Throne there were other *mestizos*, grinning at him and spoiling for a fight.

Gerard said calmly, "You are Jao Torres, I believe. And I am Gerard Fletcher."

Torres took a long, thin cheroot from a tin case and put it to his lips. Immediately, one of the men fumbled for his touch-wick, running to his master as he worked the wheel with his thumb and blew on the cotton when it began to glow, holding it out to light the cigar, watching it solicitously before snuffing out the embers with the little stone button that was fastened to the braided wick.

Gerard went on, very cool and controlled, "Your message said come and talk. I am here to do just that, to talk." His voice was mocking now. "So why don't you begin by telling me what it is you want here?"

Espada said quietly, "Be careful, Jao. I think this man is dangerous." But Torres ignored him, and a wide grin spread over his brutal face, "You don' know that?"

"I have certain ideas on the subject. I want to hear them from you."

"I am wanting your diamonds. You knowing that good."

"Our *diamonds?*" Gerard feigned surprise, and was glad to see the grin disappear.

Jao said anxiously, "This place Raman-Li-Undara, no?"

"Indeed it is. The Field of Diamonds." Gerard gathered up his *draperi* and tossed it over his shoulder, a gesture of complete nonchalance. He went to one of the wide embrasures and stared out across the meadow, waiting for Jao to speak. Jao spoke angrily, "You telling me!" Gerard turned back and said slowly, "Yes, we have diamonds here. Thousands of them, far more than a man of your limited intellect could even begin to count. Can animals count to ten? Can they count to ten thousand?"

He saw that Torres was lost in the insufficiency of his knowledge of English, but that Espada was staring at him with a strange expression in his eyes that was not altogether hostile.

Espada said softly, "How many, American *scum?*"

Gerard shrugged. "They have never been counted," he said, "there are just too many of them." He was looking at Jao Torres now, delighting in the rising excitement he saw in those tiny black eyes. He said, "This was once a volcanic area. Perhaps millions of years ago, the earth erupted, and spewed out diamonds by the thousands. Millions of years later, the local people, whoever they were, found them scattered in the surface of the soil and collected them. They stored them in a hiding-place. And they have remained there ever since."

Espada said again, his voice very hard now, "How many? And how big?"

Gerard turned to him and said blandly, "How many? A mound of them, perhaps three feet high, I have seen them. And how big? Many of them two, three, as many as four hundred carats. One of them I saw must have been over a thousand carats, and there were many others as large."

"Carrots, carrots," Jao said furiously, "I don't know carrots, carrots is vegetables!"

Espada held up his clenched fist and said, trying to control his excitement: "A thousand carats in an uncut diamond, Jao, is this size! The size of a strong man's fist! And a single one will bring more money than you and I ever dreamed of! A single one? They have a pile of them three feet high!"

There was a long silence before Jao took command again, and Gerard was glad of the greed in his eyes. He leaned forward at last and said, "Now . . . you telling me where are they."

"First," Gerard said firmly, "You release the Queen and the other women to me."

"No. First you showing me diamonds."

"When you release them, I will take you to the diamonds, not before. At this stage, I do not even know if they are still alive."

"I cut off your fingers one by one, then your toes." Jao laughed shortly and continued, "Then other pieces your body you not needing too much."

"It will not help you at all." Gerard waited for just the right moment and said, "At the very least, your *promise* that they will be released."

"My promise," Jao said blandly, "I giving it. I got five women, I giving you back all. After you taking me to diamonds."

"And I have your word that they are all still alive?"

"They are alive. Dead woman is no good for me."

Gerard sighed. "Very well," he said. "Are we agreed?"

"My promise, good promise, never breaking word."

He was lying and Gerard knew it. The time had come now for the next step. . . .

He said, "The stones are hidden in the center chamber of a labyrinth under the old temple . . ." He turned to Espada and said quietly, "I am sure that this simpleton does not know what a labyrinth is, so perhaps you should explain to him?"

Espada held his look for a moment, wondering if two

255

such different men, one evil and the other good, could perhaps have a sort of bond between them, the bond of an education in a setting where this was a very rare thing. He said to Jao, "A maze, many corridors that twist and turn back on themselves and come to dead ends. It will not be easy to find that central chamber he spoke of."

Jao grunted. "We got guide, he show us."

Gerard was aware of a thoughtful look in Espada's eyes, and he wondered if he had seemed to give way too easily. He said stubbornly, "First, I must *see* the hostages, to assure myself that they have not been harmed."

"No."

"Then I will not guide you."

He was barely aware of a look from Jao, but he tensed himself as Espada balled up his fist and drove it with lightning speed into his stomach, doubling him up in pain, knocking the wind out of his body. And that cruel foot was at his throat again, grinding as he gasped for air and could find none. Espada released the pressure, and Gerard rolled away and crouched on all fours for a while until his breath came back to him. He heard Espada's mocking voice, "You have no choice, American *scum.*"

Gerard staggered to his feet and stood there swaying. He looked at Jao and said thickly, "Your word again, then, give me your word again . . ."

Jao rose from his throne and walked over to the niche that held Shana's statuette. He ran his fingers over the pointed, polished breasts, and said, "You knowing this one? I liking too much." He touched the inscription and said, "Say here, name Shana, I reading good. You giving me any more trouble, I giving her to you *dead.* Now, you showing me diamonds."

He put back the carving and looked down at Carmen.

He kicked her and said, "You coming with me, woman."

"And I too," Espada said. But Torres glared at him and snarled, "No! You staying here, keeping watch! Maybe this trick, maybe them people coming back, we don' be sure!"

Espada simmered, wondering how soon it might be before he could make another attempt on his boss' life—a more successful one—and get all those lovely women for himself. Already assuming the role of the new leader, he thought *No, when I have finished with three of them, I will share them out among the men too, to assure their loyalty as long as I need it, keeping only the Queen and that beautiful Shana for myself . . . And the diamonds too, a few to be given to the men, and the rest for me, A fine house in one of the better Brazilian towns, perhaps, and the life of a gentleman of great wealth.* He still could not envision the worth of a pile of stones three feet high.

Gerard said quietly, "There is light down there, from bore-holes high in the rock above, only in a very few places. We will need a flare."

Torres took a flare from the wall and lit it with his tinder, and handed it to Gerard; and in his heart he was secretly rejoicing how easy this had all been. He was wondering too how he should dispose of Espada now that he no longer needed him; a quick knife in the back, perhaps, when everything had been settled, when both the women and the diamonds were his, when Gerard had been killed off . . .

Followed closely by Torres and Carmen, Gerard went to the old Temple and down into its cellars, and opened the entrance to the maze. He saw that they stared, in something akin to fear, at the carvings on the walls. Carmen whispered, in awe, "Who are these people?"

"They are Gods," Gerard said flatly. "The people who first built Raman-li-Undara. Come now. I will guide you to their diamonds."

In a moment, Jao Torres and Carmen followed the light of his flare into the labyrinth's secret depths.

Gerard was not entirely at ease, either. He forced himself to think *Three, three, three, and then six times six, and nine times nine . . . And when is the system reversed?*

He was conscious that Carmen, close behind him, was holding firmly onto Jao's arm, in an agony of suspense and that Jao himself was breathing heavily as he stared in wonderment at the confining walls, every inch of them carved with monstrous faces . . .

Chapter Sixteen

"More spears!" Emlyn said. His voice was harsher now than it had ever been in his long life.

He was a changed man; his eyes has lost their habitual gentleness and were on fire. All those years of environmental development seemed to count for nothing now, and without his conscious knowledge, his heritage had taken over. He said again, fiercely, "More spears!"

"There are men at work cutting them now," Lindsay said. "We have Gerard's chopping-knife, the swords and knives we took from our enemies, it is not enough! To sharpen their points, to harden them in fire, it takes time with so few blades! But more than three hundred Strong Men are already armed."

"Daggers for the women too," Emlyn said. "I am convinced that our good friend Gerard has gone to his death. If I am right, it means that we cannot save Alma's life, nor the lives of Shana and the other women. All that will be left to us . . . is to avenge them."

"By nightfall," Lindsay said, "every man, woman, and child of Eden who is capable of using a weapon, will have one."

The steady chopping of bamboo poles went on in the silence of the swamp.

For Jao Torres, the labyrinth was a place of infinite terror. He took great care to hide his terror, both from his woman and from a man for whom he had nothing but contempt—a man who had agreed so easily to his terms, out of abject fear, no doubt.

He did not understand what claustrophobia was, but he knew the passages were not wide enough to allow two men to walk side by side; sometimes, the ceilings were only a foot or so above his head, although on occasion they reached up into impenetrable space that was lit by tiny bore-holes casting rays of sunlight down on them. But then again there would be long and terrifying stretches of utter darkness, where the only light was the flare that Gerard carried.

The carved faces on the walls scared him badly; who were they? When the flames played over them once, he thought he recognized the long-forgotten face of a god who had been very important to his forebears, Q'asora by name, the God of Disaster, a mocking god who hated the people who had become known as Indians.

Carmen was close behind him, even holding on to his belt in a fear which she too tried to conceal. Gerard was in the lead, turning this way and that, pausing occasionally to study the carvings on the walls as though they held some kind of secret in their stone faces.

They turned left and left and left again, and then right nine more times, and then left again, or was it right? A period of utter darkness then, with a roof so low that even Carmen had to stoop. Jao muttered, "How far now? How far?"

Gerard said equably, "Thirty minutes or so, Jao, and we will be in the inner chamber. You will see a hoard of diamonds the like of which you could never have imagined . . ."

The confining walls, suddenly, were brightly lit by those narrow shafts of light, and there was the god Q'asora again, leering at them. The passage came to an abrupt stop, and Gerard squeezed through the narrow turn to his left into a passage where the darkness was absolute . . .

There was no question in his mind of what he had to do; it was merely a question of when to do it. And he thought that the time was perhaps now.

He turned another corner and dropped his flare to the granite floor and fell on it, extinguishing it at once with his woolen *draperi*. Once it was out and there was only darkness, he leaped to his feet and walked quickly in a dead straight line, his fingers on the wall as he counted the footsteps. Eighteen paces on, he found a corridor to the right, and another to the right again after ten yards, then a third to the left after four more steps. For good measure, he took eight more paces and found a corner to the right and rounded it. He dropped to his knees and said to himself fervently, "Eighteen paces right, ten right, four left, eight right . . ."

Burning it in his memory, he whispered aloud, "The reverse for the way back is . . . eight left, four right, ten left, eighteen left." He wondered if he had been wise in choosing so absolutely dark an area for his disappearance, and he fixed the numbers in his mind, knowing that a single mistake now would surely leave his bones to bleach here in the course of time, long after Eden's population had been enslaved. "Eight, four, ten, eighteen . . ."

The turns, then: "Left, right, left, left; only one right on the reverse and it is the second . . ."

The labyrinth madness, which the ancient Egyptians and the Greeks after them knew so well, was on him, an overwhelming fear that had to be forced away, its place to be taken by a cool and dispassionate calculation. He ignored the distant, muted screams he heard from Jao, "Gerard! Gerard! Where are you? Don' leave me here, I am friend now, your friend . . ." He heard too Carmen's shrieking and the scream of obscenities she was hurling at him. They were beyond—how many walls? Two, three perhaps? But there was danger even in thinking of numbers now, and he said again, furiously, "Eight, four, ten, eighteen, left, right, left, left . . ."

Under the stress, the walls seemed to be closing in on him, the eights trying to turn into eighteens and the lefts into rights . . . He gritted his teeth and ground the formula into his mind. He knew that simple as it was, that madness could drive it out of his mind. He walked steadily back.

Eight paces, and he found the corner and turned it, and took four more steps and found two corners there, one on each side of him, and unhesitatingly turned right. Ten more paces and another turn, and everything going well as he fingered the close wall in the darkness. He took eighteen more careful steps and stopped, groping, and he thought *Around the corner now is where I lost them, and I turned left, so I must turn right now . . . In God's name, no! The last of my reverse turns must be left!*

He stood still and listened; the sound of their wailing and screaming was more distant now, and he knew that they had done what he expected them to do—run off in panic to search for him. It could only mean that they were lost for ever.

He made the turn and stumbled on his fallen flare, but he had no tinder to light it with, nor any other means of making fire, but he knew that two turns further on, one to the left and one to the right, the bore-hole area started again and he would be able to see, but which came first, the right or the left? He came to the corners and forced his memory into sharper focus. He could not decide, and he groped for faces on the wall and found the sixth carving on the sixth row was turned to the right. Or should it be the third along on the third row now? Trembling, his fingers explored again, very carefully, and almost wept his relief when he discovered that this face too was facing right. He made the turn, and soon the tiny apertures high above him were casting the god-given light down into this hellhole and he knew that at last, he was safe.

It was less than half an hour before he came to the entrance again, and he fell to his knees in a kind of emotional exhaustion that he was not accustomed to. Even in the Temple cellar, there was still daylight streaking down, the red-gold now of the setting sun, and he hesitated; what he had to do out there now needed darkness. It was not easy to hold back his impatience, but he was alone and one against many, and he knew that without the friendly shelter of the night he would be powerless. One man alone, striking silently in the dark, could wreak havoc on the enemy; in daylight, he would have no chance at all of success. He steeled himself and moved away, rounding a single corner and waiting for the night. He lay down on his back and thought about Shana.

Was someone, Espada perhaps, even at this moment violating her while he waited here? There was a great urge to go on the rampage at once, but sound common sense told him that he would have no hope at all of rescuing the hostages if he acted precipitously. And so, by a deliberate effort of will, he held himself back and waited for the friendly night to come to his aid.

He remembered the first time he had loved Shana, when he had still been obsessed with the memory of a devoted wife who was still not forgotten . . . He thought of the man who had raped and killed her, lost now in the maze and sure to die. He thought too of Carmen, that savage, pathetic woman. And though she had no qualities at all to commend her, he felt guilty; he had led a *woman* to her death, and it worried him considerably: even for so vile a creature as she was, he could not entirely set aside a certain sense of gallantry. And what were they doing now, he wondered?

Had he been able to know it, Jao and Carmen were more than a hundred feet away from him, and separated by no less than ten of the Labyrinth's walls. They were still together, though three times they had almost lost each other as they turned corner after corner in the maze, looking hopelessly for a way out but being driven relentlessly deeper and deeper within it. The darkness was driving Jao out of his mind. He pulled Carmen to him by a handful of her new silk gown and slapped her furiously across the face. He screamed, "You mad woman! You telling me turning this way, we turning that way like I want we be out of here now!"

They staggered on in the darkness, and they were lost more completely than ever. In a state of semi-coma brought on by his fear, Jao fell to the ground, and found dried bones under his body. He groped and found a skeletal ribcage and then a skull, and as he threw them from him he screamed out in abject terror.

He would have been even more terrified if he had known how long the skeleton had been there, undiscovered even by the people of Eden. It was the remains of one of the labyrinth's builders who had accidentally broken the long cord they were using as a guidelines to follow back to where they had started from. Uncounted hundreds of years ago, this unfortunate man had wandered for three weeks among the walls of the maze he had helped to construct, his lips swollen with thirst, his mouth drying out, his senses slowly leaving him; and at last he had given up and had lain down to die, not moving further for a week of days and nights till the lethargy of death had overtaken him.

For Jao Torres, the bones were a symbol, a warning that his gods were angry with him, and he stumbled off into the darkness in terror, turning at random. Carmen followed him, reaching out to hold onto his belt in her fear so that she would not lose him and be alone in this dreadful place. She wondered how many more nights and days they would spend here before, after one of those nights, they would not wake any more.

As Gerard moved from the labyrinth into the cellar, he saw that darkness had indeed fallen; there was a flare burning, and two of the bandits were approaching him, grinning. One of them said cheerfully, "Jao? He get them diamonds? We all be rich now? Where he is?"

He was peering into the darkness on the other side of the stone slab as Gerard drove a fist into his throat. He seized the hilt of the man's sabre as he fell, and drew it swiftly from its sheath. He turned to counter a raised sword as the second outlaw came at him with a look of shock on his face. For a brief moment they parried each other's blows, and then the first man was on his feet again, thrusting a long dagger forward. Gerard drew his blade across the windpipe and killed him, swinging it up again to counter another downward slice . . .

For a while, the two of them fought, and Gerard turned aside a fearful blow to his head and thrust his sword through that evil heart. He ran quickly out onto the dark street, and climbed at once to the rooftop. He was alone now, and his enemies were all about him. But like all of Eden's people, he knew the township's configuration well. He ran quietly and carefully, leaping from roof to roof, peering down from time to time through the high, narrow slits of the window apertures into flare-lit rooms. He came to the quarters where Thelma had lived, the statuesque beauty he remembered so well, and he saw one of the gang asleep on her bed, another seated nearby and honing a dagger on a piece of flat stone . . . In Barbara's room there were five of the outlaws' Indian women gathered, crouched over their cooking pots and the fires they had made; one of them was feeding broken pieces of a beautiful rosewood chair into the flames.

He moved on in absolute silence, like a cat, and found Candida's room. He stared down through the opening and caught his breath as he saw Yvonne there with another of the hostages, a quiet and gentle woman named Hilda. They were both bound, and lying on the cold granite floor. A guard was seated on the bed, a barrel-chested Indian dressed in rags with a musket across his knees; he was drinking as he stared disconsolately at the two women. Gerard felt his excitement rising; but there was no sign of either Shana or the Queen.

And then, he saw Yvonne's startled eyes open, almost as if she were conscious of someone watching. She was staring straight up at him in sudden astonishment; he fancied he could almost hear the acceleration of her heartbeat, and he quickly put a finger to his lips. She looked at the guard briefly, and then turned her face away, making no more sign that might betray his presence. He was already gauging the long drop down into the room when the door opened and five more armed men entered, and he shuddered as he saw them go straight to the women and start mauling them. He watched them for a while as they laughed and joked together down there, praying that at least some of them would leave. But they seemed in no hurry to go, and he knew that the time for the rescue had not yet come. He swore silently and made a mental note of just where they were, and moved on in search of the others. A moment later, he was looking down into the antechamber to Alma's Throne Room . . .

He saw, first, Alma the Queen, *his* Queen, lying on the silk-covered divan there. And Espada was on top of her, thrusting furiously into her . . . Gerard almost screamed. When he shifted his position and widened the angle of his view he saw his beloved Shana lying on the stone floor, naked and bound hand and foot.

It was a time for caution, but Gerard could no longer contain his rage. He heard a scream of anguish escape from his own throat, saw Espada turn from his pleasure down there to stare up at the opening in sudden shock.

Gerard forced himself through the narrow embrasure, not caring that the hard floor was nearly twenty feet below him. His ankle twisted horribly as he dropped down, but he pulled himself up and hurled himself at Espada, seizing him by the throat. He knew that he needed his sword now; but the weapon was still sheathed, and there was no time or patience to draw it.

He found the windpipe and drove his thumbs in hard, seeking to rupture it. But Espada was a skilled fighter, and he threw up both powerful arms in a wide sweep and broke the hold. With a movement so fast that Gerard could not follow it, the short sword was picked up from the floor and in Espada's hand; and as Gerard drew his own weapon he saw that the needle sharp point was at Alma's throat.

He heard the harsh voice, "One move, Gerard! And I fall on my point and drive it through her! Drop your weapon! Drop it!"

Gerard could only obey, and his sabre clattered to the floor. He stood balanced on the balls of his feet and waited, and then, an extraordinary thing happened . . .

A sharp sword point at her throat, Alma rolled slowly and deliberately off the divan, the steel following her every move, and stood close by them. It moved to her full breast now, penetrating the soft skin very slightly and drawing blood. Espada's eyes seemed not to leave Gerard, but he said to Alma, almost casually, "One more move, dear lady, and I will make a move of my own." He was standing in perfect balance, ready for the expert swordsman's lunge, though there was a look of uncertainty in his savage eyes now.

But Alma spoke very quietly as though there were no danger at all in her situation. "I have been vilely abused, Gerard. And he has told me . . . Shana is next."

Espada said furiously, "One move, Gerard, and I kill her!"

His sword was steady, over the area of her heart, and there was a thin trickle of blood between her breasts. But Alma did not flinch from it or give any sign that she felt it. Her low, melodious voice was tinged with a kind of scorn. "He holds me hostage, Gerard, for your good behavior now. It is not to be tolerated."

Gerard was shaking, ready to pounce but not daring to. Espada saw the look in his eyes and shouted, "On the floor, Gerard! Lie on the floor, or I kill her now, in front of your eyes . . ."

The needle point shifted and drew blood again, and still Alma did not move or pay it any heed at all . . . She had not attained her high position without reason; she was a woman of strong character and stronger determination. She whispered, "Gerard? There is only one thing to be done now, is there not? You must save the woman you love so dearly."

Understanding, Shana screamed: "No . . . !" a long, drawn out wail of anguish. And suddenly, Queen Alma threw out her arms and clutched her tormenter by the shoulders as she screamed, "Save your Shana, Gerard!"

She hurled herself foward, impaling herself on Espada's sword. As she died, she shrieked, "Kill him . . . !"

Gerard bellowed uncontrollably, and he heard Shana's moaning too. Blind with passion, he seized that murdering arm and snapped it across his knee, and then his hands were at Espada's throat again, forcing him to his knees as he slowly throttled the life out of him. Long after Espada was dead, Gerard still held that deadly grip, shaking the body in the paroxysm of his rage, and he threw it away at last like trash to be discarded forever.

He ran to Shana and freed her, sobbing, and together they knelt beside Alma's body, even more beautiful in death. Shana whispered through her tears, "I saw . . . I saw what he did to her, what both of them did to her,

Jao Torres too. How can the act of love be so savage and brutal?"

Gerard's voice was heavy with pain. "It is how my wife died, at the murderous hands of the same animals." The tears were rolling down his cheeks as he withdrew the sword from her breast, and picked up her body to lay it down on the divan. He crossed her arms and covered her with a silken sheet, and found another to wrap around Shana's figure, fastening it at her waist with a length of llamas' wool cord. He said quietly, "I have a war on my hands now, even more personal than it ever was before. There is murder in my heart. Come, we move to the rooftops."

He changed his sabre for Espada's more efficient weapon, testing its balance and finding it quite remarkable before making the choice. He helped Shana climb up to the roof, the only place he was sure they could be safe. They quickly found Candida's room, and to his great relief Yvonne and Hilda were still there, and there was only one man with them. The guard had been changed, but he was lying beside Yvonne now and mauling her breasts with coarse hands, laughing at the anguish in her eyes.

Gerard remembered the time he had physically loved her, with an exchange of the most gentle and exquisite caresses, and he shuddered. His hand tightened on Shana's wrist as he whispered, "Wait for me here, do not move an inch . . ."

He climbed down to the narrow street, dropping from one elevation to another, favoring his injured ankle. In silence, he gently pushed open the heavy door and moved into the flare lit room. He waited only an instant for his opponent, half-naked and startled out of his wits, to stagger to his feet and reach for his pistol, and then he drove the point of Espada's sword, which had already caused so much tragedy, through a muscular chest that was deeply scarred by previous battles. He heard Yvonne stifle a scream, saw a look of horror in Hilda's quiet eyes. He said quickly, "It was necessary, one less of our enemies."

He cut them free and took sheets from the divans for them to wear as *draperies,* and together they left that dreadful room and climbed up to where Shana was waiting. Yvonne whispered in the silence, "They have Alma too, in the antechamber, and Bianca, though I have not seen her since we were captured."

Shana, the tears welling in her eyes at the memory, shook her head. She told the tragic circumstances of Alma's death and felt the depression that settled on them both as they heard her; it seemed that even the darkness was pressing on them now. "A courageous death," Shana whispered. "She killed herself to save my life and Gerard's."

They heard men running on the street below them, and there was much confused shouting. There was a distant cry, "Espada is dead!" and another, "Jao! Where is Torres?"

The outlaws were gathering together, it seemed, in fear of another raid, and the fugitives pressed themselves into the rooftop shadows as they listened. Gerard whispered, "There is an entrance to the main underground water conduit just below us. I do not think they have discovered it. I will take you along it to the outskirts of the town, and there . . . you must make your way very carefully back to the swamp without me, can you do that? It will be safe, they will not attack us tonight, they have trouble enough in the town."

Shana held him tight. "But . . . you must come with

271

us, Gerard! It will be too dangerous for you here now, they will all be searching for you."

"No. I cannot do that. There is still one more hostage to be freed. Bianca."

Her arms were gripping him fiercely as she spoke, "Yvonne and Hilda will go. I will stay with you!"

Gerard shook his head. He said gently, "It cannot be, my dearest. I cannot fight if you are by my side to be protected, and it may be that I will have to fight a great deal. I *must* know that you are safe."

"I am so frightened for you! They all know that you are here now . . ."

He laughed shortly and said, "No, that is not true. It is more likely that they imagine the township to be overrun with a hundred of us. It means that they will be on the defensive, not looking for me at all but seeking to protect themselves. And do not be frightened for me. There is a very hard night ahead of us, with almost no moon, and I always find the dark very comforting. I will not return until I have found Bianca! And you will take a message for me to Emlyn."

For a long time, she would not let him go, but she understood his argument. They found their way at last into the underground conduit that carried the main body of the water from the river to the township, it was almost dry now that the dam had been built. They crept on together to the point where it emerged among the bullrushes just beyond the walls of the furthest *conviveri*.

Gerard held her tightly, and kissed her lovingly as he whispered, "From here, it is safe. You are sure that you can find your way to the swamp in the darkness?"

"Yes."

He forced a little joke. "Remember that the tiny blue frogs that roar like heavy cannon are your friends . . ."

"Yes, I will do so."

"Find Emlyn urgently. Tell him what has happened. Tell him to take no action at all until he hears from me by whatever means I can devise. When the people learn of Alma's death, I know what will happen. The Strong Men, God bless them, will rise up in justifiable fury, and they will want to attack the town at once. They must not do this! Our enemies have taken casualties, but they are still *not* vulnerable to an assault by angry, unskilled fighting men. It will be hard for them, I know. But they *must* wait! Will you tell them this?"

"Yes, I will make sure he understands, though it gives me no comfort."

"Trust me." He kissed her eyes, sad now that she feared for him so greatly. Yvonne too held him close, and she whispered, "Already, Gerard, there is a debt to you that Eden can never repay."

And then, Hilda's arms were about him, and she was choking back her deep emotion. He knew that she was not a very demonstrative woman, but her eyes were moist as she hugged him. She too said, "A debt, greater than we can *ever* hope to pay."

"I blame myself for Alma's death," Gerard said heavily. "There was *something* I should have done, though I have not yet discovered what it was. When I find the answer to that question . . . it will haunt me all the days of my life."

Shana said in anguish, "No, no, no!" He embraced her again, and said gently, "Go now. There are still some hours to daylight, but you must hurry. Across the meadows, move only in shadow. And as quickly as you can."

He watched them moving off across the fields, faintly lit by the clouded moon, keeping close to the patches of shrubbery. When they disappeared from his sight, he moved back into the water where the bullrushes were and entered the conduit that would lead him back into the center of the town.

Somewhere back there, there was one more hostage, Bianca. He remembered her as a sweet and kindly woman of quite indefinable age whom he had loved on at least three occasions. She had always fed him apricot kernels in between their love-making and had said, 'Just a few, they will make you strong again . . .'

She was darker-skinned than most of Eden's women, but her Edenite eyes were the lightest he had ever seen, and more slanted than most. When she had loved him, he had always felt that she was searching for his soul as well as his body.

She was a close and dear friend of Shana's. He said to himself, in anger at her present situation, *I will find her, or die in the attempt* . . .

Of the five hostages the monster Jao had taken, one had been killed, three had been rescued . . . and there was one more still to be found. In the dark confines of the underground conduit, he said aloud, "Bianca! Where are you?"

Chapter Seventeen

Since the years of his infancy, Jao Torres had never wept in all of his life; but he was weeping now, copious tears of frustration, anguish, and fear.

'Corridors that twist and turn back on themselves and come to dead ends,' Espada had told him, explaining what a maze was. And at the time, Jao had thought very little of it, regarding it as some childish game to amuse idiots. But he had come to realize, now the awful danger. Turn and turn and turn again; and again and again, time after time, with still no sign of a way out . . .

He was a man of no education at all, but there was a kind of crude intelligence in him that told him his death was inevitable now, though the dying might last for weeks. And so, he was weeping. This was not the kind of death he had ever expected, slow and lingering, growing more certain as the terrifying days and nights slipped slowly by. And for company—only a woman he both loved and hated. He was lying on his back in the sealed up dark. She was crouched over him and driving her fists into his face, trying without success to pummel him into unconsciousness and screaming, "Pig! Why you bring me here to die . . . ?"

He did not even attempt to ward off her blows. Instead, he stumbled to his feet and ran off, turning corner after random corner, not even conscious of left or right, knowing only that he was still not rid of her. When he fell to the ground she collapsed on top of him, wailing, "No, don't leave me now. I don't want to die alone . . ."

She was wiser than he was, and even more aware of the fate that was to be theirs now, wandering aimlessly till they dropped from exhaustion, to be lost for all eternity, their bones to bleach like the skull that Jao had found and hurled from him in such terror, Clasped in each other's arms, and silent now in their mutual fears, they lay still, both of them wondering how long it might be before the end came.

But suddenly, he felt a stiffening of her body, a tightening of her arms around his chest, and he heard her gasp. She whispered, "A light . . ."

Instinctively, he swung round, and croaked, "I see it." It was indeed a light, amber-colored and weaving back and forth as it cast its own eerie shadows, and it was gone almost as soon as he saw it. But then it was there again, appearing mysteriously out of what looked like the unbroken face of the carved wall at the end of the long corridor. It was a flare, and there was a worried face in its light now, the face of one of their men whose name was Askula. And even more startling, Jao could see, lit by the flames, the edge of the open stone door that was the labyrinth's entrance, only thirty paces or so from where they were huddling.

Its import struck Carmen first, and she screamed and ran towards it, and disappeared from Jao's sight as she threw herself in panic through the opening. He was close on her heels, and he knocked Askula down in his haste to leave this frightening place, dropping to the ground in the Temple's cellar and lying there gasping. He would never know that the chance which had brought him to safety in his disordered ramblings was one in millions, perhaps in thousands of millions. He rolled over onto his knees, his frantic face lifted up, his cruel eyes wide as he shrieked aloud an old Indian prayer of thanks to the Gods who had so miraculously saved him.

Carmen was lying on her back beside him, emotionally drained and staring blankly up at the ceiling. And then, she was conscious that there was a dead man close beside her, his throat sliced open. As she stared in horror, she saw another corpse lying there with a great bloodstain on its chest; the flames were dancing over the ashen bodies, and the newly found safety of the cellár had become another hell. She was accustomed to the sight of dead men, but in her present state they were unnerving in the extreme, and she howled like a she-wolf.

As Jao climbed to his feet and stared down on them, Askula picked up the flare he had dropped and said thickly, "Ten, twenty, maybe fifty men come into town, we don't see none of them. They kill Jose here, and this crazy Indian Krasi. They kill Manuel, guarding one prisoner." He licked his lips and said, grinning wildly, "They kill Espada too."

Carmen stopped her howling and stared at him. "Espada . . . is *dead?*"

"Espada dead." A long, low moan escaped her lips, and she fell back to the ground, doubled up and not trying to contain the tears that would not stop coming as she rocked to and fro in utter abandonment. She whispered, "Espada, Espada, why you leave me?" In a few moments she looked up to see Jao towering over her, his face suffused with rage, and very briefly, she held his look. She did not wait for the question she knew was coming now, the accusation. She said quietly, "Yes, I am weeping for Espada. . . ."

He roared out his fury and reached down to drag her to her feet, and slapped his hand back and forth across her tearful face with uncontrolled savagery. He felt her go limp at last, and hurled her away from him as he snarled, "Now you seeing what happen, I giving you to my men . . ." He did not know whether she was still conscious or not as she lay there, nor did he care. He turned to Askula and growled, "Them people coming here? They still here?"

Askula shook his head. "I don't know, I don't see nobody."

Jao's hard eyes were on him. "You telling me fifty men."

"Maybe more, I don't know. I see anybody. I finish up like Espada, like Jose, Manuel, Krasi. I finish up dead."

Jao drove a powerful fist into Askula's battered face and screamed, "You go finding all men, Askula! Bringing women here too, all one place now! Maybe we killing one two, is hanging bodies on walls, showing them people Jao Torres, good fighting man . . ." But he broke off when he saw the look on Askula's face, knowing that worse was to come. He heard the soft, effeminate voice, "We don't got women prisoners no more, Jao. All finish, gone now."

Jao stared. "*Gone?*"

"All gone now, no more left."

Jao was in shock. His only weapon had been spirited away; and the diamonds he had come here for seemed further removed from his grasp than ever.

He fell into a deep and brooding silence.

* * *

Gerard was back on the rooftops, worrying about the oncoming dawn as he searched *conviveri* after *conviveri* for the missing Bianca. He moved from one end of the township to the other in despair; many of the rooms were devoid of flares, but would she be in one of these? He thought not. There would be at least one guard with her, and surely it would mean some sort of lighting.

The first red rays of the sun began to illuminate the gray stone walls, and he knew that he could not escape detection for very much longer. Twice, he lay still and silent as he heard men moving on the narrow streets below him, whispering together as though they knew that there was an unseen enemy nearby.

He moved on, and at last, he found her. He peered down through a high embrasure and saw her lying on a divan in Yvonne's room, very faintly lit by the approaching red-gray of the dawn. She was quite naked, her hands bound behind her back, and she was lying on her side in a position he was sure must be painful. Her eyes were closed, her face very pale; there was not enough light to see how steadily she was breathing, and he could not guess whether she was asleep or unconscious.

The drop down into the room was too deep for his damaged and unreliable ankle, but the door to the street was just below him. He climbed down the outside of the building and studied his surroundings carefully, knowing that even this faint light was a great danger. As he crept to the door, he heard a sudden shout from very close by, and spun round . . .

He saw three of the bandits racing towards him down the narrow alley, and drew the sword that had once been Espada's. He thrust out a foot and hurled the first of them to the ground, and raised his weapon to deflect

279

a monstrous blow that came at him, cutting into his shoulder before he was able to stop it. The blood pounded out and his left arm was numbed, and he knew that he was in no condition to fight against two strong swordsmen.

But there was still too much work to be done to permit him to lie down and die . . . He roared out his fury, and flailed the sword like a madman, blinded by his rage; in desperation he charged at them, through them, and past them. The unexpected maneuver disconcerted them, and he had ducked into a doorway before they recovered, running quickly down a short flight of steps and through an archway before doubling back on his tracks. He heard them racing straight on, and waited a moment before struggling with the heavy slab of a conduit cover to drop down into the welcoming darkness. The coma was already beginning to sweep over him, and he forced himself into the effort to close the opening . . .

There was blood pouring down his side, and he tore off a length of his woolen *draperi* and bound the wound tightly to staunch the flow. He was in a fury with himself now. Bianca was still out there; he knew where she was. There were some twelve hours of daylight ahead of him now when he would be powerless to help her! How great was her suffering already? And how much more would be visited on her while he waited interminably for the sun to go down? He thought for a while of a daytime attempt, and knew that it would be useless; and so, he forced all the anguish into the farthest reaches of his mind, and compelled upon himself a patience that did not easily come to him.

He had lost a great deal of blood, and he was weak, and he spent a great deal of time cursing volubly to him-

self until he realized that it was not a very profitable oc-
cupation. He found a dry elevation to lie down on,
knowing that even a few hours of rest now might bring
back at least some of his strength. He said to himself
with that stubborn practicality that was his. "*Hours* must
pass now before I can continue with my work, but they
will not be wasted; I will use them to recover, through
rest, some of my capability." But he wept at the thought
of the further tribulations Bianca might have to suffer
before he could rescue her from them.

He thought of his beloved Shana, and where was she
now? Had she reached the comparative safety of the
swamp? Had she found Emlyn? What would Emlyn be
doing now? How would the gentle people react to the
death of their greatly loved Queen? And *Shana, Shana,
Shana . . .* In the throes of utter exhaustion, he fell into
a restless comalike sleep, and he dreamed of her.

Eden, in that dream, was as he had known it—
peaceful, serene, and enchanting. He was exploring the
underground passages, measuring the depth of the
water at every fifty paces as Shana, beside him, wrote
down the figures from which he would later make his
calculations. It had been a long day for both of them,
and toward evening Gerard had said, smiling, "Out
there where the civilized people live, it will be dark
soon, I think. Shall we return to the gardens and join
the others?"

"Yes," Shana had said. "I think it must soon be the
gathering-hour. But . . . before we go back to find our
friends, will you love me?"

They were on a kind of path in the conduit, made of
flat granite stones that had been laid alongside the
course of the water, and without more ado they lay down
side by side and began fondling each other. Shana's

fingertips were tracing the contours of the strong muscles on his chest, moving over his hard, taut stomach and caressing him. There was not light enough to see what a handsome man he was, but she already knew this! There was a great excitement for her in the touch of his flesh, strong and pulsating, surely the strongest man in the world! He felt her holding him and positioning herself just so, brushing herself with him and thrusting onto him when she could no longer tolerate the arousal.

He stared up, in his dream, into the cruel face of Jao Torres, a laughing face that was saying, "Better you take my Carmen instead, she very good for you . . ." The face was weaving in and out of focus, swinging wildly around, and the features become those of Bianca, and she was whispering to him, "There is great strength in you, Gerard, you are indeed a Worthy Man."

It was Carmen's face now, and she was between the confining walls of the labyrinth, crawling to him on all fours, seeking him out with cruel hands that savaged him intolerably, and he felt the bite of her sharp teeth on him. And that huge and monstrous face of Jao Torres, painted in purples that changed to green and then to red, was suddenly the face of Espada, and there was a sword, slender and sharp-pointed, held at the breast of the woman he loved, and it was Dora, his late wife. As the sword plunged home, Carmen swooped in on him, laughing wildly, and then Torres was there again, leering.

Gerard awoke with a start and drew the sword he had taken from Espada, wondering why it seemed suddenly to be so monstrously heavy. It fell from his grasp and clattered to the ground, and, reaching for it, he fell and could not rise again. He felt the pad at his shoulder and found it soaked with his blood, and in a moment of alarm he knew that he was far more badly hurt than he had at first imagined. He struggled to his knees and removed the bandage, and reformed the *draperi* to bind it more tightly and staunchly to stop the dangerous flow, wondering how much blood he had lost, how much more he had to lose.

He forced himself to his feet with an effort of will far beyond his physical tolerance. It was a mistake; he fell again, and lost his consciousness completely.

Shana was in the swamp, with Emlyn and a hundred or more of the others who had left their hideouts to hear the news; more of them were moving in to join the group, Strong Men, Wise Men, women with babies in their arms, and young girls.

When she said, biting her lip to hold back the tears, "Alma our Queen is dead," a great wailing came from the crowd.

Then Emlyn lifted up his arms and called out urgently, "Hear me, my friends! People of Eden, listen to me!" There was an almost immediate silence. He continued, more quietly now, "Alma is dead. I believe that our good friend Gerard may well be dead too. Shana has told me that he would not leave the township till he found, and rescued, the last of the hostages, Bianca whom we all love so dearly."

He took a deep breath and said quietly, "He wants us to do nothing, and I know that to be because he fears for our lives but not his own. Even a man of Gerard's spirit and bravery cannot fight against such heavy odds, and we have been remiss in allowing him to attempt it. I believe that we should now take matters into our own hands and do two things. The first of these is . . . rescue

Gerard and Bianca if they are still alive. And the second is . . ." He raised his voice, "To avenge Alma!" The crowd roared its approval. Emlyn shouted, "Then let it be so! Lindsay! How many spearmen do we have now?"

Lindsay was carried away by his emotions, and he shook his spear and shouted, "Nearly four hundred men, and a hundred of the women who want to fight too. We are five hundred strong and more, and Gerard has taught us how to fight, and against what? Thirty or forty of our enemies? By sheer force of numbers we can overwhelm them!"

"Many of us will be cut down by their guns before we even reach the walls . . ."

"And many others will survive to do what has to be done!"

"Very well, then. But first . . ." He raised his arms again to call for silence. "Our Queen is dead, and the next in succession, as decided long ago by the full Concord, is Ferida. Is Ferida among us?"

She rose up from among the group of women where she had been sitting, and moved towards him with a strange and ethereal kind of gait, a woman of great beauty and the most extraordinary composure. There was already a regal quality about her as she said quietly, "Yes, I am next in line. And I now take Alma's mantle on my shoulders, in the hope that I can serve the people of Eden as well as she has served us for more than fifty years."

The crowd was hushed by the simple solemnity of the occasion. Emlyn said gently, "Then I await your orders, Ferida."

She stood tall and straight, her head held high. "You are the wisest of the Wise Men, Emlyn," she said. "It is your duty to advise me on matters about which I know very little."

"And that advice," Emlyn said clearly, "is that under Lindsay's command, we advance on the town in force, and see what we can accomplish."

"Then do what must be done, Emlyn," Ferida said, and that great shout went up again. The gentle society of Eden, for the first time in its long history, was on a warpath. And these peaceful, sweet-natured people, armed only with the most primitive of weapons, were ready to fight to the death in defense of all that they held most dear. Unaccustomed to action of this kind, they were disorganized and even bewildered. But they were not cowards, and there was not one among them who was not prepared to lay down his or her life to preserve the refined philosophies of their beloved community against the intrusion of a hostile outside world. Come what may, they were ready.

There was one dissenting voice, and it was Shana's . . . She waited till the uproar had died down, then she laid a hand on Emlyn's arm. She said quietly, "I know more, I think, of what is in Gerard's mind than any of us here, do you agree with me?"

Emlyn nodded. "Yes, of course."

"He told us to do nothing, and as you say it is because he fears for our lives. But were he here now, I know what he would say, and that is that an attack on the town in daylight would be foolhardy. Even a score of men, armed as they are with guns, could hold the township against a very large army in daylight. We must wait for darkness."

Emlyn sighed. "Perhaps you are right," he murmured. "But to stand by and do nothing for so long . . . it will tax our patience beyond endurance!"

"I know it. But it will not be just idle waiting. Gerard would say, 'In that time, let the men practice with their spears, have Lindsay split them up into small parties like the one he himself led that night so that all of them will not be more vulnerable than they need be.'"

Emlyn frowned darkly. "Yes," he said, "that would seem to make sense." He looked up at the sky. "But . . . so many long hours of daylight left!"

"In which time," Shana said, "one more vital objective must be achieved."

"And that is . . . ?"

"In the belief that he must continue to act alone," Shana said clearly, "Gerard will continue to take the most appalling risks, as he has already been doing. If he knows that help is coming at nightfall, he will be more circumspect, he will take no rash and desperate action that might easily result in his death. And so, we must tell him."

"If only that could be done! I agree, it would be greatly desirable. But what? Send a man into the township to look for him? We cannot even guess where he might be!"

"I *know* where he will be," Shana said calmly. "He has told me time and time again that under circumstances like these he will fight only in the dark. It means that during the daylight hours, he will be in hiding."

"Yes, but where? It makes it all the less likely that a messenger could find him."

"No. Because I *know* where he will be hiding. It will be without a doubt in one of the underground conduits that only he and I together, among all the people of Eden, know intimately. So I will go to him, and I will warn him of what has been planned."

Emlyn stared at her in shock. "Shana! You are mad!"

"No. I am a woman in love."

"Once, by a chance in a thousand, you escaped . . ."

"Not *escaped,* I was rescued by Gerard."

"And you will go back to find him, even though he may well be dead?"

"I will go back. And if he is dead, which I do not believe, then my own life means nothing to me."

Emlyn was stunned. He looked at Ferida for help, and saw only a strangely fierce light in her eyes. He turned back to Shana and said quietly, "The danger must be very apparant to you."

"Gerard's greater danger must not be his alone. He *must* be warned! And no one else can do that. I know every inch of those secret conduits, and I will find him."

Emlyn threw up his arms in frustration. Ferida had been listening carefully, and she laid a hand on Shana's shoulder as she spoke. "Go to him, Shana, if you must, a woman must always do what her instincts tell her to do, it is one of the things that make us superior to men."

"Then take two or three of the Strong Men with you!" Emlyn said desperately. But Shana shook her head and said, "No. As you say, there is danger. I will not needlessly risk the lives of men who will soon be needed for the battle."

"One man, then!" Emlyn was almost in tears. "I myself will go with you!"

"No, your place is here now. I will go alone."

She kissed Ferida quickly on both cheeks, and embraced Emlyn warmly. "I will add to what Gerard has said," she whispered. "Do nothing . . . until it is *dark.*"

And so, in broad daylight with the hot sun still streaming down, Shana began her long and difficult journey back to the town, alone and secretly terrified of the ordeal ahead of her. But she would not let her fears overcome her strong determination.

Chapter Eighteen

Shana waded resolutely through the swamp and pulled herself gratefully up onto dry ground where the forest began, and it had never before seemed to her such a lonely place. The great green trees, thickly interspersed with tall ferns, were lit with dappled sunlight.

It was only when she came at last to the edge of the woods and stared across the meadows to the distant township that she truly began to realize the enormous difficulty of her task. She stood for a while in the shade of a tall bamboo clump, and studied the ground ahead of her carefully. On the direct line to the town, there were many places where the grasses were too short to allow her sufficient cover, but they were long and thick between here and the river. It was the conduit's main exit at the river that she had to reach. She dropped to her hands and knees and crawled on, trying to remember just how high the riverbanks were here; she was sure that for most of the way they were high enough to hide her.

She wrapped her *draperi* round and around the lower part of her slender body and slid into the water. It was very cold, coming down from the top of the mountain, fresh and clear and running fast with a very pleasant sound.

Using the breaststroke—the only stroke the Edenites knew—she swam slowly and silently towards the town. Once, she heard a sudden flurry of sound like running footsteps coming from the bank above her, and she pulled in under its lee in terror, finding protruding roots to hide under. It was four or five feet above her head, and hide as she might, she was sure that she would be discovered.

A llama poked its head over the brink and stared at her briefly before cantering off again, and she breathed a deep sigh of relief; where there were llamas, there would not be people . . . She swam on patiently, and in less than two hours she could see, over the red sandstone lip of the bank, the gray walls of the town, very close now and alarming in their unaccustomed silence; two men, armed with muskets, were standing on one of the rooftops and looking out towards the forest. She pulled back below the bank, and swam on to the stand of bull rushes that masked the conduit's discharge, and clambered into the great circular tunnel, very low in water now since the dam at its other end had been so hastily built. In a silence that was frightening, she began to move slowly towards the center of the town; every few steps she made, the darkness closed in on her more and more.

But she was sure that this was where he would be! And equally sure that she would find him! She found the main subsidiary tunnel, which they had once cleared together, and there was very little water here now, hardly more than a trickle. As she moved along it, something at her feet rattled on the granite floor, and she stooped and picked up Espada's sword . . . She stared at it for a moment, trembling, and searched the darkness around her. She found him lying only a few paces away, still and silent, and she crouched beside him in an agony of alarm. There was blood all over his chest, but when she felt for his heartbeat it was strong. She found his *draperi* and wrung it out quickly, and bound it over his shoulder and under his arms, pulling it tight, putting part of it under his neck so that his head hung back a little to ease his heavy breathing.

And then, she waited, knowing that there was nothing else she could do now except dry her tears and hope. She knelt beside him, comforting herself by feeling for that heartbeat time and time again, splashing cool water over his forehead in the hope that it might revive him. She held his hand and thought of the many times they had loved each other, kneeling beside him and telling herself that if he died, then she would simply lie down beside him and wait for death to take her too.

She could not count the hours as they passed, but when he stirred at last she bent down and kissed him on the lips, and found that his breathing was more regular now. She whispered, "Gerard? Gerard my love . . . You will live, you *must* live!"

It seemed an age before he answered her. His eyes opened, and he clutched at her hand and murmured, "Shana? Is it truly you? Where are we?"

"Yes, it is your Shana, and we are safe here. Lie still, do not try to move, you have been hurt."

"Ah yes. I remember . . ." He was quite suddenly more alert, and in spite of her efforts to hold him still he struggled to a sitting position. He said, astonished, "But what . . . what are you doing here!" His voice was weak, but he was forcing the strength back into it.

"Lie down," she whispered, "you must lie still now."

291

"No, I must . . . must . . ." He gasped and fell back again, and for a few minutes the coma took hold of him again, and once more she waited, knowing that most of the danger was gone now. When he came back to his senses he sat up once again and said harshly: "No! I cannot allow myself to weaken!" Almost fighting her, he stood up and leaned heavily into the tunnel wall to stop the swaying. When the walls had ceased swinging wildly around him he muttered, "There is still . . . still work to be done! Bianca . . . I know where she is . . . And now . . . now that it is dark, I must go to her."

She stood up and put her arms around him, her head on his chest. "It is not dark outside yet," she whispered. "There are a few more hours of daylight left. How many, I do not know, though I will soon find out. Come, lie down beside me, there is nothing we can do until it is night."

"Ah yes . . ." He dropped heavily to the ground and whispered, "You are right, of course. Only when our friend the night comes can we move from here. And then, Bianca. She is in Yvonne's room." He was talking more rationally now, and taking firm hold on himself; but she knew that, for the moment at least, his mind was far stronger than his body. He said, puzzled, "And will you tell me how it is you come to be here? This is no place for the woman I love so dearly."

She told him in great detail what had transpired in the swamp, of Emlyn's plan to attack the town that night, of her own determination to warn him of what was happening. His hand was tight around hers as he whispered, "It was a brave thing for you to do, my love, and foolhardy in the extreme. You could so easily have been recaptured, and I fear that you would have been killed at once. Even so . . . I owe you my life, I am sure of

292

it. If you had not stopped the flow of blood . . ."

"Sshhh! What use would my life be to me if you were not at my side? And will you lie still and wait for me here?"

"Wait for you?"

"I must find out how much of light there is left. I will go to the end of the conduit where it reaches the river, and return at once."

"We will go together . . ."

"No! You are far too weak . . ."

"I must find out how well or badly I can walk."

"Very well, then." She helped him to his feet, and put an arm around his waist to support him, and together, they walked very slowly all the way to the exit. There, they looked out on the still bright daylight over the distant mountain. Gerard whispered, "Four hours, no more, and the darkness will be absolute save for the moon. Good."

They found a new waiting place, directly under one of the hidden access slabs that Gerard knew to be very close to Yvonne's room where he had seen Bianca's shadowy form. There was a tiny chink in the stone above them, and the light outside was still bright. The four more hours passed very slowly as they sat together in mutual embrace. He whispered, "As soon as we take Bianca, we will return to the swamp. I must lead this attack myself."

Shana protested, "No, you cannot! You must leave the fighting to Lindsay and the others!"

"It is my left side that is wounded," Gerard said. "My sword arm is still strong."

"No, I beg of you! You have done enough already . . ."

"I will have done enough, perhaps," he answered her,

"when peace has returned to Eden, not before." He stared up at the chink of light, almost *willing* it to darken, and said, "When the time comes, we will go together to Bianca, I do not want you to leave my side now. We will leave the slab open for our hasty return here, it will be for only a moment or two . . ."

"And the outlaws?"

Gerard sighed. "I would be happier, I will confess," he said slowly, "if I knew where they are. But they have taken very serious losses and they have no leader now, not even Espada, who was Jao's second-in-command. It is my guess that they will all be huddled together for mutual protection, and wondering what might happen now. But where?" He thought for a moment and said, "It is only a guess, but perhaps they will be in the Throne Room, which was their headquarters when Jao was there to lead them. In any event . . . we will move in absolute silence to do what we have to do. Then, the three of us will go back into the conduit to hurry to its discharge, across the meadow and the forest to the swamp, to see what our army is doing."

They lay close beside each other, and his hand was at her breast, seeking from the soft touch the comfort that was so dear to him. He slept for a while, seeking also the swiftest way to some sort of recovery.

The chink in the stonework showed them at last that the daylight was disappearing, and when it had quite gone Gerard eased the heavy slab aside; with only one functioning arm it was not easy, but with Shana's help it was opened slowly, and they climbed out onto the dark street and went quickly to Yvonne's *conviveri*. Very softly, Gerard eased the door open and they went inside.

It was pitch dark in there, but they moved slowly and carefully to where they knew the divan was, and Gerard reached down, groping . . .

He stifled a gasp as he touched Bianca's cold hard flesh that was the flesh of a marble statue, a body long dead, and heard Shana catch her breath too. He clutched her and held her tightly, and broke the anguished silence with a whisper, "I should have seen . . . I thought she was merely unconscious, or perhaps even sleeping."

The silence and the darkness were oppressive as they went back to the lifeline of the conduit. When the slab was firmly in place over their heads, Shana said brokenly, "Bianca was my friend . . ."

"Yes, and mine too. And now, I have even more reason to fight, as I will." He was tight with fury as they went quickly along the main tunnel to where it fed into the river beyond the city walls. When they emerged in the darkness, the sight and sounds that met them brought Gerard's heart into his mouth and tears into his eyes . . .

In the far distance where the meadows ended and the forest began, there were the flickering lights of what looked like nearly a thousand flares dancing in the night. And even from so far away the unison of raised and fervent voices came to then, singing the most incongruous of songs.

The people of Eden knew no battle hymns, those rousing choruses that had driven soldiers beyond the borders of valor since time began. But they knew, if only an ancient instinct, the value of marching songs, and so, to the accompaniment of a few musical instruments that were almost drowned by the hubbub, they were singing their hearts out. It was an old lament by an English poet, but its tempo was remarkably well-suited to the pounding of marching, determined feet:

There is a tavern in the town, in the town,
And there, my true love sits him down, sits him down,
And drinks his wine with a damsel on his knee,
And never, never thinks of me, thinks of me . . .

Shana was in tears as she watched the distant flares and listened to the singing. She whispered, "An avenging army on the march . . ."

The strong voices rose on the night breeze:

Fare thee well, for I must leave thee,
Do not let this parting grieve thee,
But remember that the best of friends must part, must part.
Adieu, kind friends, adieu, adieu, adieu, adieu,
I can no longer stay with you, stay with you,
I'll hang my harp on the weeping willow tree, And may the world go well with thee . . .

"Not an army yet," Gerard said quietly, "but an angry multitude. We will go to them now, and that is what we will turn them into—an avenging army on the march."

Together, hand in hand, they moved off to join the approaching throng of Edenites. It was an hour before they reached them, and Gerard was glad to see that two of the Strong Men, Broderick and Martin, carrying no flares and moving very carefully indeed, were several hundred yards ahead of the main body, scouting. They both embraced him warmly, and kissed Shana, and Martin turned back and cupped his mouth with both hands

296

to send his powerful voice rolling back to the others. *"Gerard and Shana! They are here . . . !"*

At once, the singing stopped, and as Gerard and Shana ran towards them, Emlyn was hurrying forward too. He threw his arms around Gerard and held him tightly, and said in deep emotion, "Thank God, thank God . . . In my weakness I had almost given you up for dead."

"And dead I would have been," Gerard said gravely, "had Shana not found me and staunched a very serious loss of blood while I lay there like an unconscious fool, not strong enough to tend to my own wound."

Emlyn's eyes were wide. He touched the bloodied pad at Gerard's shoulder and said, alarmed, "And now?"

"The blood is caking already, it is a good sign. A few days, a week or two perhaps, with constant immersion in Eden's healing springs . . . We have suffered worse wounds, you and I."

Emlyn took Shana in his arms and kissed her. He said fervently, "I can never thank you enough for what you have done, Eden will never be able to thank you enough."

Gerard told them of Bianca's death, and Emlyn groaned. "Oh, God . . . but tonight, we drive these monsters out of Eden forever."

"Yes," Gerard said. He hesitated, and then spoke, "It is about this that we must talk now."

The vast army had come to encircle them. He said quietly, "All of the flares are to be doused now." One by one, they went out, and when there was only the light of the moon he said, "Lindsay? Is Lindsay among us?"

"Here, Gerard . . ." The blonde young giant stepped forward and said, "We are ready. Ready to do your bidding, and to fight."

"Good. How many men do you have under arms?"

"Six hundred and forty bamboo spears have been cut and hardened with fire, and perhaps two hundred daggers."

"How many are in the hands of the Strong Men?"

"About half that number. I made no count of the women and children who are fighting with us."

"The women and children will lay down their arms and stay here."

Lindsay stared at him; the moon, rising over the mountain, cast a strange sheen of light over his hair. "What? But they are almost half our force!"

"I know it," Gerard said. "but I will not have women and children subjected to the dangers we must now face. This battle will be fought by men alone, as is right."

A strong yet gentle voice came to him out of the darkness, and it was Ferida's. She said softly, "Our society, Gerard, which is now yours, is matriarchal, as you know. It means not only an assumption of authority by the women, it means that we must fight too in defense of our homes."

Before Gerard could answer her, Emlyn spoke quickly. "With Alma gone, Gerard, Ferida is Queen now . . ."

"Then I will obey your orders, ma'am," Gerard said. "But with your permission, I would like to fight this battle as I see fit? I mean no disrespect at all, as you must know . . ."

"The great Alma herself," Ferida said clearly, "declared you to be a Wise Man, and it is our custom that the Queen accept, when she may, the advice of her Wise Men. Therefore, do what you think is best. You have my most complete confidence, which has been well-earned."

"I thank you, ma'am."

"Not ma'am, but *Ferida*. We have been lovers, it gives you certain privileges."

"Er . . . yes, ma'am. Ferida."

"Then tell Lindsay what must be done now."

"Yes ma'am."

He turned to Lindsay. "I say again, the women and children will lay down their arms, or better still hand them over to the Strong Men who will do the fighting, two spears are better than one. And your force will be divided into two, one small, and one large. I will lead the smaller of them in an attack on the town, and our objective will be their utter destruction. I will take with me fifty men only . . ."

Lindsay was almost wailing. "Fifty men? They will destroy you!"

"No. In darkness, they will be unaware of our numbers." He looked around at the huge crowd and said slowly, "By showing yourselves in such force, by the sound of your singing, you have broken the first rule in this kind of warfare. You have shown them some indication of our strength, which is almost always a mistake. But in this case . . ." He laughed shortly. "They have already taken heavy losses, and where there were once forty of fifty, there can only be, now, twenty or thirty of them. What will so few do in the face of so many? They will flee! In panic! Therefore, Lindsay will take the main force to the steps, their only way out. When we descend on them in the township, in small number that will be multiplied ten-fold by the darkness, they will run for the steps. And that is where Lindsay, with his major force, will be waiting for them. I must tell you that if even a single one of them escapes, the legend of Raman-li-Undara will soon become known to be true throughout the length and breadth of the Amazon Basin. It means that within a year, other adventurers will descend on us, perhaps as much as a thousand strong next time. And all of this tragedy will be played over once again, but more formidably. They *must not* be allowed to escape and spread the word of what they have discovered."

To his surprise, the new Queen Ferida rose and came to him. She took his hand and pressed it to her cheek as she whispered, "Gerard . . . Eden would be lost if it were not for you."

Her great beauty in the moonlight was stunning to the mind as she embraced him; and he wondered if it were with the emotion of her new authority, or something else. She reached up and kissed him on the lips, and said quietly, "Once, you rescued Shana from certain death. Now, go with my blessing and do what has to be done to rescue Eden too."

In the town, the battle was very brief. The outlaws, only twenty-six strong now, were not leaderless as Gerard had supposed; Jao had come back to rally them with his absolute authority. That authority was fading now that Espada was dead; many of them knew that the late lieutenant had been the brains of this loosely knit gang of murderers. They were on the walls of the township, knowing that an attack was imminent now. They had seen the flares and even heard the singing, and could not understand why it was that there was only darkness and silence now.

Jao growled, "They creeping up on us . . ." and his men tried to mask their fears. They were scattered around the immediate vicinity of the Throne Room's roof in twos and threes, and one of them, an Indian of almost pure blood whose name was Busili, heard the

300

whisper of a sound behind him and turned in sudden alarm. He had hidden himself well, and how could an enemy find him under such close concealment? He fired his musket at a shadow, and screamed out for his life as a thrown spear ploughed into his heart.

There were other shots being uselessly fired, and many of the bandits died as they dropped their muskets and drew their swords.

Gerard, alone, was prowling, with Espada's naked sword in his good hand. He saw a shadow moving, and crouched waiting . . . The shadow rose up and became the form of a man, and he stared in utter disbelief: it was Jao Torres, whom he knew to be lost in the intricacies of the labyrinth. In sudden rage, he screamed out his fury and hurled his sword like a throwing-knife. Jao fell back with practiced ease and rolled over the rooftop; Gerard ran and stared down into the abyss below him and saw nothing but darkness. He could only stare in absolute shock.

Outside of this personal encounter, the battle was going well. There were only a dozen or so of the bandits still alive now, and they left the township and ran in panic for the steps, convinced that their attackers were numbered in the thousands. As they began the long and arduous climb up the incredible twelve thousand steps, more of those deadly shadows appeared from out of bushes, from behind great boulders, from the steps above them . . . Some of them were armed with the deadly bamboo spears, but most of them had thrown their weapons contemptuously away and simply picked up their oppressors bodily and hurled them to their deaths over the cliff side.

Always, there was that furious cry: "For Alma!"

Only two of them reached the hundredth step where,

exhausted by the climb, they stopped, panting; but twenty muscular young Strong Men were there waiting for them . . . At last, a semblance of peace descended on Eden, but it was that, and nothing more, a semblance . . .

Chapter Nineteen

By the first signs of daylight, the women and children were moving out of the swamp, and in the township the task of counting the casualties was left to the Strong Men. Not one of them had been killed in the battle, though twenty-seven of them had been wounded, some of them quite seriously; these were consigned to the hot springs for immersion in the yellow waters that would disinfect and dry up their wounds and eventually cure them.

The bodies of the outlaws were gathered together for ritual burning, but to Gerard's consternation, those of Jao Torres and Carmen were nowhere to be found, and it disturbed him deeply. Shana begged him to go to the sulphur pools with the others and begin the cure of his own wound, but he would not. He muttered, "Only when I am sure that Torres is no longer a threat to us. By a miracle, he escaped from the labyrinth. He must not be allowed to escape from the valley. I will not be content until I find out what happened to him, and yes . . . to his woman Carmen as well."

"Perhaps, after all, he eluded Lindsay and his men on the steps?"

He shook his head. "It is not possible, they were too strong, the steps are too confining. Day or night, he would have been seen."

"Hiding still in the town, then?"

"Perhaps." Gerard worried about it and said slowly, "It is more likely, I think, that he will have made his way to the forest. And there . . . he can be a constant danger to us. A man like Jao Torres can live there indefinitely."

They watched the ceremonial burning of the dead bodies, and Gerard was astonished to recognize an ancient Indian ritual he had seen before in the river villages on the Outside. A platform was built and hung about with the feathers of wild turkey, pheasant, and bustard, and a fire set below it. As the flames began to consume them, one of the women detached herself from the crowd and raised her arms high to the heavens. She had discared her *draperi* and wore only her Indian skirt of beaded bark-cloth, with a similar band around her forehead. She began a strange, atonal chant in an outlandish dialect that was new to him, and the intensity of her emotion made his blood curdle.

He had seen her only once before, on the great trek to the swamp, and he remembered her well because there was something very strange about her; her face, quite unlike those of Eden's other women, was *wrinkled*. Her saffron body was still firm, and on the march he had seen her walking as steadily as the others. Now, here she was, an Indian once more, dressed in her tribal regalia and raising her voice in a chant for the dead . . .

There was a solemn silence on the watching crowd as the flames did their work. Gerard whispered to Shana,

"I saw her only once before, and have never met her. Who is she?"

"Her name is Usal-Afisa," Shana said, "which in her original language means 'The Singing Woman'. She is the only survivor from Adam Grieg's original party."

There was a tingling in Gerard's scalp. "But . . . in God's name, they came here a hundred and twenty-five years ago!"

"Yes." Shana nodded casually, making nothing of it at all. "She was one of the virgins presented to him by the Queen I-Suacher. She was perhaps fifteen years old then, she doesn't know her exact age, but it must be about a hundred and forty. She likes to tell us she'll live to be two hundred, and she probably will." She smiled. "At least, I hope so, she's a very good woman. And if you've never met her, I'll introduce you as soon as the ceremony is over."

When at last he was presented to her, he found her to be a woman of extraordinary verve and vitality. She said, her eyes twinkling, "I am glad that we met, Gerard. You will need my help very soon, I think."

"Oh?"

"The question of the Indian women who were with the bandits. Eight of them, poor savage animals who took shelter in one of the grain pits when the fighting started here, frightened and quite sure that we would kill them all. But I took a little responsibility on myself, since I know their language, and told them that they would not be harmed. Though that final decision, of course must be yours."

"Ah yes, Torres' poor, mistreated slaves." He had almost forgotten them in the nights of excitement; and they posed a problem. He said slowly, "Of course, they

305

must not be harmed, and it seems . . . it seems they will have to stay with us here."

"All they want," Usal-Afisa said, "is to return to their villages."

"Yes, I can believe it. But we must keep the secret of Raman-li-Undara, and they will spread it throughout the Amazon, as unwittingly dangerous to us as Jao Torres himself would be."

"No." Those ancient eyes seemed to be drilling into his. "No," she said again. "They know nothing of Raman-li-Undara, and care even less. They have not been taken into Torres' confidence, and I doubt if they even know the legend of the Field of Diamonds. But even if they do . . . diamonds mean less to them than a handful of maize. The one is of no use to them at all, while the other . . . It is the difference between life and death to them."

Gerard said urgently, "Can you be sure of that, Usal-Afisa?"

"I can be sure. You must know also that the Indians have a strong sense of . . . what shall I call it? A kind of stubborn honor, can you understand that? It is very hard for a stranger to know what is in the mind of an Amazonian Indian, but I am almost one of them myself, and I know them well. They know that you have saved their lives, saved them from cruel and vicious savages who inflicted the most unspeakable suffering on them. If you tell them, through me, never to speak of Eden . . . then I tell you with certainty, each and every one of them will die before that name ever escapes their lips." Her hands were gesticulating, moving with the extraordinary grace of a young dancer, and those strange eyes were twinkling again.

306

She said softly, "It will be very easy for you, Gerard. One of them knows you well, and worships you."

He was startled. "Knows me? But how can that be?"

"Her name," Usal-Afisa said, "is Gri-Sa-Puni."

"But I know no one of that . . ." He broke off. "Gri-Sa-Puni? There was a young girl of that name with my porters the night Jao Torres attached us. But surely, she must have been killed!"

"No, They found her too attractive for killing, and took her prisoner instead. She has been with them ever since, too frightened to try and escape them."

"Gri-Sa-Puni! Yes, I remember her well!"

"Was she your lover too?" Shana asked innocently, and Gerard shook his head. "No," he said, "though I think that both of my two young assistants, Welks and Dunning, had designs on her." He shrugged. "Whether they ever succeeded or not, I do not know."

"She told me," Usal-Afisa said, pressing her case, "why you were disgraced by the Government of the Outside, for trying to save the lives of her people, who were slowly being exterminated. 'Jer-Hard tried to stop them killing my people', she said, 'and for this, he became a lost man.' It does you credit, Gerard."

He frowned and turned away, remembering, "And my objections made no difference at all, I am sure of it. And protest is very foolish, is it not, unless it achieves some sort of result?"

She reached out and touched him, and said gently, "With the wisdom of my age, I will dispute that. You are very young, Gerard. Learn then, that when there is good in a man's heart, sooner or later it finds its way to other hearts, like the streams on the Outside that trickle down the mountains till they form, together, a great river like the Amazon, which is unconquerable. And shall we go to the Indian women now?"

"With the new Queen," Gerard said, and Usal-Afisa nodded.

They found Ferida, and Gerard told her what they were planning; the Queen gave her instant approval, as he had expected. They went together to the *conviveri* where the Indian women were gathered, wide-eyed, expectant, awaiting whatever fate might be theirs now with that peculiarly Indian stoicism. In the forefront of them, Gerard saw the young girl whose name meant a flower that is opening to the sun, crouched on the ground and staring up at him. Like the others, she wore only a string around her waist to which was attached a small square of leather. She did not move, but he saw that she was waiting fearfully for some sign of recognition; he fancied that she was even trembling. He was wounded by the sight of them all, feeling their fears, and he forced a smile and said: "Gri-Sa-Puni . . . It is good to find you alive."

He heard Usal-Afisa's quiet translation, and then Gri-Sa-Puni, a child no more, was crawling to him on all fours, and to his acute embarrassment kissing his feet. He reached down and pulled her to her feet as he said gently, "Soon, we will find a way to send you to your village." He knew a very few words of the Indian *lingua-franca*, and said, *"Askiha's, buru samatu,* soon, to your home."

He was aware that Shana's eyes were moist as she looked at them and suffered for them. They were all very young, and most of them were not very attractive; but there was a certain fascination both in their sombre, suspicious eyes and in the way they moved with a sort of animal grace, the feline grace of pure jungle creatures.

Their legs were bowed from too early labor, but their breasts were small and round and very hard.

He explained at great length what he was planning for them, and told them of the great need for silence about what they had seen here, hoping against hope that he could trust that sense of stubborn honor that Usal-Afisa had told him of. The old Indian woman was translating for him as he spoke. When he had finished, she said simply, "You can trust them, Gerard."

He looked at the Queen, and she nodded. "And I trust Usal-Afisa," she said. "If she tells us it will be so . . . then it will be so."

"Good, I am satisfied." He hesitated. "And there is still the question of Jao Torres."

"Tomorrow," Ferida said clearly. "It is part of our philosophy that nothing should be done today which can be put off till tomorrow."

Gerard laughed. "An excellent philosophy indeed!" he said. "Although our troubles will not truly be over until we have found him."

"And you are in no state to do that now. Go now to one of the pools, rest in it for some hours till that yellow film has completely sealed up that very honorable wound. And then, Gerard, you must *sleep*. Will you promise me that you will do this?"

He had not slept properly for three days and nights, and the thought of a comfortable bed in his *conviveri* was a magnet for him. And the soothing relaxation of the bubbling sulphur water . . .

He said wryly, "Your servant, ma'am."

He took Shana's hand and went out with her. He turned at the doorway and saw Gri-Sa-Puni's eyes on his, and suddenly recalled that Welks and Dunning, those two good English friends, had always called her

'Greasy-Funny.' He said to her again, "*Askiha'a, buru samatu*. Soon, to your home."

The Indians never cried; but tears were rolling down her grubby cheeks as she stared back at him.

For more than three hours, he soaked with Shana in one of the hot springs until that film of yellow plaster that Ferida had spoken of caked over his wound. He went then with her to his room, and lay down in the last throes of exhaustion. She stretched herself out beside him, their naked bodies very close, sharing the warmth that went from one to another of them. She whispered, "It has been so long . . ."

"Yes, too long."

"Are you strong enough to love me now?"

"If I were dead and two weeks buried, I would be strong enough to love you."

"Lie still, then, and do not strain yourself . . ."

"It is not a strain to love you, but an entrance into heaven itself . . ." He was so desperately tired! But he could not resist her, and when she sheathed herself on him he groaned aloud and welcomed the motion of her demanding hips. The long-awaited release came for both of them, and they slept together like children, clutched in each other's arms.

He awoke in the night and found her breast with his lips, and slept again in utter contentment. And he could not tell how much later it was before he awoke again at a slight sound coming out of the sleep . . .

A drop of moisture fell on his naked hip, and then another, and only half-awake he reached for it instinctively and found it to be sticky; he could not imagine what it might be, but he did not want to force the awareness on him. He thought, *Shana, my love, forever . . .*

There was suddenly a powerful hand at his throat,

gripping him and crushing his windpipe cruelly, and in a moment of sudden panic he felt that the life was being throttled out of him. Instantly, he was wide awake. He took hold of a wrist with both hands and tore it away from his neck, and he looked up into the wild and frantic eyes . . . of Carmen. The single, subdued flare was lining her startling profile in yellow light, and her upper body, covered with perspiration, was shining in the flickering flame.

But he could only stare at the blood on her breast. There was a dreadful wound there, and the blood was still trickling from it. Her face was bruised, and both her luxuriant eyes were blackened; but she was grinning with a savage kind of mockery. She said, "You sleep, Americano? If Jao find you sleeping, he will kill you, as I could have killed you! This is not a time for sleep."

Shana was already awake and sitting up as she stared at that dreadful wound. Carmen said thickly, trying to mask her pain, "Jao do this to me . . ."

Shana whispered, "Oh, God . . ."

"Some cloth, quickly!" Not waiting for her reply, he found his discarded *draperi* and tore yet more cloth from it, and as Shana left the bed he picked Carmen up bodily and laid her down on it. As he tried to bind up the wound, she parted her thighs and said, mocking him, "Look, I spread my legs for you, you take me now. Is better than your woman, I promise you, much better . . ."

He was strapping the bandage around her strong waist and over the full breast in an attempt to staunch the flow of blood. She said, whispering, "We hide together, Jao and me. But he is not my man anymore, he know that Espada was my lover, and he try to throw me out, and I call him a savage pig . . . I tell him what a

311

good lover Espada was, and Jao pull his knife and . . . and do this to me. And now . . . you want to know where he is hiding, no?"

Gerard's eyes were gleaming. "Yes, I do. But lie still now, or you will bleed to death."

"I don't care. My lover Espada is dead, I don't care if I go to him now."

Suddenly, in spite of the pain that must have been terrible, she was laughing again, a woman of great courage. "But I don't die so easy! I am a very strong woman, Jao never know this or he stab me not once, but ten times! And what will you give me if I tell you where he is hiding?"

"Nothing," Gerard said.

"You give me your diamonds. Jao want them, Espada want them, now . . . I want them."

"No. I will give you nothing."

"For nothing, I don't tell you."

Shana whispered, "If he is still in the town, a constant menace as you yourself said, we *must* know where he is hiding."

Gerard nodded. "Yes, we must. But not under these terms. I will not buy a man's life, however vile he may be, with diamonds." He turned back to Carmen. "I will give you nothing except your life. If, indeed, it can still be saved."

"What, *saved?*" She was suddenly the angry jungle animal again, and she lashed out at his face and drew blood with raking nails. She screamed, "I tell you, you don't listen! I don't die so easy! I am strong woman!"

He held both her wrists and said, "Tell me where to find him, Carmen."

She said stubbornly, "You give me diamonds, I tell you. All right, not all. You give me ten, twenty, fifty only." There was a little silence, and then she continued, "You give me one. He is not worth more."

"I will give you nothing. Tell me."

For a long, long time, she lay still, and Gerard wondered if perhaps she had lost her consciousness. But at last she stirred, and opened her eyes and looked straight into his. She whispered, "You are very good man, I think. Why don't I find someone like you twenty years ago, when Jao first take me? Why?"

He said gently, "Where, Carmen?"

"I take you to him . . ."

"No! You must not move now! Just tell me where I may find him!"

But Carmen was already raising herself up from the bed, and he could not hold her down. She said scornfully, "Little knife wound, you think it is my first? My last? Come, I take you to him."

Painfully, she struggled to her feet. "He is wounded," she said. "Somebody drive a bamboo spear through him, here . . ." She gestured at her thigh and said, "You know wounded animals? They are dangerous."

Gerard turned to Shana. "Wait here, my love," he said gently. "I will come back when I have done . . . what has to be done."

"No." She shook her head. "This is *our* fight, Gerard. Not yours alone. Mine, and Alma's, and Bianca's."

"Very well."

Shana's arm was around Carmen to help her as she led them to one of the grain pits. Gerard had taken the flare, winding it around a dozen times to make it flame more brightly, and in its light he saw that people were moving out of their *conviveries* to see what was happening now, staring at Carmen and wondering about her.

The grain pit was in a small building of its own, no

more than eight or nine feet along each granite wall. And in its center, the pit itself was a circular stone bin perhaps six feet across and twelve feet deep; the grain came up to within four feet of the lid. As they moved towards it, the flare held high, they saw Jao Torres, his body half in and half out of the millet. There were two pistols in his hand, their hammers cocked, and two knives and a sword lay on the surface of the grain. He stared up at them as Carmen said, pointing, "There is Jao. Take him, Gerard . . ."

Jao screamed in a berserk fury, "Woman! You sell me to my enemies?"

Gerard saw both fingers tighten on the triggers. One of the guns misfired; but the other sounded like the roar of a cannon in the confining pit, reverberating back and forth from its granite walls. He saw Carmen thrown off her feet as the half-inch nugget of lead tore into her throat and almost decapitated her.

He screamed, and threw the flare down into the pit and leaped after it, floundering in the shifting grain. He seized Jao by the throat and tried to throttle him, but the bandit chief was struggling under him with monstrous strength; and when he found a knife and tried to drive it up into his belly, Gerard, berserk himself, raised up that ugly head, and smashed it into the pits' stone walls. He shrieked at the top of his voice, "For Dora! For Alma! For Bianca! And for Shana, Shana, Shana!"

With each of the screams he was pounding that bullet-head, devoid now for the first time ever of its ludicrous black top hat, into the wall. He heard the skull break open at last, and knew that this murderer was dead.

For a while, exhausted by his overwrought emotions, he lay motionless, his hands still around that bull-neck as though still searching there for any kind of poisonous life.

At last, he stumbled through the quicksand of the grain and clambered up out of the pit. Shana was on her knees beside Carmen's dead body, and she was shaking. She looked up at him as he stood above them, and whispered, "A woman . . . was she truly so evil?"

Gerard's heart was very heavy. He said, trying to hold his feelings in check, "We will never know, Shana. We will never know now."

He pulled her to her feet and embraced her, and held her tight to his chest. He whispered, "But now . . . the battle for Eden . . . is over."

Chapter Twenty

It was only a few weeks after the end of the attack on Eden, but the township had already returned to its normal state.

The people were meeting once again every evening on the moss lawns, playing their games or listening to their music; it was almost as if Jao Torres and his murderous gang of cutthroats had never even existed.

Ferida, the new Queen, had been installed in Alma's Throne Room, and it seemed that she was a woman of great strength of character, knowing exactly what was best for her people and making sure that nothing less would suffice.

The Books had been brought back out of the labyrinth and set out once again in the Room of History, and no one had even bothered to make sure that the diamonds were still undisturbed; it meant nothing to them at all.

At approximately seven o'clock on a fine, warm evening, Shana and Gerard were slowly climbing together hand in hand up the slope of a hill where the llamas were grazing in the cool twilight. They found a pleasant knoll to sit on, and looked down on the peaceful gray stones of the township far below them; there were no words spoken between them for a very long while.

At last, Shana lay back on the cool grass and unfastened the knot of her *draperi*, setting it aside and waiting. Gerard stretched out beside her, propped up on one elbow the better to admire her, a goddess of the most ethereal beauty, her slender saffron thighs gilded now by the setting sun with a shining apricot blush. He thought that he had never seen as beautiful a vision as the one she presented now, the bright green meadow perfectly complementing the smooth pale copper of her glorious skin.

He leaned down and kissed her lips, her throat, her breast, and he saw that there was a strange and distant sadness in her lovely eyes, more solemn now than they had ever been before. In a moment, he eased himself more closely beside her, his head nestled into her shoulder, and the silence between them was that ancient silence of lovers who communicate only with their thoughts.

At last, Shana whispered very softly, "Will you tell me what it is that troubles you this evening, my love?"

He could not lie to her; but he felt he had to make a token protest. He said, smiling, "Troubles me? When you are at my side, my darling, there is nothing in the world that could trouble me. Unless it might be the dreadful fear that one day you will cease to love me."

He felt the tensing of her body. "Cease to love you?" she said urgently, "It could never happen, never! Surely you must know that? Oh, my loved one . . ."

"Then all is well. For without you beside me, my life would seem empty and worthless! A love like ours is a rare and precious thing, a gift from God, and nothing must ever be allowed to come between us . . ."

Her huge eyes held his, and she gently stroked the full growth of his heavy beard. "Then tell me what it is that presses on you so heavily."

He sighed. "Is it so apparant?" he asked.

She was not even blinking. "Perhaps only to me, because we share our thoughts as we share our love."

"I can hide nothing from you . . . And even so slight a fact gives me the greatest pleasure, because it reassures me of the strength of our love."

"Then will you tell me?"

"Yes, I will tell you, as I must." She waited, trying to control her trembling, sure that something dreadful was about to happen. Gerard said slowly, "In simple terms, my love . . . I am homesick."

She felt the blood was draining from her face, and her heart almost stopped beating. She whispered, in shock, "*Homesick?*"

He was aware of her terrible fear, and he held her tightly. "Yes," he said desperately, "homesick for my family, my friends, who have not seen me for five years now and do not know whether I am dead or alive! For the sights and sounds too of the great Mississippi River, with the boats at anchor there, and splendid ships coming in from the gulf from all around the world. . . . The steamboats, flat boats and barges, the bustle of commerce in the port. Never to see my home again? It is a thought, my dearest, that drives me to distraction!"

She was moaning softly, the tears streaming down her cheeks, and he was suddenly conscious of what she was imagining. He gasped, and said in surprise, "But this does not mean I want to leave you! Never, my darling, I would die! But I want to go back to America and take you with me, to be with me always, as my wife, and the woman I love."

319

Shana caught her breath and stared at him. "But . . . to leave Eden? Forever? And for the terrible Outside which you yourself have told me is filled with evil? I have *seen* the Outside, my dearest, and I know what it is like! The Outside means men like Jao Torres who nearly destroyed us, who *would* have destroyed us if you had not come to our rescue!"

The first step had been taken, and now he knew that it would be easier. "No," he said gently, "you have *not* seen the Outside, you have seen only a small part of the Amazonian jungle, which is indeed a difficult place. But beyond it, there lie great and splendid cities where men and women live together in harmony . . . Not a harmony like that of Eden, I will confess at once, and perhaps this is part of the problem too, because it is possible that Eden is . . . *too* peaceful, too comforting for a man who has spent all of his life in a struggle for survival."

"But . . . oh, my love! You have been so happy here, I know it!"

"Yes, it is true, happier than ever before! But can you understand what it means to me to spend the rest of my life in the ease and luxury of Eden? I have been brought up on adversity, on challenge, and without those two hammers battering at me . . . I do not like the thought of what I might become. I am very sure that if I ever have to cease struggling, if I ever find that there are no more challenges, no more hardships . . . then I fear not only what it will do to me, but what it will do to *us*. I fear that in the course of time, too much well-being, too much fair weather with never a storm in sight, too much creature comforts . . . these things will slowly but surely destroy me; and with it, destroy our love. This, I will never permit." He held her to him and whispered, "Try to understand the torment in my soul, my dearest Shana. It is very hard for me to express it . . ."

"I understand you," she whispered. "But to leave Eden, forever . . ."

"No." He smiled and kissed her on the lips. "I have told you of my homesickness, and I know what a strong emotion it is. I realize too how hard it will be for you when you dream of Eden as now I dream of New Orleans. And one day, I promise you faithfully, we will return and visit our dear friends here. Ferida the Queen, and Emlyn, Lindsay, Barbara, Yvonne, Thelma, and all the others whom I love so much."

Her eyes were shining brightly through her tears now, and she brushed at them with a delicate fingertip. "Then we will see them all again? It will not be farewell forever?"

"My word on it," he said solemnly. "I could not face the prospect, either, of leaving them forever. But do not make up your mind at once. Promise me only that you will think about it. And I will promise you that if the thought of leaving is too hard for you to bear . . . then we will stay, both of us together, till death do us part."

Her arms around his shoulders, she pressed his head to her breast so that he would not see the fresh tears coming to her eyes. She whispered, "It will be as you say, my love. I will face the Outside with you, provided only that you never leave my side."

He knew how hard it was for her to make the decision, and he murmured, "We will both think about it for a few days, there is no urgency at all. Indeed, I must accustom myself to it also."

He lay back beside her on the grass, an arm over her shoulder, moulding her gently, and stared at the bright moon rising over the mountain they called 'The Girl

Who Fell Asleep'. The cloud-shadows were moving slowly across her profile as though she herself were stirring. He said softly, "Look, the girl is awake, she knows that her long lost lover is approaching . . ."

Shana rolled over onto him, and her fingertips brushed the wound at his shoulder, its scar sealed up now by frequent immersions in the healing sulphur springs. She explored the whipcord muscles of his arms, the tight, hard chest, moving her gentle hands over a stomach that was hard as granite, she found him to be as strong as he ever was. She placed herself over him and lowered herself, and leaned forward to brush his lips with hers. "Do not move now, my love," she murmured, and kissed his eyes, his ears, his throat . . . All the while, he held himself back until he felt her own inevitable passions overtaking her, and she was moaning in ecstasy as they erupted together. He thrust into her fiercely, draining every last emotion from her, and they lay still at last, side by side with their limbs intertwined, and fell into that semi-sleep which was the natural result of their exhaustion.

Shana sighed a deep sigh of utter contentment as she nestled herself to him, and then there was that long and comfortable silence again as the breeze played across their bodies.

Gerard said quietly at last, musing, "At first, it will not be easy on the Outside. There will be no lack of food in the jungle, through which we will travel for two or perhaps three months, by boat once we reach the River Negro and find a trading post. But once we reach civilization we will need money. And until I can find a way to earn some . . . it may be a little difficult."

"Money?" Shana echoed. "Surely it is of no importance at all!"

Gerard laughed. "In the outside world, a man cannot live without it."

She stared at him. "Then if that is so, the solution is very simple. We have diamonds which you have told us are priceless! Carry a bag of them with you, the Queen will give you as many as you want!"

Gerard shook his head. "No," he said, "what I have done here is not to be paid off in diamonds. I will not accept a single one of them."

"Ah . . ." Shana shrugged. "Well, I think that's a very praiseworthy attitude, but is it not also a little . . . foolish? It would make it so much easier for you."

"And it is not ease that I am looking for," he said, kissing her again. "Call it . . . the first of those challenges I spoke of. Even though it is not a very severe one. I know most of the traders on the river, and they know that I am to be trusted. They will advance me whatever we need, in the certain knowledge that they will be repaid one day with full interest."

"And when we reach New Orleans," she murmured, wondering about this new adventure, "there will be so much I will have to learn!"

"That too will not be difficult."

"Do they have gardens there where people gather in the evenings to chat?"

"Oh yes, we have the most beautiful parks and gardens, and beaches too."

"And the people play chess, and *farsika?*

"Chess, and another game called dominoes, and checkers. But not *farsika*, though we have other ball games."

"And is there water running through all the houses in conduits?"

"Yes, a different system, but we have water."

323

"And does everyone work in order to help his neighbors?"

"Well . . ." Gerard thought about it. "Everyone works," he said, "yes, though largely to help himself."

"What a dreadful idea! And is there a Queen in New Orleans? What is her name? Is she as beautiful as Ferida?"

"No Queen. We have instead what you would call a Concord."

"Oh. And do you have llamas grazing with their young in your meadows?"

"No llamas. But we have sheep and cattle."

"Ah . . . and jaguars in the jungle?"

"No jaguars, and no jungle. But many very beautiful trees."

"Oh, and is it as big as Eden's township?"

Gerard laughed happily. "Perhaps a hundred times bigger," he said, delighted with her questions.

She stared. "*A hundred times bigger?*" she echoed incredulously. "But how can that be? Where do all those people come from?"

"That," Gerard said wryly, "is something we often ask ourselves."

There was a deeper gravity in her voice now. "And will I be welcome there?" she asked, her words tinged with anxiety.

"Welcome?" he said, holding her tightly. "My dearest, you will be admired, respected, and loved!" He tried to make a little joke. "Indeed, I will be hard pressed to keep the cheerful attention of my friends—of some of them at least—within the bounds of propriety! Our New Orleans women are known for their beauty, but not one of them can match your own, which by our standards is . . . quite startling. And I can count a few rakehells

324

among my friends, I'm afraid." He laughed. "Good fellows, all of them, but sometimes a little . . . bawdy."

"Ah, your friends," Shana said earnestly. "It will, of course, be my right to take any of them I please, but it is a right I willingly forego. I will love only you, Gerard! I too make you a promise—I will love no one else, ever!"

Gerard smiled and found her lips. "And I am glad of it," he said gravely.

"And shall we return now to our *conviveri?*" she asked. "We must tell all our friends what we have decided."

"Very well. I fear it will not bring them much pleasure, and I feel guilty."

"Yes, they will be sad. But they will, in time, accept. It is part of our upbringing."

Their arms around each other, they walked slowly down the hillside to the lovely old town.

Two days later, Queen Ferida sent for him, just as the last glorious rays of the evening sun were streaming through the windows and turning the gray stone to a brilliant gold.

She was gracious and smiling as he took her hands and kissed them. She said quietly, "I learn that you are leaving us, Gerard, and all our hearts are breaking." She put her arms around him and embraced him tightly as she whispered, "And there is no one in Eden who is more sad than I am."

"It will not be easy," he murmured, "and I will confess that my heart is heavy too." But she placed a finger to his lips and said softly, "No, there must never be regrets for what must be done. I myself have expected it, ever since the peace that you brought to us came once again after those fearful days and nights of anxiety."

It startled him. "You have?"

"It comes as no surprise to me at all. For one who is by nature a wanderer, a man of action if you like, it would make little sense to remain forever in the sheltered serenity of Eden, which we accept because we have never known anything else. Shana spoke to me of *challenge*, and the more I thought about it the more I became convinced that you are right. She told me also that you have promised to come back and visit us one day, and the thought of your return will be almost as exciting as your own presence among us."

"Yes, a promise I have made not only to Shana, but to myself as well. It will be hard to leave, but very easy to retrace our steps—by an easier route next time—to Paradise. I have been very happy here, as you know, and I could not spend the rest of my life with Eden nothing more than a distant memory."

The young boy Roland came in and lit the flares, and when he had gone, Ferida reached up and kissed him on the lips. Her hands were at the small of his gently arched back, pulling their bodies tightly together. "And will you love me now?" she whispered, "to make still more sure that I carry your child?"

She laughed suddenly, "All the women you have loved want to name their son Gerard, but I have exercised my royal prerogative and demanded that name for *our* son. When the time comes, it will be written in the Books: *On this day, Ferida the Queen gave birth to a son by Gerard, to be named Gerard also* . . . Come, lie beside me now, there are other things we must talk of too."

She removed her *draperi* and his, and they lay together on the scarlet silk of the divan, their warm, expectant bodies close together. She caressed him lightly,

326

relishing his great strength, and held his head to her full, soft breast. "Shana also told me," she whispered, "that you will not take diamonds with you, even though you will need money on the Outside. It is my hope that you will reconsider."

"No, Ferida," he murmured, "though I thank you. My mind is made up, for reasons which I hold to be good."

"It would not be *payment*," she said urgently. "I *want* you to take them, all of them if you will. They are a danger to us here, as you have seen. As, indeed, you yourself first told us."

"There will be no further danger if the secret is kept, as it will be. Torres and his gang found Eden only because they followed our tracks, and this will never happen again."

"I still say it is foolishness." She sighed. "But there is still time for you to change your mind. And the poor Indian women, who want nothing but to be returned to their own families?"

"I will take them to the river," Gerard said, "and find canoes to carry them to their villages. I have many friends among the traders, who will help me."

"Good. It pleases me to know that they are in such good hands. And Emlyn tells me that you must have other clothes for the journey."

"Ah yes . . . He is right, *draperies* on the Outside would excite too much attention, and therefore speculation which we must avoid."

"Then tell Yvonne what it is you need, and she will see to it. Your own breeches are still here, so perhaps a shirt and a cloak of llamas' wool . . . And for Shana, a gown like those in the earlier paintings."

He sensed an excitement on her, as though she were helping to plan a wonderful adventure, and he was glad that his decision had been, albeit reluctantly, accepted.

But there was a greater excitement on her too, and her hands were reaching for him, gently insisting. And though he soon became lost in his own yearning, in a passion he could never hide on these occasions, he still thought only of his beloved Shana.

He asked himself a silent question: *will this, perhaps, be the last time for this strange kind of physical infidelity?*

And when, an hour later, he returned to his one true love, he found that his thoughts were hers exactly, as so often happened between them. She asked her usual question, "And was the loving good for you, it is my hope that it was?" Then she whispered softly, "The last time, Gerard. It has been decided among the women that none of them will ask for you now. And I am content." He held her tightly in his arms until the sleep enveloped them both.

Chapter Twenty-One

The climb up the steps was more laborious than Gerard could ever have imagined; and in spite of his determination, his heart was heavy. As the township grew smaller and smaller with every passing Campsite, receding into the distance below them with each new day, he wondered more and more whether he had made the right decision.

He recalled that when he had left his own home—so many years ago—he had felt much the same emotions, not sure that he would ever see his loved ones again. And yet, he was now on the first stage of the long journey back to America. And surely it would be the same for the people of Eden, the sorrow muted by other excitements as time went by?

Shana comforted him constantly, even though he knew that the break was harder for her than it was for him. And the pain was lessened for the moment by the companionship of what seemed like half of Eden's population who had left their daily routines behind them to see them off. Emlyn was foremost among the party, with Queen Ferida herself, and Lindsay, and Barbara, Yvonne and Helen, with Thelma the chess-expert and a score of the other women, together with no less than twenty of the Strong Men . . . And the child Anitra, clutching her lyre and playing softly from time to time as they climbed. The men were carrying ironwood spikes and digging-tools, bags of meat, fruit, and other necessities for the journey. One of them carried an open weave basket which Ferida had prepared, containing meat and the succulent Eden cheese, topped with peaches and apricots and small clay pots of honey.

At the top of the mountain, it seemed that time stood still for them. The township was tiny down there, a toy village at the end of a snaking stairway, and a hand was clutching at Gerard's heart as he stared at it. No one seemed in a hurry for the voyagers to make the final passage through the secret cleft in the rock, and there was almost a carnival atmosphere now as they rested from their efforts. Anitra sang and played for them, some of them made fires and cooked more of the meat they had been carrying, and others soaked themselves in the sulphur springs to relieve their muscles of the stiffness brought on by the ascent. They opened up flagons of elderberry wine and drank, perhaps more heavily than was their custom, sometimes laughing and sometimes just watching Gerard and Shana somberly, as though wondering what might ever become of them.

Emlyn produced, of all things, a beautiful gold pocketwatch on a heavy chain. He gave it to Gerard and said wryly, "It has not told the time for more than ninety years, but a man does not need to know that, the sun and the moon are indications enough that the days are passing . . . but it once belonged to my father, who was one of Adam Grieg's own party, and now . . . I want you to have it, a small memento of our close friendship, to carry with you always."

330

Gerard took it from him and embraced him warmly, and said emotionally, "I will treasure it always, dear friend . . ." Anitra, strumming her lyre close by, changed the rhythm as her delicate voice lifted up in an old ballad from England:

My grandfather's clock was too tall for the shelf,
So it stood ninety years on the floor.
It was taller by half than the old man himself,
Though it weighed not a pennyweight more . . .
And it struck twenty-four
As he entered the door
With his blooming and beautiful bride.
But it stopped short, never to go again,
When the old man died . . .

She started crying softly, and Gerard put his arms around her and ruffled her hair. He said gently, "It is not forever, Anitra."

"No, so they have told me." She raised her somber eyes to his and whispered, "When you return . . . In three years, I will be of age. And I too would like to have your child." She looked at Shana. "Three years," she said with a sigh. "It is a long, long time to wait. And will you be good to him always?"

In a while, he lay with Shana in the pool, letting the hot yellow water bubble around them. Anitra slipped out of her *draperi* and joined them, holding his hand and kissing it as she tried to control her tears. The men were pulling ferns and making beds for the party, and the Indian women were huddling together in the bushes a little apart from everyone else, the instinct to hide still strong on them even though Jer-Hard was there to protect them from their enemies.

The moon rose and crossed the heavens, and at last a kind of quiet oblivion fell over the camp. Gerard whispered in the silence, "Shana, my love . . . Is it as hard for you to make this break as it is for me?"

Shana held her peace for a moment before she answered him. "It is no longer hard," she said softly. "I have taken Adam Grieg's advice and learned to accept. And how many days will it take to reach your America, my love?"

"Days? It will be months, my dearest."

"So long?"

"Three months in the jungle at least, though most of the way will be by canoe, before we reach the mouth of the great Amazon River. Then, a wait of perhaps a week or two or more for a ship . . . It is four thousand miles by sea to New Orleans, a matter of another month to six weeks, depending on the winds and the currents. But then . . . we will be home! And I cannot begin to describe the excitements waiting for you there!"

The clouds were scudding across the moon, grey puffs of cotton against a dark blue sky; the silhouettes of the trees around them had lost their green and were black now. Shana whispered, "I am afraid of what lies ahead of us . . ."

He held her close. "Do not be. Once, you were afraid of those tiny blue frogs too, you remember?"

"Yes, I remember well. As long as you are constantly by my side."

"As I always will be," he said fiercely, "never letting you out of my sight, if only because when you are not with me, the world is a dull and dreary place! I love you so much, my darling."

"And without your love, I will die . . ."

They lay with their loins cupped together as he entered her slowly, and when the excitement had reached its peak and passed it for them both, he did not stir, but lay still within her, knowing that the time would come again soon. And they slept like innocent children till the sun broke through the treetops to awaken them with its golden beams.

The camp was already astir, and it was apparent that the Edenites still could not leave Gerard and Shana alone. They all went with them through the dangerous cleft in the rock, and for almost all of them it was their first view of the Outside. They crowded the little fern-covered plateau and stared breathlessly at the immensity of the jungle far below them. They clambered carefully, in single file with Emlyn in the lead, down the narrow path that led to the lower level, and still they would not go back. At last, they came to the edge of a very high cliff where the treetops were more than five hundred feet below them. There was a river winding tortuously back and forth on itself through the dense greenery, and Ferida called a halt at last.

"This," she said quietly, "is where we make our last farewells." There were tears in her regal eyes as she embraced Gerard and kissed him, and she whispered, "You cannot know how much we will miss you, how fervently we will wait for your return, to stay with us as long as you will. You will always be . . . one of us."

"Within three years, I promise you," he said, and he found that his voice was choking too. Emlyn held him tight and could not speak, and then Lindsay was there, taking him in that great bear hug, then Thelma, and Barbara, and all the other women, followed by all the Strong Men one after the other. They were all kissing

333

Shana and wishing her good fortune on her journey into the unknown, and it seemed as though the emotional good-byes would never end.

They were over at last, and Ferida made her last remarks. "The diamonds, Gerard," she said, her head held high. "I have asked you to reconsider. Have you done so?"

He smiled. "No reconsideration is necessary, Ferida," he answered. "I repeat . . . I will not be paid for whatever help I may have been. I am not a rich man, but I have a valuable trade which will suffice for a living. No, I thank you with all my heart. But I will take nothing from Eden except the memory of the great love I found there. It is more than enough."

"Very well, then. So be it."

She made an almost imperceptible gesture to Lindsay, and then . . . there began a sort of ritual at which Gerard could only stare in shock and astonishment . . .

Ten, twelve, fifteen of the Strong Men lined themselves up on the edge of the high cliff, and started tipping leather bags over the brink, down to where the dark trees and the winding river were. Gerard gasped when he saw what they contained; they were filled with the diamonds of Raman-li-Undara . . .

At first, it was merely a casual matter of throwing away unwanted objects, but it quickly developed into an excited game, as the men took individual stones and hurled far out one by one, watching them sail out over the treetops and disappear from their sight, each of them competing with the others to see who could throw the furthest . . .

Lindsay shouted boisterously, "Norman! I do not believe that your arms are so weak, watch this one!" He hurled a great diamond that must have weighed four

334

hundred carats high into the air till it curved down and
fell among the green trees of the jungle. Norman took
up the challenge, and so did Lionel, Bernard, and all the
others, and the women gathered around them clapping
their hands in delight at each spectacular throw. They
were all laughing joyously as the men hurled millions
and millions of dollars in uncut diamonds out into the
void and tried to follow their line of flight.

Gerard felt his heart beating wildly, and he took
Shana's hand for comfort. She whispered, "It is Queen
Ferida's decision, and a very wise one, I think. No?"

He swallowed hard, lost in utter bewilderment. "But
the legend," he said, "will still live on."

"Yes indeed," Ferida said calmly. "It is a matter
which has not escaped my attention. But those adventurers you spoke of . . . If they should ever approach so
close to our hidden valley, then let it remain hidden. Let
them find a diamond or two down there, or a dozen, a
hundred, it does not matter. Let them think that the
Field of Diamonds is on the wrong side of the mountain,
down there by the river, and they will go no further. It
means that we shall suffer no more incursions. And if we
should . . ." She held his hands in hers. "If they should
perchance find that narrow entrance—and why should
they even search for it?—then we are taking another
precaution. You saw that the men were carrying wooden
tools. They are to lever away the steps between Camp
Five and Camp Six, demolishing part of the stairway entirely. Along the rest of it, we will plant bamboo in abundance, so that within the year it will be hidden completely save from those who know where it lies. When
you return to us and we see your signal fire . . . then we
will have ladders ready, ten, twenty, fifty of them, each
five times the height of a man, to carry you down over

the broken places. And meanwhile . . . Eden can rest in peace, knowing that it is now impregnable."

She took a basket of woven rattan from Norman and gave it to Gerard and said, very calm and restraining her strong emotions, "The final gesture, dear Gerard. Fruit, cheese, and meat for your journey. May whatever Gods you worship be with you both."

She turned away to hide her tears; and all the Edenites followed her as they moved slowly towards the great stone barrier that concealed the valley.

Anitra looked back as they began the climb up the broken path, and even at this distance Gerard could see the sadness in her eyes. She began plucking at the strings of her lyre, and that soft voice came to them, one of her lovely old ballads again:

Oh who will o'er the downs so free,
Oh who will with me ride?
Oh who will up and follow me,
To win a blooming bride . . .

Her voice was fading on the slight breeze, and the last notes of the song came faintly to them:

And ere the dawn of morning break,
My true love shall be free . . .

They were gone. Gerard took Shana's hand in his and held her tightly for a moment. He kissed her on the lips and whispered, "Come, let us be on our way."

The jungle closed about them as they moved slowly through it. A nearby toucan chattered at them; there was the ripe scent of a puma; a jaguar coughed in the distance; and a howler monkey in the branches of a tam-

336

arind tree was screaming at them; and the Indian women, keeping their distance, were following them cautiously, knowing that they were on the way home now in the care of this good and valiant man.

Gerard had wanted to leave his chopping-knife behind for them to use, but Ferida had sternly refused, saying, "No! We need iron tools, yes, but it is more important for you now. Emlyn has told me that in the jungle, a good knife is sometimes a matter of life, or death."

They fought their way through the dense, restricting shrubbery, always moving southeast by the sun, crossing two wide streams and dropping down a steep, muddied hillside till the sun was low in the sky behind them. They came to a clearing where great palm trees towered high above them, beneath which the forest humus was soft under their feet. Shallow water was bubbling fast over shining grey pebbles nearby, making a very pleasant sound, and there was dark green moss everywhere of a kind that was good to lie on.

Gerard set down the heavy basket of food and looked around him at the shrubbery. He said, "Yes, a good place to sleep, I think." He started breaking off pieces of dead wood for a fire, and the Indian women took it for a signal and started piling up twigs for their own little camp, closer to the concealing bushes where they could quickly hide if need be. But the young Gri-Sa-Puni crawled to them on hands and knees and rummaged through the wood to find just what she wanted; and in a moment she was twirling a dry twig dexterously at great speed between the palms of her hands, its lower end in a knothole in another piece of deadwood. As it began to smoulder at last, she blew on it, till it began to burn, and tossed dry grass on it and blew harder; the tiny flame flickered, and she placed one twig after another care-

337

fully on it till she was sure that the fire was taking hold. She began to crawl back, but Gerard said, *"Astu,* Gri-Sa-Puni, wait . . ."

He gave her meat from the basket and told her to share it with the other women. When she had scurried away, amazed at this good fortune and hurrying before he might change his mind and want it back again, he sat beside Shana and spoke. "We too will eat now. Then, perhaps a bath in the river, and a good night's sleep. Are you tired?"

Shana shook her head. "No, not tired, my darling."

"Sad?"

She reached out and touched his arm. "Not even sad." She dropped her eyes. "Well, perhaps just a little. But it will pass." She leaned over and kissed him, and whispered, "I cannot be truly sad, whatever happens, when we are together."

"Oh, my love . . ." His arms were around her. "A new life beginning for you, and I will move heaven and earth to make sure it is a happy life for you, always . . ."

When they broke away, he started unpacking the basket, setting the ripe peaches down carefully on the moss, and the apricots, and the little pots of honey, the cheese and the meat . . . He said, "Enough to last us for a long time. And how thoughtful of Ferida!"

At the bottom of the basket there was a package wrapped in woven silk, the size of his hand or larger, and strangely hard, yet pliant; and as he felt it moving under his touch, he knew at once what it must be. Even so, he could not contain a gasp as he saw the contents. There were eleven huge uncut diamonds there—eleven, he thought, one of the magic numbers of the Indians—and not a single one of them was less than three hundred carats; they even seemed to have been carefully chosen to match each other in size and shape. He could only stare at them in awe.

There was a sheet of bark-cloth with them, soft and supple and as thin as the cloth they used for the Books, and it was covered with Ferida's meticulous handwriting in indigo ink. By the light of the flames, he read it aloud to Shana, his voice hushed.

It is not payment, Gerard. It is merely a very small token of our love and gratitude. Emlyn has explained to me that you can put these foolish stones, which mean nothing to us, to good use on the Outside. You would not agree when I suggested that you take at least some of the diamonds with you, but the full Concord has agreed with this pleasing deception in the ardent hope that, faced with our insistence, you will at last realize that the will of Eden, even in such small measure, is not to be denied. May your Gods and mine go with you both on this difficult journey. And please, please come back to us one day. In undying esteem and affection,

Ferida, Queen of Eden.

He saw the slight smile in Shana's lovely, slanting eyes, sparkling now. He said, almost accusingly, "You knew, did you not?"

Smiling happily, she nodded. "Yes, I knew. I was at the meeting of the Concord where it was decided to play this little game. You yourself said that without money on the outside, life is difficult, did you not? And all you must do now is take the advice of Adam Grieg . . . and *accept*."

For a moment, he blinked at her. After a lifetime of struggle, it was not easy to envisage the change that such enormous wealth would mean. But the idea came to him that it might not, after all, be such a bad thing to be able to care so splendidly for those he loved; and suddenly, he was on top of the world, like a child again. He took Shana in his arms and hugged her breathlessly. "Very well," he said, "then that is what we will do, we will accept! And with gratitude beyond the bounds of reason, as our new wealth is . . ."

She was covering his face with little kisses as his hands explored her lithe soft body, and in a while he removed his new clothing and slipped her simple, all-concealing gown over her head. He whispered, "These foolish clothes were not made with love in mind, were they?" He lay beside her on the cool green moss, as smooth and pleasant to the touch as her own skin, and said excitedly, a loving hand at her breast, "And when we return, We'll buy iron tools by the thousand for Eden, knives, axes, shovels and mattocks . . . We'll hire porters from among our Indian friends, who are sworn to secrecy . . . Can you imagine the surprise and delight in Eden?"

The moon was high above them, casting dappled shadows in the little clearing, and the sound of the whispering water was music to their ears. It was a time for loving, and they fused their bodies together in rapture, not caring that the Indian women would undoubtedly be watching from the bushes, nor that Gri-Sa-Puni, bright-eyed with her own kind of excitement, was whispering to her companions, telling them what a fine young man this was, and how very fortunate was the woman he loved so dearly.

The night darkened as the moon passed over the palm fronds and slowly sank below the great trees beyond them. The sounds of the jungle, raucous and demanding, multiplied themselves a hundred-fold, but there was no fear for Shana now, because the man who

340

meant the whole world to her was close by her side, to comfort and protect her, to lift her hopes and her passions to the ultimate peak of contentment.

He lay with a thigh across hers, hard muscle over soft and pliant flesh, and his tousled head was at her breast as she fell into a deep and satisfying sleep, to dream of the days and weeks and months and years to come, a future filled with visions of perfect happiness, together. Gerard stirred in his sleep, and held her closer still; and she knew that even though her beloved Eden was behind her, she was still in Paradise.

The Windhaven Saga
by Marie de Jourlet

AMERICA'S #1 PLANTATION SAGA

OVER 7 MILLION COPIES IN PRINT!

Patricia Matthews

America's leading lady of historical romance.
Over 20,000,000 copies in print!